One Step Enough

Also by Carla Kelly

Fiction

Daughter of Fortune
Summer Campaign
Miss Chartley's Guided Tour
Marian's Christmas Wish
Mrs. McVinnie's London Season
Libby's London Merchant
Miss Grimsley's Oxford Career
Miss Billings Treads the Boards
Mrs. Drew Plays Her Hand
Reforming Lord Ragsdale
Miss Whittier Makes a List
The Lady's Companion
With This Ring
Miss Milton Speaks Her Mind
One Good Turn
The Wedding Journey
Here's to the Ladies: Stories of the Frontier Army
Beau Crusoe
Marrying the Captain
The Surgeon's Lady
Marrying the Royal Marine
The Admiral's Penniless Bride
Borrowed Light
Coming Home for Christmas: Three Holiday Stories
Enduring Light
Marriage of Mercy
My Loving Vigil Keeping
Her Hesitant Heart
Safe Passage
Marco and the Devil's Bargain
Paloma and the Horse Traders
Season's Regency Greetings
Regency Christmas Gifts
The Wedding Ring Quest
Softly Falling
Doing No Harm
Courting Carrie in Wonderland
The Star in the Meadow
Season of Love
The Unlikely Master Genius

Nonfiction

On the Upper Missouri: The Journal of Rudolph Friedrich Kurz
Fort Buford: Sentinel at the Confluence

One Step Enough

CARLA
KELLY

BONNEVILLE BOOKS

An imprint of Cedar Fort, Inc.
Springville, Utah

ISBN 13: 978-1-4621-2156-4

Published by Bonneville Books, an imprint of Cedar Fort, Inc.
2373 W. 700 S., Springville, UT 84663
Distributed by Cedar Fort, Inc., www.cedarfort.com

LIBRARY OF CONGRESS CATALOGING-IN-PUBLICATION DATA

Names: Kelly, Carla, author. | Sequel to: Kelly, Carla. My loving vigil keeping.
Title: One step enough / Carla Kelly.
Description: Springville, Utah : Sweetwater Books, An imprint of Cedar Fort, Inc., [2018]
Identifiers: LCCN 2018005506 (print) | LCCN 2018010948 (ebook) | ISBN 9781462128648 (epub, pdf, mobi) | ISBN 9781462121564 (perfect bound : alk. paper)
Subjects: LCSH: Married people--Fiction. | Mormons--Fiction. | Winter Quarters (Utah), setting. | LCGFT: Historical fiction.
Classification: LCC PS3561.E3928 (ebook) | LCC PS3561.E3928 O64 2018 (print) | DDC 813/.54--dc23
LC record available at https://lccn.loc.gov/2018005506

Cover design by Katie Payne
Back cover by Jeff Harvey
Cover design © 2018 Cedar Fort, Inc.
Edited and typeset by Nicole Terry and Kaitlin Barwick

Printed in the United States of America

10 9 8 7 6 5 4 3 2 1

Printed on acid-free paper

To Elam Jones (1985–2013)
because the story isn't over in coal mines.

And also to my dear friends Darren and
Verena Beazer of Cardston, Alberta,
and their children.

Lead, Kindly Light

Lead, kindly Light, amid th'encircling gloom;
Lead thou me on!
The night is dark, and I am far from home;
Lead thou me on!
Keep thou my feet; I do not ask to see
The distant scene—one step enough for me.

I was not ever thus, nor pray'd that thou
Shouldst lead me on.
I loved to choose and see my path; but now,
Lead thou me on!
I loved the garish day, and, spite of fears,
Pride ruled my will. Remember not past years.

So long thy pow'r hath blest me, sure it still
Will lead me on,
O'er moor and fen, o'er crag and torrent, till
The night is gone.
And with the morn those angel faces smile,
Which I have loved long since, and lost awhile!

Cardinal John H. Newman (1801–1890)

Chapter 1

The Number Four mine exploded on Tuesday, May 1, 1900, extinguishing the sun in Winter Quarters Canyon, Carbon County, Utah. On Wednesday, Owen Davis said goodbye to his daughter, Angharad, and Della Anders at the nearby Scofield Depot, his women in tears and reaching for him as he backed away. In a trance, Owen walked to his empty house and made a coffin for his dearest friend, Richard Evans: miner, husband, father, and choirmaster of the Pleasant Valley Ward.

Owen knew that a pine box furnished by the Pleasant Valley Coal Company wasn't good enough for Richard, the man who saved his life only yesterday. It had been Richard who had scolded him on the mantrip as they rode toward the Number Four, ready to begin a new coal contract with the U.S. Navy, and a new pay period.

He richly deserved the scold. Della had turned down his proposal earlier, declaring she would never marry a miner. To resolve this thorny issue, he had fasted and prayed as Bishop Parmley had commanded them both. Della needed to come around to his way of thinking, and so Owen told his friend.

Richard shook his finger at him as they sat hip to hip on the short ride to the mine that awful morning. Owen knew he would never forget his friend's scathing words: "You're wishing Della would change her mind? Is that any way to supplicate the Lord? I'm ashamed of you."

Even now, as he measured his intricately carved Welsh chest for a coffin, Owen felt the hot shame at Richard's rebuke all over again. Thank God he had listened to his friend.

At Richard's sharp words, Owen bowed his head, prayed, "Thy will, Lord," and received a succinct reply: "Quit." Apparently the Lord didn't waste words.

When the mantrip reached the Number Four, Owen told Richard he'd see him that night at the dance in the Odd Fellows Hall, rode the mantrip down, found Bishop Parmley—also the mine superintendent—and resigned on the spot.

Around 10:30, as he sat in his house alone, unemployed, and wondering what Della would say now if he proposed, the mine blew, spreading what every man who survived on the surface hoped was instantaneous death for those below. To compound the felony, carbon monoxide afterdamp raced through the levels and raises from Number Four to Number One and killed those miners silently.

It could hardly have been worse. Two hundred friends died, from fifty-something-year-old husbands to fourteen-year-old sons and brothers. Scarcely any family in Winter Quarters Canyon and Scofield had not lost someone dear and immediate.

Owen worked in silence. He had agreed with Della to save the top of Grandfather Davis's carved box that ordinarily held his clothing and books, and mementos of his wife, Gwyna, who died when Angharad was born. He used the box's mythic carved dragons as a headboard and footboard for Richard, as well as his own bed and Della's too, because oak was better than pine.

He had made Della a bed when she agreed to board with his sister-in-law, Mabli Reese, last August when she came to teach. Gadfreys, had he been smitten by Della's striking Greek face on his first sight of her? Mayhap. He had liked what he saw, after years of looking away when friends, the Evanses among them, had suggested other replacements to fill the huge whole in his heart.

Barely acquainted with her, something told him that Della was worth using his oak for her bed. Yesterday she gave it up without a murmur for Richard's coffin, even though no one would ever see all that oak and glorious carving once it went into the ground, holding Richard's remains until Resurrection Morning. Eventually, only God and Richard would know, and that was sufficient unto the day.

The morning before his daughter left with Della, Angharad had rested her forehead against the unfinished coffin and dissolved in tears. Her whole body shook as she gasped for breath.

Alarmed, he turned to Della. "You must take her out of the canyon."

He and Della had another matter to handle first, and it required Bishop Parmley, a man too busy and blasted by his own grief and work digging out the dead to see them, but the man they needed.

Hand in hand—under protest, Angharad had agreed to stay with her Aunt Mabli Reese—he and Della had walked the canyon, searching for the bishop. They passed silent homes, empty boardinghouses, and tried not to flinch or cry out in sympathy at anguished screaming, or keening in that low, thoroughly disconcerting way that Celts mourned.

Surprisingly, they found Bishop Parmley in his office, staring at and through the door when they opened it to his "Come." Sister Parmley must have brought him a meal, but it congealed on his desk.

"Bishop, the last thing you need is us bothering you," Owen began.

Their reason for being there, taking up his time when so many needed him, dawned on the bishop. He sat back and regarded them with a faint smile.

"You need a temple recommendation to Manti," Bishop Parmley said. "Della needs an endowment interview, and you two need wedding interviews."

"This is our only chance, Bishop," Della said. "Owen wants me to take Angharad to Provo tomorrow."

"This afternoon," Owen amended, and he braved a glance at his darling woman. "Angharad is shaking and having trouble breathing. I want her out of here *today*."

Della nodded, not happy with him, but willing enough.

"I agree with Owen. The Knights will give you every assistance in Provo." Bishop Parmley beckoned her closer.

Owen nearly had to pry her from his side, but she went forward, holding out her hand to the bishop. He grasped it and she sobbed.

"Sister Anders, thank you for all you have done," he said. "Especially among my Finnish families."

"We sauna together and I know the women," she said softly. "It wasn't anything."

"It was everything. I told you once that the Lord was mindful of you." He looked up at Owen. "Go out on the landing. I must interview your dear lady privately for her own endowment before your wedding interview."

Owen went onto the landing of the outside stairs, closed his eyes, and wished he could shut out the shrieks of the bereaved that seemed to carry on the wind.

The interview was short. Bishop Parmley called him back in as Della folded a piece of paper.

Bishop Parmley gestured to the chairs. "Sit down, Owen. Della, give that to the stake president in Provo, and he'll provide your second interview."

The bishop took out a tablet with the Pleasant Valley Coal Company heading. "I have proper church forms in my office at the meetinghouse, but I am not going over there." He passed his hand in front of his face. "There are too many bodies. I can't. The stake president will understand."

"At the school, I put our paper flowers we made for the dance last night on each body."

Another ghost of a smile. "I applaud your courage, Della. Two schools are morgues, and so is the church."

Bishop Parmley uncapped his fountain pen and dated the page. "I'm going to interview you two together and include a note, so the stake president will understand when you go there for your wedding interview." Again that fleeting smile. "I know this is irregular, but tell me what is regular about what we have experienced here?"

Bishop. Superintendent. The two duties of his life seemed to struggle against each other, now more than ever. "Do you know Gomer Thomas, Owen?"

"The state mine inspector? Aye. He arrived last night from Salt Lake."

"Gomer told me this is now the worst mine disaster in the United States. My mines. My men. My own brother. My friends. My congregation. Good God in heaven."

Their voices were hushed as Thomas Parmley, in his role as their bishop, questioned their church activity, their payment of tithes and offerings, their belief in the restored gospel of Jesus Christ, and their allegiance to President Lorenzo Snow. They assured him of their chastity and their willingness to be sealed for time and eternity.

When the bishop finished his interview, he held out the paper for them to sign and added his own signature. "I have no doubt that you two will make an excellent marriage," he assured them. "Would that matters were easier now."

Owen heard someone coming up the steps in a hurry. Bishop Parmley sighed, the sacred moment gone. "I wish I could be in Manti Temple with you next week." Tears filled his eyes. "If only everyone who would have rejoiced with you could be there! God Almighty, how I wish it."

The three of them stood up. Bishop Parmley put the paperwork in an envelope and handed it to Della. He stared at Owen then, his exhausted eyes energized.

"No more mines, Owen. No more."

Owen shook his head. He turned Della toward the door just as Frank Cameron, Castle Gate mine superintendent, opened it. He stepped back, apologizing, but the bishop ushered him inside, his business done with Owen and Della.

If the walk back to Mabli Reese's house next to the mortuary that the Edward's Boardinghouse had become hadn't strengthened Owen's resolve sufficiently, it came when Angharad hurled herself into his arms the moment he opened the door to his sister-in-law's house.

"Owen, she is desperate," Mabli said.

"Da, I kept seeing you on a stretcher!" Angharad sobbed into his shoulder as he picked her up.

"I was never on a stretcher, dearest," he reminded her gently.

When she had calmed down enough to relax her grip, he knelt on the floor with her in his arms. Better do this right now.

"Angharad, you're going out on the next train," he told his daughter. "So is Miss Anders."

"I am not certain I can leave you here alone," Della whispered. "Please no, Owen."

"I've been alone before," he countered.

"Not like this."

Trust Della to cut right to the heart of the matter. He knew he wanted Angharad away from this canyon of death, but Della was another matter. The last thing he wanted was to watch the train carrying the woman he loved grow smaller and smaller.

"You must go," he told her, hoping he sounded firm and husbandly, even though Della hadn't said aye to anything yet over the altar in Manti Temple. "You must."

Della turned to Mabli. "Watch him carefully for me, please."

"You know I will," was Mabli's quiet response.

He knew his sister-in-law was broken in half too, widowed several years ago by a mine bounce and now mourning for William Goode, a shy Englishman she had kept company with since Christmas. He also knew she would never fail him.

Owen put them on the next train heading away from Scofield. "The burials will probably begin on Friday," he told her as she stood on the steps of the railcar, Angharad close to her side. "Andrew Hood said something about a funeral service on Saturday, with church leaders coming from Salt Lake. I'll leave here Monday morning."

He kissed Della, supremely unwilling to let go. So much for brave words. The last thing he wanted was solitude.

Della took Angharad firmly by the hand and entered the railcar. Owen stepped away as the train began to move.

If only the train could have picked up amazing speed and shot from Pleasant Valley. Della, his calm, steely, brave woman, leaped to her feet and banged against the closed window. The last he saw of them was two people holding tight to each other, their mouths open in silent wailing.

Owen backed away until he stumbled against an empty coffin brought from Denver, and he sat down on the lid. He leaped up, hoping no one had witnessed his stupidity, and returned to his empty house and Richard's unfinished coffin.

For the first time in his musical life, he had not a single song or even tune to hum. In silence, he measured and cut, planed and sanded, glued and nailed. It wasn't warm, but he found himself sweating. The sawdust clung to him even tighter than Angharad and Della had.

He worked in complete silence. When the work was done Thursday morning, he knelt and prayed in Welsh, as always, and steeled himself for his next ordeal.

He walked to Martha Evans's home, one of the many where he had carved the family name and installed it over the front door one year as a Christmas present. On the Evanses' sign, he had also carved Richard himself, mouth open in song. He looked away, saddened nearly beyond his capacity to bear it.

Andrew Hood, their Scottish Sunday School superintendent, was already there with Dr. Emil Isgreen, the man who had competed with Owen for Della's affections. While Martha and her children went into the kitchen, the three of them removed the canvas bag covering Richard and dressed him for burial in his temple clothes.

The task was grim beyond belief, considering that Richard must have been thrown against the roof of the mine. Owen had spared Martha the added horror of trying to identify her husband because he recognized Richard's hand with its little ruby ring, still wrapped tightly around his pickaxe. In his dreams, Owen knew he would unwrap that stiff hand from the ax over and over.

After a prayer, Owen cradled his friend in his arms and wrapped him in the quilt Martha had left in the front room. He carried Richard to his new home of oak, surrounded by carved dragons of his homeland. Owen wailed every step of the journey, keening his sorrow to the sky.

He thought he was alone, but he saw Della's friend Eeva Koski and her husband, Kari, out of the corner of his eye. He took in their sympathy and something else on Eeva's face as she looked behind him.

Startled, he turned around to see Martha Evans following him, resolute and courageous.

"Martha, no."

She ignored him, walking ahead to open the door to his house. Her face calm, she carefully took the quilt from her husband's ruined body and arranged it just so in the coffin, a pat here a pat there.

"It's a lovely coffin, Owen, my dear."

"I didn't want you to see him like this."

"Silly man. Do you think I did not look at him in the canvas bag?" she said, reminding Owen again of the strength of women.

She watched as Owen gentled the body of her husband, lover, friend, and confidante into his new home. Without a doubt—no words passed between them—they both knew Richard Evans, choirmaster dubbed the sweetest singer by Bishop Parmley, had probably assembled the men's section of the choir into some corner of paradise. Owen could almost hear them tuning up with "Men of Harlech," all his lovely, dead friends.

After kissing Owen's cheek, Martha left as quietly as she came, to be followed into his house by Eeva Koski, looking not a bit pleased.

"Kari tells me you made Della and Angharad get on the train," she said, poking his chest for emphasis.

He looked over his shoulder at Kari, who was regarding him with something close to amusement. "Aye. They don't need to be here."

"*You* need them."

"I'll be fine, Eeva," he insisted, knowing how feeble he must sound to an audience of one irritated Finn and another trying not to smile.

"You are *not* fine," she said. "I am going to do something."

She turned on her heel and left his house in a swish of skirts that somehow managed to sound angry too.

Owen stared after her. "What in the world . . . ?"

Kari shrugged. "I learned that my life is much happier when I do not argue with someone who is probably right. It's late. Go to bed."

"I don't even have a bed."

"No, and you probably can't sleep," Kari agreed. "You'll stagger around until you drop dead too." He shook his head. "I've seen it happen. So have you. What a waste, considering that there is an almost-wife who would like to see more of your sorry carcass."

"I'll try to sleep, Kari."

"See you later."

He tried, but he couldn't. Kari was right. He was going to die without Della.

Chapter 2

Bishop Parmley must have wired ahead after Owen put them on the train. Both Amanda and Jesse Knight were waiting for them at the depot in Provo three hours later.

Della stared at the Scofield-bound train with a stack of coffins waiting to be loaded. She longed to sprint across the platform and leap aboard, hang decorum. She belonged nowhere but with Owen.

At home, trust Amanda, Della's shirttail relative, to know what Angharad needed. She helped the child from her coat. "Are you hungry? Your Uncle Jesse is famished and says I don't feed him enough."

Angharad couldn't help smiling at that, but then she put her hand to her mouth. "I shouldn't laugh."

"Of course you should." Amanda whispered theatrically in the child's ear. "I know I feed him enough, but he always sneaks nuts and candy when he thinks I am not looking. When did you eat last?"

"I don't remember."

"Then it's time for food." She ushered Angharad toward the kitchen. "There is cinnamon bread cooling, and my cook is ready to slice some. What do you think?"

Angharad nodded. "I think I could eat it. Might there be butter?"

"Always," Amanda said. "Scoot on into the kitchen."

"I can do dishes when I finish," Owen's daughter said, not one to neglect a social nicety.

"That's not . . ." Amanda began, but then she stopped. "Actually, Mrs. McNulty could use some help. Yes, please. I'll take Della to the parlor because she looks tired."

With a backward glance at Della, Angharad went into the kitchen. As one, the Knights each linked an arm through Della's and took her into the parlor, sliding shut the pocket doors behind them.

Della told them everything that had happened. Beyond tears now, because her eyes hurt too much, she told them of sudden death, vacant-eyed widows, bewildered children, screams of anguish, and paper flowers intended to decorate for a dance that night strewn instead on miners' torn bodies.

"Owen used my bed and his and part of his grandfather's carved box to fashion a coffin for the choirmaster and his best friend," Della concluded. She accepted Uncle Jesse's handkerchief. "He insisted that Angharad leave the canyon, but I belong with him. Tell me, why is life so hard? I want to go to sleep and wake up when all this misery is over."

"I've wished that a few times," Uncle Jesse said. "We all have."

"What did you do?"

"I rolled up my sleeves and went to work," he said simply. "Go back tomorrow, Della. We'll try to convince Angharad to stay, but I doubt we will win."

Leaning against Amanda, she closed her eyes. When she woke up hours later, she lay on the sofa. She put her hand to her eyes and felt a soft, damp cloth over them.

"Your eyes were so red," Amanda told her from the wing chair close by. "I thought a cloth might help."

Della sat up suddenly, looking around. "Angharad?"

"She has more sense than you do," Uncle Jesse said from the archway. "We ate our way through half a loaf of cinnamon bread. What a sweet child—she asked me quite politely if she could lie down in the fairy princess bedroom in the turret."

"She loves that room," Della said. "So do I."

His expression turned contemplative. "She wanted to rest her eyes before she went back up the canyon to Da."

"We have to go back," Della said. She sat up and felt the parlor spin around. "Oh, I am dizzy."

Uncle Jesse came closer. "You've not let an ounce of your guard down since the mine blew, have you?"

"How could I?"

She closed her eyes but there it was—the explosion, the bodies, the shrieks and moans, her little students adrift in an adult world with no anchor, her own horror at finding Owen's blue-and-white-striped shirt on the pile outside the boardinghouse where the dead were being washed, and the shock of seeing Owen in his own kitchen later, when she thought he was dead.

There was another matter. In the middle of all this, she was back at the Molly Bee again, waiting to hear if her father was alive or dead. But that was years ago. She didn't have time for Papa now. Maybe later. "I must go back."

"In the morning," Amanda told her. "Go upstairs to your daughter."

"My daughter. I wonder what Angharad will call me, after I marry her father."

"As she was drifting off to sleep, she asked me when Mam was coming to bed," Uncle Jesse told her. "She means you, Della."

~

Della woke in the morning as the sun seeped around the window blind, her mind empty of everything except the reality that she had slept all night.

She listened to Angharad's even breathing. Soon there would be funerals and more tumult as widows and fatherless children went away . . . somewhere.

But where? She lay there, upset, thinking of her friends, and now there was her father in the background, gone these twelve years in his own mining mishap. Hadn't she put his memory to rest? Why was he here too?

She closed her eyes, remembering a sermon given Sunday before the world fell apart in Winter Quarters. Nahum Powell, Tamris Powell's husband and now a dead man, had spoken on the topic of hardship, something everyone who mined coal was already well acquainted with.

Della remembered how Brother Powell had leaned on the pulpit in that casual way of his and reminded the congregation that no matter how hard things were mining coal, they were still in God's hands, and He was mindful of them.

She turned on her side, only to gaze into Angharad's dark Welsh eyes, open and questioning. She touched the child's hair, smoothing it down.

"Da?"

"We're going home."

~

Two telegrams waited for Della as she came downstairs with her arm around Angharad. Growing up in a Colorado mining camp and later in a lawyer's house in Salt Lake City, Utah, she knew two things about telegrams: one was always bad news; two were worse.

Calmly she slit one envelope, read the few words, and handed it to Amanda. *Be still and know that God is God,* she thought, remembering Nahum Powell's sermon. She asked Angharad to go into the dining room and bring her an apple from the fruit bowl. The obedient child gave her no argument.

"Eeva Koski is one of my Finnish friends in the canyon. I teach—taught—her daughter Tilda. She says Owen isn't sleeping, isn't eating, and she fears for him."

"Are you surprised?" Amanda asked.

"No. He seems to feel some . . . some odd remorse that he is still alive."

"I've noticed that after mines collapse," Uncle Jesse said from the doorway, looking as serious as she had ever seen him. "A rock crushes one miner, and the man working next to him is unscathed. It drives . . ." He stopped. "It causes some distress to the survivor. Let us leave it at that."

Della opened the other telegram and felt the tiniest bit of hope. "This is from Mary Ann Parmley, the bishop's wife. Bishop says please return, and he also has a solution for us. I wonder what he can mean."

"Parmley is a shrewd man," Uncle Jesse said. He clapped his hands once, decisive now. "I'll go hold the train." He started out the door then leaned in, smiling. "I can do that, you know. It's a perk of stockholder power, and now and then I have no qualms about collecting."

"While you're at it, send a telegram to Sister Parmley," Amanda said.

Jesse gave his wife a little salute. When Angharad returned from the dining room, Della took the apple from her, looked at it, and laughed out loud.

"I didn't know those apples were wax," she exclaimed. "They look so real and I wanted one."

Angharad struggled not to laugh. Della touched her shoulder. "It's all right to laugh," she said simply. "You know your father would laugh."

"Even now?" Angharad asked, as her grin widened.

"Even now, because it's funny," Della assured her.

They packed and were on the train in twenty minutes. As Della left for the depot where Uncle Jesse waited, Amanda whispered in her ear that she would find a house for them, and not to worry about it. Della was too shy to suggest that they look for a bed too since Owen had used both of theirs to make Richard's coffin. They could work out that little detail after a wedding in Manti.

At the depot, Jesse told her to be brave and kissed her cheek. He had another telegram in his hand. "It just arrived."

He must have noticed the sudden alarm in her tired eyes because he smiled and waved the yellow sheet at her like a fan. "It's from your great Salt Lake friend, Mr. Auerbach himself. See the return address?"

She opened it on the spot because she knew Uncle Jesse wanted to know what was inside. "'Courage, Della,'" she read out loud. "'I'll have a little something for everyone in the canyon. I have employment, if you need it. Your friend, Sam.'"

Della rested her forehead against Uncle Jesse's chest. "Please tell him thank you and that I will see him soon."

"Consider it done," he said. "Better get moving."

Della grasped his arms. "Thank you and Amanda for what you are doing for us," she said.

"You know she would call this one of many back payments owed to you," he said gently. "She still anguishes that she had no idea how difficult life was for you all those years in Salt Lake with her cousin Caroline."

"I was told never to complain or say anything to anyone."

Uncle Jesse sighed. "If only we had known." He brightened then with the same resolve that had made him famous and wealthy in Utah mining circles. "But we're moving forward now, and so should you. God keep you these next few days, Della."

She and Angharad made themselves small in their seats on the train, two people in a railcar full of older boys with shovels, and serious men in suits and carrying briefcases. Della watched the boys and saw the grim purpose on their faces. Either church leaders or scoutmasters must have recruited them to dig graves.

The men in suits must be lawyers, or state officials, or perhaps insurance agents. She couldn't imagine all the paperwork involved in catastrophe, but there it sat with her and Angharad on the train.

She noted with odd satisfaction that this time there were no coal cars barreling through the canyon. Coal had never stopped for one or two deaths. Maybe two hundred men and boys meant something.

As Angharad slept, Della recalled a song Sammy Padfield had taught them during a lull in the school day, something his English father, dead now, had sung. How did it go? "'On a May day morning early,'" she sang softly. "'Here a moo, there a moo, here a pretty moo.'"

The words changed in her mind, and she appalled herself by singing, "'On a May day morning early, here a death, there a death, here an awful death . . .'"

In Colton, where they changed trains for the steeper pull into Scofield, Mary Ann Parmley met them, little Willie on her hip with Mary and Maria close by.

"Mr. Knight's telegram arrived two hours ago, and I decided I couldn't stand another moment in the canyon," Sister Parmley said as they came aboard the branch line. Her eyes took in the boys with shovels crowding on too. "It's hard, Della, but you know that."

Bless Mary Ann Parmley for bringing along her daughters. Maria and Mary took Angharad with them down the aisle. In moments, they were playing cat's cradle, heads together.

"I'm worried, Sister Parmley," Della said. "There was a telegram from one of my Finnish friends and . . ."

"You should have seen her corner Thomas and demand that he do something to get you back into the canyon," Mary Ann said. She gave Willie a cookie, which settled him down. "You have fierce watchdogs among the Finns." She smiled. "Must be all that sauna and rolling bare in the snow."

Della nearly smiled. "They're loyal and true. Poor Owen. It's too much, isn't it?"

Mary Ann nodded. "Too much for a man who escaped certain death. He wonders why he is still alive." She sighed, as if irritated with herself. "Della, I get exasperated when someone says the Lord will never give us more than we can bear. He doesn't *give* it to us, so I can't blame Him. But sometimes too much is too much."

"I can't argue that." She looked at Angharad sitting with her friends, concentrating on the string passing between their fingers, children again, where only a short time ago Owen's daughter wore the face of someone six times her age.

"We're going to feel almost normal again someday, aren't we?" she asked Mary Ann. "Not now, and not tomorrow, maybe not for weeks or months, but we will, won't we?"

"I think we'll be different," Mary Ann said finally. "My household is in turmoil. My brother-in-law William . . ." She bowed her head and Della leaned closer to her. "My sister-in-law and her little ones have moved in with us, and Della, did you know she is expecting a baby this fall? What has coal done to us?"

It was a question with no answer.

"Maybe *not* the same then," Della said. "Maybe we will be better, stronger, braver, and kinder. As for coal, I have had enough."

"Has Owen?"

"He said he has, but I don't know," Della said honestly. "Eeva once mentioned something called the lure of the mines." Her voice trailed off as she remembered everyone gone now because of coal and mines.

Better, stronger, braver, kinder. The words seemed to match the *clack-clack* of the train. Better, stronger, braver, kinder.

Chapter 3

They reached the Scofield Depot and the engine hissed to a stop. Della thought she was prepared, but could anyone be prepared? Hand in hand, she and Angharad stared at coffins stacked on top of each other.

A carriage waited for them. Sister Parmley wasted not a minute getting the girls inside as she tried to turn them from the stark view. Angharad looked back, distress written all over her face.

"These are the last of seventy-five coffins that arrived from Denver earlier today," Mary Ann said, her voice low in the quiet carriage, as the driver started into Winter Quarters Canyon. "There weren't enough ready-made coffins available in all of Utah."

"The ladies of Salt Lake and Provo are gathering flowers to send tomorrow. Amanda Knight told me."

"How kind of them," Mary Ann said simply. "Everyone wants to help."

Mary Ann glanced at her timepiece when the carriage pulled up to the Parmley residence. "The bishop said he would be in the Wasatch Store and that he would have Owen with him. I'll take Angharad with me because it's time for lunch."

Angharad took a moment to convince, her dark eyes rebellious. "Da needs us both," she insisted.

"I know, but the bishop wants to see me and your father," Della said, wishing she knew what lay ahead. Time to try some negotiation. "Sister Parmley mentioned pancakes with butter and maple syrup."

"Perhaps," Angharad said, after giving the matter some thought.

"You'll see us soon. I promise."

The driver indicated he could drive her to the store, but Della shook her head. "I'll walk. You need to be moving coffins." *Besides that, I can't sit on a wagon carrying coffins.*

"Aye, miss," he said, tipping his hat to her.

She thought she could walk briskly to the Wasatch Store, eyes in front, but that proved impossible. Every single home on the narrow road had at least one coffin in the front yard, and she knew those homes.

In them were her children, the whole lower grade she had last seen trailing after their mothers on that horrible day of the explosion. Here they were, smiling at her shyly, which meant she had to stop at each house for tears and a hug.

"Will we go back to school next week, Miss Anders?" Will Thomas asked her, as they stood among the coffins in his yard, the setting so cruel but duplicated everywhere she looked.

"Miss Clayson had me determine your final grade from your last test scores," she said. "No more school until autumn."

"Not for me then. Mam is taking us to Springville. She has a sister there. Aw, miss, we'll be all right. Don't cry."

"Springville is a lovely town," she said as she held Will's hand, not wanting to let go because she was losing all of her students, as sure as their mothers had lost their husbands.

On she walked, her heart breaking, staring at the ground because suddenly it was too hard to see one more coffin. If only she could blot out the occasional shriek, the low moan. She stared down at her own shoes.

She stopped when she bumped into someone. "Beg pardon," she murmured, and she would have stepped sideways, but familiar hands grasped her and pulled her close.

"Taking your time getting to the Wasatch Store, miss?" she heard, as Owen Davis held her so tight that even Sister Parmley would probably *tsk* a bit. "By the way, what are you doing here? Don't you listen to sound advice?"

"When I hear it," she said. "Leaving you yesterday wasn't sound advice."

He held her close. Her hat fell off, or he pulled it off because the stupid, floppy thing was getting in his eyes.

When Owen let go, Della saw the exhaustion in his eyes and gray in his hair that hadn't been there even yesterday. She touched his hair then ran her fingers in it, as if trying to wipe off the gray.

"I got two telegrams this morning, and both of them commanded me to return here," she said. "Don't ever make me leave you again, because I won't."

He pulled her to him again, this time to talk into her hair. "I can't eat, I can't sleep, I can't sing, I'm barely breathing."

"Then it's a good thing I didn't waste a moment getting here," she replied, wishing for serenity, even as her voice shook and her nose ran.

He gave her his handkerchief, the one that always smelled of laundry soap and traitor coal. She blew vigorously on one corner and wiped her eyes with the other. The third corner went back to its owner, who did the same.

"I hope Bishop makes this brief," he said, steering her toward the outside stairs at the Wasatch Store. "I'm loading my friends into coffins and trying to comfort people who cannot be comforted."

You are one of those, she thought.

After telling two more of her students that she would see them after a meeting with the bishop—most canyon children understood a summons from the bishop—they walked up the outside stairs.

"In here," Bishop Parmley said as they came to the landing and the open door that led into the library—her library, where she had presided all year.

My lovely library, she thought, wondering who would manage it after she left. For one terrible moment, she thought she saw Remy Ducotel, Nicola Anselmo, and Levi Jones in their usual places by the newspapers, with David Evans running his fingers through the D books, because he loved Dickens. She turned her face into Owen's shoulder.

He seemed to know what caused her distress, and tightened his grip. "There'll be others here, *m cara*," he whispered. "Give it time."

She patted his chest, took a deep breath, and saw who else stood in the library. She smiled to see Dr. Isgreen, who had taken her to dinner on Saturday nights for months. The last time she saw him, they had struggled together to get Mari Luoma off the railroad tracks, where she had waited for the coal train to strike her dead.

Next to him was a man holding a sheaf of papers. "What is going on?" she whispered to Owen.

"Whatever it is, I hope it's fast. There is so much to do."

Bishop Parmley grasped her hand and held it, as though he expected her to bolt. To her surprise, he put her hand in Owen's.

"Perfect," he said, a busy man with his mind made up, apparently.

He looked into Della's eyes. "Sister Anders, you are planning to be sealed to Owen in Manti Temple by the end of next week?"

"Yes, sir," she said, mystified. "You know that." He had written a recommend for a temple wedding only two days ago. "It's our temple district and not so far."

"Della. Owen. I prayed about what I am going to ask of you," he said, and she had never seen his expression more serious. "I'm not taking this lightly. Sister Anders, will you let me marry you civilly right now to Owen Davis?"

Owen's head went up in surprise, but he only tightened his grip on her, as though she had suddenly become a lifeline.

"But next week . . ." she said, and then she turned for a good look at the man who held her hand. One look was enough.

Her free arm went around his waist, as she realized she was holding him together, and not the other way around. She found strength from somewhere because Owen's was gone, and she needed to share hers. She had one question only.

"Bishop, this doesn't mean we have to wait an entire year to be sealed in Manti, does it?"

"Not at all," Bishop Parmley assured her. "If you or this man clutching you as though his life depended on it hadn't been church members for a year, you would have to wait. That's not the case."

He put his arms around both of them. Della breathed in the coal, the sweat, and the exhaustion. Bishop and mine superintendent, Thomas Parmley was a man with far too much to do, who had taken the time for a small kindness.

"I don't want either of you separated by one more night in this canyon," he said in firm tones. "This is no place to be alone, no matter how excellent your intentions are to wait a week to marry. Too many hearts are broken. Is it yes then?"

Della turned in Owen's grip to face him. "Yes. Owen?"

He nodded. Captains on ships far out at sea could have heard his sigh of relief.

"Well then," Bishop Parmley said. "Let's deal with the paperwork first. Abraham?"

"You don't have to do this, Della," Owen said, maybe wanting to give her a moment to reconsider. "It's only a week's wait."

"Yes, I do," she said calmly, all fear gone.

"Very well, you two," the man she didn't know said. "Owen, you know me." He turned to Della. "Miss Anders, I am Abraham Ketchum, Justice of the Peace and Scofield butcher," he announced proudly, leaving Della to wonder whether he was prouder about the title or the occupation. "Let's do the paperwork so dear to the state of Utah, and then Mr. Parmley can marry you."

Bishop Parmley touched Della's arm. "Della, I wish I could turn Owen over to you for the rest of the day, but he's still my elders quorum president, and I need him to help me in the homes."

"Bishop, it's your lucky day. You'll be getting two for the price of one," she said. "Once we're married, I'll help him, if you don't mind."

"I won't turn you down."

Della leaned away from Owen and kissed Bishop Parmley's cheek. "Thank you. I always wanted to be married in a work dress with my hair in a knot. It was my life's dream."

"Any time, my dear, any time."

Della smiled when Dr. Isgreen chuckled.

Ketchum sat down at Della's library desk. "Your bishop already filled in the information from his church records," he said, indicating the forms. "Owen, he showed me a copy of the death certificate for your late wife, and I have noted that here." He looked at Della next. "Any impediments I should know about, Miss Anders?"

"None, sir. I've never been married, and I am twenty-four."

He indicated where they should sign. Owen picked up the fountain pen and signed with no hesitation. He handed it to Della, a question in his dark eyes.

"I'm unemployed, I have about forty dollars to my name, I turned my bed into a coffin for my best friend, and I'm going to hurt for a long, long time," he said, his voice barely audible. "You can withdraw and feel no reproach from me."

"Withdraw? I suppose I could, but why would I?"

Della took the pen. She thought about the school year, the choir where she served as secretary, her friends—many of them gone now. She stepped closer, wishing they were alone, but speaking to him as if they were. "I have this vast and fierce love for you, Owen Davis."

The simplicity of her words brought tears to his eyes. "Oh, now," she said, and dabbed at them. "You Welsh think you're the only people with a gift for language. We Greeks were writing poetry when you were probably worshipping trees and painting yourselves blue."

Dr. Isgreen laughed out loud. "I guess she told you, Owen."

"I guess she did."

Della signed the paper with a sure hand and dated it where Abraham Ketchum indicated. Ketchum asked Dr. Isgreen to sign as a witness, and he signed as the other witness.

Their bishop stood in front of them, cleared his throat, and married them. When he finished and the state of Utah was satisfied, he nodded to Owen. "Have you a ring, lad?"

"I wish I did."

"I'll loan you this one."

Della looked in surprise at Dr. Isgreen, that self-assured man who suddenly didn't look so confident.

Maybe it was the moment for truth telling. "I would still prefer to give this to you myself, but your . . . your husband beat me fair and square." He nodded to Owen. "I expect this back when you get your own ring for this good lady." He took a simple gold band from his vest pocket. "Yea or nay?"

Owen nodded. "Give me six months."

"Fair enough."

Owen took the ring from Dr. Isgreen and slipped it onto Della's finger. "Six months," he told the doctor and kissed Della.

The doctor picked up his hat and kissed Della's cheek. He shook Owen's hand. "Treat her right or I'll thrash you and not stitch you up afterward, no matter what Hippocrates thinks I should do." He winked at Della. "And do what she says."

Abraham Ketchum left after telling Owen that he always gave advice to a new couple. He shook his finger at Owen. "No more coal mines," he said. "That's an order."

Bishop Parmley put his hands on their shoulders. He kissed them each on the forehead. "I have no doubt this will be a good marriage."

Finally it was just the two of them standing in the library. Without a word, they wrapped their arms around each other. After a moment's hesitation, he moved his hands a little lower and patted her hip.

"I don't know how or if I will ever measure up to Gwyna, my love, but I will try," she said into his chest.

Owen held her off from him and gazed deep into her eyes. "Let's clear this now. There will be *no* measuring on my end of this marriage. Gwyna was Gwyna and you are my Della. I have a big heart." He touched his forehead to hers. "Wife, Richard would become my own *bwca* and haunt me if he knew he saved my life just to have me ruin yours with pettiness."

"Thank you, Owen. I needed to know that. I hope Gwyna doesn't mind that I already think of her daughter as mine."

"Mind? I have no doubt that she is pleased and relieved," he said.

They stood at the window, looking down at coffins and women in black. She wished they could get some blankets and bed down here tonight, above the tears and tumult.

"Wish we could stay here," Della said.

"So do I. Sister Davis, you're now the wife of the ward elders quorum president. Both my counselors are dead, so . . ."

He stopped speaking and she tightened her grip on him. "We have work to do, my love," she finished and bumped his hip with hers. "We're not always going to be sad."

Chapter 4

After eating a hurried sandwich with Angharad at the Parmley house, Owen and Della worked until the stars came out, going from house to house, comforting, listening, taking notes on what, by now, the widows were beginning to realize they needed. They mourned with those that mourned.

To say it was difficult would have been to understate the matter. The one bright spot, besides Della's presence, that held Owen firm was Angharad's smile of delight when they told her Bishop Parmley had married them. Blushing with shyness, Della held out her ring hand to Angharad.

That ring. How soon could he come up with enough cash to replace it? The irony was not lost on Owen.

He dismissed any further contemplation of the matter because there was enough to worry about. He left Della and Angharad standing close together long enough to go into the kitchen and thank Sister Parmley for her help.

"No difficulty there, Owen," she said. "Your Angharad and my girls are all distracting each other and helping with William's wee ones." She touched his hand. "Thank you for letting my Thomas marry you two. I know you wanted to wait until Manti next week."

"I thought I did. I need her right now, don't I?"

"We all see it. You need to sleep tonight. Having Della close by will help." Her face flushed. "Too many widows are sleeping alone tonight and hereafter. I imagine they are cuddling their children close, but it's not the same."

"I know," he said. "I remember." He thought of days that stretched into years without Gwyna as near as his fingertips, his refuge from unrelenting hard work and worry and struggling to make ends meet. "We can be sealed next week all the same, Bishop says."

"He's right." She gave him a little push. "Go out there and slay some dragons, you Welshman!"

Bless Sister Parmley's English heart. He would have to explain *y draigh och* of Wales to her sometime.

"We don't slay them, dear sister," he said, congenitally unable to leave his beloved dragons undefended. "They protect us."

A shadow crossed her face, as if she wondered where the dragons had been sleeping when so many miners died. He couldn't say anything, because he had the same thought.

As dusk neared, Owen wondered how it was that even in a coal camp preoccupied with death and sorrow, word of their decidedly impromptu wedding preceded them. Where they had no right to expect even a kind look from distracted people, there were smiles. Tamris Powell even managed a theatrical hand to her forehead and a heartfelt, "Thank the Lord," before she fell into Della's arms in tears over the loss of her dear Nahum and her older brother, William Jones, and his two sons.

When a thoroughly shaken Della let him pull her from the Powell house, they had to sit in the wood shed until she gathered herself together. She shivered beyond any possibility of his warming her, outside of getting her in bed and wrapping himself about her, which he longed to do as the day wore on.

"Married men's mines," she managed to say. Her voice shook with anger. "Over and over everyone told me these mines were safe for families because they weren't gassy mines, prone to explode over nothing. You know, like the Castle Gate in April, where you had to shore up the timber. The Winter Quarters Mines are family mines!" She practically spit out the words.

"I have no answers," he said simply. "Not one."

She began to droop as sorrow replaced outrage. "Now Tamris's lovely Winifred will never know her fine father." She made a visible effort to control herself. "I wish I had known *my* father longer. Twelve years is never long enough. Where now?"

He listened to Della's disjointed words as she jumbled this disaster with her father's death in Colorado years ago and with April's Castle Gate, all of it tumbling out fresh and raw, as if they happened yesterday. She didn't seem aware of it.

Home to bed, if I had a bed, he thought. *You've had enough*. "To Martha's."

They walked up the canyon as dusk settled, smoothing away the harsh white of the coffins outside everyone's homes, and inside them too.

She stopped him, and he tensed. Despite the low light, he saw the affection on her face.

"Owen, my first night here, all I saw were shacks. Gradually they turned into houses, and then into homes." She turned to him, her face suddenly bleak. "Will they become homes again?"

"They will, *m cara*," he told her as he pulled her close. "And we'll do the same thing in Provo with our home."

Her voice was muffled against his chest, but he heard her. "I needed to know."

He led her up the steps to the Evanses' house, stopping this side of the door, wanting to brace her against the sight of Richard's coffin. He whispered to her what lay within, and she nodded.

He knocked. Martha opened the door and smiled to see them. She was dressed in black, as were all the other women in the canyon. Owen had lived around mines and death all his life, and it still mystified him that a normally colorful coal town could suddenly plunge into mourning. Where did all those black dresses come from?

"Martha, I'm all out of words," Della said.

"Then let us be silent together."

With remarkable poise, the two women sat in the chairs next to Richard's beautiful coffin. Heads together, arms around each other, they sat in silence until Martha called Owen's name.

"Owen dear, Mary Evans and I have a favor to ask of you," Martha said.

"Anything."

"You heard that, Della," Martha said, and visibly gathered herself together. "We have our own family plots."

"I know," Owen said, remembering other sad days when little ones were placed there so tenderly from both Richard's and David's families.

"Our lovely men will be buried in our plots on Saturday. We want you to sing 'Lead Kindly Light' for them."

Owen bowed his head. Martha, one of many canyon women who had nursed Angharad in the desperate days after Gwyna's death, had asked the impossible.

He could not tell her aye, nor could he tell her no. He raised his head and conveyed everything in silence to Della, his wife of no more than ten hours, trusting her as he had never trusted anyone in his life.

To his infinite relief, Della understood. "Owen will stand with Angharad and me, and we will all try to sing." She drew a shuddering breath. "I cannot say it will be our finest performance, but we three will try. Depend upon it."

"I can ask no more," Martha said, her voice serene even as her twined hands shook.

Polite hostess to the end, she saw them out the door and closed it quietly behind them. Owen knew she would sit close to her husband's coffin until morning. Seven years ago, with an infant in his arms, he had rested his head against Gwyna's casket and wept until exhaustion claimed him.

They had visited every home Bishop Parmley had requested. They walked to the Parmley home, left the list of instructions with Mary Ann, and picked up Angharad and Della's carpetbag.

In silence, they walked to Owen's sister-in-law's house next door to the Edwards boardinghouse, where the pile of dead men's clothes remained. Della sighed, and he knew she was remembering her distress at finding his blue-and-white-striped shirt on that scorched pile.

Mabli had finished serving dinner in the boardinghouse and had leftover food on her own table. "I made too much," she said, her head down. "There are only ten men there now, and I forgot."

Almost overwhelmed by the urge to sleep, Owen dragged out his timepiece. Half ten o'clock. No wonder he was tired.

Della put her arms around Angharad. "Dearest, would you stay here with your Aunt Mabli?"

"Oh, I . . ." Angharad started, her eyes full of distress.

Bless his wonderful sister-in-law, so protective of Gwyna years ago and equally kind to Gwyna's daughter now. She rubbed Angharad's cheek with the back of her hand. "I would rather not sleep alone tonight, my love. I need you."

He watched his daughter with real appreciation as she looked from him to her aunt and back. "Would you mind if I stayed here, Da?" she asked, and then she gave him a look both practical and womanly, which touched his heart. "Mabli would be alone, and you have . . ."

Her eyes questioning, she touched Della's arm. "What do I call you now?"

"Whatever you like," Della said, and then she laughed. "As long as it's not Miss Anders! I may have started the day as your school teacher, but I don't appear to be ending it that way."

Angharad gave Owen an apologetic look this time, full of tenderness because she was a thoughtful child. "Da, I never knew my mother. I love her, but would you mind if . . . if . . ."

She paused and Owen could nearly see her child's mind at work, wanting to be polite, but uncertain of the right words, especially since they were speaking English because of Della. He could also tell she did not want to hurt his feelings. With real appreciation, his tired mind threw off exhaustion and let him journey through their years together, father and daughter. Now there was Della too, and he saw no resentment in Angharad's eyes.

"Would I mind if you call her Mam now?" he asked, finishing her thought.

Angharad nodded. Deep in his heart, Owen could nearly hear Gwyna's sigh of satisfaction that he had finally taken the step she had probably been waiting years for, since she was a kind woman and a practical one, much like her daughter, and she had loved him.

"I think . . . I know . . . your mother is probably rejoicing right now," he said quietly. "Before she passed, she told me to do my best. Aye, call this nice lady Mam."

Della sniffed back tears and then folded his daughter in her arms. "Mam it is," his new wife said.

Here we are, Gwyna, Owen thought. He felt no sadness, only relief. His arms around Della, Angharad, and Mabli, he wanted to tell everyone in the canyon that life was going to go on. It might not seem so this evening, but it would. Seven years ago, he wouldn't have wagered even a groat that he would ever feel happy again.

Maybe even more than happy, as he watched Angharad and Della so close together, as if they belonged that way. If he had died in the mine, he had no doubt Della would never abandon his daughter. She was not a woman of half measures.

Angharad inclined her head toward Della.

"I'm sorry to tell you this, Mam, but he snores, and more's the pity."

Della laughed, the sound wonderful to his ears.

Chapter 5

"Funerals tomorrow, starting with the Finns," Owen said as they walked up the canyon. "I'll need my . . ." He shook his head as if to clear it. ". . . my something. Della, I'm losing my mind."

"You're tired. Maybe your suit and a good shirt?"

He replied in Welsh, and she reminded him to speak English. "Aye. A suit. Shirt."

They walked in silence to his house, which seemed strangely out of place because there was no coffin in front of it.

He opened the door. "I'll warn you. It's a mess," he said, ushering her in.

He was right; it was a mess. The remains of two bed frames and the rest of the large carved box littered the floor in the front room, along with wood shavings and sawdust. Della peeked in the kitchen. Her heart pounded as she remembered that late-night sight of him, stoking the stove, when she thought he was dead.

She walked to the door of his room, which looked surprisingly spacious with the carved box and his bed gone. Owen just stood there, as if wondering where he was.

"Your suit?" she reminded him. "I hope it doesn't have sawdust on it."

He gave her a strange look. "I doubt anyone would notice." He sighed. "This place is a wreck. How did Angharad and I live here?"

"I know it looked better than this."

"Not much."

The bare mattress and the pillows and blankets appeared as forlorn as the cardboard boxes, stenciled "Pleasant Valley Coal Company," with his possessions inside. Della knew Angharad's little room lay beyond, built out of his larger room, so she stood in that doorway, admiring the dollhouse, seeing the bed neatly made, the child's clothes on their wooden pins. The tidiness soothed her soul. *It will be this way again*, she reminded herself.

He found his suit and brought it to her. "No sawdust. I have one of those new shirts you bought me at Christmas, still in its package. Here is my green cravat. Angharad likes it best."

She carried the clothing into the kitchen, draping it over a chair. He followed behind with his new shirt, and she put it on the chair too.

She tensed to hear the sound of a wagon heading deeper into the canyon toward Finn Town. She thought of her friends Eeva and Kari Koski and all the mourning in the sauna, where Eeva had told her the men would be laid out and shrouded for their coffins.

Have I done enough there? she asked herself and went to open the front door.

Owen stopped her, his hand on the door. "Don't open it. I can't bear to see one more coffin and hear one more wail, and . . . and feel like a black-hearted cur because I survived."

It was finally too much. "No more what-ifs, my love. You can't change the fact that you survived," she told him as she walked him toward the bedroom.

"I don't want to change the facts. Am I a coward?"

"That is the *last* thing you are, Owen Davis," she said, at a loss in the face of his great sorrow.

She saw all of his confusion, as if he sat on the man-trip up to the Number Four and it was Tuesday again. "Richard scolded me and told me to pray better. I did what he said, the Holy Spirit answered, and I listened. I *listened!* My last view of Richard Evans was his big smile that I had finally done what I should have done sooner: petition the Lord for a *real* answer and not what I wanted." He kissed the top of Della's head. "I wish I could tell Richard what I learned."

He must not have been aware of how much he leaned on her. She braced herself, not willing to stop the words that poured out of him.

"I know I did the right thing, but it's hard to bear," he continued. "For years, I mined coal beside my friends, and now they are gone."

"You are here," she reminded him.

"God's mystery. Evidently I have work to do."

But not in a mine, she thought.

He leaned against her, and she closed her eyes, so tired. He felt heavier and heavier until she realized he was asleep standing up.

"Silly man," she whispered.

Unsure of what to do but unwilling to wake him, she backed herself toward a chair where he had set a box of stockings. She bumped it off with her hip and sat him down. Now what?

She watched him a moment, satisfied herself that he wasn't going to fall off the chair, and hurried into the kitchen, where she lit a fire in the stove to warm some water.

She leaned against the table, wondering how to face two days of funerals, then felt ashamed. She had lost no one in the disaster. The Lord Almighty must be tired of her, and she couldn't blame Him.

When the water in the reservoir was barely lukewarm, she dipped out a basin, found a washcloth, soap, and a towel, and returned to Owen's bedroom. She lit the kerosene lamp and almost wished she hadn't because his dark eyes were disconcertingly half-open. Cautious, she passed her hand in front of them. Nothing. *I certainly hope you don't sleep like that every night*, she thought.

How to proceed? She closed his eyelids. She wetted down his hair, remembering a time he joked that Welshmen mostly had black hair because the Lord knew they would be mining coal.

The water was black now, so she threw it out the kitchen door, wondering how to get him down to the mattress on the floor. Although they were much the same height, he far outweighed her in muscle. She had taken off his socks and was washing his feet when someone knocked.

The door opened, and she heard footsteps then, "Sister Anders? I mean, Sister Davis?"

She could have sunk to the floor in relief to see Bishop Parmley. "I really need your help," Della said, then put her hand to her mouth. "Oh, but you probably came here to ask us to help you with something. I'm sorry!"

"I had a distinct impression that *you* needed some help," he said. "Let's get this man to bed."

Della didn't mean to babble, but she did anyway, sounding like a child plucking at her mother's sleeve with the news that she was trying to clean him up, but she didn't want to wake him and had no idea how to get Owen in his nightshirt and down on the mattress on the floor because he weighed more than she did.

She stopped, tears on her face, embarrassed and so lonely for help from someone who had to be more tired than she was. "I'm sorry, Bishop," she said.

"No fears, Della. In good days and bad days, you know I walk this canyon every evening with my lantern. Something told me to stop."

She hugged Bishop Parmley, grateful for his assistance. Between them, they stripped Owen of his clothing, pulled his nightshirt down over his head, and set him gently on the mattress, all without Owen doing more than mumbling and opening his eyes once to stare around owlishly, then returning to slumber.

"When he wakes up, tell him the Finn's funerals will start at nine. The Koskis want you there." She heard his sigh. "We Parmleys will be going to Provo in the afternoon for my brother's funeral, and all the Gatherums' too," he said.

"We'll be there for the Finns," Della said, even as she trembled inside.

"Thank you. I've just come from Finn Town, and every woman there requested your presence in particular."

"They're my friends."

He kissed her forehead and left the house.

Della stood in the doorway until he was out of sight. She locked the door and stood a moment in the front room, wondering if the Knights had found them a place to live in Provo, something modest because they didn't have much and were currently unemployed.

She pulled her nightgown from her carpetbag and couldn't help smiling as she put it on. "I came to a canyon to teach school," she said softly, even though she probably could have banged a gong and Owen wouldn't have heard a thing, "and look what I found: a snoring Welshman."

Chapter 6

Della woke in the morning to Owen Davis raised up on one elbow, looking at her with eyes fully open now and appreciative, even though she knew her hair was a mess.

"I'm a sight," she mumbled, patting the bedclothes for the hairpins she had neglected to remove and trying to tug her nightgown down.

"You're beautiful," he said, and he kissed her.

Early that morning, in a quiet house in a silent coal camp, Della truly became Owen's wife. For precious moments, there was no grief in the Davis house, nothing but each other, and it felt supremely right.

Della had to laugh when Owen assured her, "With more rest, I will amaze you."

"What a relief to know that I am married to a modest, circumspect man," she told the ceiling.

"Della, Della," he murmured. "You're going to keep me humble, aren't you?

"Someone must," she said, which made him laugh out loud.

He sobered quickly and pulled the blankets up around them. "I don't even want to face this day, but you made it a little more likely that I can. There aren't sufficient words to convey my gratitude," he said frankly.

"I believe that is what our bishop intended," she said as she sat up and stretched, then shrieked when he tugged her down to tickle her.

Before his eyes closed again, she reminded him that the Finnish funerals and others would begin at nine o'clock.

"I wish I didn't have to even think about it," he said. She heard his sorrow and something more. He put his hands behind his head. "I have already told you about what happened to my father and brothers, dead in the Abercarn Horror back in Wales and sealed in that mine, never to come out."

"Don't," she said, putting her hand over his eyes.

"I must. There were more than one hundred graves for the men who . . . who were brought to the surface before the mine was flooded to put out the fire. I was ten. I still remember."

"And I remember my father's funeral," she said. "I cried and cried and no one held me."

Silence. Owen slept. "But he was only one man," she told her sleeping husband. "You saw one hundred there and here are hundreds more, the Finns first. Does anyone need this much death in large numbers?" She sighed. "Or one by one?"

The thought brought her to her feet, and she began searching for her clothes. Eeva Koski had said Mari Luoma wanted to see her, and there was no time like now, even though it was early. *Who could sleep?* she wondered and then shook her head in amusement. *Except maybe a newly married man too long on a fallow field.*

She looked down at her sleeping husband. "I'd rather stay here with you," she whispered, then reminded herself that she had other matters to attend to. Owen would keep.

Mari and Heikki Luoma had come to her at the beginning of the school term, Heikki asking so politely if his bride could join the lower grades class, sit in the back quietly, and learn more English. And so Mari had, until her pregnancy became obvious, and Miss Clayson, a stickler for propriety, had said that was enough.

Miss Clayson. Della dressed quickly. Surely there was time to see both Mari and Miss Clayson before the funerals.

She walked quickly to Finn Town, hands rubbing cold arms, head down because she didn't want to see the coffins, now filled and loaded onto wagons that trundled down the canyon, heading for the cemetery. She stood in silence by the Finnish communal sauna, where she had enjoyed many happy evenings with her now-widowed friends.

Her heart sore, she watched as other Finns removed coffins from the sauna and loaded them onto a waiting wagon. Some of the men nodded to her, those lucky miners on the afternoon shift who had been home sleeping when their countrymen died in the Number Four and Number One. She nodded back.

Kari came to her when the coffins were tied down. With tears in her eyes, she watched as he patted two coffins. "Your brothers?" she whispered to the wind.

She wondered at the enormous swell of grief that filled her heart, then realized her mind had taken another odd turn back to the Molly Bee on the Colorado plateau. She remembered she had done that precise thing.

The memory compelled her forward to stand beside Kari and pat those two coffins, as well. His arm went around her as the wagon moved away.

"My father died in a mine," she told her friend's husband. "I patted his coffin. Funny that it should take me this long to remember."

"Not so funny," Kari said. "I have noticed, dear friend, that the mind pretty well does what it pleases at times like this."

They walked to his house and there was Eeva with her welcoming smile. Standing with her was Mari Luoma, dressed in black from head to toe, but her own smile wide as she held out her arms for her teacher.

Della held her close as she could, considering that Mari's pregnancy was far enough advanced to make it more convenient to stand a bit sideways. Her last view of Mari Luoma had been near the railroad tracks as Dr. Isgreen pulled her away from the approaching train. The vacant look was gone now, to Della's relief.

There were two other people in the room. When Della released Mari, her friend introduced them.

"Isaak and Leena Mako, cousins of Heikki from Belt in Montana," she said with a gesture. "Dear teacher, they are taking me home with them today." Her lovely face softened as she rested a hand on her belly. "Heikki and I . . . This is *our* little American. I cannot return to Suomi." Her head went up. "No. This land will do, and so I told the parents of Heikki only yesterday. I cannot return with them. I will not."

Della regarded the couple and saw kindness. She squeezed Mari's hand. They embraced again.

Della left as quietly as she had come. Her steps slowed as she neared the schoolhouse and then quickened as she saw Miss Clayson, dressed for travel, with a suitcase in her hand. She knew her prickly principal was not a demonstrative woman, but suddenly it didn't matter. She held out her arms and embraced

Miss Clayson, who set down her suitcase and hugged her back.

"I hope you weren't planning to leave without a goodbye," Della scolded gently when she released her principal.

"Farewells are hard," Miss Clayson said. She visibly gathered herself together. "Remember in the library a few weeks ago when you gave me that classified section of the paper?"

"I teased you about job-hunting, didn't I?" Della said. "Cheeky of me."

"You do have that tendency," Miss Clayson said, but with only a touch of her former asperity. "I'm going home to Boise to teach sixth grade and live with my mother." She looked toward the cemetery. "I'm leaving now. I have not the courage for funerals of miners."

"Good luck to you, friend," Della said. "I wish you well in Boise."

"And good luck to you and your miner. I hear you were married yesterday morning." She handed Della a note. "Here is my Boise address. Let me hear from you." She looked up the canyon. "Here he comes. I envied you for a while, you know."

"No, I didn't," Della said, touched.

"He had better take good care of you," Miss Clayson said, and as Della had heard all year from her steely administrator, it *wasn't* a suggestion.

"Goodness, Dr. Isgreen already threatened him in person," Della said, which made Lavinia Clayson laugh. "Thank you for more than I can ever say."

"Thank *you*." Miss Clayson squeezed Della's hand. "You're not the only one who learned a lot in the Winter Quarters School this year." Her chin quivered, but her gaze never wavered. "So did I."

Angharad had insisted they stop for her, but her Aunt Mabli came outside to tell them she was still asleep. "She doesn't need this. I will keep her here," Mabli said, and then she went back inside and closed the door so there was no argument.

Della would have given her none. Her eyes on her husband, she watched him carefully as they walked to the cemetery, with its long trenches of coffins in place.

Owen stood in silence for the brief service, head bowed and bare in the cold wind. He took her arm after the final prayer. "They came from so far. France, Switzerland, Germany, Finland. Same as me, seeking better lives. God bless us all."

She wasn't surprised when he joined the boys and the mourners with shovels, a man with strength in his back from years of shooting down coal, then digging it out and loading big lumps onto ore cars.

She wanted to turn away from the awful sight of so many coffins in trenches. The rain had turned to sleet that the wind tossed back at their faces, but she knew she would not leave until her husband finished his work. It touched her heart to see him look back at her, as if reassuring himself that she was there.

I will never leave you, she told him silently.

Her wait became immeasurably easier when she felt a gloved hand in hers.

Startled, then delighted, she saw Kristina Aho, her blond loveliness set off by the immaculate cut of her gray suit. And there was her son Pekka, who had been Della's first student to leave her class after his father died in a Number One cave-in last year.

"I came for Viktor, my brother-in-law," Kristina said in her ear as they hugged each other and then made room for Pekka, tidy in Finnish short pants and embroidered vest. "Reet is too young for this, so she stayed with my landlady in Salt Lake."

Mrs. Aho indicated the tall man behind her. Della held out both hands to Mr. Whalley, Menswear manager at Auerbach's Department Store in Salt Lake, where Della had found the newly widowed Kristina Aho a job. A quiet man, he had been Della's boss the summer before when she sold shirts and sundries in his department.

Mr. Whalley shook her hand and then looked beyond her. "A size sixteen medium," he said. "Miss Anders, is this the man you bought the shirts for?" He chuckled. "And claimed he was just a friend?"

Della turned around as Owen approached the little gathering. He leaned the shovel against the shrinking mound of dirt, wiped his hands on his trousers, and held out his hand.

"My dear, this is Mr. Whalley, who knows shirts," Della said. "Mr. Whalley, I'm Mrs. Davis as of yesterday."

She had only known Mr. Whalley as a manager who suffered no fools gladly, even though the customer was generally right. She saw sympathy in his eyes now, and tenderness when he glanced at Mrs. Aho and her son.

"Pleased to make your acquaintance, Mr. Davis, and congratulations to you both," Mr. Whalley said. "I wish it were under better circumstances, but I wasn't about to let Kris . . . Mrs. Aho travel all this way unescorted." He smiled then, and the look he gave Pekka told Della worlds about his fondness for both Ahos. "Not that she was unescorted, eh, Pekka?"

And the smile Pekka flashed back told Della even more about how matters stood with her friend. *We keep on living*, she thought, grateful to see evidence of it, even on such a sad day.

Kristina's eyes were on other graves farther away. She touched Pekka's head, and they started toward the row where her late husband, Matti Aho, lay. Della's hand in Owen's, Mr. Whalley beside them, they followed at a respectful distance.

"I have been keeping company with Mrs. Aho for several months now," he said. "You know I am a staunch Presbyterian, but lately I have come to enjoy Lutheran sermons, because that means Sunday dinner with the Ahos. Ahem, I suspect that the God of the Presbyterians and the Lutherans is one and the same."

"I couldn't be happier," Della said, impressed with Mr. Whalley, partly because that statement was as close as he had ever come to a bit of humor, at least in her hearing. "I think you should keep company with the Ahos right now."

"So I shall." He tipped his hat to them, reached inside his suit and pulled out a white envelope. "Everyone in the store took up a collection for the miners' families, and Mr. Auerbach doubled it." He put the envelope in Owen's hand. "There is one hundred dollars for each widow, and a little more."

Mr. Whalley wasn't a man who ever appreciated dramatic overtures, so Della offered a sedate handshake and heartfelt thanks, when she really wanted to dance around and hug him.

"We'll see that Superintendent Parmley gets this," she said. "You couldn't have done a kinder thing."

"Death is hard even when you expect it," he replied, his eyes going over the rows of coffins. "And like this? Who can bear it?" He nodded toward the widow and her son standing with heads bowed by another grave, one filled in last fall. "And here is something else: Mr. Auerbach insisted that Kristina received one hundred dollars too, even though Mr. Aho died months ago. She and I are going to arrange for a proper stone for his grave. Good day, Mr. and Mrs. Davis, and good fortune to you both."

"Good luck to you too, Mr. Whalley," Della said, touched at his generosity and affection, grateful for this glimpse into the heart of a quiet man who bore sorrows of his own.

"I should shovel some more," Owen said, but she heard reluctance in his voice.

"No. You should walk me to the Wasatch Store, where we will slip this envelope under Bishop Parmley's door," she said decisively. "I have a key to the library. We're going to go in there and just sit."

She thought he might object, but he did not.

"Just sit?" he asked, and she heard a sliver of humor. "You wouldn't mind if I kissed you once or twice?"

"I was counting on that."

Chapter 7

The ordeal of burying Richard Evans on Saturday would have been impossible without Della and Angharad beside Owen, holding his hands.

He had spent a sleepless night sharing his mattress this time with both Della and Angharad, because his daughter had seen too many coffins and weeping classmates and refused to be away from them.

Bless Della's heart. She made the best of the situation, sitting there in her nightgown, with her funny Magic Paper, those sheets of flexible cardboard found inside men's shirts. She had given Angharad the task of drawing her own bedroom in their new house in Provo, something none of them had seen yet, if it even existed.

"What if there isn't a house when we get to Provo?" he spoke into Della's neck when he held her close after Angharad slept.

"I don't know. I'm trusting Uncle Jesse."

He wanted Della, but there was no way, not with Angharad sleeping beside them. When he could tell Della slept, he got out of bed, dressed, and walked to Martha Evans's house. He knew she would be awake, the same as other widows of men he had mined with mere days ago. There were flickering lights all over the canyon, pointing out the homes where husbands waited for burial tomorrow.

Martha seemed not even slightly surprised to see him when he tapped on her door, and she opened it, the perfect hostess at midnight. She patted the chair next to hers as she leaned against her husband's coffin. "No sleep for you either?"

"None. I'm sharing my mattress with Della *and* Angharad tonight." He took a deep breath, wondering if he was about to add to her burden. "And there is this: Richard's last bit of kindness to me was to scold me into petitioning the Lord in the right way, and not seeking my own interests at the expense of truth. I owe him this visit."

"I, for one, am glad you listened, even if it was likely a royal scold," Martha replied.

He heard all the strain in her voice. "Martha, my answer from the Lord was to leave the mine, so I did. I am all that is left of the day shift and the men's choir, and I feel it acutely. Why me?"

She held him as he wept next to his best friend's coffin, with its magical dragons and its leeks and daffodils, symbols of Wales, carved years ago by a miner grandfather he never knew, and handed down to him following his father's death. What better place for such a box than underground?

"Forgive me, Martha," he said when he could speak. "I have no right to burden you."

"What are friends for? Promise me that you will find another occupation in Provo, as I know you told Della you would."

Her eyes bored into his. Maybe she knew him too well, the bereft father who had taken his infant daughter from nursing breast to nursing breast in the canyon, hers included, after Gwyna's death. It was an admittedly odd intimacy. He had to look away from the intensity of her gaze.

When he averted his face, she forced him to look at her. "Don't go back on your word to the best woman you could ever have married. Don't even consider it, Owen Rhys Davis." She gave his face a shake.

"I should stay here and help you and the others."

"And how would you do that? You must move on," Martha said firmly. "Bishop Parmley has already asked me to manage a boardinghouse in Clear Creek, only eight miles from this man of mine. When this awful week is done, I will be going there with my little ones. I will manage, Owen."

"And the others?"

"They will manage too," she said. "Your obligation is to Della and Angharad now. Don't forget that."

What demon drove him on? "Martha, maybe I can convince her, change her mind. She could teach here. You know how hard it is to find a single woman to teach in the canyon and the district might make allowances. I could go back to the mine. I know I could."

He hadn't felt Martha's wrath since that time three years ago when the Pleasant Valley Ward Relief Society turned on him for not pursuing a lovely lady, friend of the Parmley's, who came to visit and seemed interested in him. He felt that wrath now, only worse.

She pulled his face close to hers, and he saw all the anger and exhaustion in tired eyes. "Owen, if you make that good woman—your wife—have to choose between you and a paltry mine, I'll have nothing more to do with you. For shame!"

It had to be said. Maybe he needed her anger to jolt him back into reality. He had made a promise to another lovely lady. He had already married her. In a few days they would be sealed for eternity in Manti Temple. He had no business waffling and dodging. He kissed Martha Evans's cheek, hugged her, and stood up to rest his head against the coffin he had fashioned out of his own Welshness and his regard for the best of men.

"I'm sorry for whining, Martha," he said quietly. "And yes, I will sing for Richard and David tomorrow."

"We thank you."

His hand was on the doorknob when she stopped him. "Didn't Della's father die in a mine cave-in?

"Aye, and so she was sent to Salt Lake to live with wolves," he said, not mincing words, surprised at his own bitterness.

"How is this horrible week upsetting her?"

"That was years ago."

She gave him another leveling look. "And you think a body can ever forget? One man or . . ." Her voice failed her for a moment and then returned stronger. ". . . or two hundred. It doesn't matter. Think about Della in all this." She managed a smile. "Now go away and leave me here with Richard."

He blew her a kiss and walked through the sort of dark he knew so well underground, pierced here and there by little points of light. Women mourned in silence now, and despair roamed freely up and down the wagon road like the last plague of Egypt.

He only thought Della slept. Shawl around her nightgown, she stood on the porch, moving from one foot to the other because she hadn't bothered with shoes. The sight of her warmed him, and made him shy, because he was a modest man, and here was a pretty woman in a nightgown on his porch.

"You'll catch your death," he said as he took her by the arm and steered her inside. He held her close in the front room.

"I watched you walk to Martha's," she said, caressing his face.

"And here I thought I was quiet and discreet."

"You were, but I missed you. One day and I already missed your warmth." Della turned her face into his shoulder. "I know you are unemployed and this is a terrible time. Please don't regret what we have done. Bishop Parmley did move us along rather quickly."

What could he say to that? He led her back to the bed they shared with his daughter this night, dazed with the enormity of his regrets and unable to articulate any of them to the one person to whom he should share them all.

"I said my goodbyes to Richard," he managed to tell her.

"Did you?" she asked, as if she knew what he was thinking.

The burials continued Saturday after a funeral under the direction of church leaders from Salt Lake City.

The newly completed Odd Fellows Hall, supposed to be the scene of Tuesday night's dance celebrating Dewey Day, was the only building large enough to house all the mourners, everyone wanting some reassurance, some hope. They sat on chairs brought in from everywhere and stood against the walls when chairs ran out, a congregation exhausted by anguish and tears.

Only the little ones, children who couldn't understand what was going on or know why their mamas seemed so distant, looked around in delight at the veritable garden of flowers, furnished by women from Salt Lake City and Provo, where husbands and fathers didn't die by the hundreds on a single day.

God bless Della Davis. She kept her arm firmly around his waist and her hip cemented to his as they stood close together, Angharad in front of them, almost as if they were unconsciously—or consciously—serving as his buttresses. Packed together as they were, somehow Della managed to lean even closer and shush him when Elder Reed Smoot, an apostle of the Lord, counseled the miners to "say no rash words, do no rash act. Take no especial steps demanding what you may think is right from the Company."

He saw he wasn't the only surviving miner listening and being shushed. Other men around him stirred and whispered and then returned their attention to the church leader from Salt Lake City who maybe didn't understand what had happened. Elder Smoot had never shoveled coal, picked out stones, eaten endless oatcakes when the money ran out in summer, wished he could give his children new shoes. What did he know of grievances?

Apostle or not, Elder Smoot, you could have said anything but that, Owen told himself as he listened, shocked. But no, Elder Smoot stood there at a pulpit brought in from the Scofield meetinghouse and said, "Don't let men come among you to harrow up your souls."

"He's telling us not to strike, Della," Owen whispered in Della's ear. "Couldn't it wait?"

She patted his chest and his arm went around her shoulder. He didn't want to remember those words. He wanted to remember what the well-meaning man said next: "There is a bishopric here that loves you . . ."

Maybe he should have stopped there because it was true, but no. He continued, ". . . and we hope the conditions of each family may be learned."

Conditions of each family? Owen thought, wondering where this enormous surge of bitterness in him was coming from, he who paid his tithing, lived the Word of Wisdom, attended his meetings, and fulfilled his church callings. *I'll tell you the conditions,* he wanted to shout. *There are widows and fatherless children, and the coal company will turn them out soon. They have no income, I'm unemployed, and we feel so terrible.*

"I have to leave," he whispered.

He towed Della from the hall, Angharad trailing after. Outside, he leaned against the wall and gathered himself together, Della close beside him.

"I can't bear it. I simply can't."

"No one can," his wife said, "but we have to. Just a little longer."

She was right; he knew it.

"You needn't go back in there," his practical darling continued. "It's stifling, and you're the only man in there who smells good to me."

Who couldn't laugh at that? "Della, you're hilarious," he said.

"I know. Angharad, see if you can find Da some water."

His daughter darted off, and Della kissed him, no simple peck, but a full-bodied kiss that made him grateful everyone else was still inside.

Angharad got him a drink of water from somewhere, and Della sat him down on a bench. In a few minutes, his breathing turned normal. He listened as the choir sang "Wanted on the Other Side."

The words irritated him; they always had. "I ask you, Della, how is it comforting to tell someone mourning a loved one, 'Service he has gone to render, wanted on the other side?'"

"I know," she said, plunking down beside him.

Della did a strange thing then. She pulled up her knees, sitting there on the bench in her best Sunday dress, and rested her chin on them, arms wrapped around her legs like Angharad might sit. "I remember a sacrament meeting once where my Salt Lake bishop said we wouldn't mourn if we saw how good things were on the other side." She chuckled, a cozy sound that stirred his heart, even as he sat there so miserable. "I almost didn't believe him, then decided I would be happier if I did. It might be true, even though we on this side can't see it."

With an exasperated sigh, she seemed to realize how unladylike she looked and put her legs down. "It's your decision, Owen. I can't make it for you. Maybe you should ask yourself what Richard would want you to do."

"Maybe I'd rather wallow in misery for a while," he said frankly.

She shrugged. "I wouldn't blame you."

"Thank you."

"This is the easy part," she reminded him. "When people pour out of here, we're walking to David and Richard's family plots, where you are going to sing 'Lead, Kindly Light,' the miners' song."

"I can't."

"I know *you* can't, but *we* can, and we will, my love."

They did later, but not before he had helped shovel dirt on more rows of coffins, this time men like himself who had joined the Mormon Church in the British Isles and followed the call to Zion. Many of these were single men. Only last Monday, he had teased shy William Williams about saving his money to send for Mary Jones in Merthyr Tydfil. Who was going to tell Mary Jones what had happened to the man she waited for?

But there was no putting off the worst of the ordeal, standing by the more remote family plots of miners who had been living in Pleasant Valley longer. After older brother William Evans dedicated the graves of his two brothers until the morning of the First Resurrection, the Davises stepped between the two plots. Propped up by his women, Owen Rhys Davis gathered all his strength and sang "Lead, Kindly Light" to David Evans and Richard Evans, while their surviving brothers and nephews who had been on the afternoon shift joined them on the final verse.

As if they had planned it, all the other excellent voices dropped out as he sang the first verse again, loathe to let go. Owen felt his breaking heart soar with the spirits of his two friends far out over the valley and the mourners and gravestones. Others nearby at their own burials turned to listen.

"'Keep thou my feet; I do not ask to see, the distant scene—one step enough for me.'"

It was done. After shoveling soil over his hand-made casket with the beautiful symbols of Wales on it, Owen turned away after one last look into Martha's grieving face. He wondered if he would ever be able to sing again.

Chapter 8

Owen put his wife and child on the last train to Provo that evening, along with Angharad's furniture, his handcrafted sofa from the front room, and his promise now to meet them in Manti on Thursday morning at the temple. Della couldn't argue when Bishop Parmley said he needed Owen's help with company paperwork for the deceased miners' widows, although she wanted to.

"The company is forgiving all last month's debts in the company store and providing five hundred dollars for each widow," Owen told her as they walked toward his house. "Other donations are coming in. I'm going to help Bishop with those for a few days."

"And sleep where?"

"I have a mattress."

"And a marvelous mattress it is, husband," she teased.

Their path had been smoothed enormously by the arrival of their stake president, who had come up from Provo for the funerals and had no problem furnishing them their last interview for temple sealing. He waved away any explanations about their hurried civil wedding days ago.

"You've been through enough," he said, and he took both of them by the hand. "Bishop Parmley explained it all, and I am happy to sign away an eternity for the two of you."

Della smiled at that, looked at Owen, and wished he would smile too. He frowned instead, which made her wonder what was going through his head. When she touched his arm, he seemed to remember where he was, and smiled. It came too late. *Poor, poor man,* she thought. *You need some rest. Something better than a mattress in an empty house.*

She left Angharad and Owen to quickly pack out her room and walked to Finn Town alone, head bowed against the force of the wind. Her mind rebelled at leaving the canyon's grieving inhabitants to their own devices, even as she knew there was nothing more she could do for any of them.

Eeva Koski hugged her and said she must return to sauna with them, but in Clear Creek.

"Kari thinks it best we go there to mine with other Finns," she said as she stood in her doorway. "There seem to be hard feelings here." She sighed and looked down the winding road Della had walked. "Why must things change?"

The visit to Annie Jones was harder because there was Myfanwy, one of her best pupils, dressed in black and standing by the door as Della had watched her after school all year, waiting for her father to walk up from the mine, ready to hand off his lunch box and sit on the porch to hear about her day. "Da makes the time for me," she told Della once.

Myfanwy had written a story about her father that Della had submitted to the district office in Spanish Fork for a writing contest. The results wouldn't be in for a few weeks. The Winter Quarters School was closed now until fall, but the school year hadn't entirely wound down in the rest of the district. In other classrooms, teachers and students still worked and wrote little essays about what they would do this summer, while Myfanwy's classroom had become a morgue. Bishop Parmley had already said they would repaint the interior of the school because the odor of burned flesh remained. No one wanted an essay about that.

Della sat with Annie, reminding the woman of her gift of oat bread and salt when she arrived.

"And now it will be Owen Davis for you," Annie said and smiled. "Take care of him, as we took care of him during his worst hours after Gwyna died."

"I promise. What will you do?"

"I'll stay here. Probably take in washing. Our oldest boy still lives with me, and the mines will reopen." Annie's eyes filled with tears. "As I told you a few months ago, we keep busy with our children and try not to think about what could happen." She took a deep breath, and Della marveled at the strength in Annie's calm face. "And since it did, we carry on with the help of the Lord Almighty." She kissed Della and went into her bedroom, closing the door quietly.

Martha Evans held her close for a long while. "I could give you all manner of advice," she said finally, holding Della off to look into her face. "Just love the man. He has some serious doubts about his life right now."

"About me?" Della asked. "Tell me, Martha. About me?"

"Probably about everything. He wonders why he is alive and . . . and other things."

"Provo is only seventy miles from Gwyna's grave," Della said, filling in what she knew Martha would not say. "I can't do anything about Gwyna."

"No, you can't. He loved her and she died. Now he loves you."

"Does he? Is it enough for him?" Della made herself put words to her fears.

"Aye, he does, my dear," Martha assured her. "He also loves the mines. I could box his ears for that and shake a stick at him, but there is a lure that wives don't understand."

"What should I do if he breaks his promise to me and the mines win?"

"You'll know what to do wh . . . if it happens."

"You're not easing my mind, Martha," Della said, and then she hated herself for questioning a woman newly widowed who had more important things to consider. "I'm sorry, friend." She took Martha's hand. "I probably will know."

"Of that I have no doubt; nor should you doubt." Martha said with certainty, as though she spoke to one of her children.

The Davis house was starting to look as bare as the houses already abandoned by widows and children who waited for the train to take them away from their homes. Della, Owen, and Angharad walked behind the wagon taking their paltry effects to the depot. They stopped at the hospital at the mouth of the canyon, where Emil Isgreen kissed Della and dared Owen to do anything about it.

Della had to smile inside when Owen held up his hand. "Dr. Isgreen, you have already threatened me with dire things if I do not do my duty by Della Davis. Kiss her again and I'll lay you out, even if you are taller than I am."

"I know you could," Emil said, good-natured as always. "Good luck to you. Stop by, if you're ever in the canyon again."

"We will be," Della said promptly. She glanced at Owen, who nodded, his eyes still tired, but not so sad. *So there, husband*, she thought.

Goodbyes at the station were easier this time. "Eight in the morning at the Manti Temple," Owen said to Della. "You have the paperwork, and I'll provide the Welshman."

"Where will you sleep tonight?" she asked.

"Probably on Mabli's sofa. I'd rather sleep with you, all things considered. My goodness, but you can blush. Blush away, Della. I'll see you Thursday, with Mabli and we'll see who else."

Who else could there be? she asked herself, and she knew he was asking the same question. Gently, she took his face in her hands and kissed him carefully and so slowly that the conductor finally walked by and cleared his throat.

"We have a schedule, ma'am," the man said and then walked on.

Owen pulled away first and chuckled at that. He didn't say anything as he helped her up the steps, ruffled Angharad's hair, and stepped back. He gave her a long look, then "*Fi cariad ddau ohonoch*," and a kiss blown to them both.

All of a sudden Della felt like it was the two of them against the world, with no buffer, no Owen, nothing. "What did he say, Angharad?"

"'I love you both,'" the child replied. "Why does Thursday already seem so far away?"

Oh dear, Della thought. *One of us is going to have to be the adult, and I suppose I am elected*. "It's not so far away, dear. Think of it like this: it's already practically Saturday night, and we can't count Sunday because that is church, and we are busy all day. I think the Knights will have a house for us, so we will be busy on Monday and Tuesday, putting things away."

"We don't have much," Angharad pointed out. "How can that take two days?"

"We'll work slowly. We'll have to find a market and buy some food and arrange for ice deliveries for our icebox," Della said. *If we have a kitchen with an icebox, and an address.*

"Then it will be Wednesday, which we can't even count because it will go so fast," Della concluded. She had to smile because it was preposterous. "Don't look so skeptical, Angharad."

"It's hard not to. Will Da be all right by himself?"

"He'll be better when we're together again," Della said honestly. "Remember: we're just counting Monday and Tuesday. Nothing else matters."

Chapter 9

Only a woman in deep and abiding love could turn five days into two and a half, but Della succeeded as well as was humanly possible, considering.

She couldn't help her feeling of relief to be out of Scofield, at the same time she regretted leaving. *You're not running away*, she scolded herself, and then she wondered why she felt so bereft. The canyon she had come to love with all her heart had turned on them. She knew she wanted to treasure up each memory of teaching, meeting lovely people, half of whom were gone now, going to sauna with her Finnish friends, managing the library, discovering her own worth, falling in love.

Her long list of positive emotions that should have been rightfully hers struggled against the massive, overwhelming sorrow she felt. She wondered if that would change, or if the Winter Quarters disaster would remain the darkest cloud of her life, never quite out of sight.

Once over Soldier Summit and in Thistle, the train uncoupled one of its helper engines and let off passengers, some of them her young students. Forcing herself to smile, she hugged and kissed each one and their mothers, heading to other relatives in other towns, scattering like leaves in autumn. As absurd as it sounded, she wanted to turn back time to Tuesday, May 1, and run from door to door in the canyon, imploring each miner to stay home that day. That way, 10:28 a.m. would come and go with nothing more interesting than a spelling test. There would be the dance that night in the Odd Fellows Hall, and she would tell Owen that *yes*, she would marry him, no matter what. Martha and Richard would gather close and wish them well, and she and Owen would make happy plans for a Manti Temple wedding with all their friends in attendance.

Shaken, she sat down with Angharad and held her close when the train started again, craving the child's arms around her neck as they clung together, wishing for . . . what?

"I wish we could turn back time, Angharad," she said softly. "Do you?"

The child nodded. She sat up on Della's lap. "Remember how Da and I touch fingers before he leaves for his shift, and he says, 'Leave it in God's hands?' We do that every morning." Angharad shivered. "We *used* to do that. Please, Mam, let's still leave it in God's hands."

Della felt a shard or two splinter from the boulder on her heart and soul. Trust the daughter of the man she loved to be the adult in that moment. "I do believe that will be the best course," Della said. She held out her forefinger and Angharad touched it with hers.

"In God's hands," she whispered.

"*Ddwylo Duw*," Angharad echoed.

Amanda Knight waited for them at the depot. "Owen sent us a telegram," she said, holding off Della for a better look. "'Look at her hand,' it said."

Della held out her left hand. "I tried to argue, but Bishop Parmley insisted."

Amanda laughed, such a welcome sound.

"Bishop said Owen and I needed each other now and not next week, so he married us then and there," she said. "He was right. Why do I argue with a bishop?"

"Because you're Della," Amanda said promptly. "Come on, you two. It's late, and I want to get you and your possessions to my home. We can stack them in the carriage house and sort it out on Monday."

"We don't have too much," Della said. Her good humor began to reassert itself. "I take that back: Angharad has a completely furnished house."

"Mam, you know it's a dollhouse," the child reminded her, her eyes bright too, for the first time in days.

"And what a house it is, built by a master," Della agreed.

The carriage started for Center Street. Angharad tucked herself close to Della, but her eyes were on Amanda Knight. "Please, mum, what should I call you?"

Amanda laughed. "You hear Uncle Jesse and yet Della calls me Amanda."

"I am confused," Angharad said with some dignity. "Are you and Mam related?"

"Sort of," Della said, well aware how little she wanted to ever tell this child about Aunt Caroline Anders, a cousin of the kind lady seated beside them, wife to her Uncle Karl who took her in after her father died. "We're what people here call 'shirttail relatives.' What are we, Amanda?"

"Caroline and I are distant cousins, and she is your aunt, Della. Perhaps I am a distant aunt," Amanda said with a laugh. "Does that simplify things, Angharad?"

Angharad shook her head.

"Do this then," Amanda said. "You call me Aunt Amanda, please. Uncle Jesse is Uncle Jesse to everyone in Utah, I think." She peered closer. "Have I completely confused you?"

"Not yet," Angharad said. She closed her eyes. "I'll think about it a moment, if that is all right with you and Mam."

"'Mam,' is it?" Amanda asked.

"Yes, and I love it," Della replied. She leaned back against the cushions. "My word, is it possible to feel so tired and still be alive?"

"What a terrible week for you. All you need to do when we get home is go to bed. Sunday we'll be in church. I don't intend for either of you to lift a finger."

Angharad felt heavy against her arm. Della heard even breathing. She inclined her head against the child's, hoping her father slept, but knowing he didn't.

"Owen stayed to help Bishop Parmley with insurance paperwork." Della struggled as her own eyelids seemed to droop of their own accord. "Imagine this: Mr. Auerbach sent a check for fifteen hundred dollars. People have been so kind."

She looked around, missing Uncle Jesse for the first time. "Where is . . ."

"Jesse? He tried mightily to change his plans, but he couldn't," Amanda said. "He and our son Raymond are on their way to Alberta District, in Canada."

"What on earth for?"

"Business. I think he's going to buy a lot of land."

At the house, the driver carefully lifted Angharad from the carriage and at Amanda's quiet command, took her upstairs to the turret room, where he set her down just as gently. Della undressed her down to her shift while Amanda pulled back the covers and popped her in.

Della watched the sleeping child, envious of the peace on her face. Amanda took her hand and tugged her from the room, leading her downstairs.

"Just a few words, dear," Amanda said as she led her into the parlor.

Della wanted to object, but that would have taken more words than she was currently capable of. She rested her hand against her cheek as she fought sleep.

"I want to put your mind immediately at rest, Della, even though it seems like mighty small potatoes in the face of this week. We found a house for sale and we acquired it."

"Heavens, I didn't expect you to go to such trouble and expense," Della said, dismayed.

"It was no trouble and very little expense, and you will be renters," Amanda replied. "Two bedrooms, a front room, a kitchen and dining area, and believe it or not, an indoor lavatory."

"I didn't expect that," Della said, perking up. "How in the world can we afford such a place?"

"Is twenty dollars a month agreeable?" Amanda asked.

"That can't possibly be, but yes, provided we both find work, and soon."

"There is a sort of shed that would easily serve as a shop for a man inclined to work with wood," Amanda added. "You know, someone like your Owen."

"Someone like," Della agreed. "Make it completely perfect, and tell me it is not too far from here so we can visit, and convenient to walking everywhere."

Amanda clapped her hands together. "It's perfect! Wait until I tell Jesse."

She put her arm around Della. "If twenty a month is too high, we'll lower it to fifteen—anything to help you two get a good start."

Della was certain she had cried every tear in her body, but she was wrong. She leaned against Amanda and wept in the dark parlor.

"Dear, dear me," Amanda crooned. "It's going to get better. I just know it. Whatever we can do to help." She cleared her throat. "Since you're already crying, this shouldn't burden you too much more: Don't worry about furniture. Mr. Auerbach himself telephoned me and asked what you might need. He brought it by yesterday. In person."

Della accepted a handkerchief from Amanda. "A house. Furniture." She blew her nose. "How can I even begin to thank you?"

"No need," Amanda said, her voice serious. "This is many long overdue payments for what you richly deserve, Della Davis. You may tell me not to, but I will always regret that no one helped you when you came from Colorado with that nametag around your neck, after your father died. I wish I had been more aware of your . . . your difficult life in my cousin's household."

The dark room began to work on Della. All it lacked was Owen. "I'm so tired," she murmured. "Could I . . . could you just cover me with a blanket right here?"

"I can and will," Amanda said. "Need any help?"

Della shook her head. She was down to her shift by the time Amanda returned with a pillow and blanket. Without a word, she lay down on the sofa, curling up because it was too short. Amanda tucked the blanket around her, kissed her cheek, and closed the pocket doors as she left the room.

Must pray, Della thought. She got off the sofa and knelt by it, resting her head on the seat.

Amanda found her there in the morning, still kneeling, still sleeping, Owen on her mind and in her heart. She barely remembered a blanket wrapped around her as she followed her hostess down the hall to another room, where she returned to sleep in a real bed. She remembered Amanda telling her something about Sunday School, and that she would take Angharad, but that was all.

She woke late in the afternoon to find Angharad curled beside her, asleep. Della watched her face, remembering that Owen had told her how much she resembled Gwyna, with her long eyelashes, heart-shaped face, and prominent cheekbones. "You're going to be a beautiful woman, Angharad," she whispered.

She dressed quietly and brushed her hair, hungry now and hoping there was something left over from Sunday dinner in the kitchen. She peeked into the parlor first, where she had started her night.

Amanda looked up from the book she was frowning at and closed it.

"Thank goodness you're awake. I was getting tired of pretending to read an improving work, when I really want to show you your new house." She laughed. "After some roast beef and mashed potatoes?"

Della nodded, happy to turn herself over to someone else to make decisions and smooth her path.

"Angharad will be fine and I know you don't want to wake her," Amanda said a half hour later as they walked the short two blocks to Della's new home. "My housekeeper will keep an eye on her when she wakes up, and we won't be long. Here it is."

She gestured toward a white frame house with a porch, set back among the trees. "I think it was a tree lot originally," Amanda told her. She took a key from her pocketbook. "Here you go. I know it's the Sabbath, but I couldn't wait. I took the liberty of asking my yardman and his wife to arrange the furniture you brought. Go on. Open the door."

Her fingers shaking with excitement, Della opened the door and couldn't help her sigh of pleasure.

"I have some lace curtains that will just fit these windows," Amanda said. "Della, what do you think?"

"Mr. Auerbach, what have you done?" Della asked out loud.

Too shy to even sit in one of the new armchairs, she perched on Owen's more familiar handmade sofa. The sofa's two cushions looked suddenly shabby and needed refurbishing. Sitting on the sofa gave her a glimpse into the kitchen, with cabinets that smelled newly painted.

"We had our yard man touch up a few things," Amanda explained as she followed Della into the kitchen. "While he was at it, there was time to put down some of that new-fangled linoleum. The salesman said the tile pattern is the latest thing back east."

"You're determined to make me cry, aren't you?" Della teased. She admired the oak table and four chairs in the corner. It was a snug fit, but there were only three of them, and no one was oversized.

She opened one of the cabinets, charmed to see dishes in place already. She turned to Amanda, delighted to see the normally dignified older woman looking so pleased. "I suppose you will tell me that you had a few dishes just lying about, languishing from boredom."

"It would be the truth. The icebox is on the back porch, and we already have food cooling in it. The ward Relief Society hasn't had so much fun in years, I think."

Della opened the door onto the back porch, admiring the linoleum there too and the brand-new icebox. Someone had put an ice cream churn on the bottom shelf, next to two Red Wing crocks.

It was too much. She leaned her head against the doorsill, determined not to cry over an icebox and the kindness of strangers.

"You haven't seen anything yet," Amanda assured her. "If you want to cry, save it for your bedroom."

"Which way?"

Amanda led her down a short hall and opened a door on what was Angharad's room, with all of Owen's homemade, carved furniture and the magnificent dollhouse. The room was even large enough for Angharad to play there without having to move the dollhouse into the front room.

"I am really hoping that husband of yours will have time before Christmas to make a dollhouse for Ray's daughter," Amanda said. "Uarda will be the envy of nations. All right now, close your eyes."

Della closed her eyes. Amanda opened the door across from Angharad's room and gave her a little push against the small of her back.

"Open them."

Della obeyed and put her hands to her mouth, her eyes wide. "Mr. Auerbach, what have you done?" she asked again.

"I told him it wasn't a large room, really, and needed a simple bed," Amanda explained as she gave Della another little push. "Will this do, do you think?"

Della stared at the simplicity before her, an oak bed with a modest headboard and footboard. The grain of the wood fanned out in the perfect design of nature, requiring nothing beyond a good finish. She ran her fingers over the whorls, knowing that even a carpenter like Owen would be suitably impressed. Her good humor took over. *If you even notice the wood, after I'm in this bed*, she thought.

She touched the bedspread, remembering it from Domestic Wares, second floor. She had admired just this brand during a noon break last summer, wanting to take something like that with her to Winter Quarters as she finished her job and made plans to teach miners' children in a distant canyon. The five-dollar price tag had put an end to that little dream, and this was the ten dollar spread for a double bed, the kind married people needed.

"I like that burgundy color," Amanda said. "He absolutely insisted that you needed sheets and pillows too. Mr. Auerbach is a hard man to argue with, so I didn't put up much of a struggle. And look how the bed matches this bureau."

Overwhelmed, Della sat down on the bed, enjoying the feel of the rug as she admired the dresser that matched the two nightstands with their lamps. She got up to open the closet door, which was already furnished with hangers and two blankets on the shelf above. Sister Knight's Relief Society hadn't forgotten a thing.

Unable to speak because she knew she would cry, she followed Amanda to the room at the end of the hall, which turned out to be a real lavatory, with a toilet and sink. "My goodness," she managed, but that was all. Thick towels already hung on the racks.

"Alas, the bath is still a tin tub hanging on the porch," Amanda said. "Maybe we can squeeze a tub in here eventually."

"This is luxury right now," Della assured her. "How can I ever thank you enough?"

"Just be happy here," Amanda said simply. "That's all Jesse and I want for you and your husband."

Chapter 10

Owen and Mabli took the last train north on Wednesday evening, unwilling to chance a late arrival to Manti and his wedding to the second woman he loved. It was just a bare sixty miles to Manti through canyons west and south, but he wanted the train to go faster and faster. He wasn't certain if he wanted out of Winter Quarters Canyon worse than he wanted to see Della and never let her go.

The trip to the turnoff at Thistle was hard enough, with widows and their children on board, all looking as blasted and numb as he felt, scattering to the four winds. He spent some time going down the aisle, making certain he had addresses where they could be reached—those he hadn't talked to earlier in the canyon—and giving them the good news that there would be a settlement from the coal company. He knew he could give his list to Mabli for Bishop Parmley when she returned to Winter Quarters.

"I almost don't care to return to the canyon either," Mabli told him when he sank back into his seat.

"I know your David is buried there," he reminded her, thinking of her sister Gwyna, but not wanting to mention Mabli's twin sorrow.

"He is, but I must tell you, darling Owen, maybe I should move on too. I've been thinking about it."

They changed trains at Thistle, and he slept all the way to Manti, leaning against Mabli. Delays kept them from arriving until two o' clock in the morning, so they decided to remain in the depot and save a few dollars at a hotel. Bless her heart, Mabli knew unemployment weighed heavily on a Welshman's heart, and she did not argue.

Perhaps trying to keep himself alert, the stationmaster's assistant pressed Owen to know more about the mine disaster. Normally a polite man, Owen shook his head, hoping the assistant would understand.

The assistant nodded and wandered off. Owen watched him out of half-closed eyes, wondering if anyone could adequately explain the catastrophe to someone who knew nothing of mining and hadn't been in the canyon.

Mabli was far too much of a lady to recline on an unoccupied bench, except she did precisely that without a qualm. Owen sat on the floor in front of her, his back to the seat, ever the gentleman, even though he knew he must look like a bum, unshaven, eyes smudged with exhaustion, jaw clenched. He hoped no one would mind if he shaved in the men's room before heading to the temple to be married.

He woke at seven in the morning, when the train from Salt Lake arrived carrying Della, Sister Knight, and Angharad. He rubbed the sleep from his eyes, wished himself clean-shaven and tidy, and grabbed both of his girls into a tight embrace.

"I know I look a sight. I'm going to find the men's room and shave. I'll meet you at the temple at eight."

"I'll wait here, husband," Della said, and she walked to the bench where Mabli was sitting up and looking around.

Of all the things she could have said, "husband" was utter perfection. "Very well, wife," Owen responded.

"I think you had better find the men's room, my dear," she reminded him when he just stood there. "I'm not in favor of kissing stubble across an altar."

He laughed at that—who wouldn't?—picked up his suitcase, and made a dignified retreat to the men's room. He tidied himself, changed, and came out neater. To his further joy, Della sat by herself on the bench. The others must have gone ahead, which added to his pleasure because he didn't feel like sharing her with anyone, not even Angharad.

She was reading a newspaper and hadn't noticed him yet, which gave him the further luxury of admiring her handsome looks without having to say anything yet. Wife, lover, friend, and probably she who must be obeyed, on occasion. Thanks to Gwyna, he already was well-acquainted with the necessity of bending to someone's will besides his own, especially when the alternative might be a night on the sofa, mulling over marital felonies and misdemeanors.

He was a grown man, former widower, and eager husband. Why this sudden rush of heat to his face?

"Owen, for goodness' sake, you're too old to blush," Della said.

"I was just thinking that there isn't a luckier man in all of Utah and its contiguous states, nearby territories, and ships at sea," he told her.

She blushed then. They sat together on the bench in the depot, holding hands, seizing one small moment of calm, just the two of them.

They were sealed together in Manti Temple three hours later, kneeling across from each other with an altar between them, her hand in his. Bless Andrew

Hood, Pleasant Valley Ward's Sunday School superintendent, for arriving from Scofield in time to serve as one of the witnesses. In the quiet room, Owen looked down at Della's hand in his and felt the benign presence of friends gone now, friends with whom he had crossed the Atlantic and mined in Utah, friends who bore his sorrows, and he theirs, and also their joys. It was life complete, taking everything into account.

Della touched his face, and he looked in her dark eyes. She nodded slightly, and he knew she felt the same emotion.

After a multiplicity of blessings, each one grander than the last, they stood together, man and wife earlier in the week, but now united for eternity. God seemed to work His wonders in strange ways, but that was certainly His privilege, Owen decided.

"Today is May 10," Brother Hood told him as they changed back into their street clothing later. "Never forget it, lad, or you'll be in the blackest of black books with the missus. They never forget, so you daren't."

"I know good advice when I hear it, Andrew," he replied. "Thank you from the depths of my heart for coming."

"I couldn't have been anywhere else today," the Number One foreman said.

"Is it back to Scofield for you?"

"Aye. We'll be reopening the Number One next week."

"And the Four?" Owen asked, both wanting and not wanting to know.

"Bishop says by the end of May. There's plenty of work for you."

Work I'm good at, Owen thought, even as he shook his head. "I promised Della I would not."

Andrew held out his hand. "That may be, but don't forget us. Come and visit."

"I will. We will."

Nothing remained now except to hug Angharad outside of the temple and thank her for being a good guest at Mrs. Knight's aunt's house during the wedding. All that remained was to buy tickets for the trip to Provo and resume worrying about how to feed his family in a new town where he had no prospects.

Mrs. Knight had other ideas. "Not yet, Owen," she said as they started toward the depot. "Before he left for Canada, my husband wanted you to have this."

She handed him an envelope. Owen glanced at Della, but she appeared as mystified as he was.

"Open it, Da," Angharad said.

He did, and he drew out a receipt for two nights at the Manti House. "I can't deny I am pleased, Sister Knight," he said. "Thank you and Uncle Jesse."

"Angharad has agreed to stay with me," Mrs. Knight said, her arm around his daughter. "And here is a piece of good fortune. I have convinced Mabli to stay with me for the rest of the week and cook. Mrs. McNulty is visiting her ailing sister, and I am all thumbs in the kitchen. There. I admit it."

"Well, then, Mrs. Davis, it appears we are spending two nights in Manti," Owen said, which earned him a round of applause from their little wedding party on the steps outside the temple and kind glances from other people going inside. "Mrs. Davis, what do you say?"

Della knew who needed her attention. She knelt by Angharad, who couldn't help her worried look, and said, "I'll take good care of Da and bring him back safely to Provo." She hugged the child. "I know you don't want him out of your sight, but he will be in my sight. No fears?"

Angharad nodded. "No fears. Da?"

He held out his forefinger and touched her finger. "No fears."

They walked their friends to the train station and then went to the Manti House. Once inside, Della handed over Sister Knight's receipt and had a word with the front desk clerk, who gave her a room key.

"Upstairs and to the left," the man said. "We serve dinner at six, and there is also room service."

Owen didn't remember much else. Della helped him off with his clothes while he protested, his eyes closed. There was a soft pillow, and a few minutes later, a warm wife tucked close. He wanted to say something about promising to be more amorous after he had some sleep, but nothing came out of his mouth.

"I'll keep," was the last thing he heard. How kind she was.

He slept twelve hours straight, waking up shortly after midnight. Warm, comfortable, peaceful, he lay there in the cocoon of a sleeping world. He shifted in bed, careful not to wake his wife, because he wanted to look at her.

She hadn't bothered to close the drapes, and the full moon spilled its light across the bedspread. She lay on her side, facing him and the moonlight, her black curls wild around her head, which made him wonder all over again how she managed to tame that mop.

Fascinated with her, he ran his finger above her elegant nose—no better word for it—to outline it. He didn't want to wake her, even though he needed her more with each passing minute, now that he wasn't blasted with exhaustion.

He could wait. He wanted to expand the moment, without thinking about the canyon. Absolutely no one in Manti needed them for anything.

She had wonderful, full lips that he was already well acquainted with. The Almighty may have given the Welsh amazing gifts, but He had skimped on full lips. He admired Della's, thinking that some day they might be fortunate to have children who looked more like her than him, especially any future daughters.

And those eyelashes. They seemed to brush her cheek. He looked closer, but the room really wasn't light enough to confirm his suspicion that she seemed to have a double row of them. Was that even possible?

He touched her cheek, which made her put up her hand and cover his.

"I thought you would never wake up," he teased.

She burst out laughing. "Twelve hours." She sobered immediately. "And you needed every single minute, my love."

"I did," he agreed, his hand on her head now, enjoying those curls and well aware that he could do this whenever he wanted, and he wanted to now, in the quiet and comfort of the Manti House. How kind of the Knights to give them this loving time.

Chapter 11

All dividends of tender, wifely affection aside—and what man could ever blithely dismiss those?—Owen spent a goodly portion of the next day reveling in the joy of what he always thought of as bed chat, or pillow conversation, as *she* preferred to call it. He had explained the matter while examining and then kissing Della's kneecaps with their charming dimples.

"It's this way, *m cara*," he told her after he lay back down beside her. "We can be as silly as we wish, and not have to make an accounting to anyone except ourselves. This is where I tell you what I like and don't like, discuss national politics, and oh, I don't know, quiz you on the state of our pantry. And tit for tat, naturally."

She settled more comfortably into his loose embrace. "Welshmen and words," she commented to no one in particular, but perhaps to him, because there he was. She stretched her arm across his middle and tickled the opposite ribs, which made him forget words and substitute deeds until she was profoundly satisfied.

"As you were saying?" he began later.

"I like you," she said suddenly, and then she amended that with a laugh. "I love you, and you have ample proof of that already."

Indeed he did, and it was making his eyelids droop. "Explain yourself."

She raised up on one elbow and stared at him until he laughed. "Owen, you have a certain rascally charm I really hadn't anticipated. I like that. I *like* you."

She said it so simply. "And as for national politics, I will remind you that women have the vote in Utah. We might argue about issues because I tend to prefer the Democrats and there isn't much you can do about it." She peered closely again. "Heavens, are you even a U.S. citizen?"

"No, actually," he admitted. "What with one thing and another, I am still a citizen of Great Britain. I haven't sung 'God Save the Queen' in ages, though. Give us a kiss, my pretty one."

And so it went until they were famished and realized it was imperative to find food or die.

Even food tasted better. For lunch and dinner, Owen polished off Manti House's roast beef and apple pie with whipped cream, pleased to see that Della did the same thing. Gwyna used to pick at her food. He had married a healthy woman this time, and it relieved his heart.

Another night with no one but Della on his mind fortified him for the two-hour ride north to Provo. He knew he didn't imagine her sigh when they left the hotel.

"Let's return here someday," she said.

"Either that or never leave," he teased, which made her laugh.

"You say Uncle Jesse is in Canada?" he asked when they were settled on the train for the return to reality, Provo, and hopefully employment.

"Amanda said he wants to buy land in the District of Alberta," Della said, making herself comfortable against him. "Ranching, I think. Owen?"

He couldn't stay awake, but his dreams were pleasant, consisting mainly of Della, and a far cry from the desperate images that robbed sleep all last week.

So he thought. He woke up after the conductor walked through the car and said everyone was changing trains at Thistle. He knew there would be more widows and children from Scofield leaving the canyon and coal for good. Della's hand was tight on his arm, so he wondered how peaceful his sleep had been.

He steeled himself for more widows, but it was the late train. He did see Samuel and Ada Fergusson, staunch Presbyterians who looked disapprovingly on all the Mormons in Winter Quarters Canyon. Still, he knew them, a childless couple, and he trusted Sam, who worked in the fan house and kept air flowing faithfully over Mormons, Baptists, Catholics, and Lutherans alike.

As the train picked up speed on the descent into Spanish Fork Canyon, he walked through the swaying car and squatted in the aisle beside Sam, who greeted him with a smile and a nod.

"Out of the mines too?" Owen asked.

"Ada insisted. Even aboveground wasn't enough for t' woman," he said in his spare way. "I could argue, but why? And you, lad?"

"I made a promise too," Owen said, with a glance back at Della, who slept. "Off to find something to do in Provo."

"Ya will. You're a clever mon with wood."

Fergusson patted his shoulder, and Owen returned to his seat, cheered somehow. He sidled in next to Della, touched how she turned toward his warmth and burrowed closer, depending on him to keep her warm, apparently. Two women depended on him now. He had less than forty dollars to his name.

He leaned back, thinking of Mr. Bullock, a friend of Uncle Jesse's, who had chatted with him last Thanksgiving about installing wainscoting in his dining room. Hopefully, he hadn't found someone to do it yet. Uncle Jesse had also mentioned something about cabinets and bookshelves needed at Brigham Young Academy. Summer was a good time to build such things, before the start of a school year. With any luck . . .

Silently he blessed the Knights for their gift of two nights in Manti. Della had hinted at amazing wonders in their new home on Third Second South, not far from the Knight's house. Part of him preferred to keep his distance from what he never wanted to call charity, while the other part of him, the part now the sole support of three instead of two, welcomed such kindness, for kindness it was.

He glanced down at Della, barely visible in the darkened car, lit only by a lamp at each end. He knew he should never second-guess his decision to marry again. Gwyna had meant the sun, moon, and stars to him, but so did Della. If matters had been different, he would have taken some time on a slow day in the Number Four to sit down in a quiet place with Taliesin Llewellen, whose first wife had died years before and who had married another a few years ago. He wanted to ask Tally if he had felt any guilt at giving his heart to another. Tally could have reassured him, more like, but Tally was dead.

Are you destined to overthink everything? he asked himself. Ah, well. He matched his breathing to Della's and slept too as the train clacked and swayed through Spanish Fork Canyon.

The depot in Provo was shuttered. They retrieved their luggage and strolled through Provo's darkened streets, passing the Knight's home. He noticed that no lights were on there, which meant Angharad could be retrieved the following morning.

"Here it is." Della stopped in front of a tidy place with a porch, the kind of spot that might be nicer with some seating. He could tip back his chair, put his feet on the railing, and hear nothing but birds twittering in the morning, a far cry from the nearly constant rumble of coal in the tipple.

The reminder of coal made him turn automatically east toward the sheltering mountains, visible in the moonlight. Twists and turns through two canyons and he would be home again in Winter Quarters Canyon. *You don't live there anymore, boyo*, he told himself, and looked away, but not before he saw the shadow cross Della's face. She seemed to know what he was thinking.

"Hand me the key," he said. He took the porch in two steps and unlocked the door, returned for their valises, and set them down while Della watched, her head tipped to one side, as if wondering what he was doing.

"Hang on."

He picked her up, carried her handily up four steps and bore her over the threshold as she laughed.

"No electricity," she said as he put her down. "I know where the matches are."

"First things first." He kissed her soundly. "Mrs. Davis, we have arrived."

She had the most tender lips. She evidently also wanted him to see their new house because she didn't linger in his embrace. He heard some fumbling in the kitchen and the sound of a match striking, and then—illumination. She held the lamp high and returned to the front room.

"Mr. Auerbach has been at work here," she said. "And look, Amanda found lace curtains while we were in Manti. Guess we'll have to call it a parlor."

He looked around the room. "Tell me, *m cara*, your da was a miner. Did you ever live in a house with lace curtains?"

"The Anderses' house in Salt Lake," she replied. "A *home* with lace curtains? Not until this one."

Her words touched his heart, the same heart that had been beating in unison for pleasant hours with the marvelous woman now his wife. "It's already a home?" he asked, curious.

"The moment you carried me over the threshold."

Chapter 12

Owen slept late. Della observed him carefully, wishing he didn't sleep with his eyes half open because it still unnerved her. She would have to ask him sometime about her little quirks that made him shake his head.

She also wished he slept more peacefully. She doubted he was aware how he twitched and how he spoke in Welsh, sometimes sounding urgent, as if something terrible hung in the balance, which she didn't doubt for a second was a result of May 1. Maybe time would change that.

And how many years before you didn't think about the Molly Bee mine and your father dead under tons of rock? she asked herself as she watched her man. She realized it hadn't been more than a day or two since she had remembered those awful days on the Colorado plateau, waiting and wondering if the three miners underground would come out alive or dead.

When it happened, she had tried to crowd close to the windlass that brought up the cage from below, calling, "Papa! Papa!" at the top of her lungs. Grownups had pushed her back, and she was never allowed to see him.

Della put her hand to her heart, amazed how fast it beat. She reminded herself she did not have the time, the energy, or even the reason to be reminding herself of something that happened twelve years ago. The wounds of the Number Four and Number One were fresh and raw too. Time to tamp down her own memories, force them back to wherever it was such unrest came from. After all, she was not alone, and her husband needed her.

Owen lay stretched on his back, arms out, reminding her of his propensity to take the whole bed. And why not? He had spent many years alone in a bed for two. She had no trouble fitting herself in with him. Her eyes on him, she dressed quietly and closed their bedroom door behind her.

Barefoot, shoes in hand, Della walked through her little house, laughing at herself because what pleased her the most was the lavatory, with its toilet and sink. The tin tub hanging on the wall in the screened porch off the kitchen signaled that bathing was still a kitchen affair, but Aunt Amanda had already warned her.

She sat in one of Mr. Auerbach's wingback chairs in the parlor, silently blessing his thoughtfulness. She knew stationery lurked in one of the unopened boxes on the back porch. By tomorrow there would be a letter of thanks heading to Salt Lake City, even though her words already seemed inadequate. She leaned back, acutely aware as never before of the many people determined to help the Davis family.

She peeked in on her husband, still asleep, put on her shoes, and quietly left the house, pleased with the neighborhood already. One of her earliest memories was walking with Papa through such a neighborhood, with trees just being trees—not cut down for fuel or to widen a narrow canyon road or timber up a mine until there were no more trees aboveground.

Hardly aware of what she was doing, Della turned and faced approximately south and east toward Scofield and nearby Winter Quarters Canyon, imagining the sadness hunkering down over that narrow canyon road, maybe planning to stay like an unwanted guest. Owen had done this very thing last night, and here she was, remembering too. She looked away from the mountains, focusing on a leafy street in a quiet community, where birds chirped and a cat sunned itself on the neighbor's porch.

"This is better," she said. She reminded herself that it was a lovely spring morning, and she was going to see Amanda Knight and retrieve Angharad. She smiled at the mailman as he passed her and tipped his hat. *Provo is my town now,* she thought as she continued down the street and knocked on the back door of the Knight house. *I'm going to like it here.*

Wiping her hands on her apron, Mabli Reese opened the screen door and hugged her. "No Owen?" she asked.

"Still asleep," Della said, hoping her husband's sister-in-law wouldn't tease her and make some comment about wearing out the man. "What do you think of the Knights?"

"Mrs. Knight asked me if I could stay through the week until her cook returns from Logan," Mabli told her. She smiled, the first smile Della had seen on her face since breakfast in the Edwards boardinghouse on May 1, when Mabli whispered that Will Goode, all blushes, said he would see her at the dance that night in the new Odd Fellows Hall, the dance no one attended.

"You realize that Owen will hang about the back door all week, in the hopes of receiving one of your cinnamon buns," Della said.

"I hope he does," Mabli said. She gave Della a nudge. "I don't see Owen hanging about *here*, not a newly married man. I can always find ways to keep Angharad here helping me, if you'd like."

This was a new Mabli, one willing to tease a little. Della felt her heart grow lighter, even as she blushed.

Angharad came through the kitchen door then, smiling and holding out her arms for Della, who hugged her.

"Where's Da?" she asked.

"Still asleep, my dear," Della told her. "I know, I know. You've told me he never sleeps past six."

"I'm still tired," Angharad said, sounding seventy instead of seven.

Della held her close. "We won't always feel tired."

"So this is where everyone chooses to hang around?"

Della looked up to see Amanda Knight, eyeing them all from the door. She gestured them inside as Mabli sniffed the air and hurried to open the oven door.

She feigned relief and Angharad clapped her hands.

In minutes they were seated around the kitchen table, eating sausage and baked eggs and glancing at the cinnamon buns cooling too slowly for all of them.

"This will never do," Amanda said at last. "Mrs. Reese, I am out of patience with cinnamon buns that refuse to cool off. Please bring them over. We'll take our chances."

Not usually one for theatrics, Mabli presented the buns with a flourish that made Angharad laugh and then look around, surprised, as if she shouldn't have laughed. Della put her hand on the child's arm. "Laugh all you want," she said. "We need to hear it."

Silence then, as everyone ate. After Angharad's second bun, she set aside a third "for Da" and then asked Della if she should gather her things.

"Yes, please," Della said. "Da will be awake and wondering where his little girl is."

"Girls," Angharad amended. "I'll be quick."

Amanda nodded her approval as the child hurried upstairs. "You seem to have made two conquests, Della."

"I love them both. You've come to know Angharad better now," she said, "and thank you again for keeping her here so we could have two days together in Manti."

"I know her better," Amanda agreed. "I can completely imagine you taking her to Arizona Territory and starting over if . . . if things had gone differently in the mine on that awful day."

"I would have," Della said simply. "I could never leave her alone. Sometimes I wish . . ."

She stopped.

"Wish what? Tell me, my dear," Amanda asked gently.

"It's nothing," Della said. *Papa, I wish I could tell you everything has turned out better than I ever imagined,* she thought. No need to trouble someone else with what was decidedly in the past. Funny to be thinking about it so much lately.

Angharad bounced downstairs then, her few belongings in a little bag. "Sister Knight said every girl needs her own luggage," she announced, holding out a leather satchel. She dipped a true British Isles curtsy to Amanda. "*Diolch yn fawr iawn.*"

"What do I say to that?"

"You're welcome," Della said.

"You're welcome, Angharad," their kind hostess said. "Come to visit me anytime. Oh, take that cinnamon bun for your father."

"I'm always here to listen," Amanda said to Della as Angharad skipped on ahead toward the door.

"Maybe later."

"Don't wait too long, my dear."

Chapter 13

Amanda walked Della and Angharad out through the front door, her arms linked through theirs. She stopped suddenly. "I forgot something. Don't move." She darted back inside and returned with a folded sheet of paper for Della. "Here you are. This could be well worth your consideration."

Della opened the note and gasped.

"It's not bad news, is it?" Angharad asked anxiously. "Please no."

Della knelt beside her stepdaughter. "Heavens no, my dear one. It's the best news." She looked at Amanda. "Does this Mr. Holyoke know I'm married? I'm not allowed to teach school now."

"And more's the pity," Amanda replied. "Women may have the vote in Utah, but there is certainly work to be done." She glanced at Angharad. "Better read it out loud, Della."

Della interpreted the glance correctly and pulled Angharad closer. "Are you ready for this?" She cleared her throat. "'Dear Mrs. Davis, I am the principal at Maeser Elementary School, and I can possibly use your help here this summer. Please stop by at your earliest convenience.'" She looked at the signature. "'Allen Holyoke.' My goodness, Amanda. Am I correct in suspecting the fine hand of the Knights in this summons about employment?"

"Guilty as charged," Amanda replied serenely, walking them to the carriage block. "What was I to do? The Holyokes came to dinner two nights ago, and I might have mentioned your name."

"Might have?" Della teased.

"Just a casual mention that you were a teacher at Winter Quarters School with impeccable credentials, seeking to start over in Provo."

"Between the soup and main course you did all this?"

Amanda laughed and gave Della a swat to the back of her skirt. "Angharad, you need to see that Della behaves!"

"Da tells me that too," the child said, which meant they were all laughing as they left the Knight house.

"Sister Knight has a candy dish with nonpareils," Angharad said as they strolled along, in no particular hurry.

"Any left?"

"A few," Angharad said with a laugh. She stopped. "Maeser Elementary? Mam, I know right where that is. Sister Knight said I will be going there in September."

"We had better find it then, so I don't get lost tomorrow."

Two long blocks and a short one, and they stood in front of a two-story tan brick building with an impressive arched entrance of darker brick.

Angharad held her hands up, framing the lettering over the door. "Maeser School. I will learn great things here."

"You will learn great things wherever you go, dearest, because you want to," Della told her. Her heart sore, she thought of her lovely Winter Quarters children, as she stood on a peaceful street where, from the look of things, nothing terrible had ever happened.

Angharad pointed to the row of windows above the second story. "Is that a half story? What is it for?" she asked, thankfully oblivious to Della's disquiet.

Della swallowed down her tears, suddenly wanting Owen beside her to buoy her up, even though she knew the folly of that. Wasn't he suffering enough?

"It might be an assembly area," she said, striving to keep her voice light.

"When can we find out?"

"When autumn comes and you start school."

She didn't imagine Angharad's satisfied sigh. "Do you think my teacher will put spelling words on autumn leaves made of construction paper, like you did, Miss Anders?"

Della knew she was teasing. "Miss Anders went away and came back as Mrs. Davis, also known as Mam."

Angharad put both her hands in Della's. Her heart seemed to swell, or maybe she had laced her corset too tight that morning.

"Mam, come closer."

Della knelt on the sidewalk beside Owen's daughter. Angharad transferred her hands to Della's shoulders and leaned close. "When we did not think Da had survived, you said you would take me to Arizona Territory with you, where you would teach and I would go to school. Did ye . . . did you really mean that?"

"With all my heart," Della assured the serious little girl. "You were never going to be left alone to shift for yourself in the household of strangers."

Forehead to forehead now. "Did that happen to you?"

Funny how one small question could take a woman back twelve years to that time she was a child and alone on a train to Salt Lake City, desperately sad, and with no one to comfort her. "It did happen to me," she managed, as her eyes filled with tears.

Angharad touched Della's cheeks with the end of her pinafore. "You didn't want that for me."

"Never."

"*Diolch yn fawr iawn*," Angharad whispered back. "Thank you ever so very much."

Hand in hand they returned to their house, pleased to see Owen sitting on the front porch, his feet on the railing and hands behind his head, as Della had mentally predicted. He had taken a kitchen chair to the porch and he looked like a man at peace with the world. At least until she came close enough to kiss his cheek and see his old eyes.

The chair came down on all four legs and he plopped Angharad onto his lap. She sighed and leaned back, in her good place again, as far as Della could tell.

"Da, I missed you, but not too much because Sister Knight has a candy dish in the parlor," she said, which made Owen laugh out loud, smack his head and exclaim, "I have been supplanted by lemon drops."

"No, Da, nonpareils," Angharad said, which made him laugh louder. "And Mam has a note from the principal of the school where I will go in September."

Owen turned his attention to Della, still bent on humor apparently, which soothed her as nothing else could. "It can't be a note for misbehavior. She never went to Maeser School."

"Da, be serious."

"There's time enough for that."

Owen held out his hand to Della and tugged her closer. She kissed the top of his head this time and handed him the note. "That's good news," he said, handing it back when he finished. "We'll both be doing a little bit here and there, it seems. George Bullock still needs someone to put wainscoting in his dining room. He stopped by earlier. Just missed dragging me out of bed by a matter of minutes."

"Da, you've never slept so late before," Angharad said. "Are you sick?"

"My heart's a little sore," he told her. She nodded and he held her closer. "Yours too?"

She nodded again and then brightened. "Da, I have a cinnamon bun from Aunt Mabli. It is for you."

She held it out and then shrieked when he growled and snatched it, opening the paper bag to breathe deep and flutter his eyelashes until Della laughed out loud.

"You are very nearly certifiable," she told her husband. "I love a maniac."

He shrugged and took a bite. "I would almost commit felonies for one of Mabli's cinnamon buns."

"Is that a good thing?" Angharad asked doubtfully.

"It is to me," he replied. "Della, if you roll your eyes anymore, they will get stuck."

Della blew a kiss to them both and went inside, seeing again with pleasure Mr. Auerbach's wingback chairs. *My first real home*, she thought. She looked toward the porch and her husband, wondering if there might be a baby born here, knowing it was probable. She thought of Mari Luoma, heavily pregnant, and on her way to Montana. And from the look of Mary Parmley, William Parmley's widow, there would be another baby in a few months without a father.

I can't be thinking of children with no fathers, she thought. *Stop it,* she ordered her weary mind. *I have a husband and a daughter, and maybe employment, to worry about.*

Dinner was handily taken care of that afternoon with the arrival of the ward Relief Society president bearing a platter of chicken and followed by daughters carrying mashed potatoes, well-peppered white gravy, canned corn, and an apple pie.

"I can't imagine you felt like cooking today," the lady said after introducing herself and four daughters. "Here you are, a new bride."

Della thanked her for her kindness, which also included a calendar with Relief Society meetings marked in red, through to the end of the year, and Primary for Angharad. She silently thanked Amanda Knight for sending out ward members to gently fold them into this new congregation of fellow Mormons.

When she walked Sister Forsyth out to the porch, Owen was chatting with a man about his age who introduced himself as the elders quorum president. Coming up the walk was another young man.

"We'll soon need someone to manage the traffic," Owen said. Della saw the pleasure on his face, reminding her, as if she needed reminding, of the gregarious nature of all sons and daughters of Wales.

The smile left Owen's face when the newest arrival introduced himself as the ward choirmaster.

"Of course, we know what singers you Welshmen are," the man said after he nodded to the Relief Society president and her daughters, who waved to Della and picked their way through the crowded porch. "Can we expect to see you on Sunday after Sacrament Meeting?"

"Most certainly," Della told their latest visitor at the same time Owen shook his head and said, "Not for me."

"Oh, but . . ." Della began, until she took another good look at Owen's face and saw all the pain resurface. "Perhaps not right now, Brother . . . Brother . . ."

"Smart," the young man said. "I am studying music pedagogy at the Academy." Obviously not a fellow to surrender without a fight, he leaned closer. "Tenor? Bass?"

"Second tenor," Owen said, "but not now. It's too soon."

"After what?"

"The death of the entire Pleasant Valley Ward Choir men's section on May 1, except for me," Owen said. He set Angharad off his lap and went into the house. The young choirmaster stared, open-mouthed, as the door closed.

"I don't . . ." Brother Smart began. His eyes widened then. "The mine?"

Della nodded, wanting to hurry him off the porch and go to her husband, but too polite to say more.

He appeared to be a fellow with some sensitivity. Brother Smart tried to speak, but couldn't summon anything equal to the occasion. Della patted his arm.

"He will be all right. Give him some time," she said, even as she wondered if she spoke the truth.

She glanced at Angharad and absorbed all the surprise and distress on her face. "Don't worry about Da, my love."

"He has to sing," the child said after Brother Smart tipped his hat to them and beat a hasty retreat.

"I know. Let me see to Da. Would you set the table please?"

Angharad went into the kitchen without a word. Della peeked into the room, saddened to see the child plump herself down at the table and rest her chin in her hands, her well-ordered world given another jolt.

What can I do for both of you? Della asked herself. *I wish I knew.*

Her heart in her mouth, she knocked softly on their bedroom door. When Owen didn't answer, she went inside anyway.

There he sat, facing away from the door on his side of the bed, his head bowed and his shoulders shaking. Her heart crumbling, Della sat beside him. After too long a time to suit her, his arm went around her waist and he pulled her closer.

"It's not that I can't sing," he managed, tears on his face, the raw hurt evident. "I almost don't remember why I want to, and that's nearly criminal."

She pulled his head gently down on her shoulder.

"I don't really like this Owen I have become," he said into her neck. "Do you still like him?"

"I even love him. Singing can wait."

"How long?"

"Until it's in your heart again, Owen."

They sat close together until Angharad tapped on the door and reminded them that dinner was getting cold, and was she the only one who liked chicken?

Chapter 14

Early in the morning, Della nestled close to Owen, listening to him breathe his way into sleep again after a most pleasant interlude, relieved to give her dear man some solace. She thought of husbands and wives, grateful to be among that number now.

Dinner had been so solemn, everyone trying to cheer everyone up and failing. Owen had finally apologized to his ladies and returned to the front porch, where he read through a stack of newspapers from Merthyr Tydfil that Della had used to cushion his few plates and bowls from the Winter Quarters home. Della played checkers with Angharad in the kitchen.

He had come into the kitchen later that evening and sat down with them. "I'm sorry," he said simply. "I know that time will smooth things over, but right now . . ." He shook his head.

"Da, you can't not sing forever," Angharad said, her voice firm.

He winced at her words. "Right now, I feel as though I could, and that's an honest answer, dear child."

"Time, Da," Angharad reminded him. "You said so yourself just now, think on." She glanced at Della and then back at her father. "Would you mind if Mam and I sang in the choir?"

He smiled at that. Della felt optimism, just a little sprig, struggle to the top of the sorrow in her heart and perch there—exhausted, but *there.*

"Mind? Never. Go right ahead."

She was a persistent child, the daughter of a father who, months ago, had refused to take no for an answer when Della told him she wouldn't sing in the abundantly gifted Pleasant Valley Ward choir. "I might need a round note from you, Da. You know, just to make certain I am on key if Mam and I practice here at the house."

"I could probably muster a round note on demand," he said.

Della felt optimism perk up, wisely careful not to jump up and down. "That sounds fair enough, Owen."

"It'll do for now, you pretty Davis ladies. I do feel like carving, though. Let me show you where I put my tools."

He took the kerosene lantern from the table and led them out the back door and into the shed behind the house.

"Angharad, when you were eating nonpareils out of Sister Knight's candy dish, I swept out here and discovered a right fine bench."

Della looked around in delight. Her husband had found a place for his carving tools. He picked up a partly carved box. "I can finish this by the end of next week," he said. "Della, what would you think if we went to Salt Lake City to take it to Mr. Auerbach as thanks for the furniture?"

"Me too, Da?"

"Absolutely. We travel together."

But that was last night. Della closed her eyes now and thanked the Almighty that the man sleeping beside her hadn't found anyone to suit him until she came into Winter Quarters Canyon, riding the flat car with the Scofield miners heading for their afternoon shift, and wondering if she had lost her mind to teach in a coal camp.

She turned over to see Owen watching her. She saw the admiration in his eyes, and no sorrow.

"I astound myself with how pleasant it is to lie here and wonder how Greeks ended up with an abundance of everything," he said. "Maybe it is the warm Mediterranean air. Your nose, all those curls, your lips. If I think about anything else, I'll break out in a sweat. Give me an hour to recharge."

Della laughed out loud and then put her hand over her mouth, not wanting to wake up Angharad. "At which time, we'll be up and eating our porridge, and I will be worried about what Mr. Holyoke might have for me this summer."

"Alas, it is true," he said, addressing the ceiling. "I am ever grateful for night."

"You're a bit of a scoundrel," she teased.

"Guilty as charged. Would you think me boorish beyond belief if I catch another forty winks while you make said porridge?"

"I would think you most manly," she said, willing to be generous to this good fellow she had married.

"After all, I am thirty-two to your nearly twenty-five. Not decrepit, by any means, but . . ."

She kissed him soundly, and he laughed when she leaped off the bed as he grabbed for her.

"More of that Welsh balderdash I was warned about," she said from the safety of the door. "See you at breakfast, O Ancient One."

The three of them made plans over breakfast, which meant that all of them set out with Della for her interview, Owen to continue on with Angharad to see Mr. Bullock about wainscoting. The plan was to meet at the Knight house, where Angharad hoped there might be more nonpareils in the candy dish.

As plans frequently did, this one fell apart right away, to everyone's benefit.

"We'll walk you inside," Owen said as he stared up at Maeser School's impressive façade. "Do the arches repeat?"

"We'll find out," Della replied, happy to have an escort, especially one with her best interest at heart.

Inside the door stood a man who surely had to be Principal Holyoke, by anyone's deduction. The teachers were already in their classrooms, and he had a magisterial air that reminded Della of Miss Clayson, and also her principal back in Salt Lake's Westside School.

"Mr. Holyoke?" she asked, coming forward and putting on what she hoped looked like her brave interview face. "I am Mrs. Davis."

She held out her hand first, because that was what etiquette books said to do.

"And I am Professor Holyoke," he said, shaking her hand. "This is your husband?"

"Aye, sir, Owen Davis." The two men shook hands and Owen indicated Angharad. "My daughter Angharad."

"Who should probably be in school," Mr. Holyoke said from his great height, though kindly.

"Sir, we finished the term already in Winter Quarters Canyon," Della explained. "My principal turned in our grades early because . . ." She couldn't continue because Angharad made a low sound in her throat.

"I should have known that," Mr. Holyoke said, interrupting her. Della heard all the sympathy in his few words. "In that case, Angharad, we look forward to seeing you in September in grade . . ."

"Two," Angharad said. "Mam was my teacher last year."

"So Mrs. Knight told me."

To Della's gratification, the tall principal knelt down to be on eye level with his prospective second grader. "Angharad . . . dear me, I hope I am pronouncing your name correctly."

"Close enough, sir," she said. "We Welsh make allowances."

Mr. Holyoke laughed. "And I believe you are also famed for singing and for extreme patience with the less gifted linguistically."

Angharad frowned. "That's a new word for me."

"Your former teacher will explain it," he said, standing up, amusement written all over his face. "As for now, there is a slide and a swing set behind this building you are welcome to try out while I visit with the grownups."

"Thank you, sir, but I will take her with me to *my* job interview," Owen said.

"Finding work aboveground, Mr. Davis?"

"I am, sir. Good day to you." He held out his hand for Angharad.

Holding hands, father and daughter left the foyer to Della and Mr. Holyoke. He indicated his office and she followed him inside, feeling suddenly as assured as a salamander on a hot rock.

Mr. Holyoke put her at ease at once. "Sit yourself down, Mrs. Davis. My compliments on such a charming daughter."

"She is the daughter of my husband and a fine student," Della said, wishing they were sitting beside her. "I know enough Welsh for 'hello,' 'goodbye,' and 'thank you,' but I expect I will learn more."

"I expect you will." The smile left his face. "Tough times in the canyon."

"I'm not certain I could adequately explain to you how difficult things are," Della said. "So many of my pupils are fatherless now, and uprooted too."

"Your husband is among those choosing to find a new livelihood elsewhere?"

"He is, although I do not think his heart is entirely in it," she said. Something about the sympathy in Mr. Holyoke's eyes told her she could trust him. "But here I am, because Mr. and Mrs. Knight are so kind to us."

"You have excellent advocates," he told her. "Uncle Jesse is a most persuasive man, and Mrs. Knight not one whit behind him. I wish I could offer you a teaching position, but I cannot."

"I know, sir."

"What I *can* do this summer is call on your assistance in the school library." He smiled at her. "Mrs. Knight informed me of your weekly stint as librarian at the Wasatch Store."

This was no time for the sweetest memories to flood her heart of watching the modest men and women of the canyon read newspapers from their native countries, devour magazines on American life and customs, and read through all of Dickens and Mark Twain and Thackeray. The memories poured out like a spring freshet, and she had to look down at her lap for a moment to regain her equanimity.

"It was a joy and a delight," she said when she could speak. "Too many of my avid readers are gone now."

The principal sighed. "I wish there was something we could use besides coal to warm our homes and fuel our industries, but that is an issue for another day." He cocked his head to one side and regarded her. "Would you be willing to help us this summer? As soon as school adjourns, my librarian is heading to New Jersey for a summer course in the Dewey Decimal System at Rutgers University."

"My goodness, I would love that," Della said. "You keep the school open in the summer?"

"No, but it is an excellent time for a fairly monumental task, even in our modest library. You've heard of the Dewey System?"

"Oh, yes. Our little library in Winter Quarters used fixed positioning, but I've read about Mr. Dewey's system."

"Seems smarter to shelve by subject rather than height and date of acquisition, eh?"

"Considerably," Della said. "But you said your librarian is studying the system this summer? Why would you need me?" *I don't mean to be suspicious*, she wanted to tell him, *but you're talking to the lady who was railroaded into the Pleasant Valley Ward choir by someone seeking certain advantages. I wouldn't put it past the Knights, but I won't do busy work.*

"It's not superfluous work, Mrs. Davis," the principal assured her. "If you agree to this, you'll find yourself with stacks of books all over the place in here. I want you to do a preliminary sorting into category." He moved a book across his desk toward her. "This is one of Dewey's later editions that explains the whole thing."

She picked up the book and ruffled through the pages. "I've been curious about this approach."

He laughed. "Now that is a response worthy of a diplomatist!" He held out his hands. "Mrs. Davis, you see before you a man who is seriously outranked in seniority by our librarian, Miss Temple, who has been working in our school system for twenty-eight years, as opposed to my paltry nine. When the Rutgers course is done, she has informed me she intends to visit relatives in Maine. She is planning to arrive back here two weeks before school starts, and I don't have the seniority to demand anything else."

"I begin to see your dilemma," Della said, as she itched to start reading Mr. Dewey's tome. "You need someone to classify without the benefit of a university course. Or get started, at least."

"I do, indeed. It will mostly be tedious sorting. Five days a week at hard labor, Mrs. Davis, for the princely sum of six dollars a week, and my undying gratitude. I dare you to tell me if you've ever had a better offer."

Della laughed and held out her hand, which the principal shook. "Excuse my slang, but it's a deal, Mr. Holyoke."

She had immediate second thoughts. Five days a week? Well and good for the family purse, but what about Angharad? "Almost a deal, sir."

"What? Regrets about such munificence from the Provo School District? Come now, where's your courage?" the principal joked.

"My stepdaughter. She is but seven, and I can't leave her alone," Della said. "Her father will be working too, hopefully, and . . . well, I don't know what I was thinking."

He gave her another kind look. "No problem at all. Bring her along, and set her to work dusting the books and shelves. I can guarantee her fifty cents a week, with ample time for the playground, when she starts to sneeze from all that dust."

Della sighed with relief. She nodded. "Yes, please. She will be delighted to earn a little money to help out."

"I understand tight times, Mrs. Davis," Mr. Holyoke said. He stood up, and Della rose too. "I well remember shining shoes at the Hotel Washington in Madison, Wisconsin, to earn tuition money for the university."

"I was a kitchen flunkie for a crew stringing telephone wire in Cottonwood Canyon to pay *my* tuition."

"School is out here at the end of next week," he said. "Show up the following Monday, you and your little helper, and I will have contracts for both of you."

He escorted her from the school just as the bell rang.

"Time for an assembly, Mrs. Davis," he said, turning to go up the stairs. "Why is it, I ask, that students have trouble concentrating as the school year draws to a close? We will now hear recitations from grade six, and hope they are sufficiently entertaining to tide us over until the noon hour and blessed lunch. Good day, Mrs. Davis, and thank you."

"Thank *you*," she whispered as he bounded up the steps and went inside. "Twenty-four dollars a month. I believe we can do this, Owen."

Chapter 15

If she hadn't been nearly twenty-five, well-educated, and a matron now, Della would have skipped all the way home. She reminded herself that just as cleanliness was next to godliness, so was dignity. She knew it was best to walk sedately up the front steps to the Knight home when she wanted to bang open the door and shout for joy.

As it was, she grabbed Amanda Knight in a bear hug, gratified to feel the woman's arms tight around her. Amanda held her off and looked into her eyes. "Summer work?"

Della nodded, almost as out of breath as if she had run from Maeser School. "Six dollars a week and work for Angharad too. My corset is too tight."

"I don't think Owen would mind a bit if you didn't lace so diligently," Amanda joked.

"True. Vanity, thy name is Della," she said, happy to laugh at herself, and grateful that for a few months at least, they could pay the rent. She knew Owen would find work and they would manage. Angharad would go to school at Maeser, and maybe the pain of May 1 would start to fade.

She was silent then, knowing they would never forget. She sat down and stared at the cut glass candy dish with its nonpareils that Angharad liked so well.

"What's the matter, my dear?" Amanda asked, sitting down beside her.

"It's difficult to explain," said Della, she who never used to tell anyone about herself. The hard school of life in the barren Anders house in Salt Lake City had taught her that the less said, the better.

"Try," Amanda said, her arm around her as they sat together in the parlor.

"All I want to do is forget that Winter Quarters ever happened," she admitted, after several deep breaths. "All that does is make me feel guilty."

"Give yourself time. You have time."

"I do." Impulsively, she kissed Amanda Knight's cheek. "I'd better go home and see if the other two-thirds of the family had good luck."

She left the house, wishing she could shake off the chill that had descended on her with Amanda's kind words. No point in telling her shirttail cousin that Richard and Martha Evans had said precisely the same thing when she told them last winter that Owen was too indecisive about revealing his own feelings. As it turned out, no one in Winter Quarters had any time left. No one had time left in the Molly Bee in Colorado, either.

No one need ever know how foolish you feel for believing your own loss of your father was worse than the loss of two hundred, she thought.

The postman was getting ready to deposit a letter in her mailbox. He tipped his hat to her.

"Mrs. Davis?" he asked.

She smiled inside, wondering when it would fully sink in that she was Della Davis now, not Anders. "Yes, sir. We moved in two days ago."

He handed her the letter and said good day. She looked at the return address and wanted to hand it back, telling him politely that she didn't want it, and could he please exchange it for something better?

Inside, she stared at the envelope, wishing it would go away, then picked up a paring knife from the drain board and slit it open.

It was a short message from her Uncle Karl, probably dictated to her from his office, because the envelope's return address was Anders, Court and Landry, Attorneys at Law. He congratulated her on her sealing in the Manti Temple and invited them to visit in Salt Lake City. She kept reading and knew what to expect: "Had I known you were getting married last week, I probably would have come to your wedding. Thank you for at least sending a note that you were moving to Provo, with your address."

That was it, the scold that she had not informed them. On the positive side, there was no suggestion as to when this visit to Salt Lake should occur, which relieved her. Also there was no pernicious paragraph stating that she simply needed to contact Aunt Caroline, who would make all the arrangements. All too familiar with years of non-arrangements, Della decided to consider that a small victory.

"I am never going to visit there again," she told Owen later, when she sat on his lap in the kitchen after Angharad had gone to the Knights' house to spread her good news about a library job for her too.

She hadn't said anything about it when Owen and Angharad came home with the good news that Mr. Bullock was agreeable to having Owen install new wainscoting, as they had discussed last Thanksgiving, but never committed to.

"Forty-five dollars for the project," Owen had announced. "I start next Thursday."

She had been properly delighted, which wasn't hard. She also knew she could not fool this man who knew her well now, even beyond intimacy. After Angharad banged out the screen door and down the back steps, heading to the Knights' and more nonpareils, she handed him the letter she had stuffed behind the sugar bowl.

He read it, sat down, and held out his arms. "The beauty of this is you don't have to go to that house ever again," he told her. "We want to see Mr. Auerbach so I can give him the box I am carving. Why not send your uncle a note saying we will drop by his office that same day?"

"But I don't want to see him," she said politely, as if she explained it to a six-year-old.

What a clever man she had married. He saw right through her teacher's façade. "I'm no fan of burning bridges," he said. "I have an aunt in Merthyr Tydfil who disowned my mother when she joined with the Mormons and compounded the felony by marrying my father. I still send her a Christmas letter every year. I have no idea what she does with it, but it's not on my hands or my conscience."

"You're going to make me see my uncle again?" she asked, feeling only a little militant.

"Aye, miss, but mind you: his office and not the house," he said. "But mark me well, *m cara*: you'll never face him alone again."

During that week, he continued his wood carving in the kitchen, rather than the workshop, where the light wasn't too good. Angharad was equally pleased to join them with her pad of paper and colored pencils at the table, as she practiced her letters and numbers while Della read to them both from Sherlock Holmes collected stories. They all agreed to listen to "The Speckled Band," which kept everyone up too late, and led to Angharad needing to sleep with them.

"From now on, we'd better read Beatrix Potter," Della said as Angharad slept between them. "Peter Rabbit is slightly less frightening than a swamp adder."

Owen laughed softly and reached around his daughter to tickle Della. "Aye, miss."

The swamp adder didn't keep Della awake, but she did toss and turn at the thought of visiting Uncle Karl, even in his office. He had never been more than a distant figure, spending more time in his office than in the imposing house on the Avenues. His only comment about Della's care had been to inform his wife of her needs and expect her to take care of them, something that never happened. An office visit sounded innocuous enough, and Della almost believed it.

She believed it all through the rest of the week, where she fell into the pleasant pattern of cooking, cleaning, and then writing a letter to Mr. Auerbach describing her new life in Provo and saying they would visit him on Monday. She steeled herself to respond to Uncle Karl's note by reminding herself she was an adult. She sent a chirpy note stating a brief visit to his office on Monday afternoon, signed yours truly, Della.

On Saturday afternoon, when Mr. Bullock picked up Owen in his carriage to select the right wood at the lumberyard for the wainscoting, there had been time to visit Amanda. Two days away from her return to Winter Quarters Canyon, Mabli Reese had put her niece to work helping make tarts while Della visited in the parlor.

"I have a letter from Jesse," Amanda said, after pouring lemonade for them both. "He and Ray are thinking of buying up a prodigious amount of land in the district of Alberta."

"To what purpose?"

"A ranch for one, but he mentioned so much land that I wonder if he has a larger enterprise in mind."

Della took a sip and set down her glass. "Amanda, how many fingers does Uncle Jesse have in how many pies?"

"The Tintic Mining District, of course, plus our ranch in Payson—my, but that was a hardscrabble time—and you know the Knight block downtown, plus investments here and there."

"And a few houses in Provo, one of which we live in," Della reminded her. "Why is he so kind?"

She knew it was a silly thing to ask, and regretted it immediately. "I didn't mean . . ." She stopped and faced her own fact. "I have known some who are not so generous with their money."

"So have I. Jesse is not one of those." Amanda smiled, and Della saw a faint blush. "I asked him that after the Humbug Mine came in. 'Why so kind to others?' I asked. With no hesitation he said it was a mandate from heaven, given to him right there by the Humbug. I have never questioned his generosity since."

"We have certainly been the recipients," Della said. She couldn't say any more. Amanda covered Della's hand with her own and they sat quietly together until Angharad brought in two cherry tarts and asked why they were just sitting there.

"My dear, we were waiting for tarts, and here you are," Amanda replied, and squeezed Della's hand. "Take them outside and get another for yourself. And one to take home to Da."

"Don't fear what happens, Della," she whispered as Angharad went to the porch. "You have champions now."

Chapter 16

Sunday School in a new ward was filled with the usual discomfort of knowing no one and the realization by afternoon services that Owen truly could not sing a note. As Della and Angharad sang and exchanged worried looks, he bowed his head and sat in silence, eyes closed, at the mercy of memory. Holding him close that night had helped, but she had still found him in the kitchen after midnight, putting the final touches on a carved box that needed no final touches. She watched him a moment, kissed the top of his head, and returned to bed.

She must have had restless dreams of her own, because the next thing she remembered was Owen gently shaking her awake and calling her name. She opened her eyes, remembering for a moment a young girl standing by a deep hole in the ground, shouting for someone. The bad memory drifted away like smoke, and she looked into her husband's face.

"That was some nightmare," he said. "I heard you from the kitchen." He got in bed.

"I wish you would sing to me."

"I wish I could," he told her. "Will this do for now?"

"Almost. At least say the words to 'Ar Hyd y Nos.' In English if you please."

"'Sleep, my child, and peace attend thee, all through the night,'" he said, speaking all the verses until she slept, safe in his arms.

In the morning, with their own suitcases in hand for Salt Lake, they all walked Mabli to the depot and put her on the train back to Scofield. Mabli told them Mrs. Knight had given her twenty dollars for her services that week. "I didn't expect such generosity," she told Della as Owen bought her train ticket. "I was happy to help."

"The Knights are like that," Della said. "Just accept it."

"I can't help but wish the Knights' cook would decide to visit her sister more often," Mabli said as she kissed Angharad, hugged Owen, and let him help her onto the train.

Della watched Owen's face as his sister-in-law sat down in a window seat. He took an involuntary step toward the train. With heaviness in her heart, she knew he wanted to return to the canyon, and coal, and maybe Gwyna. He stopped himself and looked at her, embarrassed.

"It's all right, Owen," she said and tucked her arm through his. "We'll visit in a few weeks."

"No," he replied, surprising her. "We have work to do here in Provo. I cannot help my friends."

He bought their tickets to Salt Lake and began to relax on the train, a route he said he had not traveled since his arrival in Utah almost eight years ago.

"But it's only forty-five miles," Della said.

He shrugged. "Might as well be four hundred and fifty miles, if you work six days a week and have a small child to care for." He patted her hand. "But here we are now."

Feeling like a world traveler, Della pointed out the little towns between Provo and Salt Lake to both Davises. Angharad stared in amazement at the width of Utah Valley, before they slowed down for Point of the Mountain and Salt Lake Valley.

Della had to suppress a laugh when the child turned to Owen and asked him so seriously if he had any idea what it was like not to be wedged in a canyon.

"I have some notion," he assured her. He nudged Della. "Richard used to tease her that Winter Quarters Canyon children all had one leg shorter than the other one because they walked on slopes."

Della laughed out loud and nudged back, touched in her heart that he could mention his friend without apparent sadness.

The sight of Salt Lake City was almost too much for the little girl, her mouth open over tall buildings and streetcars and the general bustle of people hurrying about on wide sidewalks.

"Would you like to live here?" Owen asked her as they walked almost as purposefully as the other pedestrians, following Della.

Angharad shook her head. "I will leave it to them."

"You chose wisely."

Della slowed her pace a little. "You might change you mind when you eat a cream cheese sandwich on date nut bread from Mr. Auerbach's store."

Angharad stopped in the middle of the sidewalk, which meant that several men in dark suits with briefcases had to step around her. "I cannot even imagine that, Mam," she told Della.

"I can," Della replied and set Angharad in motion again before there was a pile up of pedestrians. "Easily as good as nonpareils. Believe me?"

Angharad thought a moment. "I'll believe you, even though thousands wouldn't."

It was an answer worthy of the man who held his daughter's other hand and was laughing now. "Oh, you Welsh," Della murmured, delighted.

One amazement piled on top of another for the wide-eyed little girl. When they reached the corner of State and 300 South, she stood a long moment at the nearest Auerbach's window display, with mannequins dressed in the latest summer fashions.

"You actually worked here," she said to Della.

"I actually did. There's something even more exciting inside."

"Third Floor, please," Della said to the elevator man on the main floor.

Even Owen jumped when the white-gloved attendant closed the filigreed metal cage, followed by the heavier door. "Fair takes me back to the hoist in a colliery," he said as they began to move up. "Cleaner, though. No coal. And we're going up, not down."

Della looked down to see Angharad clutching her father, her eyes huge in her face. "You'll be fine," she assured the child. "It's her first elevator ride, Seth," she told the elevator man, an old fellow she knew well from trips up and down from Menswear to the offices.

When they came to a smooth stop, Angharad relaxed visibly. With a real flourish, Seth took a wrapped caramel from a small bowl in a niche. "First time riders always get one of these," he said.

Angharad took it and thanked him prettily, which made him beam at her. With a grand gesture this time, he opened the cage and then the larger door and bowed her out. She gave him her best curtsey and led the way.

"How in the world could you tear yourself away from Auerbach's to come to our canyon to teach?" Owen asked Della as she directed them toward the frosted glass door at the end of the corridor.

"It was on a whim that I came to your canyon," she told him. "Even last Christmas, Mr. Whalley said he would hire me full time if I was too afraid to take that train back to Winter Quarters." She leaned closer. "Besides, by then I had decided I was in love with you."

He took her hand and kissed it. "No words, Della, no words."

"Da, *tyd yma*."

"Look now, I've been summoned."

Owen walked down the corridor and stopped, his turn to stare and hold Angharad close. Della hurried to stand beside them and gaze at the framed art on Magic Paper, done with Franklin Rainbow Colors that her lower grades class had drawn for Mr. Auerbach last fall, when she wanted to show her summertime boss something about her canyon children.

Her voice hushed, Angharad stepped forward and touched her drawing, the picture within a picture of her father helping her sketch a dragon, the one Owen had confessed he had a hand in creating.

"There we are, lovely one," he said.

He walked slowly down the hall, stopping at the longer sheet of paper showing the canyon train taking Kristina, Pekka, and Reet Aho to Salt Lake City, the picture with a dragon on the roof waving to the dragon standing beside a lady with bountifully curly hair, surrounded by her students even now dispersing throughout Utah.

"We thought the Ahos needed a dragon," Angharad told her father. "Mayhap we all did, think on."

"Mayhap we still do," he said. Blindly, he held out his hand for Della, and she took it.

Chapter 17

"Come in, come in, my lovelies," Mr. Auerbach said, ushering them into his office. "At last I am privileged to meet another canyon child and the happy couple. Mr. Davis, you've found yourself a peach."

No denial from him. With a sideways glance at Della, Owen shook hands with the powerful and kind man. "I have, sir. The man who married us said if I do what she says, I'll be a happy fellow."

"I trust you know wisdom when you hear it," Mr. Auerbach told him.

Salt Lake's department store king turned his attention to Angharad. He gave her a courtly bow. "Angharad Davis?" he asked.

"I am, sir," she replied, with enough poise to make Owen smile inside.

She tugged on Owen's sleeve. "Da, is this where I . . ."

"Aye, miss." He watched with appreciation as she carefully unwrapped his carved box, setting on the lid and giving the box a little pat.

With a curtsy good enough for Queen Victoria, Angharad handed the box to Mr. Auerbach. Her courage deserted her and she stepped back until she leaned against Owen. His hands went to her shoulders.

"What did we want to say?" he prompted.

That was all she needed. "Thank you for the beautiful furniture," Angharad said, and then she extemporized, to everyone's amusement, "Mam tells me I cannot eat on the parlor chairs on pain of being sold to gypsies. The bed is big enough so I can sleep in the middle if there is thunder and lightning. We all agreed."

"Your gift was so kind, Mr. A," Della said when Mr. Auerbach regained his composure. "So are the towels and sheets." She laughed. "How did you know I had been admiring that particular bedspread?"

"A lucky guess, Della." Mr. Auerbach touched the box and removed the lid. "Fancy this," he said and took out a piece of paper with a dragon.

"Da says everyone needs a dragon."

All we can get these days, Owen thought, as Mr. Auerbach beamed at Angharad and tucked the paper back in the box.

"And now my dears," he began, turning his attention to Della. "Do you suppose Miss Davis here would care to try a cream cheese on date nut bread sandwich?"

"I am certain she would," Della said.

"I would?" Angharad asked.

"Yes. It's even better than those cherry phosphates at the Palace Drugstore in Provo."

"I'll prove it to you," Mr. Angharad said. He opened the door. "Miss Milton, would you take Miss Davis to the mezzanine for cream cheese on date nut bread?"

"I would welcome the opportunity," said the dignified and magnificent Miss Milton. She held out her hand for Angharad.

Mr. Auerbach gestured to the chairs, his face serious, now that Angharad was out of earshot.

"We were all appalled to hear of your sad news," he said. He leaned back in his chair. "I find myself looking at my Winter Quarters art gallery in the hall, wondering who is left and who is gone."

"Many of my students are fatherless," Della said, her voice low. "They are scattering to the four winds now, as their mothers take them to live with other relatives."

"And you, Mr. Davis?" The gaze he turned on Owen was unflinching. "We know what it is to suffer, we Auerbachs. Life is not kind to Jews in Europe or, I think, coal miners anywhere."

"No, sir, it is not," Owen said, when he regained *his* composure. "I send you special thanks from Thomas Parmley for your generous contribution to the canyon's widows. He would write you, but he is so busy, and I . . . I have left the canyon."

"We were happy to help. May I call you Owen?"

"Aye, please."

"Owen. Della." Mr. Auerbach came around his desk and took their hands. "I am ready this moment to offer you both employment here in our store. Della, Mr. Whalley will be in my debt forever if you will come aboard as his assistant. Owen, I can always use a good carpenter." He smiled. "And from the look of this box, you could easily do a brisk business making this an Auerbach's exclusive offering. What do you think?"

Della would do this in a minute, Owen thought. He felt cold fingers patter down his spine.

He was wrong. His wife gave her former employer her kindliest smile but shook her head. "Sir, I think moving to Salt Lake would put us too far away from our remaining friends in Scofield, and . . . and other considerations. We have temporary jobs now, and hope for the best for this fall."

Owen had to give Mr. Auerbach credit for trying. "I know I could pull a string or two and find you something to do at your old Westside School besides teaching. I own considerable rental property over there. I could make you quite a deal on a house."

Owen could feel Della wavering. He knew how she felt about her first school, but his dear wife touched Mr. Auerbach's sleeve. "You're so kind to worry about us. I must say no, but with all my thanks. We'll manage, sir."

Mr. Auerbach was made of sterner material, and obviously not used to someone turning him down, even though he appeared to remain good-natured about the matter. He threw up his hands in what Owen hoped was mock frustration. "Humor me, Della. Bear in mind, at least, that my offer is always open to both of you."

"That we will do, sir," Della said.

Owen watched her eyes fill with tears. She brushed them aside, leaned closer and kissed Samuel Auerbach's cheek. "You're the best man I know, perhaps with the exception of this husband of mine. Thank you, Mr. A."

"And you're as good as any daughter," Mr. Auerbach replied. "Will you let me know how you are getting on? If any of your former students are in need of something, I can always help." He gestured toward the door. "After all, I have their art gallery outside my office."

"I promise. Thank you again for the wonderful furniture."

"Anytime." He cleared his throat. "Ahem. If you're ever in need of a crib, you need only contact me."

Owen felt his face grow warm. A glance at Della showed him her own adorable confusion, which made Mr. Auerbach laugh at them both. "Two sillies sitting here in my office! Maybe three. I have eight children of my own!" He glanced at the clock. "And now I have a shareholders' meeting."

He escorted them into the hall, and whispered to Della that her old boss in Menswear had been discovered last week looking at engagement rings before the store opened.

"I know he's sweet on Mrs. Aho, and nothing could please me more," Della said. "Mr. Auerbach, are you a little bit of a matchmaker?"

"Eveline says I am a meddling old *meshuganah*," he said. "Is there Welsh word for troublemaker?"

"*Gwneuthurwr drafferth*," Owen said promptly and then laughed.

Angharad waited for them in the narrow snack bar in the mezzanine. While Della thanked Miss Milton and wiped cream cheese off Angharad's face, Owen didn't say no to a nut bread sandwich of his own.

"My word, Della. We might have to return here every few weeks to let Mr. Auerbach know how we're doing," he told her as she dabbed at *his* cheek.

"That's fine with me," she said, amazingly complacent. "That way you'll be too stout to wedge yourself under a shelf of coal and chip away."

"Method to your madness, eh?"

"No. Self-preservation," she said without a smile. He did not doubt this was a word to the wise, with the hope that it was sufficient. "Now I suppose we must face my uncle."

Why he had thought that was a good idea escaped him, and they put it off long enough to eat fish and chips in the basement cafeteria and pay a visit to Kristina Aho, who was painting the Saltair Pavilion in a display window. Paintbrush in hand, she said there would be real sand and mannequins cavorting in the latest swimwear.

Owen admired Kristina's blond good looks, rendered more lovely because her hair was caught back in a red western bandana as she painted. As she and Della chatted, he marveled that a Finnish woman widowed by the Number One could move so gracefully into a confident lady who could support her family. *Give it a generation*, he thought, touched. *Pekka will graduate from the university here and find himself an American wife. In another generation, Finnish customs will become quaint, except at Christmas.*

He considered Angharad and knew she would be the last of his line to speak Welsh. The thought might have saddened him a few years ago, but not now, not with Della in his life and the sure knowledge that she, too, could carry on confidently, if needed. *Hurrah for the ladies.*

"There's no avoiding a visit, I suppose," his wife said as they walked one block, crossed a wide street, and then stopped in front of an imposing building. *Anders, Court and Landry, Attorneys at Law*, Owen read silently.

"The firm occupies two floors," Della said as Owen opened the door for her and Angharad.

She had gone noticeably pale and he worried. "We don't have to do this."

"We're here. Might as well."

He admired her show of confidence as she asked the superior-looking woman seated at a desk to announce their arrival. He stood there, acutely conscious of his well-brushed but shabby suit and Angharad's dress that had seemed perfectly appropriate for a warmish spring day, but which now looked rumpled and worn. *Show no fear, Owen*, he told himself.

They seated themselves in the lobby and waited five minutes, and then ten. Della leaned closer. "Five more minutes, and then we leave," she whispered. "We have a train to catch."

Owen's smile froze when Karl Anders opened a door, nodded to Della, and came in their direction. It wasn't lost on him that the receptionist stood up when he passed her desk.

"Della, what a delight to see you," he said as his cheek brushed past hers but didn't quite touch. "You should have told me you were getting married last week. I would certainly have tried to be there."

Owen, who had sat out cave-ins in the dark, had to remind himself not to be intimidated. Still, there was something chilling about a man in a perfect suit who could walk across a perfect carpet and snatch the light from his wife's face.

He should have known better than to underestimate the woman who shared his bed and loved his daughter.

"Uncle Karl, it was a trying time all around. We're sealed together now and wanted to say hello. We were already in Salt Lake on other business and the Interurban doesn't leave for an hour. How are you?"

Oh, Della, Della, he thought with admiration. He kept a straight face as Karl Anders took *that* in and realized, somewhere in his perfect mind, that he wasn't the first choice.

"Good enough, niece," Anders replied. Then it was Owen's turn. He held out his hand. "I remember you from last Thanksgiving, Mr. Davis."

They shook hands, and there it was, just the smallest glance down to see if there was coal dust on the attorney's fingers.

"Aye, we met in Provo," Owen said, wanting to match his wife's cool reserve. "I'm out of the mines now, so no fears about coal dust on your fingers."

A small frown, but that was all. "I wish you both well." Anders gave Angharad a glance. In her kindness, just a child who had no idea what was playing out in the lobby, she gave the lawyer her sweetest smile. "Your . . . your . . . daughter?"

"Aye, sir, Angharad. Your niece taught her this school year in the canyon."

Uncle Karl nodded, evidently not a man who felt comfortable around children. Owen tried to imagine years of sterile life in the Anders household and silently cheered Della's fortitude.

There was not going to be an invitation into Karl Anders' office. That fact was as plain as if a judge had banged down his gavel and declared a mistrial.

"Caroline will be distressed that she missed seeing you," Anders said, as smooth a lie as Owen had ever heard. No wonder he was a successful lawyer.

"She'll recover, I am certain," Della replied.

"She has been under the weather for some months now."

"Please tell her for me that I hope she feels better soon."

Oh, Della, you could have been a barrister too, Owen thought, amused.

"I will pass on your best wishes," Anders said. "Now I must return to my office. So much to do."

Owen shook hands with his wife's uncle, hoping never to see him again, but nodding and smiling because he understood prickly relatives himself. Who didn't?

"Uncle Karl, take care of yourself," Della said. To Owen's astonishment, she took his hand in grip so firm her knuckles whitened.

Owen held his breath. He knew that look of hers, the one that turned steely when she narrowed her eyes.

"I only wish one thing," she said, her voice low, after a glance back at Angharad, who had already started for the door that led mercifully to the street. "I wish Aunt Caroline had given me that letter from my father years ago."

"Oh, but . . ."

"I couldn't have done anything about it, because I was powerless. I would have at least known that my mother loved me and would have stayed in my life, had her own father not dragged her away. Can you imagine what a difference that would have made in my life? No, I see you cannot."

How odd: a lawyer with nothing to say. Owen almost pitied him.

"Too many years have passed, and I will never find my mother, thanks to what my aunt did," Della said, her head high and her voice firm. She stepped back and took Owen's arm; he felt her tremble. "I would like to have known my mother. Good day."

She turned on her heel and left the lobby, hanging onto Owen now, her dark Greek eyes stormy.

Years ago—who knew where—Owen had come across a copy of *Antigone*, Sophocles's great tragedy about a young woman with the courage to bury her brother in defiance of her tyrant uncle. He never forgot Antigone's determination to do the right thing, no matter the consequences.

Here was his own Greek woman, braver than armies. *I had better measure up*, he thought, as they walked in silence to the depot. *I would dread a confrontation with a thoroughly convinced woman.*

He looked at her with admiration, shocked to see a frightened child staring back.

"Della?" he asked. "Are you all right?"

The look vanished, leaving confusion on her face. "I don't know what I am."

Chapter 18

"I don't know what got into me," Della told Owen that night, long after Angharad was asleep in her own bed. She burrowed close to him.

"A bitter serving of righteous indignation?"

"You Welsh and words," she said. He massaged her shoulders and she relaxed. Her hand went to his chest. "I know the Molly Bee closed about eight years ago."

"If you know that much, can you find out more?"

"I doubt it. It was two paragraphs on a back page of the *Tribune*. I was working in the library after school and read it there. I imagine all the miners moved away."

"She's somewhere," Owen said.

"You'll think this is silly, but . . ."

"I doubt it. I have a seven-year-old daughter, remember."

They laughed together. "After I got that letter last spring from my uncle, I dreamed about writing to my mother, and addressing it to 'Anywhere, USA.'"

Owen heard all the wistfulness in her voice. "Did she get the letter in your dream?"

"Every time," Della said, her voice soft and low. She snuggled closer and closed her eyes.

Owen held Della close as she slept. He breathed deep of her rose-scented hair and turned his thoughts from letters of the heart to the mines, which, if he were honest, formed another kind of love in his heart.

Almost four weeks had elapsed since the double mine catastrophe. It was too early for anyone so close to it to view the matter dispassionately, but he tried. Lying there comfortable and breathing cool air that smelled nothing of sulfur, he knew how familiar he was with chance. So did every man who ever entered a mine. The odds were in a careful man's favor, but for how long?

He had sat out his fair share of mine collapses, never alone, always with companion miners because most men worked in twos. Sometimes there was no spare air, so they sat in silence to conserve it, candles blown out to save on oxygen. Other times, especially in the high caverns of Utah mines, a group of singers could get up a respectable chorus, especially if there was a high tenor like Richard Evans.

Then when rescuers poked through the rubble, and the trapped men saw tiny points of light from the small open flames—amazing how bright they seemed after total darkness—everyone could laugh and shake it off, dig out, and return to work.

"Papa."

Della said it again, but louder. "Papa." Owen kissed her head, which made her sigh and return to deeper sleep.

Some men never came out, Della's father among them. Owen knew little of hard rock mines, but he tried to imagine the Molly Bee of Della's childhood. He knew the boom and bust of mining coal. Summers were always harder because no one needed to heat their homes. The price of silver fluctuated too, depending on politics.

Della had told him something of her hard times. In that brief span of mere hours when he left the Number

Four and the explosion, he knew he wanted more information from her—not because he was interested in another's misery, but because it pained him to see the distant look on her face now and then, when he knew she was miles away.

He didn't care for that distant look in a woman's eyes, especially *his* woman's eyes. Here in Provo, there should be time to change that odd stare into the soft glance she more often gave Angharad and him.

Another thought plucked at him and demanded attention like a toddler. A realist down to the soles of his feet, Owen knew there was not one thing he or anyone else could have done to prevent the deaths of two hundred men, once the chain reaction of coal dust exploding and killing in the Number Four began its split-second work. The rapid spread of invisible afterdamp that raced through the levels connecting the Four with the One was just as inexorable.

He knew he could not bring back his friends, but he wondered if there were some way to make a mine safer. There he lay, satisfied, relaxing as sleep claimed him. Deep breaths of clean air and rose talcum powder gently pushed him into the mattress. He could think tomorrow.

Or not think. Owen knew it was easier to let himself be borne along on the pleasant tide of springtime in Provo. People being what they were, maybe it was a kindness to begin a new routine somewhere not far removed from sorrow by distance because he saw the mountains every day, but mentally, miles away in a town where no one dug coal.

A methodical man, Owen settled into a pattern of lying in bed after Della woke up, stretching, and heading to the lavatory. After a week or so, he knew her routine of cleaning up, dressing, kissing his cheek, and going to the kitchen.

He heard the coal tumbling into the cook stove and soon sniffed the fragrance of porridge, or perhaps flapjacks, as Americans called those delectable cakes. There was also the novelty of milk to drink, because their nearest neighbor had a cow and Della knew how to bargain. His morning routine included knocking on Angharad's door and then entering to admire his daughter, who continued—through hard years and better ones—to wake up like a flower turning toward the sun.

He stayed in her room long enough to reply to her Welsh greeting and remind her that time waits for no girl. When Owen finally made it to the kitchen, Della had spread out the *Daily Enquirer* so he could read, as carefree as a lord. The paper was a luxury they had both agreed on, especially since the paperboy lived just down the street. Della had already worked out an arrangement to help the affable child with his reading, once the boy's mother had confided before Sunday School that he needed some tutelage, and with new twins, she hadn't time. Della did have time, which meant summer school for James the paperboy in exchange for the news.

Morning meant a kneeling prayer in the parlor before breakfast, when the three of them thanked the Lord for another day, prayed for friends hurting under an unimaginable load that Owen could very well imagine, and asked for whatever blessings the Lord thought they might need, since the entire matter was in His hands, anyway.

Lunch packed in his old miner's bucket, with the water reservoir below and the food compartment on top, Owen walked his girls to Maeser School, kissed them both, touched forefingers with Angharad from habit, and then walked four blocks north to the Bullock home.

He quickly learned that the Bullocks were a prolific bunch. This particular Bullock, an accountant who knew what he wanted, carefully informed Owen of the project and his expected conclusion and turned him loose to work.

"You're highly recommended by Uncle Jesse, and that's enough for me," Mr. Bullock said as he put on his hat and checked his timepiece. "My family is gone for a few weeks, so you can work uninterrupted. If you need anything, stop by my office." He handed Owen a business card. "Any questions?"

A man of few words indeed. He was no Welshman. "I do have one, and it's because I am curious," Owen said. "Does everyone call Brother Knight 'Uncle Jesse'?"

"Everyone I know," Mr. Bullock replied. "As an accountant, I can tell you he's given away a lot of money to people in need and many see him as a rich uncle." He looked Owen over, maybe wondering if Owen was one of those. He must have decided he wasn't, because his tone changed. "I would hate to be his money man and have to bite my tongue every time Uncle Jesse wanted a little something for a widow or orphan. Not that I'm against charity! Oh, no. Still, it must be hard to reconcile a generous man's ledgers. Good day, Mr. Davis."

Hard in this life, easy in the next, Owen thought as he took a pry bar to some less-gifted carpenter's version of wainscoting.

It was easy work, probably good for two weeks. He worked steadily every day, with time out for lunch with his girls at Maeser School, where Della explained the Dewey Decimal System to him, and Angharad showed off the books she had dusted and stacked where Mam said.

Routine soothed his heart, and he watched it work on Della too. She smiled more, and she didn't carry her shoulders so high, the way a person did who had too much tension stored up to ever relax.

As they moved deeper into their personal relationship, Owen could have gone to his knees in gratitude for a healthy, vital wife. Gwyna was his joy, but he had watched her sink and suffer from a heart weakening each year of her short life. Toward the end, he could only stand by, helpless, as something as simple as breathing at high altitude in a coal camp finally became impossible.

In the proper footgear, Della could probably have beaten him in a race. They were much the same height, but he knew her legs were longer than his. He enjoyed her economy of motion as she worked about the house, cooking, cleaning, ironing, tutoring the paperboy, and taking meals to old Brother Scott down the street.

"It's like this, Owen," she told him one night as he brushed her hair. "We take turns casually dropping in at suppertime with a dish of something or other. It's been going on for months since Brother Scott's wife died. Now that *we* moved in, all the days of the week are covered."

"Surely he knows what you're doing," he said. "Sit still, Della. Your hair requires intense concentration."

She laughed at that. "Amateur!" She leaned against him and looked up. "We tell him there was too much for supper and ask if he would mind. He maintains his dignity, and we get to do good. Everyone wins."

Normally an articulate man, he had no idea how to tell his wife how *he* had won. She had never heard flowery sentiments in her hard life. After a sweet moment of love one night that practically made his heart stop, she had stared deep into his eyes. "I haven't sufficient words," was all she said.

He knew another way to touch her heart. Owen had noticed how often she took off her wedding ring, the one he had borrowed from her former suitor—oh, the irony—because he could afford nothing. He found the pretty thing on the windowsill in the kitchen after bread making, or another time on the sofa in the parlor.

He drew the inside of the ring on a scrap of paper and took it to Brother Thomas Taylor. Recommended by Mr. Bullock, Owen had moved on from wainscoting to lining closets with cedar in all the bedchambers at the Taylors'. Brother Taylor and Julius Jensen owned a jewelry store.

Della approved the closet project in particular because he came home every night smelling of cedar. When he told her Mr. Bullock had also asked him to help in the teardown of the old Bullock Hotel at Center Street and Fifth West, she had hugged him, pleased that word of mouth was getting around and jobs seemed to be falling his way. He could work on both projects at the same time.

What he didn't tell her was that Brother Taylor had agreed to barter cedar closets for a wedding ring. The amiable jeweler had laughed over his story of Della's ring given to him by a former rival and agreed that

Owen could pick out a very nice ring when the closets were done.

He selected a wide band with a simple flower etched in the gold. Inside, Brother Taylor himself had etched OD to DA, 1900, and found a small box. "What will she do?" Brother Taylor asked as he handed it over.

"Cry, more like," Owen said, "and I'll mail the other one back to my rival."

After supper, when Della was sitting on the porch with James the paperboy and Angharad, taking turns reading *The Jungle Book,* he had set the ring box on the ledge in the kitchen next to Emil Isgreen's ring.

He joined them on the porch to read *Mediation and the Atonement* and casually glanced at Della, who sat on the top step of the porch, cuddling two readers.

"Did you forget your ring again?" he asked when Mowgli and Bagheera were preparing to fight Shere Khan.

Della glanced at her bare finger and sighed. "It won't do to lose it," she muttered, handed the book to James. "I'll be back."

Silence from the kitchen. Owen waited, then folded down a corner of the page and took his chances.

She stood in the middle of the kitchen, ring box in hand, staring down at the lovely thing inside. As he watched, enchanted, she poked at it, maybe wondering if it was her imagination.

"Brother Taylor and I did a barter for those cedar-lined closets," he said. "I'm getting good money for the hotel teardown. No one's going to starve in the Davis house if you have a wedding ring from me and not Dr. Isgreen."

Without a word, she grabbed him around the neck and planted a kiss of startling proportions on his lips.

Kissing her back was never a strain, even if his shoulders did ache a bit from prying out old wattle and daub all afternoon, once he finished the closets.

She pulled away first, but not far, and gave him her intense stare that made him wonder how other husbands managed without Della Davis in their lives.

"Put it on my finger," she ordered and held out her hand.

"If you'll stop shaking," he teased. Then he laughed at himself because he was shaking too.

He slid it on. "Will it do?"

"Forever," she whispered.

Chapter 19

In retrospect, when he had time to repent at leisure and think about the matter, Owen never should have listened to Uncle Jesse. And in retrospect (that devil in the details), he never would have done anything different. Owen knew himself too well to think he could ever ignore a plea from a mine owner who wanted a safer workplace. And who could say this wasn't the reason he was still alive?

As it turned out, the cost was higher than he would have reckoned. At the time it seemed reasonable, but he was wrong.

The whole matter started simply enough, a mere conversation among men after dinner at the Knights' house, where the women adjourned to the parlor to chat, and the men stayed in the dining room. Angharad had been content to help the cook in the kitchen and eat in there.

Although the Knights had invited them over to dinner several times this summer, he wondered if he should have been wary of this gathering. One mining magnate, a mining engineer, two investors, and him: a part-time handyman looking for permanent work. He didn't blame Uncle Jesse later, not at all. The man was worried, and he should have been.

Owen smiled to himself when the two investors from back East looked around for a servant to bring in after-dinner coffee or brandy. To earn a little money in Wales, his mam had served meals in the owner's house back in the Powell-Williams Colliery. She would come home late and sit on his bed and tell him about coffee in small cups and snifters of brandy and another drink, served only after really good news, that popped and fizzed.

Not in the Knight house. Fruit and nuts went around, chased down by cold water. Owen was partial to baked and salty walnuts. He had taken a handful of nuts when he noticed everyone was looking at him. He briefly wondered what kind of manners felony he had just committed. Or maybe he should have been listening to the conversation.

"We need your advice, Owen," Uncle Jesse said. He took some nuts too, giving Owen permission to follow through with his initial plan to eat them. "Gentlemen, do you have any idea how hard it is to judge that fatal moment when ten seconds more will burn the nuts?"

Everyone laughed. Owen could almost imagine them as well-dressed cartoon figures in the newspaper, with little thought bubbles: "What is *really* on Uncle Jesse's mind?" or "No one will believe this back in Pittsburgh," or maybe even, "Let's get to it. Time is money." Owen ate his handful of walnuts and waited.

"I have a problem, Owen," Uncle Jesse said, not wasting a moment on preliminaries. "I've had two cave-ins in the Banner, my newest mine in Tintic, and I don't know what to do."

"I'm no hard rock miner," Owen countered, uneasy already.

"You know wood. You've been in cave-ins."

"Aye to both," Owen agreed, "but I promised Della I would not go in a mine again."

That earned him eye rolls and chuckles from the fat cats around the table. The mining engineer didn't smile. Maybe he had a wife like Della, who worried every time he went underground and the mine trembled.

If he was anything, Uncle Jesse was persuasive. How else did a man get so rich? "Would you consider a short time underground to give me some advice?"

"Tell him yes, lad," one of the Easterners said. "Who wears the pants in your family?"

"We've only been married since May," Owen replied before he thought. "I don't wear them much, either."

The table exploded in laughter. *I could have gone all week and not said that*, Owen thought, ashamed of himself. His mortification increased when Amanda Knight stuck her head in the doorway and asked what was so funny. The men laughed louder when her husband said, "I will never tell you, not in a million years."

"Forgive that," Owen muttered, his face flaming hot.

"I haven't laughed so hard in ages," the Easterner said. "We'll pay you a sizeable consulting fee. Think about it, at least. Should we offer him sixty dollars, Mr. Knight?"

Three months' rent. "I'll think about it," Owen said. Maybe that would hold the man off. Maybe the investor would take a train back East. Maybe full-time employment would suddenly materialize. Maybe he should reconsider Mr. Auerbach's offer.

"When can we expect an answer?" the man asked. "Tomorrow? Next week?"

Owen looked away, knowing how men with money operated. They wanted answers and they wanted to make more money, hang everyone's feelings, even a tender wife who sometimes woke him up at night saying, "Papa," in a little girl's voice. Or a coal miner still prying his best friend's fingers off a pickaxe every other night or so.

"I'll answer when I can," he said with enough force to silence the investor. "You don't know what we've been through recently. When I can, gentlemen. Excuse me, please. It's time to walk my girls home."

"Girls, is it?" the other Easterner said, after a sly look at Uncle Jesse. "'Pon my word, I thought polygamy was outlawed."

"My daughter and my wife," Owen said, irritated with himself for his conversational blunderings.

A moment in the kitchen with Mrs. McNulty and Angharad took the edge off his embarrassment, especially when his daughter presented him with another slice of cake with thick frosting and little silver doodads in curlicues.

"I told Mrs. McNulty that you like white cake better than any other kind," Angharad said.

The Knights' cook handed him the rest of the cake. "It'll just go bad here," she said, and she frowned when he started to object. "Don't tell me that you know more about cooking than I do, Owen Davis! If I say it'll go bad, it'll go bad."

"I try not to argue with the ladies," Owen said, backing out of the kitchen, cake in hand. He tapped on the parlor door, and Della looked up, relief in her eyes. She said her goodnights and joined him and Angharad.

"You have a friend in the kitchen," Della said as she eyed the cake.

"Best place to find a friend."

The night was cool. When Angharad skipped ahead, Della leaned closer. "You couldn't have rescued me at a more opportune time."

"It was getting a little close in the dining room too," he admitted, more willing to listen to her than to explain his discomfort, mostly of his own making.

"You probably won't believe this, but those two ladies, the wives of those rich men from back East, just about assured me that you would be working underground for Uncle Jesse in the Tintic District," she said as they strolled along.

Maybe he waited too long to reply. She stopped. "Of course you told them no such thing. Didn't you?"

"Well, I . . ."

"Owen Davis, what are you doing?"

They were passing one of Provo's little pocket parks, a spot with trees and park benches. City workers must have uprooted the summer flowers that were fading. Only yesterday Angharad had gathered up some of the bewildered things and put them in a vase for the kitchen table.

Her expression militant, Della sat down on one of the park benches and patted the spot beside her. He knew better than to do anything except sit.

"It was a bit of an ambush," he said. "Uncle Jesse and the mining engineer, Steve something . . ."

"Henry," Della said. "His wife, Maryetta, was in the parlor. They've been married about six months."

That's right. Mrs. Henry hadn't much to say during dinner, but he did notice that she had no waist. "She's in the family way, isn't she?" he asked, hoping to buy time.

"Five more months. You're observant."

"He was so solicitous of her. Easy to spot."

"They're living in Knightville," Della told him. "Uncle Jesse wanted him here specifically to talk to you. Did you?"

Bless the ladies, Owen thought with appreciation, even as he squirmed. "Stick a handful of ladies in a room, and all truth is revealed," he teased. "Any idea what her china pattern was when they married?"

She laughed and flicked the side of his head with thumb and forefinger. "You think you're so funny, but she said something about cave-ins, and she looked mighty worried."

"No, he didn't talk to me directly, but Uncle Jesse mentioned two cave-ins." He took a deep breath. "He wants me to go with him to Silver City and give him my opinion."

He knew she wasn't slow. "And you plan to do this by killing a chicken and checking its entrails?" she asked. "Probably at high noon on Main Street there?"

"He wants me in the mine, Della. You know he does."

"You told him no," she said, but he heard the defeat in her voice.

He looked her in the eyes and, to his dismay, watched hope slide away. Better face it. "I told him I would think about it. I made no promises."

"Owen, no."

She started to move away from him. He tightened his grip on her shoulder and held her there. "Don't pull away from me, Della, not ever."

"Then don't go in a mine again."

"He's offering me sixty dollars to go below and look around. Three month's rent, Della, and I'm about done with that teardown of the Bullock Hotel. No other prospects at the moment. When's the librarian returning from Massachusetts?"

"In three weeks. Owen, no," she repeated in a quiet voice. "We'll manage somehow. You know we will."

"Very well," he said. "No."

Chapter 20

Two weeks later, he was on his way to Silver City in the Tintic Mining District, sitting beside a bleak Jesse Knight in his private railcar. Della had seen them off with tears in her eyes. To his relief, only half of those were for him. More were probably for Steve Henry, new husband and prospective father, buried under a ton of rocks in the Banner mine.

The Banner had been on his mind for two weeks, even before the accident that plunged Maryetta Henry from wife to widow. After work each day, he went to his backyard workshop, first to think and then to draw a timber frame. He knew hard rock mines typically used square sets or wooden boxes—for want of a better term—to shore up all sides of a passageway. This frame would be something in addition to a square set.

Maybe a hard rock mine like the finicky Banner needed more attention to make it safer. His idea would take more wood, but what was a life worth?

He didn't say anything to Della, who had worries of her own. "No one is hiring right now," she told him one Saturday, after a visit to Provo Cooperative Mercantile Institution. She had plopped down next to him on the front porch.

"Put your feet up on the railing," he said, smiling at her. "It always makes me feel better."

"Knucklehead. And entertain the neighbors?"

"You do have lovely legs, Mrs. Davis."

"They're for you alone, you rascal."

He had married a thoughtful woman. After a day or two, it became obvious to Owen that Della knew he had something more important than her legs on his mind. Being that thoughtful woman, she knew precisely when to ask him what was on *his* mind one night.

"You can't fool me, you know. You're thinking of Uncle Jesse's offer."

"Aye, miss," he said to tease her, but he found he couldn't joke about the matter. "I think of my friends, gone now. I know there is nothing I could have done to save them."

He both felt and heard her sigh.

"But I have an idea that might save other miners."

She was an honest wife. "I went in your workshop yesterday. What are you making?"

"It's a . . . I don't know any architects' language. Call it a tiny model. I don't know what hard rock mines look like inside, but I know mines, and I've been listening to Uncle Jesse."

"My father thought he knew mines."

In a moment, his chest was damp with her tears. He knew she was thinking of her father's death in the Molly Bee. Two weeks ago in Tintic, Winter Quarters Canyon back in May, and then Colorado twelve years ago: mining deaths never grew old in the heart and soul, never mind the brain. Still, she had asked. Better bumble ahead.

"I'm wondering if a more—again, I don't know the words—more solid structure beyond a mere square set might make it safer, or at least allow better refuge until the miners can be dug out."

"How could you get such a structure into a mine? It would be too large."

"True. I would build it in units aboveground, then dismantle or partially collapse it some way to go into the mine."

She rose up on one elbow and put her face close to his. "No mines for you, Owen. You promised."

"It could save lives."

And there the matter ended for the night. All the next day as he tore down an old hotel, wondering if his life was destined to take odd jobs from now on, he had a better idea. A quick stop at the hardware store after work and the matter of a penny kept his plan alive.

Della and Angharad were still at Maeser School, so he cleaned the dust and plaster from his hair and body and hurried to his workshop. He had made his model of balsa wood because it was plentiful and cheap. In a matter of minutes, he had cut out a miniature timber, and then another. Working carefully, he attached the tiny hinges to the wood.

"There you have it," he said in quiet triumph. He folded in the balsa logs, hinged now. If he could somehow slant the unit's roof and reinforce it, possibly the rock and rubble would slide down the side, instead of crash through the square set. He could write a letter to Steve Henry, Uncle Jesse's mining engineer, and ask about rocks in motion and at rest. Three or four of these units in a row, then regular housing, then more units might give miners a place of refuge when the mountain started to move.

He wouldn't know, though, unless he went underground, and that was his frustration, one Della didn't understand. *Why are you doing this?* he asked himself, even though he knew the answer. *I can save other lives.*

Another week passed, and August turned the corner toward September. Owen knew his wife was a careful spender, her eyes trained to a bargain. PCMI had a special on two gingham dresses. Those, plus her clothes from last year, would be enough for Angharad to start school. His daughter had proudly showed him the four silver dollars she had earned dusting and moving books around that summer, plus one dollar more for what Mr. Holyoke termed her bonus.

"It feels good to earn money, doesn't it, Da?" she said, as she watched him fiddling with more balsa units in his workshop.

"It does, Miss Davis. What sort of plans do you have for your salary?"

He knew she had been considering the matter when, with no hesitation, she announced, "Once I pay the bishop fifty cents for tithing, I will buy a pair of shoes and maybe stockings and save the rest." She leaned against Owen. "Mam tells me that Brother Esplin at PCMI said he has shoes just my size."

He made himself pay attention to Angharad, who seemed to have more on her mind than shoes. He knew this daughter of his.

"Da, my new teacher is going to be Miss Wilkins. Mr. Holyoke told me. He asked her if she needed some bulletin board help. I am to help her tomorrow instead of Mam." She grabbed his arm. "Da, she especially needs someone who can color in the lines and cut evenly. I can!"

"I'll wager you will be her best pupil, same as you were Mam's best," he said as he put away his tools. "Let's see if Mam needs some help with dinner."

Hand in hand they went in the back door in time to see Della marking an *X* on the kitchen calendar. Her back to them, she sat down at the table and stared at Miss August carrying a fishing pole.

His hand went to her shoulder. She sighed and leaned her cheek against his hand. "I'm getting impatient," she whispered, her eyes on Angharad, heading to her room. "Four months. Shouldn't I be a little bit in the family way by now?"

Maybe she could take some joshing. "My experience suggests that no one is a 'little bit in the family way.' It's an all or nothing proposition."

"You know what I mean."

"Aye, miss." His hand went to her neck, so soft. "Patience is a virtue, or so I have been told."

"It's highly overrated." She kissed his hand on her shoulder and then sniffed. "You smell of plaster. I liked the cedar better."

"So did I. What's for supper?"

"Beef stew and sliced peaches. No oatcakes yet."

He knew she was teasing him in turn, but there was worry in her eyes. What if neither of them could find jobs? Perhaps it was a good thing she wasn't with child right now. Still, he watched her droop as another twenty-eight days rolled around, and it pained his heart.

If Della was down, Angharad made up for her silence during supper, almost bouncing in her chair, eager to help Miss Wilkins. Owen was happy to let her run on and then dart outside for Kick the Can with the other children.

"So much energy," he remarked as he helped Della clear the table. He picked up a dish towel. "Cramps? I can do kitchen duty."

She flashed him a smile. "Nothing a hot water bottle can't cure, when we go to bed. I'll wash. You dry."

And they would have, except for a pounding on their front door.

"What in the world?" Owen asked as he threw down the dish towel. "Stay here." He went into the parlor, stunned to see Uncle Jesse staring through the screen door, his face bleak and reminding Owen of every bad moment in May at the Numbers Four and One.

"What has happened?" he asked, opening the door. "Can I get you . . ."

He knew Jesse Knight as a cool man, a calm one, someone used to high stakes and well-earned rewards that he used to benefit others. This was a different Brother Knight, one in the grip of sorrow.

Uncle Jesse accepted the glass of water Della gave him. She sat on his other side, her hand on his sleeve, but he was looking at Owen. "Steve Henry died in a cave-in today in the Banner," he said, and then he put his hand over his eyes. "Owen, I need your help. This can't go on."

Della bowed her head. Owen knew what was going through her mind, as sure as if she had stood on the table and shouted it. A young widow, and her expected baby fatherless because of rocks containing silver, gold, and lead. What did that wealth even matter?

Uncle Jesse was speaking to Della now, pleading with her. "Della, I need Owen to walk that mine with me, measure it, evaluate it, and help me decide what to do."

There was a long, long pause. She sat with her head still bowed, looking at neither of them. "Then do it for Mrs. Henry, poor woman," she said finally. "Don't do it because you need more money."

When she raised her head, Owen knew what he would see. He knew Della's intense gaze startled Uncle

Jesse. The man sat back slightly, as if wanting to distance himself from the light that burned in her eyes.

"Take Owen, but promise me he will not be underground long. *Promise* me."

"I cannot make you a promise like that, Della," Uncle Jesse said, his voice equally firm. "Can you compromise?"

"Don't ask. I know Owen has been making little models of . . . of timber units for a mine." She looked at Owen. "You can't bring them back."

She was right. He could not raise from the grave Richard or David Evans, any of the Farish brothers, the Gatherums, Hunters, and Strangs, or the Davises and Joneses. Barney Dougall, Bishop Parmley's mining engineer, was gone too, and any number of skilled men in the wrong place at the wrong time. And Frederick Anders, whose Colorado death years ago left a child at the mercy of relatives in Salt Lake City.

"Can I save others? May I try? I won't know until I look," Owen said.

He couldn't bear her expression. Even worse than Della's fierce gaze was the sight of a woman without hope. Worst of all, she was his wife: bone of his bone, flesh of his flesh.

"Do it," she said, rising from the table. "You won't rest until you try." She started for the door and then turned back suddenly and slapped the table with her fist, hard enough to make the saltshaker topple.

"I love you both," she said, her words coming out strangled, as though they needed oxygen. "But ask any lady what compromise means; ask Mrs. Henry, in fact, I dare you. She will tell you it means that women lose."

Chapter 21

"I'm not used to sprawl like this," Owen told Uncle Jesse the next morning as they stood on the depot platform at Eureka, largest town the Tintic Mining District. "Canyons are certainly more constricting. I'm also not used to seeing headframes, at least not recently."

"Jokers call them gallows," Uncle Jesse said. "Some of my mines have levels and raises, such as you're accustomed to from Winter Quarters. Those are called drift mines here. Other have the windlass and hoist."

"I'm familiar with hoists from collieries in Wales," Owen said. "Sure enough there is always a fool every year who sticks his head out on the ride and loses it."

"But only once," Jesse joked, and they laughed, gallows humor from miners.

Owen stared a long time at the town. The street nearest the depot had the customary cafes, and sure enough, one was a Chinese restaurant with pretensions, titled The Grand Dynasty. Closer to the area where a few forlorn cattle waited in the slaughtering pen, he noticed a row of doors and windows and women wearing less than a man would suspect, considering that the air was still cool.

So that was Eureka, with another row of saloons, with names like The Golden Nugget, Lil's, and oddly enough, Buyer Beware. He saw pawnshops for the less fortunate, and more doors and windows with wary-looking women a bit past their prime.

"This is why I started Knightville," Uncle Jesse said, correctly interpreting the shake of Owen's head. "None of this."

"You get miners to stay there?" he asked, half joking. A redhead in a barely there camisole and petticoat was giving him the eye.

"You know I do," Jesse said. "Many of you British Isles miners followed the siren call of the gospel, thank the Almighty. There is a fair smattering of Methodists in Knightville too. They sing almost as well as you do."

As I did, Owen thought. "There is a school?"

"A good one. I have a story about it. I built the school for Knightville and tried to get county funding for it. 'Nothing doing,' I was told. It seems we didn't have enough students to qualify." He snapped his fingers. "That was an easy problem to solve. I hired Brother Higginson, father of eight school-age children, to come to my mine. Huzzah! School funding."

Owen followed Jesse Knight from the depot to Hancock House Inn, where he secured two rooms and they left their luggage. Owen realized this was the first time he had seen Uncle Jesse as a man of business. Up to now, the dignified fellow had been a dinner host, a friend, and a refuge for Della. He had kindly bought them a house, even though he brushed it off and called the little place useful rental property. Twenty dollars a month gave them comfort and privacy and another sort of refuge. He thought of Della, probably eating lunch with Angharad at Maeser School right now, and wished he had not come to Eureka.

Owen looked down at his shoes, the steel-toed boots he wore in the Number Four. He had changed into the familiar overalls and black sweater he had never thought to wear again. He smelled of coal in this busy town dedicated to silver, gold, copper, and lead.

"Owen?"

He looked up with a start, aware his mind was wandering far afield and deep into the Number Four again. "Just thinking of Della." Might as well face facts. "And coal miners too."

"Think of the Banner now. I know I'm distressing your wife, but I need your advice."

"You shall have it."

They boarded the railcar to Silver City, some two miles farther into the western desert of Tintic Mining District. Owen leaned back, his eyes on the stark silhouettes of headframes. The desert floor was a mottled olive green, which contrasted with the gray of mine tailings and tan of stones and hillside. No one could call this country attractive. Still, the sky was deep blue, with a few scudding clouds dimming the sun momentarily and then blowing on.

Silver City was a smaller replica of nearby Eureka, right down to the seedy cafes, cribs for sporting ladies, and saloons. He knew he never wanted Della or Angharad to see this ugly side of mining. True, there had been a saloon at the mouth of Winter Quarters Canyon, but in his role as bishop, Thomas Parmley railed against it regularly over the pulpit. On the other hand, the superintendent in Thomas Parmley knew he had to tolerate it, although not with any good grace.

He must have sighed too loudly to suit Uncle Jesse. "I know it isn't much. When we're done here, we'll take my spur line to Knightville."

Two horses pulling a surrey took them west past other mines, some with headframes and hoists, and other drift mines opening through portals. "The Bullock Mine. The Swansea over there," Uncle Jesse said, pointing. "And up there for all the world to see, my aptly named Mammoth. Ajax, Sioux, Yankee, and so on, mines as far as you can see." He nodded to the left. "The Banner."

They left the carriage and walked in silence to a headframe like all the others, except there was no indication of work underway. A half dozen men dressed much like Owen stood by the hoist. They straightened up when they saw who he walked with.

"Men, this is Owen Davis, who used to mine in Winter Quarters," Uncle Jesse said. "He and I are going down to walk around a bit. Is the debris cleared?"

"Aye, sir," said one of the miners. He held out his hand to Owen. "Perry Timothy. From Spring Lake, outside of Merthyr Tydfil."

"I know it well," Owen said, shaking hands. "Did you know the Perkins family? I was married to Gwyna Perkins, God rest her soul. Mabli Reese is my sister-in-law."

A nod and a smile, and all connections were established and quietly acknowledged in that way of Welshmen. "Many of you here?" Owen asked.

"Enough so that we have to number our Joneses," Perry said with a grin. "A fertile lot, eh?"

Both men laughed. It was an old Welsh joke.

Uncle Jesse gestured toward the open cage on the hoist. "After you," he said. "And you and you. We need some light."

Three of the men stepped forward, but the fourth hung back. Uncle Jesse merely nodded, which impressed Owen. Not every mine owner would accept the fact that one of the four was too superstitious to go below so soon after a death.

Owen felt in his pocket and smiled. He never left home for a shift without a cracker or bit of potato to appease the restless Tommyknockers or *bwca*. As the cage descended with a groan and a creak, he took out the oyster cracker and tossed it below into the dark.

He sniffed the air as the cage descended. "How far down?" he asked Jesse, speaking loud to be heard over the grind of the cables.

"Three hundred feet so far," Jesse said. "I didn't know you were superstitious."

"You caught me in the act," Owen replied, too long a master of his business to feel the need to explain himself or even care.

They left the hoist, lit their candles, and started through the mine, eerily silent with no drills banging away at the rock face. Owen looked at the beams above and the wide space between them, put in place by miners or engineers eager to get to the ore and move on. He recalled with a pang Steve Henry's comment to him at Uncle Jesse's dinner a few weeks ago that something had to be done before another miner died. And now Steve's unborn child would never know its father.

"You're still exploring here, aren't you?" he asked Uncle Jesse. "Things aren't well shored yet."

"True and more's the pity," the mine owner admitted.

Uncle Jesse returned to the hoist, but Owen walked the mine silently, guided by the lights of the candle he carried and the one in his cap. His quiet words to the miners meant they paced with him, adding whatever light they could throw on the deadly Banner mine. He made note of the wood and the spaces free of any framework. He had a plan, and he knew it would work, provided Uncle Jesse and his backers were willing to spend more on timber, and give him a free hand to measure and calculate. The Banner was no place to dash in and prop up ill-fitting beams. This mine was a killer and needed to be tamed.

He also knew Della would fear every second he spent below the surface of an already lethal mine. After the mind-numbing losses in Numbers Four and One, he had made her a promise, and he was about to go back on it, if Uncle Jesse made him an offer. If he didn't, the matter would end right here.

Just as silent, Owen walked back with the miners. They seemed to understand he didn't want to talk. One of them sang "Lead, Kindly Light," under his breath while the others hummed in harmony. Owen smiled inside, thinking through the lovely words. *One step enough for me*, he thought, touched, as he walked forward from one weak light to the next, minding his stride but confident because he knew mines.

Soon enough they came to the better-lit hoist, where Uncle Jesse waited. Owen nodded to him and looked back down the dark corridor. "I'll do it for you, Steve Henry," he whispered in Welsh into the gloom. "And you, Richard and David Evans, and you, William Parmley."

Uncle Jesse stood beside him as they watched the three miners travel up the hoist. When all was silent before the hoist came down again for them, Jesse put a hand on Owen's shoulder. "Talking to spirits?" he asked.

"I suppose I was. My dead friends."

"At times I think mining is too cruel," the mine owner said. "Then I remind myself that men have jobs and can support their families honorably because of what I do. Am I wrong?"

"Only if the mine is too dangerous to work. Let me do some measuring tomorrow, and some calculating."

"I'll be grateful for your opinion, Owen. One more day?"

"That will suffice."

Sitting at the desk in his room in the Hancock Inn, he was done by noon on the third day.

The second day he had measured the height and the length of the drift on Level Three and showed his balsa wood model to a handful of miners. He spent some time in the carpenter's shack in Silver City, mindful of changes to make there to accommodate the bigger timbers he envisioned, above and beyond the wood of a square set. One of the artisans in the machine shop next door said he could fashion a large enough hinge for a demonstration model.

Without any words spoken, Uncle Jesse took Owen through one of the larger empty houses in Knightville, located close to the school that currently did double duty as LDS meetinghouse and a gathering place after hours, with a few books and magazines. For a sweet moment, Owen thought of Della in the library of the Wasatch Store in Winter Quarters Canyon, sharing her enthusiasm about Charles Dickens and Horatio Alger and Robert Louis Stevenson with readers young and old.

He wondered what she would think of Knightville, a pleasant-enough little village, but one bare of trees and grass. He thought of their lovely street in Provo, with spreading elms and the flowers his wife had cultivated all summer, perky in their window boxes, even though coming autumn had begun to fade their vibrancy.

With Uncle Jesse standing silent in the doorway, he walked through the empty house, noting the size of the bedrooms, which would be Angharad's and which he would share with his wife. Maybe they would make a baby here in Knightville; Provo hadn't proved particularly fertile. They would raise mining camp children.

He turned to leave the empty house, stopping to pick up a pencil stub the former owner had left behind.

"Who lived here?" he asked, knowing what Jesse Knight would say, because this house was a cut above.

"Steve and Maryetta Henry," Jesse said with no hesitation. "Are you superstitious?"

"You asked me that before and I said I was."

Owen waited; he knew what was coming. How was it possible to want this, and dread it at the same time?

"I'm paying you sixty dollars for your consultation and opinion."

"My opinion is in the folder back at Hancock Inn. I think you'll find everything in order."

"Then let's go home. I'm ready for a night in my own bed. I'll read it on the way back."

He did, turning each page and nodding. Owen pulled out Della's copy of *Treasure Island* and read as the private railcar attached behind the ore cars clacked and swayed to Spanish Fork and then Provo.

"Let's walk," Jesse said as they left the depot.

They walked one block and another, and then Jesse Knight stopped. "You'll want better cutting and shaping tools for stronger timbers. I realize this plan means a lot more wood and more expense."

"Aye, if you want the Banner to be safer and not kill husbands."

Maybe he had gone too far. Uncle Jesse frowned at him. Did it matter? Owen knew the sixty dollars in his pocket was already safe.

"You would run the carpenter shop to your satisfaction and go below only to measure and install the timber."

"Aye, sir, and Della will consider that a reach."

Jesse Knight held out his hand. "Well then, how about a furnished house and fuel, plus eighty dollars a month?"

It was more than a generous offer, but still one he knew Della did not want. Owen thought of his friends, the dear ones he could not bring back. He thought of the lives he could save in the future.

Still, he had promised Della. Did his word mean nothing? Slowly, haltingly, he tried to explain this to as good and kind a mine owner as he knew he would ever meet. Jesse stopped him.

"I know I am asking a terrible sacrifice from Della," Jesse said. "I would never ask it, except that I know you are the person who can solve the problem."

"How do you know that?" Owen asked, angry with himself, distressed to be torn in two, trying to honor his wife's wish on the one hand and thinking of his dead friends on the other, and his plan to make this situation better.

"You are a man with great skill," Jesse said. He raised his hand as if to ward off a comment. "I don't say this to flatter you, Owen; you're far too realistic to be swayed by blandishments. In another time, another place, you would have gone to university and become a skilled engineer." He leaned closer. "You still have those skills. I need them now. I am honestly desperate for them."

Owen closed his eyes, weary with words, tired of turmoil. All he wanted to do was lie down with Della and hold her close until they both stopped hurting.

"If I do this for you, will you let me train a crew that can carry on in my place? I can't keep hurting my wife. I know I will need to be underground, but not forever. I don't want this job, but you need help."

"I do. Six months?"

Sick at heart, knowing Della would never understand even six months, he shook Jesse Knight's hand.

Chapter 22

From the wary look in his eyes when he walked in the front door and set down his valise, Della knew what was coming. Uncle Jesse must have offered Owen a job, and he was trying to figure out when to spring it on them. She returned to the kitchen without a word.

He must have realized there was no good time. He kissed the back of her neck while she stirred the pot of stew, unwilling to look him in the eyes, unhappy with him and with herself for even thinking he would keep a promise wrung out of him in a time of high distress.

As they sat down to eat, Della felt even worse for Angharad. The moment the blessing on the food was over, she told her father that school was starting next week, and she already knew she would be in Miss Wilkins's class.

"I helped her with bulletin boards, Da, and she was pleased." She took the bowl of stew he handed her, but set down her spoon, too excited to eat. "There will be a parents' meeting on Friday. I'm glad you're back in time for that. Mam is making *cage bach* for the meeting."

And what do you say to that, husband? Della thought as Owen took a deep breath and set down his own spoon. It was small and mean satisfaction, watching him squirm, and she disliked herself for feeling that way about the man who shared her bed.

"Angharad. Della. Uncle Jesse has offered me a position as chief carpenter of his mining interests in the Tintic District. We're moving on Friday."

Angharad gasped. Tears sprang into her eyes and she lowered her head to hide them. "No, Da," she whispered. "Not a mine."

Della put her hand on Angharad's arm, and she quietly pulled away, hugging herself, drawn in tight as Della had watched her during the awful afternoon in May when the two of them were certain Da was dead. For a fleeting moment, Della remembered another little girl standing by herself, head down, by a grave in a Colorado mining town. The awful moment passed, but not as quickly as Della wished it would. She felt icy chips traipsing down her spine.

Someone had to speak. Might as well be her, since Della knew when Owen left her at the beginning of the week that this would be the logical outcome. Her man was smart and savvy, and he knew mines. "I am hopeful we will come to like . . . wherever this is," she said.

"You promised, Da," Angharad said, and Owen flinched.

Good, Della thought, shocked to her core by the bitterness that rose in her like bile. *You did promise us. Explain a compromise to your daughter, if you can.*

"For the most part, I will be working above ground in the carpenter's shop, preparing timbers for installation in the Banner Mine," Owen said. "I already know what needs to be done there to make the mine safer for the men who do the work."

Silence. He looked at Angharad's bowed head and sighed. He kept his gaze on Della and held it. "If I can help prevent even one death in another mine, I will consider my efforts worthwhile. I promised Uncle Jesse I would work for six months and train my replacements."

More silence. Della's heart broke when Angharad got up from the table and left the kitchen. She winced to hear the door to her room close quietly.

"Owen, is this worth it to you?" she asked, unable to help herself.

"How can you ask such a question?" he snapped, then sat back in surprise, as if startled by his own vehemence.

Della sat back too, unable to say what was in her heart.

"I know what I am doing," he said finally. "Trust me."

"I suppose I must." Della looked down at the stew—one of her better stews—that might as well have been gall and wormwood.

"That's not precisely a ringing endorsement."

"No, it isn't," she said honestly. "I'm not a fool. I knew when you went to Eureka with Uncle Jesse that you were coming home with a job offer."

"You gave me your approval to go." A muscle worked in his jaw.

"I knew you would go, whether I approved or not." She took a deep breath because she had to say it. "Only six months? Owen, I am not certain I believe you."

He stared hard at her and she leaned back in her chair, blistered by his expression.

She had no intention of looking away. She maintained her calm gaze and watched his expression change and soften. "What can I say to that?" he asked finally. "You don't trust me?"

"I want to," she said calmly, as her insides writhed. She leaned forward. "I have sat in sauna and listened to wives speak of the lure of the mine. I have listened to Martha Evans and Annie Jones talk about that obsession. I fear it. That is all."

"Try to trust me," he said finally, quietly. "Six months."

She had lost; she knew it. Della managed a smile, because she knew that where he would go, she would go. Maybe if matters went well in the Banner Mine, the little girl in the Colorado mining camp would go back to wherever she generally stayed in Della's mind, biddable and silent. "Let us begin again. Perhaps you should tell me where we will live."

She could nearly feel the relief that poured off her husband, never mind that she had to force herself to speak. He sat back and she saw pride replace the wary look, or at least mask it. How could she tell?

"First, let me tell you I will be earning eighty dollars a month."

"My goodness," she said, impressed even though she didn't want to be.

"It gets better," he said, sounding more like the Owen she knew and loved. "Included in my salary is a furnished house waiting for us in Knightville, the town Uncle Jesse started because he didn't want saloons and sporting houses anywhere close by. It isn't furnished right now, but he assured me it would be." He tried a joke. "We'll have to take Angharad's house, of course."

She laughed because he expected it. If she was honest, the thought of the dollhouse in transit truly was a funny image. "Is there a school?" she asked, knowing it would look nothing like the Maeser School, where Angharad had already invested herself.

"Aye, miss," he teased, but gently.

Maybe he knew he had broken her heart by going back on his word. He had no idea how badly, but neither did she. This man-woman business was new to her. She dug a little deeper, thinking of her husband now, and the relief he must feel to know he could provide comfortably for a wife and child. *I must bend*, she thought, *but how far?*

"Uncle Jesse said the enrollment now is large enough to be funded by the county," he told her between bites. "Good stew, *m cara*. I don't know much about counties here, but he said increased enrollment means there will be a new building soon."

"Is the . . . the . . . mine close by?" She even hated to say the word.

"Five miles away, but there is a rail that travels the distance several times of the day and night and on special demand. I am not certain I could recommend Silver City to you, but I doubt you will need to go there. Eureka looks a little better. Well no, it doesn't."

She set down her spoon and touched his arm, just a small touch. "I need to know how often you will be in the mine. Please be honest with me, Owen Rhys Davis."

"The dread three names! I measured for a solid day already. I'll be in Salt Lake soon with one of Jesse's other mining engineers, who knows where to get the wood I need. One of his machinists will craft the hinges. You saw my model."

Della picked up her spoon and set it down again. The last thing she wanted to do was anger her husband, but a wife needs to know. "You didn't answer my question. How often?"

He threw up his hands. He seemed to reconsider the matter, and gave her a wry look instead. "I'll be more carefully measuring the length of that one level or drift, which should take me quite a few hours. I'll be underground for the installation, of course. I am also going to train a good crew to do the work." He shifted his chair closer to hers. "I know I made you a promise, *m cara*. I also know I can help save other lives. Can we leave it at that for now?"

Whatever Della had hoped for, this was more than she expected. "We can, but you have a bridge or two to mend with your daughter."

"Aye. I don't like breaking her heart." He kissed her cheek. "Or yours." He looked toward the hall and Angharad's room. "I'll give her a moment." Again that wry look. "I'll give *me* a moment, if I'm honest. Della, do you ever feel helpless and wonder what to say? The women in my life are tasking me."

Someone has to, she thought, and not with much charity. Still, he was her eternal man, so she'd better cheer up. "I think we both have a lot to learn. Now I will tell you about my day with Mr. Dewey and his decimal system."

He laughed, and the cloud hanging over the kitchen seemed to lighten, if not disappear altogether.

"You could assign yourself one of those essays, 'What I did during my summer vacation,'" he suggested as he buttered the heel of the loaf, his favorite part. "You know, you and Mr. Dewey." He winked. "Or maybe you and Mr. Davis."

"I couldn't show *that* to anyone. Not even you."

"Pray, why not?"

"You'd get a swelled head." She buttered a slice of bread too. "You certainly know how to show a girl a good time, and at very little expense."

He laughed at that. When he sat back, she nodded her head in the direction of the hall. "Good luck. She's terribly disappointed."

Serious now, he nodded back and left the room. Della heard a soft knock on the door, a muted "Come in," and then the door closed quietly.

She went about her work in the kitchen, thankful that for some reason she had not thrown out the boxes they had used for their move from Winter Quarters. She took a moment to rest her hands in the hot dishwater because it felt good. She wondered what she would find to do in Knightville to distract herself from the knowledge that her husband would be underground again, probably more often than he would ever admit. Teaching was out, and she doubted Mr. Dewey was well known in the Tintic Mining District.

Owen came out later and went directly to the porch, where he sat with his feet up on the railing and the backs of his hands over his eyes. Indecisive, Della stood in the parlor and then went down the hall to Angharad's room, where it was her turn to knock on the door, go inside, and console a little girl.

Angharad's eyes were swollen with tears, but she took a few shuddering breaths and laid her head in Della's lap. "He shouldn't be in a mine, no matter what he thinks," the child said, reminding Della of the many times Angharad had seemed much older than her seven years. Maybe that was the fatalism of mining camp children, because Della remembered grown-up dread on the Colorado Plateau, the kind that gnawed at her stomach even more than hunger, when the mine didn't pay.

Mustn't think of that, she told herself. *Mustn't think of Papa.*

"When are we moving?" Angharad asked finally, when the shortening shadows of early September yielded gracefully to nightfall.

"Friday. We'll start packing tomorrow."

Chapter 23

They left Provo on Saturday, delayed because of one piece of good luck. Her sister-in-law, Mabli Reese, had been hired by Amanda Knight to replace their old cook, who gave her notice and said she was moving to Logan to live with her ailing sister. Mabli's telegram to Owen had been followed a day later by the now-former cook at the Edwards boardinghouse, eyes bright, two stuffed valises in hand, and the happy news that the Knights wanted her to move in the Davises' house when the Davises moved out.

"They will have an apartment above the carriage house for me, but it isn't ready yet," Mabli said, over chamomile tea in Della's kitchen. "And since you're leaving your furniture here, at least for now, I agreed." She peered closer at Della, who tried to look happy. Her eyes narrowed, but she glanced at Owen, all smiles.

"Darling boy, I left a small trunk at the depot and I believe the driver was taking it to the Knights. Could you bring it here instead?"

Owen did an Oriental salaam, which made Mabli giggle. "Your wish, madam, is my command." He said something in Welsh that made her roll her eyes.

"My dear, you do not look happy about this change of address," Mabli said as soon as Owen left.

"He's going back in the mines, this time in Tintic," Della said, hoping Angharad, moping in her room, wouldn't hear.

"Duplicitous man. He told me he will be head carpenter and running the shop in Silver City." Mabli set down her cup with a decisive click. "I will have his hide."

"He *will* be head carpenter, so you needn't flay him. He's contracted with Uncle Jesse to timber up the levels strong enough to withstand what the Banner seems inclined to dish out," Della said, trying to keep her voice neutral. "He has a plan to make the Banner safer for miners. I believe the job will extend to other Knight mines, as needed."

"He'll be underground measuring and putting beams in place, won't he?"

Della nodded. "I can't keep him out of the mine."

"I suppose he said he was doing it so other miners wouldn't die, and that is somehow going to bring back all the friends he lost."

"Mabli, you have a way of going directly to the heart of the matter," Della replied, impressed.

"I've seen this before, Della."

"From Owen?"

"From my own husband, God rest him," Mabli said simply. "And probably dozens of other miners, both the quick and the dead." She shrugged. "Is this how they make sense of death? Who's to say?"

How did I make sense of my father's death? Della thought later, after Mabli was unpacking. It was something for her to think about. With Angharad busy helping Mabli, Della had managed to sneak out of the house. Mentioning she was going to Maeser School would likely have set off another storm of tears from Angharad, and Della wasn't up to that.

She walked purposefully enough, but she slowed her steps when she crossed the street and turned the corner. Owen had nudged her awake last night, muttering something about waking him up with her talking. "Over and over, you're asking, 'What will I do?' or something like that," he told her. He had been kind enough to cuddle her close until he thought she returned to sleep.

Owen didn't wake up when she got out of bed and tiptoed to the porch, where she sat, arms wrapped around her legs and chin on her knees, until dawn began to announce its appearance with preliminary throat-clearing from the rooster next door.

No point in telling her husband that one night he was gone, she had sat upright, heart pounding so loud ships at sea could have heard it, as she relived the Molly Bee cave-in. For the first time in years, she stood at the portal to the Molly Bee screaming "Papa, Papa!" until she was hoarse. The room was cool, but she had found herself in a puddle of perspiration. Afraid she had screamed out loud, she had hurried to Angharad's room, only to find her asleep.

The next night had been worse, as she remembered the last time she saw her father. He had teased her about something she couldn't even recall now, and she had stomped away down the path to school, not letting him kiss her cheek. The first few years she had been in Salt Lake City, under Aunt Caroline's thumb, she woke up nearly every night in tears, thinking of Papa standing there (she had looked back once), waiting for his daily kiss.

She came to a stop on the sidewalk close to Maeser School, still covered with regret after thirteen long years now and shame so thick she could nearly touch it. She had wanted to ask Aunt Caroline when the hurt would go away, but her aunt would have just scolded her, as she had scolded her for bursting into tears at the dinner table one night because the cook served meatloaf and mashed potatoes, her father's favorite dinner.

"'It's been four months, Della. Stop it,'" Della whispered out loud, remembering Aunt Caroline's angry words with perfect clarity. "'Your father was a ne'er do well, and your mother deserted you.'"

That last bit wasn't quite true, but Della had only known that less than a year, from a long-delayed letter that Frederick Anders had written to his brother, Karl, in 1876, mourning the fact that Olympia Stavrakis had been dragged away by her father, screaming and reaching for her baby, when Frederick was in the mine and unaware.

Twenty-four years Aunt Caroline had kept that letter from her own husband, a letter rightfully Della's. She had the letter now, but too many years had passed, and the mine had closed. How could she ever find her mother?

Irritated, Della ordered herself not to think about her father or her mother as she quickened her pace and arrived at Maeser School. Just stepping inside the building, quiet all summer, brought back memories of another kind. As she walked toward Mr. Holyoke's office, she passed classrooms where educationists were adding the last touch to their bulletin boards or writing on the blackboard using colored chalk saved for special occasions, like the first day of school.

For the life of her, she wanted to be doing precisely that. Why on earth had a progressive nation like the United States decided that only single women could teach? What in the world would she find to do in Knightville? She had no idea, but Della already knew that it would not include staring hard at the calendar every twenty-eight days.

She tapped on Mr. Holyoke's door and walked in. She held out the Dewey Decimal System manual, hoping to make this quick before she started to cry.

"Thanks so much for letting me help this summer," she told the principal, who took the book from her and gestured for her to sit down. She shook her head. "I have a lot to do, sir. My husband took a job in the Tintic Mining District, and we are leaving as soon as possible."

For a small moment, Mr. Holyoke's evident dismay gratified her starved heart. To her embarrassment, she felt tears gather from wherever it was they lurked, ready to show up when she least wanted them. "You'll . . . you'll let Miss Wilkins know that Angharad won't be in her class after all?" she managed to say in a rush, ready to bolt from the office.

His eyes troubled, Mr. Holyoke nodded. "We'll miss you both." He opened his mouth, closed it as if he thought better of what he was planning to say, then opened it again. "I've been doing some checking around on your behalf, you know, something in the assistant librarian realm. Brigham Young Academy has an opening, and I would have recommended you highly. I was going to tell you tomorrow."

"It's nice to know," Della said quietly. "Thank you."

"If things don't work out for Mr. Davis in Tintic, check back with me. That position will go quickly, but there will be others," he said, coming around his desk and holding out his hand, which she shook. "You will be a valuable resource anywhere you live, Mrs. Davis, and I don't mind saying so. Good luck to you three."

Unable to work up the courage to talk to Miss Wilkins, Della walked home slowly. September had come, hot still, but with cooler nights that had started fading the marigolds lining the walk of an elderly lady who sat on the porch and tatted. All summer, Della had smiled and waved at her. She did it now, wondering if the woman would wonder where she had gone, when she didn't smile and wave at her again.

From the somber look on Owen's face as he sat on the porch, no one was probably happy in the house, either. "I arranged for my last paycheck to be sent to the carpenter shop in Silver City," she told Owen, sitting down beside him.

He nodded, his eyes so distracted that she felt a chill on the back of her neck. "What's wrong?" she asked, not wanting to know, not really, because nothing was right.

"Angharad asked Mabli if she could stay here with her so she could attend Maeser School." Again that muscle worked in Owen's jaw. "I reminded her that we are a family, and we go together. Della, what have I done?"

She couldn't think of a thing to say, but he expected some consolation, someone to tell him, "There, there, everything will work out." She wanted to remain silent, should have remained silent, but she couldn't.

"You're going back into the mines." She left him on the porch, unwilling to console him because he had created this situation. She went into the kitchen to continue packing her few dishes.

He must have followed her so quietly. "I'm also responsible for supporting this family," she heard from the kitchen doorway, and she felt a different sort of shame cover her. Of course he was responsible for them all, and he was not a man to shirk such a stewardship. *Forgive me*, she thought as she turned around and let him fold her in his arms.

She couldn't bring herself to say it out loud, but his arms felt good, so tight around her. Better to look ahead and not think about May 1 in Winter Quarters Canyon, or her father's pained look as she flounced away from him on that last day of his life. She shuddered at the memory and closed her eyes against it. Maybe she could sleep tonight and not dream.

Chapter 24

Uncle Jesse's word was good. Della stood back while Owen unlocked the door to their house in Knightville, peeked in as if he wasn't certain and then stepped aside.

"Furniture," he exclaimed, and then he touched his daughter's head. "Angharad, you needn't share your dollhouse, thank the Almighty. None of us are tall, but we're not *that* short."

"Do be serious, Da," Angharad said. "I was willing to share."

Della sighed with relief to hear Angharad tease back. Something unspoken between them assured her that this lovely daughter of Owen and Gwyna Davis was going to do her best to like this situation not of her choosing. If she could, Della could. *I should write, "I am the grownup" on a blackboard fifty times*, she told herself.

The thought stayed with her as she walked through the house. It was small to be sure, and it contained no indoor bathroom, which made all three of them sigh, but the two bedrooms were large enough and the parlor almost spacious.

Della had to smile when Owen pressed the mattress a few times in what would be their bedroom and frowned. "We should have brought our mattress along," he said.

"And turn out poor Mabli?" she teased. "Besides, oh picky man of my dreams, you already have the best component of any bed standing beside you."

He laughed at that. "Aye, miss, I do. Did you ever hear such a whiner?"

"No! Martha tried to warn me about Welshmen, but I didn't listen."

He grabbed Della around the waist and gave her such a smacking kiss that Angharad stuck her head in the door and covered her mouth with her hand, her eyes merry.

"Good for us," Owen said much later, after the supper of stew and cornbread the Knightville Ward Relief Society president brought over, along with an offer to go grocery shopping in Eureka tomorrow, "so you won't be cheated by the Italians."

They had prayed as usual with Angharad, kneeling alongside her bed. With the child asleep, they adjourned to the parlor.

"It's to the carpenter shop for me tomorrow," Owen said. Della tucked herself close to him as they sat on the sofa. "School for Angharad?"

"Yes, and then Sister Pritchard and I will shop in Eureka and beware of Italians and Greeks, I believe she said." Della felt her eyes closing.

They opened wide when Owen carried her to bed.

"I know it's not what you wanted," he spoke into her shoulder. "But I have some good ideas for the Banner Mine. You can keep house and be a lady of leisure."

"I'd rather look for a job," she said, trying out the idea on a man who was at the moment most mellow.

"No need. I can't tell you how relieved I am to support my family. I liked Provo, but odd jobs weren't going to pay the bills." He tugged at her tangled curls. "Neither would Mr. Dewey."

"Is that an emphatic no, or may I use my mind too?"

She heard a rueful chuckle in the dark. "You should have been a barrister, complete with wig and gown. What can I say to that that wouldn't incriminate me as an unfeeling husband?"

Well done, Della, she thought. *Don't give up.*

After boiled eggs and porridge, Owen caught the train to Silver City. Della and Angharad walked hand in hand to the one-story clapboard building that also served as the Sunday meetinghouse. As they passed tidy houses like theirs, Della had to admit that Uncle Jesse knew how to build a town, even though she didn't want to be there.

She remembered Hastings, the village at the foot of the mountain where her father was buried, with its streets going off in all directions at the same time. Winter Quarters was scarcely better, with a canyon so narrow that the houses seemed to cling to the rocks.

True, there were no shade trees here, but she had not expected to see any, not in a mining camp. Knightville was built close to several mines, one with a headframe bearing a startling resemblance to a gallows. She noticed two other mines with timbered portals, or drifts, where miners just walked in and went to work, without being lowered down hundreds of feet. One of those was the fabled Humbug Mine, which had started the Knight fortune.

"It's better than I thought," she told the girl holding her hand so tight. "There's a baseball diamond."

They could never have gotten lost. All they had to do was follow the children. Della's heart softened a little more to see an older woman standing by the entrance. Her hair was white and confined haphazardly into a bun, with tendrils bolting for freedom, and her gaze was kind. She dressed neatly in a simple shirtwaist and dark shirt, reminding Della for one sweet moment of her own teacher clothes.

"I think you will be fine here," she whispered to Angharad.

"How do you know?"

"I just know. Trust me."

Della towed Angharad up the few steps to the front door and introduced herself to the teacher, who gave her name and held out her hand.

"Miss Baldwin, this is Angharad Davis, my stepdaughter," Della said, feeling the pull of the classroom in a way she hadn't expected. "I was her teacher last year in Winter Quarters Canyon. She is qualified for second grade, and possibly third."

"Actually, it's Mrs. Baldwin. I'm a widow, and I live with my son, who is Mr. Knight's surface superintendent. Do come in."

She led the way into the one-room school, small for certain, and if not crowded, then at least cozy. Della breathed deep of chalk dust and the industrial strength floor cleaner that all Utah schools seemed to use. For a blink of time, she was back in Winter Quarters, anticipating her first day teaching the lower grades. Any moment now, Israel Bowman would come out of his classroom and wink at her, and Miss Clayson would stand there patting her ruler.

But no. Israel and his pretty Blanche Bent had married in Provo in June, and Miss Clayson was teaching in Boise. *And I am here,* Della thought. In a blink, she saw another little girl in her first school in Hastings, Colorado, her lunch bucket a lard tin and the contents crackers and a carrot, the same as Papa took into the Molly Bee when times were tight.

She shook her head, wondering where these unnerving blinks were coming from. "You are in good hands, my love," she told Angharad.

They hugged, and Della put her hand on Angharad's shoulder, as other students, already in class for a week, walked around them with smiles, maybe remembering their first day in class. They were all children of the mines, and mines opened and closed without regard to school schedules.

"You're getting a lovely student, Mrs. Baldwin," Della said. She felt a strange tug at leaving Angharad here, no matter how nice the teacher.

"Mrs. Davis, I understand what it feels like to turn over my child to another. We'll do well."

That was all Della needed. She stepped back and smiled at student and teacher. "Angharad, I'll be buying groceries in Eureka. You can find your way home if I am not here at three."

"I'll make certain she heads home with children who live close by," Mrs. Baldwin assured her. "You're in the Henry's house?"

Della nodded, watching a shadow cross the teacher's face. "A sad business, but my husband is here to make it better."

"So we have heard. Tell me, if you know, what has become of Mrs. Henry?"

The teacher whispered this last question after she turned Angharad toward the classroom door.

"Mrs. Henry has gone back to Iowa, where her family lives," Della said.

"My late husband was a miner too."

Then you know, Della thought. *Does it never end?*

Angharad was already talking to a girl about her size, who patted the empty desk next to her. Della walked down the steps and stood in the schoolyard, with its amazing view of the valley below. She gazed across the broad plain toward distant mountains, everything a shade of gray and faded olive. She saw the multicolored slag heaps and the gallows-like headframes.

Is this to be my life? she asked herself. No answer. Again for a blink of time, she felt like she was in another canyon in another state, twelve years old.

Chapter 25

Owen told Della and Angharad that night over dinner that he could find no fault with his carpenter crew. He had ridden the train home with other miners and with the bishop of the Knightville Ward, who was already eager to enlist Owen's services in the elders quorum.

"Bishop McIntyre told me that the last quorum secretary kept the minutes in Welsh until he convinced him otherwise," Owen told his ladies as Della passed him two sausages she said had come from an Italian butcher shop in Eureka. "Sausages? This time last year it was oatcakes, eh, Angharad?"

Angharad nodded, her eyes bright, because he knew she liked sausage too. "What about your day, my dear?"

"Da, it's not the Maeser School, but I don't mind so much."

Owen glanced at Della, who put her hand to her breast and heaved a sigh of relief, which eased his own heart. *And what about you?* he wondered. "You found an Italian butcher in Eureka?"

"I did. Sister Pritchard warned me that he sometimes puts his finger on the scales when he weighs meat."

"Did he commit such a felony with you?" he asked, happy to see her eyes livelier.

Della touched his arm. "No! Here's the beauty of it. He looked at me, kissed his fingertips, and said, '*Que bella, signora.*'" She laughed out loud. "I thought Sister Pritchard's eyes were going to pop out of her head."

"I trust you did the honest thing and told him you weren't Italian?"

"It gets better," she said, hiking her chair closer to his in a way that eased his heart, after her unhappiness of the last few weeks. "When I told him my mother was Greek, he pointed next door to the Andromeda. It's a Greek coffee house."

"Mam, you didn't!" Angharad asked, her eyes wide. "Coffee?"

"I did, but not to drink coffee. Greek coffee shops are just for men." She laughed, and took another bite of sausage.

He already knew his wife was part of the female species, which he had once told her was a breed apart. She could spin a tale as well as a Welshman. "And?" he prompted, as she took her time chewing and swallowing. "As a husband, should I worry?"

"Not in the slightest." She gave him a sly, sidelong glance. "However, I do not think Sister Pritchard will ask me to be a Relief Society teacher anytime soon."

"Must I tickle you right here to get the rest of this story out of you?" he asked.

Angharad gasped. "Da, do you *tickle* Mam? I've never seen you do that."

"Only now and then," he said, his face warm. *Long after you're asleep, daughter.*

Two spots of color waged their own war in Della's face, but she held up her hands. "You two will try me to death! I went into the coffee shop—it was too early for the men to congregate—and introduced myself to the proprietor, Archimedes Stath."

"Stath doesn't sound so Greek," Owen said. He speared a bite of sausage from his wife's plate, and she smacked his wrist with her knife. "Ow!"

"Da, really," Angharad murmured. "Your manners . . ."

"It's short for Stathopoulos. When he came to Castle Garden in New York City, a customs official shortened it for him, whether he wanted him to or not, I suppose," Della said. She generously gave Owen the rest of her sausage.

"Da, were you in Castle Garden too, you and my other mam?"

Her other mam. Owen's heart softened as he remembered two frightened young people, holding hands, hoping there wasn't any reason they wouldn't be allowed into the United States, considering that they had twenty pounds to their name and no urge to recross the Atlantic.

"Your mam and I came later, so we went to Ellis Island." He chuckled at the memory. "The admitting officer changed *my* name from D-A-F-Y-S to what we use today."

"You didn't ask him to change it back?" Angharad asked.

"I was too afraid to argue. It was enough to be here, and I'm used to Davis now."

"Was I there too, Da?"

"You were, but so small inside your mam," he said, and he felt the red returning. He wasn't used to such frankness, but why not tell her what she wanted to know? "There we were, the three of us, in a new country."

He glanced at Della and saw tears in her eyes. He could tickle her later. Time to reel in this interesting conversation. "Where were we now? Sister Pritchard was shocked at you, Mrs. Davis, when you went into a coffee house."

"Mr. Stath was so kind. I told him that Mr. Randazzo next door said I should introduce myself." Della smiled at them both. "Angharad, imagine this! He kissed my hand and told me my face could launch a thousand ships, except we live in a desert."

"Your face? Mam!"

Yes, her face, Owen thought, admiring his lovely wife, trying to see her through a Greek's eyes. The Welsh may have been blessed with silver tongues and throats, but the Almighty had lavished everything on Greek women. *I was a lost cause the moment I saw her. I'll tell Angharad some day.*

"Helen of Troy, the wife of King Menelaus of Mycenae, was supposed to be so beautiful that her face could launch a thousand ships. Don't look so skeptical, daughter!" Della said.

"Launching ships? What does that have to do with anything?"

Here came another sidelong glance from his wife, who appeared to have mastered the art of delivering humor with a straight face. "Angharad, it's a sad fact but true that men don't make much sense when they fall in love."

"Really, Mam?"

"Yes, really, Angharad." Della clapped her hands together. "That's enough! Here's the best part. Is everyone ready for dessert?"

Owen looked at Angharad, and she nodded. "Aye, Della Olympia Davis. Your daughter and I are ready and willing."

She gave him such a tender look, then opened the bread box and took out a small plate. "Baklava," she announced. "No one does desserts better than the Greeks."

Owen felt his mouth water. "I had this once at a Winter Quarters Christmas party. A very small piece, please."

Della poised a paring knife over a little corner.

"Well, slightly more."

She sliced off a similar piece for Angharad, who took a tiny bite, sighed, and took another bite. After the third bite, she eyed Owen's plate. He put his hand over it, and she laughed.

"Da, she's right. We don't have anything like this."

"We do not," Owen agreed. He ate his piece slowly, rolling around the overpowering honey goodness in his mouth. "There is nothing subtle about the Greeks."

Della took one bite and divided the remainder between his plate and Angharad's. "I'm only half Greek, and that's too sweet."

Baklava required more milk, which Della poured before she sat down. Owen looked over the table, with its leftover sausage—probably going in his lunch box tomorrow—applesauce, and bread still warm. Winter Quarters and oatcakes seemed a long way from Tintic Mining District.

Angharad pushed away her plate with a sigh. "Can you make this?"

"No. I'll never have the patience," Della said. "Mr. Stath told me he makes baklava every Monday, and he'll save me a piece. He also said he makes *spanakopita* on Wednesday. You will like that, Angharad."

"I will?"

A veteran father, Owen knew dubious when he heard it.

"Spinach, Greek cheese, and eggs, in the lightest crust you can imagine," Della said.

"Maybe," Angharad said, still wary.

"Trust me. Now let us do some dishes so you can have the table for homework," Della said.

"Did your mam make you spinach pie?" Angharad asked.

"I never knew my mother," Della said. She set the dishes in the sink and sat beside Angharad. "She was taken away from me and my father when I was a baby."

"Who would do that?" Angharad asked. She placed both her hands in Della's, which touched Owen's heart. His child was as tender as his wife.

"Her own father," Della said. "I don't know why, and I don't know where in the world she is."

"Would you like to find her, Mam?"

"More than I can possibly express in words."

He took that thought to bed with Della later, breathing deep of the hint of olive oil she used to straighten out her tangle of curls.

"I wonder how we could find your mother," he said.

"I have no idea," Della said, as she composed herself for sleep. "A few years ago, I wrote a letter to Hastings Dry Goods, Hastings, Colorado. Papa sometimes let me pick out penny candy there. It was the only store I remembered. I asked if anyone had ever heard of Olympia Stavrakis."

"What did you learn?" he asked when she remained silent.

"That the Molly Bee had closed five years earlier, and there weren't any miners left in the county. End of story."

She slept, but not for more than an hour or two. By the time the moon rose and rested its mellow glow across their bed, he heard her speaking in a small voice, asking for her father. "Please let me see him. Please," he heard, each word louder and more frantic than the one before. "Frederick Anders. You know him. This is his mine!"

Before he could grab her she leaped out of bed and stared down at the floor, seeing something that wasn't there. "Don't hide him from me," she said. "It's cruel! Cruel!"

Then she dropped to her knees, pleading with someone equally unseen to him, but clearly larger than life to her. "You don't understand what I did!"

She put her hands over her face and sobbed. Afraid to upset her, Owen got out of bed slowly. He gently rested his hands on her shaking shoulders. She turned her face into his nightshirt and wept.

"Della, Della, whatever it is, you're safe with me," he whispered.

She opened her eyes, startled, and looked around at the two of them kneeling together on the floor. "Owen, what happened?"

"I don't know." This wasn't the first time. He thought she didn't need to know that.

Chapter 26

Della settled into life in Knightville, almost but not quite welcoming the first snowfall near the end of September. She had missed Owen the week he was in Salt Lake City, accompanied by a mining engineer, as they arranged for timber shipped to his carpenter shop, located between the Union Pacific tracks and the Denver and Rio Grande tracks.

At least she had spared him another of her nightmares, one of those dreams that found her waking up on the floor on her hands and knees, staring down into what, she had no idea. She began to dread falling asleep, wondering if she would wake that way again, or if the image would be one she could bat away like a lone mosquito flitting around in a darkened bedroom.

Owen came home with presents from Mr. Auerbach. "I went in to pay a friendly visit, and what did he do but send me home with enough date nut sandwiches for everyone in your class, Angharad."

"Da! Really?"

"Would I tease about something so serious?" he asked her. "I did eat one."

"I'll forgive you, even though thousands wouldn't," she teased back.

"From me to you," he told Della later in the privacy of their bedroom, when he pulled out a pale yellow silk nightgown, one she remembered from the corner of Lingerie where shoppers went for a peek but seldom bought.

"How did you ever work up the nerve to go to the lingerie department?" she asked.

"I just walked in there like a Welshman, looked the frosty old dame behind the counter right in the eye, and told her to wrap up her favorite one. This is it."

Della laughed until tears ran from her eyes. "That was Miss Marchbanks! I hope you didn't tell her who your wife was."

"I might have mentioned Della Anders. Can't be certain of that because the number she pulled out fair blinded me."

"It doesn't mean anything to you if I'm rolling my eyes in the dark, does it?"

"Not even a little. Go to sleep."

She kissed him back and closed her eyes, happy to obey, except that he shook her shoulder.

"You still there, fairest?" he asked.

"Barely."

"Here's something else I did. The engineer had some shopping of his own to do, so I went to your uncle's office."

Funny how the mention of her uncle snapped her wide awake. "And?"

"I stopped in to say hello." He nudged her. "Remember, I am a gregarious chap."

"That you are, Owen Davis," she agreed.

"It was just a short visit, to tell him how things were here in Knightville."

She heard him move a bit and turned to see him up on one elbow, the better to see her. "Say on, sir."

"He said your aunt simply isn't getting better."

Is that all? she thought, irritated. *Well, boohoo, Aunt Caroline.* Immediately ashamed of herself, she tried to muster up a sentence of sympathy, but nothing came out, except, "Salt Lake has good physicians. I am certain they'll find one."

"That's the thing: they've been to several, to no particular relief for your aunt. Her throat hurts all the time. He said she's eating mostly pureed foods now and losing weight."

Best to be honest. "I wish I could tell you how many times I wanted her to curl up into a little ball like a mealy bug and roll away."

"I don't doubt that. Still, he looks so worried." He lay down again. "I said I hoped things changed and left it at that. He sends you his best wishes. He sounded sincere."

"Sincere?" She curled up close like a mealy bug herself. The nights were getting colder. "I wish he could have worried about me a little during Aunt Caroline's regime."

"I felt the distinct impression he wishes the same, *m cara*."

Once or twice during the week, Della thought about writing to Uncle Karl. The thought passed quickly enough. She had a more pressing matter to brood about, when she should have been pleased that Angharad was enjoying her shabby little overcrowded school, and Owen had found good work that mattered to him, even if it terrified her and always would.

Even here in remote Tintic Mining District, the calendar still mocked her. She swallowed down tears and marked another *X*, twenty-eight days after the *X* in the preceding month. Could a calendar be cruel? This one was. It had been hanging on the wall when they moved into the Henry's quickly vacated house. Newly expectant, Maryetta Henry must have received it from Mellin's Food for Infants and Invalids. October featured a baby improbably smiling and sucking at the same time. Della had looked ahead to November, relieved to see an old man in a wheeled chair smiling, too.

She stared at the baby through a blur of tears and jumped a little when Owen put his hand on her shoulder. She leaned back against him.

"We need a different calendar," he said. "I have one in the carpenter shop that features tenpenny nails arranged around scantily clad women."

She smiled through her tears because she knew he expected that. He sat down next to her and took her face in his hands.

"Della, I didn't marry you because I wanted to get children. I married you because I love you, and the idea of being anywhere out of your orbit was unthinkable."

"But I want a baby," she whispered into his chest now as he held her close.

"I know. I'd like one too, but that was never my first thought," he assured her. "You were my first thought. You still are."

"Just don't tell me to be patient," she said, finally. He was as comfortable as a man could be, but she was already going to make him run for the train. She took a handkerchief from her apron pocket and blew her nose.

"I will not tell you any such thing." He kissed her forehead. "Other than the obvious answer, how can I help you feel less dismal, once a month?"

"I need more to do. I need a job."

He was on his feet now, reaching for his coat and lunch bucket. "Very well. Take the midmorning train to Silver City and come to the carpenter's shop. Let's see what happens."

He blew her a kiss and darted out the door. Della gave October Baby a menacing scowl and took off her apron. She was going job hunting.

Della was the only occupant of the railcar that left from Knightville at ten o'clock. She thought long and hard about what dress and hat to wear and settled on her favorite brown skirt and shirtwaist with little green flowers, a relic of her teaching days. Her second-best hat would do, with its modest brim and simple grosgrain band.

There were no terrors to this train trip, nothing compared to the winding, narrow canyons from Spanish Fork to Scofield that had frightened her so badly last year. This trip was almost leisurely, with the view to the west and away from eastern mountains wide open and welcoming.

There it was at the foot of the mountain: Silver City, named for the wealth of silver within, plus the gold and lead to be found as well. The treeless plain did not dismay her. She knew better than to expect charm in a mining district.

Three distinct rail lines wound their way from nearby Eureka and points east and north, an iron necklace of commerce circling the streets. She saw row on row of miners' housing and was grateful for Uncle Jesse's Knightville, even though other mine owners mocked the Mormon miners with their strict rules. All the buildings looked raw and weathered.

She stared in fascination mixed with dread at the headframes silhouetted against the sky as the sun approached its zenith. It was easy to imagine road agents and other assorted bad men swinging from these hoists, and she had imagination in abundance. She knew one of the headframes belonged to the Banner Mine. Just the thought of Owen deep underground made her turn her head and look at the town instead.

Everywhere she looked she saw slag heaps, mine tailings raised up and dumped out, to slide down slopes. The lighter off-color stood out in contrast to the drab gray and olive of the hillsides and valley floor.

The train stopped, and the station agent came out of the depot and helped her down. "Mrs. Davis?" he asked.

"Why, yes," she said, puzzled he would know her name.

"Your husband told me to expect a pretty lady with curly hair," he told her. "I am to point you in the direction of the carpenter shop." He started to point, then lowered his arm. "I'll escort you there. The mail is already sorted, and no one else appears to need me."

She walked with the agent to another nondescript, blasted-looking building, this one larger and possessing a chimney that covered one end of the structure.

"Does it get that cold here in the winter?" Della asked, pointing at the chimney.

The agent laughed, and she felt foolish. "You can tell I don't know much about mining."

"That chimney heats a boiler, which runs the saw using steam power," he said. "Noisy around here."

He opened the door, ushered her inside, and tipped his hat. "G'day, Mrs. Davis. Train leaves at three."

Della breathed deep of pine and other wood she did not know. What looked disorderly at first glance turned into order, with uncut logs arranged by size and type on one side of the main room and planed boards on the other. And there was her husband, a pencil behind his ear, standing in the doorway of what looked like an office.

Edging around the machinery, Della picked her way toward him, minding her skirt. Owen took her hand, pulled her inside, and closed the door, which cut down the noise immediately.

"Someone should take a dust cloth to this office," she said, after kissing his cheek and tasting sawdust on her lips. "And maybe to you."

"That would be a forlorn hope, *m cara*," he said. "The big logs we ordered are coming in. The machinists are working on the hinges. Maybe next week we can start hinging the timbers and getting them ready for the mine."

"You're sure they're the right measurement?"

"As close as can be," he replied, "although I don't mind admitting that if you hear me awake and tossing about some night soon, it's because of nerves."

"Owen Davis, you can pretty much do anything," she said, pleased with him for no other reason than he was aboveground and in charge of the carpenter shop. Maybe there was hope for her and Silver City, as long as she didn't remind herself that the man installing the beams underground was going to be this same man.

"Now the question of the ages is, what about you, oh fair Olympia, since you appear before me in your second-best hat, quite a trim skirt and shirtwaist, and determined to work?" He took the pen out from behind his ear. Turning to his drafting table, he rapidly drew a storefront with a sign reading, "Apprentice wanted. Must be able to read bad handwriting. Will train." He handed it to her. "Cross the tracks where they come together in a *V.* You'll see this sign on a shack I will laughingly call an office. It's next to Henry Nailor's Pool Hall. Take the sign out of the window and tell Saul Weisman you're the man for the job."

"My goodness, I doubt he is expecting a lady to apply, is he? Will he agree?" She pointed to the sign. "'Read bad handwriting'? Is this a joke?"

"That's up to you, Mrs. Davis." He kissed her cheek this time. "He's hiring, and so is Andy Wilkinson at Wilkinson Mercantile. The madam always wants pretty women at the bordello, so I am informed by sources who should know, but I do not recommend *that* drastic step."

"Oh, you," she murmured. "I'm quite happy with one husband."

"Music to this Welshman's ears," he said cheerfully. "I never reject a bargain. Ow! That's my foot you're stomping, in case you're wondering. Now go and impress Saul Weisman."

"Bad handwriting. What does he do?" she asked, letting him head her toward a side door, where there weren't any boards to step over.

"He assays gold and silver using heat and chemicals."

"Owen, I don't even know what that is," she said, and she felt nervous knots gathering in her stomach.

"He samples the ore that comes from Uncle Jesse's mines and determines the percentage of gold and silver that can reasonably be expected from, say, one drift. They vary, depending on the seam. What the assayer finds often determines where the miners work."

"Owen, I don't know anything," she said, suddenly afraid.

"I thought you wanted to work?" He put his hands on her shoulders and gave her a gentle shake. "You can do this. Saul needs someone smart, and that's you."

"You know as well as I do that he wants—is expecting—to see a man apply."

Owen shrugged. "The sign has been in his window for a couple of weeks now. He hasn't found the right person yet. Once he sees you . . ." He tugged her hat down over her eyes, and she protested again. ". . . he'll know he needs you. Look, Della, I weighed the mercantile, the bordello, and Saul's place, and Saul came in number one, far ahead of the pack."

"You are a rascal, Mr. Davis!"

"And *you*, Mrs. Davis, are the man for the job."

Chapter 27

She crossed the tracks and came to the *V*, just as Owen had said. The sign for Henry Nailor's Pool Hall had missing letters. She smiled to see "Poo Ha" proclaimed for all and sundry and figured the three *l*'s had blown over Denver by now.

A first and a second look at the shack only made her frown. The building seemed to lean toward the east, supporting her suspicion that if the wind stopped, the structure would topple, and Mr. Weisman would need new accommodations.

There was the sign with its odd requirement, nicely lettered. *Nothing ventured is nothing gained, Della*, she reminded herself, and she knocked.

"Come in, please."

Her hesitation past, Della did as requested, going first to the window to take out the sign and then turning to face a small man seated at a table, his hands folded, surrounded by brown glass vials and a jumble of papers.

"My husband told me I was the man for this job, Mr. Weisman," she said, well aware how stupid that sounded.

"Come closer."

She did, surprised this time to see a man with a surprisingly young voice. The most remarkable things about him were a hunched back and eyes as dark and deep as hers.

"I'm Della Davis," she said, finding her voice because only kindness seemed to come out of those eyes. "My husband Owen was newly hired by Uncle Jesse—Mr. Knight—to run his carpenter shop. I see to it that my stepdaughter Angharad is in school each morning, but I would like to work."

"No one else at home to care for?" he asked.

Maybe prospective employers had to ask questions like that. "I wish there were, but no," she replied. "I taught school last year in Winter Quarters Canyon, but school districts don't hire married women to teach."

He nodded. "Seems a waste of a good brain," he said. He had a lovely accent, not beautiful and Welsh like Owen's, but German or Swiss. "Mrs. Davis, did you know that six hundred years ago, there was a female professor at the University of Padua?"

He gestured to a chair close to his own, and she sat.

"I believe she taught the wisdom of Aristotle. Pretty good for an era most historians today scorn as unenlightened and stultifying, no?"

"Something happened in the past six hundred years then," Della said, convinced there had never been a job interview like this one, if that's what Mr. Weisman was doing. Whether he was or not, she found him fascinating.

"Indeed something did happen," he said, "and that's also why some of my brethren of the Hebrew persuasion don't teach at major universities even now." He held out his hand to her. "Can you type, Mrs. Davis?"

She shook his hand, marveling at the smoothness of his fingers. She doubted anyone in a mining camp had hands like his. She knew Owen didn't. Della looked into his eyes because it was impossible not to.

"I learned to type this summer," she told him, her hands in her lap again. She took out a folded paper from her purse, straightened it, and held it out to him. "I worked all summer implementing the Dewey Decimal System in the Maeser School in Provo. I'm not speedy, but I'm accurate."

He took her resume, which suddenly looked no bigger than a postage stamp to Della, because she knew what little employment history it contained: one year in Winter Quarters, the year before at Westside School in Salt Lake City, and one summer as a kitchen flunkie in Cottonwood Canyon, working for a crew stringing telephone wire. She could have added six years shelving books at a library to buy her basic necessities, one item at a time, but he knew enough to make a decision.

"I want to work, sir, and I can type. Would you like me to demonstrate?"

He shook his head, handed back the paper, and her heart sank. She looked toward the door, wondering what kind of help the Wilkinson Mercantile wanted.

But no. The little man with the big hunch, lovely eyes, and precise accent wasn't finished with her. "I need help in keeping up with paperwork."

Maybe this was time for a joke. "You aren't worried that I might ask you to write an essay on what you did during your summer vacation?" she asked.

He laughed, and her heart eased. His face turned solemn then. "I could write you an essay someday on slipping away from a pogrom in Prussia, my chemicals on my back, clinking away and making noise. I had to leave them behind in the snow."

"My goodness. You're a survivor," she blurted out, wanting to know more.

He nodded emphatically. "Luckily, the gold I had sewn into my overcoat was a lot quieter." He spread his hands on the table. "Now I am here, not in the lap of luxury, but at least off the bony knees of poverty and terror. I need a secretary."

"There's a lot that must have gone on between abandoning your chemicals and sitting here in Silver City," she said, fascinated now, her fear gone.

"A story for another day," he replied. "Mrs. Davis, would you please work for me?"

"You still don't want me to demonstrate my typing proficiency?" she asked, looking toward the big type-writing machine on a table closer to the door. To her continued relief, it was an Olivetti-Underwood, just like the one Mr. Holyoke had lugged from his office to the library.

"You would never lie on a resume, would you?" he asked in turn.

"Heavens, no. Who would do such a thing?"

"You would be amazed. I can't pay you more than fifteen dollars a month, so let us pray that your husband is a steady man with no intemperate habits that might get him fired."

"Not Owen," she said promptly. "He doesn't smoke or drink. I was going to add gamble, but he's working in a mining camp, so you can draw your own conclusions about that."

Mr. Weisman laughed and sat back as much as he could, considering the hump of flesh on his left shoulder that extended nearly to his waist. "Have you ever been accused of being witty, Mrs. Davis?"

"No. Am I?"

"You are. Now, to recapitulate: you need to be home in the morning long enough to see your daughter off to school. What about the afternoons?"

"School lets out at three. I believe I can make arrangements for her to stay with friends until almost four, when the three o'clock train arrives in Knightville," she said, hoping this was true, because she knew she wanted the job.

Mr. Weisman eyed her, and she gazed back. "I think this will work quite well, Mrs. Davis. Here from ten in the morning to three in the afternoon, Monday through Friday? Twenty-five hours a week, toiling in an assayer's office?"

"I can. I will."

"I might have to ask you to deliver assay reports to the various mine offices here in Silver City, if the engineers are impatient and demanding." He shifted and winced. "You understand."

"Perfectly."

"I can guarantee you a faithful body guard, if you are reluctant to traipse about this lively town by yourself."

"You have other employees?" she asked, curious.

"I suppose you could call him that. You'll meet him tomorrow." He smiled at her. "If you have a soup bone with some meat on it, bring that along too. Saladin likes treats."

Saladin. Pogroms. University of Padua. *My goodness*, Della thought. She remembered the bad handwriting portion of the sign. "About your handwriting . . . Should I read something before you hire me unaware and discover I am a fraud?"

"If you must. I only put that there to amuse myself." He handed her a letter.

She stared at it and laughed. "Mr. Weisman, it's written in another language."

"You passed," he said. "It's Yiddish. One hopeful fellow tried to read it."

He stood up then, and she saw how short he was, and how crooked. She also saw how the effort made him frown. How did a man like this escape a pogrom? Maybe with something named Saladin.

"I will wager you never expected to be taller than your employer, did you?"

She could blush and deny and look away, but why? "No, but I also never expected to find myself wanting to hear the story of how you got here," she said frankly.

"It's a good one. I also would wager that you have a story too."

I do, she thought as she shook his hand and promised to see him tomorrow at ten o'clock. *I'd rather hear yours, Mr. Weisman.*

Chapter 28

Finding a place for Angharad after school was simple, thanks to Mrs. Baldwin. After a breathless stop in the carpenter shop where she gave Owen the good news and asked him to find a meaty soup bone—he blinked at that one—Della hurried to catch the three o'clock train that got her to Knightville at half three, as Owen would have said.

"I can't always guarantee such a quick trip, Mrs. Davis," the engineer told her.

"Just as long as it eventually gets here," she said. "I'll catch the ten o'clock tomorrow morning."

"You found employment?"

"Oh, my, yes I did. See you tomorrow."

She dashed from the platform as the miners on the afternoon shift prepared to board. The men from church tipped their hats to her as she hurried toward the nearby school, where she found Angharad and two other little girls cleaning Mrs. Baldwin's blackboards and dumping trash.

"I decided to put everyone to work," Mrs. Baldwin said as Della took the steps two at a time. "Slow down! You'll have to loosen your corset strings if you rush too fast."

"I hurried as fast as I could." She turned to Angharad, who was wiping down the blackboard. "I found a job."

"Mam! Doing what, pray?"

"I'll be typing up assay reports for an interesting fellow name of Saul Weisman." She sat down because Mrs. Baldwin—once a teacher, always in charge—was frowning and pointing to a chair. "Maybe I did run too fast."

"As you can see, there was no alarm," Mrs. Baldwin said. "Finish your work, girls, and then you can pick out a book to borrow." She turned back to Della and leaned closer. "Angharad is such a leader already, and a good student."

"She is," Della agreed, her voice low too. "When I took over the class in Winter Quarters last year, the students in grades one through three had been monumentally short-changed by their teacher. I started out with everyone at a grade two level, even the newest students like Angharad, and then challenged them until most were at a grade three by the end of the school year."

"It shows. Angharad is reading as well as my third graders. Excellent, girls! Go pick out your books and wait outside for Mrs. Davis, will you?"

"I'll be needing to find someplace where Angharad might go after school until I get home," Della said. "Do you know of anyone?"

Mrs. Baldwin didn't hesitate. "Mrs. Tate, who lives three doors to the south of you. Her daughter Minnie is the one with the red hair standing by Angharad. Mrs. Tate's husband has experienced some ill health and works only part time at the Humbug Mine. If you were to offer her two dollars a week, it would help them."

"I'll do it." She held out her hand to Mrs. Baldwin. "Thank you for not making a face about my wanting to work. My Aunt Caroline . . ."

She stopped, wondering why Aunt Caroline had even crossed her mind. It felt like a breath of cold air in an otherwise lovely afternoon. "Well, she used to make fun of ladies who had to work." She couldn't help her wry expression, or maybe she didn't try. Mrs. Baldwin seemed like the sort who would understand. "She would probably be appalled at women who *want* to work, and I do."

"I don't make light of working women. I'll wager you don't either." Mrs. Baldwin walked Della to the door. "Besides, your work will help Mrs. Tate. Sometimes the Aunt Carolines of the world don't think of that, do they?"

No, they don't, Della thought as she joined the girls on the outside steps. The oldest child peeled off pretty soon to her own house. When redheaded Minnie stopped, Della followed her up the walk for a word with her mother.

The matter was concluded quickly, with Della studiously overlooking the tears in Mrs. Tate's eyes at the idea of eight extra dollars a month, which told her all she needed to know about hard times here.

"I can drop off eight dollars for the month tomorrow morning, when I take the train to Silver City," she said. "I always pay ahead."

"I'd be grateful," Mrs. Tate said simply and with real dignity. "If you happen to have any ironing that needs doing, I charge a nickel a piece."

"That would be a great relief for me," Della replied. "I absolutely hate to iron, and this job means I won't have time for it. I can drop off four shirts tomorrow. Isn't it amazing how men can get themselves so wrinkled?"

They laughed together, Della with her fingers crossed behind her back. Owen was neat and did his own ironing. She was going to end that tonight because

Mrs. Tate needed whatever nickels came her way. She knew Owen wouldn't object.

He didn't. As he brushed her hair after Angharad was asleep, their nightly ritual now, he listened to the whole saga, starting with Mr. Saul Weisman, segueing to Saladin, and then ending with Mrs. Tate.

"She can do my ironing starting tomorrow," he said. "Take twenty cents out of the kitchen jar." He kissed the top of her head. "I admit to more curiosity about Saladin."

She tugged him down on the bed beside her. "Is it a wolf?"

He laughed. "I guess you will find out, think on."

"You are *not* reassuring me, Mr. Davis."

"In that case, how about I cuddle with you?"

"Talk's cheap."

"Cuddles aren't."

In the morning, she dropped off Owen's shirts and eight dollars and twenty cents with Mrs. Tate. With a meaty soup bone carefully wrapped in brown paper, Della took the train to Silver City after Angharad waved goodbye and good luck from the steps of the Knightville School.

In Silver City, she had to wait a few minutes for the track to clear as a Denver and Rio Grande Western ore car picked up steam and headed toward Salt Lake's smelters, some eighty miles to the north. All around she heard the noise of money being made, whether from the whine of boards going through the saw in the carpenter shop, the clang of metal on metal in another building, or other ore cars bumping each other like impatient children.

As the caboose passed, she still stood on the boardwalk, thinking of Winter Quarters. She knew Martha Evans was running the Clear Creek boardinghouse now, and Tamris and Winifred Powell were living with Tamris's sister in Springville. She thought of the men gone and then looked toward the carpenter shop, thinking of a man still hurting and attempting to assuage his grief by working harder for other miners.

And what about you, Della Davis? she asked herself. A wary look at Owen each morning was enough to tell her if she had cried out in her sleep, missing her father as she hadn't missed him in years. For the umpteenth time since May 1, she wondered if *that* mine disaster had jogged something loose in her mind. The loss of her father and the death of two other hard rock miners on the Colorado Plateau did not compare to two hundred, did it?

Apparently last night had featured only peaceful sleep. Nothing on Owen's face indicated she had jerked him from sound sleep with her tears. And here she was, ready to knock on Mr. Weisman's office door and meet Saladin.

She knocked and entered, looking around quickly and relieved to see only Mr. Weisman, scribbling on a yellow pad.

"Pull up a chair, Mrs. Davis," he said. "Your first challenge is to read this and make sure you can decipher what passes for my handwriting. Out loud, please."

Amused, she took the strip of paper from him. "'October Twenty, Nineteen Hundred, Dear Mr. Utley, Mammoth Mine.'"

She frowned and peered closer wondering if she was about to lose the job she just accepted. He did have dreadful penmanship. Mr. Weisman slid the lamp on his desk closer to her chair. "'Swansea Mine, fourth drift west, fourth room. Mineral content . . .'"

She read the mineral percentages slowly, glancing at Mr. Weisman for affirmation. "My goodness, there is money to be made here," she said when she finished, which made Mr. Weisman laugh and throw off about ten years from his appearance. Maybe he wasn't as old as she thought.

"I don't even know what this means," she said, handing back the list.

"You will learn. And even better, you can read it." He rummaged in his desk drawer and pulled out a handful of printed sheets. "This will simplify matters. Most analyses can be typed onto these forms. Simple, no?"

She nodded, pleased. She took off her hat and hung it next to her cloth bag containing lunch and a soup bone. She handed the brown parcel to Mr. Weisman. "This is for Saladin, as requested."

Mr. Weisman took it out and slid his rolling chair back far enough for her to see a black form under the desk where his feet had been.

"Meet Saladin, your body guard and escort, should the two of you agree on that."

Della started in surprise and looked closer, hoping not to see sharp teeth or hear something growling at her. She saw a benign face gazing back at her. Mr. Weisman's kneehole desk admitted little light, and Della had no idea how large Saladin was, or even *what* he was, in the dog world.

"Mr. Weisman, was Saladin under your desk yesterday when I came in?"

"Indeed he was." He reached down and patted the dog. "You may have wondered why that Help Wanted sign was in my window so long."

"Owen did mention it had been there ever since he started."

"And long before." He handed Della the bone she had brought. "Give him the bone."

"It's safe?" she asked, dubious, but sensing that her employment really hinged on Saladin and his likes and dislikes.

"Quite safe. Saladin is somewhat—how shall I put this?—somewhat discerning. If he had declared you *persona non grata* yesterday, you would have heard him growl and seen him tug on my pant leg. Obviously no such thing happened. Go on. Don't be afraid."

Della stooped down and held out the bone. Saladin sniffed at the meat, edged a little closer to her hand, and then delicately took the bone from her. With a sigh that sounded nearly human, Saladin settled down and began to gnaw.

"What breed of dog is he?" she asked.

Mr. Weisman shrugged. "He is my lucky charm, Mrs. Davis. When I abandoned those noisy glass vials in that Prussian forest, snow all around, he bounded out of nowhere." He blew out his cheeks at the memory. "I thought he was going to eat me, but he stayed by my side all the way to the railroad depot and the train heading to Berlin. Could I leave something so faithful behind?"

"I suppose not, but how did you get Saladin from Europe to here? Aren't there ship rules?" she asked, curious.

"Would you argue ship's passage with a hunchback guarded by something this formidable?" Mr. Weisman asked in turn.

"I suppose I would not," she agreed.

"Did you ever have a pet?"

"Never. My father was a miner in the Molly Bee in Colorado," she said, kneeling down again for a better look at Saladin. "My mother disappeared when I was born, and Papa could barely keep the two of us fed."

She sat back on her heels, surprised at the sudden anger in her voice. Saladin looked up and cocked his head. "I mean, you know, times were often hard in the mines."

"It's not for the faint," Mr. Weisman said.

It was time to take her place behind the typewriter and scroll in the printed form. Time to get to work and not wonder why she was talking now about her father, the man she loved and lost so many years ago, with this man she barely knew.

She completed the first form and took it to Mr. Weisman, who had moved slowly and painfully to the next room. She sniffed chemicals and heard the pop of a little fire. Saladin padded along behind her, which might have told her worlds about his intention to protect Mr. Weisman from everyone, even the well-meaning woman who brought him a soup bone.

Mr. Weisman set down the vial, held with tongs, that he had poised over a lump of ore. He read through the form, nodded, and handed it back after signing it.

"That is the business of the day, Mrs. Davis," he said. "Please put it in the Out basket, get the next miserable bit of scribbling from the In basket, and carry on. Glamorous work, yes?"

She laughed and returned to the main room. As she scrolled in another form and prepared to stare at Mr. Weisman's writing until it became legible, she felt something by her shoe. She looked down and there was Saladin. She patted his head, impressed with the silkiness of his fur. Not sure what to do with dogs, she touched his dangling ears, then gently rubbed the spot on the top of his head where the ears began.

After a minute of this, Saladin snuffled and curled up next to her shoe. "Mr. Weisman?" she called, but softly. "I think I have a friend."

"Mrs. Davis, you have two friends."

She smiled at that and returned to her work, content.

Chapter 29

Heavy snow came to Tintic in October. The first fire Owen built in the parlor's stove smelled of dust and something ineffably like the end of summer. Autumn had been leisurely, which meant time to visit a little between the houses and get to know neighbors in ways that didn't happen at church, because they were all busy there.

As time passed in the lovely company of his wife, Owen felt himself sinking into the pleasant complacency that comes from love, and plenty of it. Amazing how the smallest glance from Della across the table during breakfast was enough to make his heart merry. That she loved him he had no doubt. She scolded him when he needed it, brushed the lint off his coat before he left for early-morning Priesthood meeting on Sundays, and liked to curl up next to him on the sofa as he listened to Angharad read on his other side. It was the rare moment when her hand didn't inch over to rest on his thigh.

There was nothing he could do when she drew another *X* on the calendar except put his arm around her shoulder until she took a deep breath and changed the subject.

Granted, her employment seemed to ease her heart by giving her something to do that took her away from home, and neighbors with babies. He knew she would never begrudge other women their bounty with children, but her deep-set, expressive eyes told him worlds about the state of her heart. She wanted a baby, such a simple thing. Wasn't it?

All personal matters aside, it amused him how quickly she found herself at home in a ramshackle office run by an Austrian hunchback and his equally unusual dog Saladin, a black monster with a feathery tail. Owen admitted to his own qualms, having once or twice stepped back into the carpenter shop when Saladin strolled by on the loose. The beast had a way of curling his lip and growling in a soft, malevolent tone that threatened peril, at the very least.

Owen admitted to terror the first time Della invited him to share lunch with her at Saul Weisman's office. She gave him one of her exquisitely perfected, down-the-nose looks, sidled close, put her hand inside his shirt and whispered against his skin, "Are you a man or a mouse, my darling?"

Armed with another soup bone, he braved the assayer's office, his coal miner's lunch bucket held out in front of him for some puny protection. Saladin had been lying asleep at Della's feet. When Mr. Weisman invited him to come inside, the dog raised his head and fixed him with a glance remarkably like Della's.

"Do I drop it and run?" he asked, which made Mr. Weisman laugh.

"Not at all. Della, perhaps you had better stand up and give your husband a kiss. That way Saladin will know he comes in peace."

Della, is it? Owen thought as his wife patted the monster, stood up, and kissed him. He looked at Saladin, who let out a *wuff!* consisting mostly of bad breath and put his head back on his paws, monumentally uninterested, now that the female of the pack had established her connection.

After that, he generally ate lunch with Della and Mr. Weisman—who insisted on being called Saul—and Saladin, who did him the signal honor of heaving himself onto his back and demanding Owen rub his stomach, whether he wanted to or not.

As much as he wished Della could have stayed home and waited for the birth of a child, he had to admit that she sparkled in the work place. He had noticed this in Winter Quarters, where she taught school, and he saw that same energy in Saul's office. He laughed when she proudly showed off her typing and, to Saul's amusement, also held up what the Austrian called "Exhibit A," containing the worst handwriting known to man.

She learned quickly and did her job well, which made Owen both grateful and proud. Because Saul Weisman's disability made walking uncomfortable, he turned over the delivery of assay reports to Della. Any hesitation Owen might have felt to see her abroad in a town full of miners quickly dissipated the first time he saw her walk with real purpose toward the Swansea mine office, Saladin matching her stride for stride.

She hadn't bothered with a leash, which meant every man between the assayer's office and the mine office gave her a wide berth. Some of the more adventuresome sprites tipped a hat her way, or tried to speak, which meant Saladin administered his thoughtful stare. No one troubled Della.

During supper, Della entertained them with Saul's stories of life in Vienna, Austria, going to university for a year to study medicine and then leaving its storied halls because he ran out of money after his father's death. "I told him about your dragons, Angharad, and he wants you to draw one for him," she said.

"Do you think Mr. Weisman needs a dragon?" the child asked.

"Everyone needs a dragon," Della replied. "He said he would send me home with one of *his* drawings, if you would draw him a dragon."

And so Angharad had spent the better part of one evening drawing a Welsh dragon for an Austrian Jew who had learned to assay ore, landed a job in Prussia and found himself in the middle of a pogrom, and came to America—and then Utah, somehow. One dragon turned into two and then three as Della edited the difficult parts of an interesting man's life for Angharad.

"Someone like Mr. Weisman needs more than one dragon," Angharad explained as Owen and Della tucked her in bed. "I should draw a dog too."

He leaned against the door and listened as Della and Angharad sang "Ar Hyd y Nos," the lullaby he had sung to his child even before she was born, but which the mine disaster had sucked completely out of his life.

Maybe the dragons intended for Mr. Weisman made Angharad especially brave. Before he closed the door to her room, his daughter sat up. "Da, you need to sing again."

"Oh, I don't . . ."

Her hand went up imperiously. "Da! I am a fine soprano. Mam sings a very good alto. We are not complete."

He thought about that the next morning as Della packed their lunches and carefully placed the dragon sketch between two pieces of cardboard. Angharad's words of the night before had turned his wife quiet. He could tell something else bothered her, and he knew what it was. She had wakened him from sleep last night, crying for her father. He had soothed her back into slumber, but he knew this time she was aware, unlike other times when he mentioned her nightmares and earned himself a blank stare.

"Do you know, Saul told me about dreams," she said as she spread butter on Angharad's cheese sandwich. "He had a friend in Vienna, a medical student, who thought dreams were our way of expressing things we can't talk about."

She put down the knife and leaned against the table. "I don't seem to remember my dreams, or at least not for long. Should I?"

It was a question for the ages. He kissed her forehead. She laughed and picked up the knife again. When she made no more mention of the matter, he couldn't help his relief. He was at that critical moment when the hinged timbers, measured specifically for the Banner's third-level drift, were being moved toward the mine. He wanted to concentrate on that and not worry about dreams, his or anyone else's.

His hands gentle on her shoulders, he told her in his most matter-of-fact way that he would be late coming home that night because he did not know how long it would take to swing the beams into place, lock them securely in the passage, then put down a layer of stronger slabs across the whole affair. She seemed to shrink inside herself, her eyes huge, but the work had to be done, and so he told her.

"I'll be along as soon as I can," he said as he enveloped her in his arms, touched to the depths of his soul how she clung to him. "I can tell you not to worry, but I know you will."

He took his lunch bucket. She jumped when the waiting train gave three blasts, and put her hand to her throat. She shook her head at this and walked him to the door, her arm around his waist.

"I'll be waiting up for you," she said.

"It might be late. You needn't . . ."

"I'll do it if I want to."

She patted his waist and let go, but then she grabbed him again by the belt. "Do this for me," she said, and it was no suggestion. "If you can't sing, you can't sing, but do at least *think* those words to the miners' song."

He nodded, and thought about the words, finding himself repeating the last line over and over: *One step enough for me. One step enough for me.*

To his relief and pleasure, he found the entire verse reverberating through that corner of his mind that seemed to reside just below the part that governed the actual duties of the day. He had reason to appreciate the team he had assembled in the carpenter's shop. Yesterday he had talked them through the entire installation, assigning each man to a portion. He told them to be ready for anything and watchful, and they did not fail him.

They only installed the first set of timbers, with their sturdier-than-usual braces and beams, which created a solid unit. He let out the breath he felt he had been holding for a month as the beams swung into place and anchored themselves against the ribs and roof of the drift, leaving plenty of space to wield the drills that extricated the ore. This was twice the strength of a regular square set, and hopefully what the Banner Mine needed. Time would tell.

He felt a measure of pride when the mining engineer from one of Uncle Jesse's other mines joined them in late afternoon, nodding to see their day's work. He looked at the angle of the roofed structure and nodded again. "In theory, it should work," he said. "There is every likelihood that a rock fall will slide down, because the roof beams are too strong to collapse now. The rocks will reach that angle of repose and stop."

"In theory," Owen said.

"I have no doubt it will be tested," the engineer said with a shake of his head. "I have to tell you: I don't know about the Banner Mine. The assayer's reports are promising, but I have to ask myself, is it worth it?"

By the time all the tweaking and fitting was done, the sun was long gone and the stars had come out. Tired and hungry, Owen rode the train home to Knightville, certain he would find Della up and waiting for him.

The lights were out in all the houses except those belonging to the two men with him from his team. The others lived in a Silver City boardinghouse.

"We tell them to go to bed, but they never do," he murmured.

"And we love them for it," his crew member said.

Della leaped up from the sofa when he opened the door and threw herself into his arms. "I prayed and prayed," she whispered in his ear as he held her tight.

"Thank you, *m cara*," he said, humbled down to the core of his soul. "It went just the way it was supposed to."

Della let out the breath she had been holding all day, took his hand, and pulled him to the kitchen, where stew and hot bread waited for him. He ate, and she never took his eyes from him.

Sleep came easy and quick. In no time, it seemed Owen was on the train again, lunch pail full, headed back to Silver City. A light snow fell, but he doubted anything was capable of making a mining camp look good. He rested his cheek against his hand and found himself thinking about Provo, where the leaves were probably gone now, but where snow could turn into snowmen that weren't grimy from mine dust.

But the work was here. Looking as tired as he felt, but also quietly triumphant, his crew was already in the shop, preparing more timbers for the finicky, contrary, arbitrary Banner Mine.

They stopped an hour later when a warning siren blared across the valley, earsplitting and immediate. One of his crew opened the door, making the piercing scream louder until it drowned out the whine of the saw.

They all stepped into the street, wondering, and then looked toward the Mammoth Mine in the distance. Looking, concentrating, they soon saw miners pouring from the mine.

Owen shook his head, wondering at the state of the timbers in the Mammoth, wondering why he didn't quit and go back to handyman work in Provo. They could be on the train tomorrow morning.

The moment passed as he thought of Richard and David Evans and all those Farishes and Gatherums. "I owe it to you," he whispered. "I can make this safer."

"Should we go, Owen?"

"I'll leave it to you. It looks to me that there are plenty of men."

As he spoke, a wagon full of men in mine rescue suits and helmets raced toward the Mammoth. Hands on his hips, he stared after them, shook his head, and went back inside his shop.

But who can concentrate after that? He looked at his timepiece. He might be a little early for lunch at the assayer's office, but Della had seemed edgy this morning, gasping when Angharad dropped a pan and then putting her hand to her stomach and managing a weak laugh. He could surprise her.

And he would have, except someone pounded on the door. He hurried to open it, wondering if he should have taken his men to the Mammoth after all.

Saul Weisman stood in the door, panting. Owen took him by the arm and tried to lead him inside, but the little man resisted. Hands on his knees, he bent double until he caught his breath. When he spoke, Owen felt the blood leave his face.

"It's Della. When the siren started, she screamed. She fell on the floor and she's still screaming."

Chapter 30

Why was she lying on the floor, cheek pressed against the wood, as if trying to burrow underground? Her head already ached from someone's screams, which were even louder than the steam whistle from the mine.

When she realized she was screaming, she stopped, opened her eyes, and looked at her floor's eye view. His head cocked to one side, Saladin stared back at her. He lay near her and stretched out flat, his face level with hers.

Relieved not to be alone, she touched his snout. He inched closer. "I'm sorry for the racket, Saladin," she said. "Don't know what got into me."

She shuddered and closed her eyes again, wishing she could block out the sudden sound and the panic that filled every part of her, all from a steam whistle. She knew Owen wasn't in the Banner Mine today because he had told her over breakfast that he needed to prepare the next unit of timbers. Why, then, this sudden terror?

She tried to sit up, but the floor felt more comfortable, soft almost. Maybe she would stay there until the mining boom in Tintic faded away, as they all did eventually, and everyone left her alone. She could turn into the floor and then maybe the dirt underneath.

But no. She heard people running along the boardwalk and Owen shouting her name and saying something in a language she didn't understand. She winced when the door slammed open and he threw himself into the assay office, dropping to his knees beside her. Luckily Saladin didn't seem to mind. He whined and moved aside to nose Saul Weisman, who trundled in and collapsed in his chair.

That was the end of her peaceful time. Ten to one, Owen would want to know what had happened, and she had no idea what to tell him. Already she was having trouble remembering what had happened. It was as though a cosmic hand was closing over her mind.

She let Owen help her to her feet and sit her down at her desk.

"What happened?"

She couldn't speak to tell him, and then she realized he was not asking her, but Mr. Weisman.

"Get your breath, sir," Owen told her employer, who still gasped for air from the exertion of running fast in a body so crooked.

Della breathed quietly on her own. She felt her heart slowing. For one dreadful moment, she wished it would simply stop, putting an end to . . . something. The moment passed. A woman couldn't sit knee to knee with Owen Davis and want to die.

"I can talk now," Saul Weisman said.

Please don't, she thought in sudden alarm. *I have no idea what I said.*

"Tell us, please."

Mr. Weisman swung his wheeled chair closer. Della felt his light touch on her wrist and then realized he was feeling her pulse.

"Better now, Della?" he asked.

She nodded. It wasn't true, but he expected her to be better. Owen probably did too.

"Della, you screamed when the whistle blew. You dropped to your knees, kept screaming, and stared down at the floor." His voice changed and he sounded uncertain. "It was strange. You were speaking in a child's voice."

"She's done that a time or two in bed, with a nightmare," Owen said.

When he kissed the top of her head, she suddenly resented him for speaking to Mr. Weisman as if she weren't there.

"What did she say?"

Nothing at all, she thought in panic, as the hand in her mind closed shut and removed all memory. Oddly, it felt like a mercy. *Nothing.*

"Owen, I'll never forget. It was, 'Papa. Papa. I didn't mean it.'"

She wanted to close her ears against Saul's words. "I wish I remembered."

"I wish . . . well, I do not know what I wish. I do know for certain that when the whistle blew, you started to scream," Saul said. "Did it set off something in your mind?"

Owen kissed the hand he held, his eyes troubled. "*M cara*, did something like this happen to you on May 1?"

She gave herself permission to think of that unforgettable day. She remembered glancing at the classroom clock just before the whole canyon rumbled with the explosion. She remembered one of the windows bowing inward from the percussion of the blast and throwing herself across her students closest to the window, in case the window shattered.

"I didn't scream," she said.

"There wasn't any whistle at the Number Four," he said.

She felt the hairs on her neck rise as a tiny memory struggled to the surface. "There was a whistle at the Molly Bee," she said slowly, remembering. "It was about one in the afternoon, and we heard it all the way to Hastings."

"What did you do that day? Think for a moment."

She didn't need to. "I screamed," she said simply, and turned her face into his shirt. "I couldn't stop."

What was there to say? Della heard the calming tick of the Regulator. Saladin was not a young dog, and he had started to snore, now that his people seemed rational again. Outside, a wagon rumbled past and someone laughed. She heard Mr. Weisman get up and shuffle into his kitchen lean-to off the main room. He returned with a glass of water for her. Obediently she drank, and she thanked him with her eyes.

He sank into his chair and wheeled himself closer. "Would you mind a personal ramble? It might have some bearing, or it might not. Let us say I am thinking out loud."

"Ramble, by all means," she said.

"I went to university in Vienna, with the hope of becoming a physician. I've told you this before. My father died unexpectedly, near the end of that first year, so my dream ended. I stayed in Vienna, however, and learned the assayer's trade."

"Things can change, can't they?" Owen said.

"Indeed. I had a friend at university named Sigi. After I left school, we met in Vienna's coffeehouses. You could stay warm in one of them and sip a cup of coffee, and if times were plush, eat *sascher torte*." He kissed his fingers. "Food from the gods. Chocolate cake. Apricot jam."

"I have a jelly sandwich," Della said, and Saul smiled.

"Sigi is now a famous doctor in Vienna, but back then he was a poor student. We talked for hours. He told me he had a theory about dreams. He felt then, and probably still does, that dreams hold clues to our minds. Sigi thought it took little triggers to set them off. Like a mine whistle, perhaps."

Della considered it. "Even now, I have only the faintest memory of the mine whistle that just blew. And you say I was on my knees, looking down a hole? Why don't I remember that?"

"I've found you that way a time or two, Della," Owen said.

Startled, she had to know. "Before we came here?"

"Once or twice, but not regularly until we were here and around mines again."

"I wish I knew more of what Sigi must know now. I haven't seen him in years," Saul Weisman said. "Well, questions seem to beget more questions." He slapped his knees. "I am making an employer decision now. Mr. Davis, please take Mrs. Davis home, tuck her in bed, put a hot water bottle at her feet, and let her sleep."

"I second your motion," Owen said. "Della, let's eat those jelly sandwiches in Knightville. I'll tell my crew. They might have news for us about Mammoth, and I'd like to know."

"Here's what happened," he said when he returned. "It seems the earth rumbled a little up at Mammoth and shifted. Everyone is all right. Shall we go?"

They rode home in silence, Della dozing, then waking, and then settling in more comfortably against a comfortable man. They ambled home hand in hand to a silent house, where he helped her out of her clothing and put her to bed. He lay down beside her on top of the blankets, his hands behind his head.

"'Papa, Papa, I didn't mean it,'" he said. "What didn't you mean?"

"I wish I knew." She suddenly felt that odd hand in her mind open a little and then close almost as if it were teasing her. "Maybe I don't want to remember. Could that be possible?"

"I suppose anything is possible. Too bad we cannot ask Saul's friend Sigi."

Della felt the mattress begin to claim her, but she struggled awake because there was something she had to say. "You won't like this, Owen, but we need to leave here. We need to leave now."

"I'm half beginning to agree with you," he admitted. "However, I have another unit ready to install in a few days. I'll have one more ready after that, and then we'll take a few days and go to Provo for Thanksgiving."

"I mean we have to leave for good."

"I know you do. I made this promise to myself and to my dead friends."

He said it in such a matter-of-fact way, as if the spirits of Richard and David Evans and all the others hovered over him. In some way, they probably did. She knew the Welsh were superstitious, and miners times two.

"You made me some promises, Owen."

There. She had said it. Maybe she had wanted to say it ever since he told her they were going to Tintic, a place she was coming to dread, as much as she liked

Angharad's school, and her pleasant association with the assayer, and Owen's position of responsibility and increased wages.

"You're going to keep reminding me that I broke that promise, aren't you?" he said finally. He got up and stood in the doorway, his back to her.

"Until you come to your senses, my dearest husband."

The door closed. "Or until I lose mine," she added to herself, because he was gone.

Chapter 31

Even though Owen had admitted he was wavering, they declared an unspoken truce on the matter of staying or going. As Della thought of what Saul had told them, she began to wonder what else was lurking around in her mind that felt no free rein to come out until she slept. In consequence, more and more she found herself wide awake and staring into the dark, wondering if she wanted to sleep, because sleep meant trouble.

Owen bore the brunt of her distress, which increased the guilt she felt over making demands of him when he had his own sorrow to deal with. He woke up weary because more and more, she kept him awake with restless movements.

"Della, you made my heart stop last night," he said early one morning before the sun was up. "I woke and you were standing over our bed, staring down at me. I fair had heart palpitations."

"I'm not even aware," she said. "I swear I am not."

"I believe you, even though thousands wouldn't," he joked.

She knew it was a British Isles bit of wit, but it made her feel helpless and then angry. "I wish you wouldn't say that," she said, leading to an argument all the more fierce because they kept it quiet, since Angharad still slept in the next room. She wanted to weep because after six months of marriage, it was their first fight.

He left for work without his usual kiss. He didn't come to the assayer's office to eat lunch. He apologized that evening, blaming his foul mood on the tension of making sure of the precision of his measurements.

She accepted his apology, all the while wondering if she should apologize for that which she could not control. Maybe he expected her to. When she didn't, she felt his subtle withdrawal. The casual observer might not have noticed, but Della could tell by his long silences.

He no longer told her when he went into the mine, but from Saul's office window, she saw Owen and his crew with their load of prepared timbers, riding a flatbed up to the Banner Mine on Uncle Jesse's railroad spur. It stung her that he said nothing, but she knew better than to comment or, heaven forbid, nag him, as she remembered Aunt Caroline berating Uncle Karl. Maybe Owen was trying to spare her more anxiety. Or maybe he didn't care anymore.

Or perhaps it was all in her mind, because her husband continued to love her, which, truth to tell, relieved her of considerable anxiety. She treasured the pleasant aftermath when he cradled her head with his hand and held her close to his chest. For those precious moments, her life seemed normal. She was a new bride in love with her husband. If all wasn't precisely well, whose life was?

Owen's placid good nature at such times gave her courage to hope tranquility had returned. She asked him one night if she still had those dreams. His hesitation told her all she needed to know, even though he said there probably weren't so many.

She lay beside her husband, warm and comfortable but wishing she had the courage to ask again if they could leave Tintic as soon as he finished the timbering on the third drift. She had begun to dread the train ride from Knightville to Silver City each day, to the point of hunching down in her seat when the little spur train rounded a curve that opened onto the western plain, stark with headframes and slag heaps. Below ground, miners were busy with their jackhammers as patient mules pulled the ore cars from the mines, one car after another. Gold and silver assayed out in high percentages and men made money.

She longed for trees with leaves, sidewalks, grass, substantial buildings of brick and stone, and lemonade on the porch in the afternoon. Everything here was unpainted wood scoured by constant winds and windows darkened by soot and particles blown from industrial chimneys that turned washing hung out to dry into gray rags. If the wind blew hard enough, she could taste grit in her jelly sandwiches. Lemonade on the porch would have been laughable.

Still, she had promised to honor and obey the good man she married, as much as she yearned to be somewhere else. A strange curtain made of two parts unease to one part disillusionment settled on her mind and refused to let any light through.

She could almost fool Owen into thinking she was content to live in a mining camp. She could almost fool Mr. Weisman by laughing and joking with him. The only creature she couldn't fool was Saladin. Every morning, the sad-eyed behemoth greeted her at the door and then came close to rest his head against her shoes as she sat at her desk and typed. Every so often he raised his head to look at her, just a sympathetic stare, as if he understood her turmoil.

They were three days from returning to Provo for Thanksgiving with the Knights when Owen announced over breakfast that they were going into the Banner that afternoon, once the morning shift finished, to secure the next timber unit in place on Level Three.

"Da, did you forget that tonight is our Thanksgiving celebration at school?" Angharad asked, the dismay evident in her voice and on her expressive face. "I am to be a pilgrim by the name of Priscilla Mullins. There is a wonderful poem too, which we are going to recite."

"'The Courtship of Miles Standish,'" Della said. "My goodness, Angharad, you get to tell John Alden to think for himself."

"Mrs. Baldwin says it is a very American thing to do," Angharad replied. She tried again. "Da, there are two men interested in Priscilla Mullins, and you will miss the fun."

Owen laughed at that, and winked at Della. "Think on, daughter, but there were two men politely fighting over *this* mam who decided to cast her lot with you and me. Perhaps it is also a Welsh thing."

Angharad gave Della a wide-eyed look. "Mam!" She thought a moment and Della nearly smiled to see the gears turning in the child's head. "Dr. Isgreen?"

Della wanted to hold the moment in her hands, watching father and daughter look at her, with all the kindly regard she was familiar with, from life among the Welsh.

"She made the right choice," Angharad said.

"Aye, and so I tell her often," he replied. He gave a sigh. "I do hate to miss your debut on the American theatrical stage, but tonight is the perfect time to install the timber. The miners on the second level have reached a point at the face where they need to blast. When we finish installing the unit, we will set off their charge on the second level on our way out, and they can start work there in the morning. Forgive me?"

"I am doomed to disappointment," Angharad pronounced in round tones worthy of a Siddons or a Bernhardt.

"Alas and alack," Owen said. "I'll get home in the wee hours. Tomorrow after I wake up, what do you say you sit on my lap and we read the poem together?"

"If that is to be my lot," his daughter replied.

"You'll still like me, won't you?"

The hand in Della's mind, the one that had closed after the whistle blew at Mammoth, seemed to open again, but only far enough for her to remember another little girl, another time, and that same unanswered question. It closed again before she had more than a glimpse of her father on a path, he going one way, she another, but not happily. She opened her mouth to speak, and Owen looked at her expectantly. She closed it.

"It's nothing," she said, wondering why her heart beat a little faster. "I'll watch for both of us tonight and give you a full report, since you must do this."

Maybe he heard the bitterness. She truly hadn't intended for her sudden fear to translate into anger. He gave her an appraising look and returned to his porridge. When he said goodbye later, he took her gently by the chin and gazed deep into her eyes.

"I could tell you not to worry, could I not?" he asked.

"You could," she said, suddenly weary. "I doubt you would listen if I protested."

"That's unfair, wife."

"It's how I feel."

Silent, he joined his friends on their way to the tracks.

Della made herself deliberately cheerful at work, which Saul Weisman saw through immediately.

"He's in the mine this afternoon, isn't he?" her boss asked when he handed her three more illegible reports.

"Yes, he is, drat the man," she replied. She picked up the reports. "Mr. Weisman, your handwriting should be taken out and shot."

He laughed at that, and Della had to smile, in spite of the fear that gnawed at her, and something else: the knowledge that she and Owen had not parted on kind terms. There it was again, that hand opening and closing, teasing her with some memory.

The day was warm for November. She stood in the door as three o'clock approached and watched, waiting, her hand shading her eyes. She was rewarded with the sight of Owen and his crew sitting on top of the hinged timbers headed to the Banner Mine. Each shaped and sized log was numbered. Owen had begun drafting his own approximation of blueprints for each unit. On the third drift he would lay out the blueprint and make sure he had timbers of corresponding numbers in the right places, everything as orderly and accurate as one talented man could possibly contrive.

Maybe when the level was completely timbered and vastly safer he would consider his emotional pilgrimage to the graves of his friends fulfilled. Or would there always be another mine to shore up, another mining camp to seek out, another promise to dead men? It seemed unfair. Still, she owed him an apology for her shortness this morning.

Distressed, Della walked toward the slowly moving car. As the train picked up speed, she walked faster, wanting to wish him good luck, eager to tell him one more time how much she loved him, except she wouldn't say anything that brazen anywhere except in their home. She *could* say she was sorry.

The train had picked up real steam now, because the slope to Banner Mine required it. *Turn around*, she thought. *Just wave at me one more time. I can tell you I'm sorry tonight.*

I didn't mean it, Papa. I didn't mean it, popped into her mind. With her heart in her mouth, Della whirled around, wondering what mother had allowed her child so near to the tracks. She looked closer. Nothing. Thoroughly chilled, she wondered what had just happened. She turned back to the train, but Owen was a small figure by now. *Too late*, she thought.

Supper was a hurried affair, with Angharad repeating her lines as Della French-braided her hair, gave it the critical eye, and pronounced it a success. Pilgrims probably never resorted to anything as stylish as a French braid, but Angharad knew what she wanted and sat patiently.

"When we go to Provo, we should visit a photographer's studio for a family portrait," Della said as they hurried to the well-lit schoolhouse with other children and parents. "I'll braid your hair and we can twine ribbons in it."

Della gave the child a gentle push toward the front of the classroom, where two blankets had been strung to serve as a curtain. She took her seat next to Mrs. Tate, the lady who had opened her home to Angharad for that hour after school before Della arrived. She took the smallest Tate on her lap, gratified when the child leaned back against her with a sigh.

She glanced at Mrs. Tate with satisfaction. Della knew two dollars a week was helping feed a family where the father wasn't getting well fast. He had stayed home tonight, probably marshaling his forces for the day shift. Della gave silent thanks for her own healthy man and wondered if she could think of a convincing reason to tack another fifty cents onto her weekly payment without making Mrs. Tate feel poor. She would ask Owen what he thought. *After I apologize to my good man*, she reminded herself, as if she needed reminding.

With a lurch of the blanket curtains, a consultation between two little boys about what to do, and then another more successful lurch, the blankets parted and the pageant began. Della silently praised Mrs. Wilkins as her carefully rehearsed pupils pronounced their lines with energy and enthusiasm. Della knew from experience that a teacher couldn't ask for more, not with little ones eager to impress and buoyed up with the idea of a few days off soon for turkey and stuffing.

The program continued with Angharad's Priscilla Mullins and her charming Welsh accent, politely asking John Alden to speak his mind. As John Alden opened his mouth to reply, the steam whistle in the valley started to shriek.

Cast and audience alike froze. *Please no*, Della thought. Forcing down her panic, she listened, knowing that each mine had its own series of short and long whistles so rescuers would know where to go. Three long blasts for the Mammoth. She knew that one all too well, but this was different—a short, a long, a short, and another short.

She didn't know the code, but that made no difference because the audience did. She gasped when everyone turned toward her.

Maybe they were looking beyond her. Della turned to look in the same direction. Everyone on the other side of her was looking at her too.

"Oh, God, please no," she whispered.

Immobilized with horror, she felt a cold breeze on the back of her neck as someone opened the door. The blast grew louder until it filled the classroom—a short, a long, a short, and another short.

She tensed when she felt a hand on her shoulder. "It's not the Banner," she said distinctly. So there. Whoever he was could find another woman to terrify.

The hand didn't leave her shoulder. "Sister Davis, you'd better come with me," she heard Bishop McIntyre say above the great roaring in her ears.

Chapter 32

Della didn't take the time to get Angharad out of her long black pilgrim dress with the starched white collar and into her own clothing. She clung to her stepdaughter when the bishop's wife and Mrs. Tate tried to convince her to let Angharad stay with them. "You know, until you find out what is going on," the bishop added.

"No," Della said. "We stay together, don't we, Angharad?"

"Aye, Mam," came her child's quiet voice.

She held Angharad tight on her lap as they rode the special train to Silver City. Wearing his overcoat, Saul Weisman waited for her by the tracks, his face as white as she knew hers was.

"I'm riding with Mrs. Davis to the Banner," he told Bishop McIntyre, who had the good sense not to argue.

She looked for Saladin, and heard a mournful, wolfish howl from the assayer's office.

"He's in my bedroom," Saul told her. "I don't know what he would do."

To her relief, the whistle stopped its unholy shriek. She looked around for other wives of miners, and saw none, which chilled her heart. Bishop McIntyre was talking to a man she recognized from the Knightville Ward who also mined in the Banner. Desperate to know what was happening, it was all Della could do to stand still beside Angharad, who shivered uncontrollably, even after Mr. Weisman took off his overcoat and draped it over her shoulders.

After what seemed like an epoch or two, the bishop joined her. "Here's what we know, Sister Davis. The men came out of Level Two after setting a charge, which Owen was to set off after they finished on Level Three, and came out." He took a deep breath. "For some reason, that charge went off as the Level Two men started up the hoist."

Della gasped, remembering that Bishop McIntyre's first counselor was a Level Two man. "Brother Cable?"

He shook his head. "The blast caught him."

Della bowed her head, thinking of Sister Cable and her three children and then of Martha Evans at Winter Quarters with her three children and Annie Jones and Tamris Powell on and on and on.

Bishop McIntyre visibly collected himself. "The Level Two brought Brother Cable up and then took the hoist down as far as they could, but Two is blocked now and they can't get to Three. The hoist was weakened, but they're repairing it."

"Dear God," Della whispered. She knelt beside Angharad, who was weeping openly, her whole body shaking. She grabbed Owen's daughter and held her close until the shaking stopped. Someone gave her a handkerchief for Angharad's face.

"Angharad, we're going up to the Banner," she said.

"Stay here," Bishop McIntyre said. "I insist."

"Insist all you want, Bishop. We're going up to the Banner. Don't even try to stop me. We'll walk the slope if we have to."

She stared him down, even as her heart broke into a million pieces.

"Very well," he said, wise enough to know when he was defeated. "Hop on the flatbed with Angharad. Here's what they're going to do, after the rubble is off the hoist: clear the rubble inside Two up to a winze between the Two and Three. Owen and his crew will be tunneling toward the winze, most likely, so they can come out on the Two, above the blockage." He put his hand gently on both her shoulders. "And we will wait."

"I'm coming too," Saul Weisman said. "Saladin and I."

"There's no arguing with you people, is there?" the bishop said.

"No, nein, nyet," Saul said cheerfully. "Pick a language, any language."

In silence, hanging on to each other, they rode the flatbed to the Banner Mine, tucked in the side of the mountain, not far from probably the only remaining stand of trees where the slope leveled out. Someone had built a fire and placed folding camp chairs around it. Bishop McIntyre usher them toward the blaze.

Della resisted, looking toward the headframe, which was still some distance away. "I'm going *there*," she insisted.

"No, you're not," the bishop said, and she heard no hesitation this time. "The miners are going up and down and spelling each other as they dig out. You'll be in the way, and I won't allow it. Don't argue this point with me, Della."

"Very well," she said.

He handed her several blankets and gestured for one of the miners to bring over a cot. "If you get tired, lie down. Maybe Angharad can sleep. The men have soup and bread. I'll see that you get some too. We'll keep the fire going."

He put his hands on her shoulder again. "Kneel down, both of you, and I'll give you a blessing."

Without a word, they did as he said. With one hand on each head, he blessed them with comfort and serenity. When he finished, he helped them up, kissed the top of Angharad's head, and walked up the slope to the headframe.

Della handed back Mr. Weisman's overcoat. She wrapped Angharad in one of the blankets and led her to the cot. "Lie down now," she said. "It's going to be a long night."

"Will they get Da out?"

"They know what to do. So does Da. They're digging on their level too." *If they're alive to dig*, Della thought, *but you don't need to hear that.*

"Sit close, please, Mam."

"I'm right here. I'll never leave you."

"I know that. Do you think Da is singing the miners' song?"

Break my heart some more, Della thought. "I don't know," she managed to say.

"If he won't, we must. We have to." Angharad started to cry. "He's not here to pitch it just right. Oh, Mam!"

"I can pitch it," Della said, as her mind, heart, and soul murmured *no more. No more. No more mines, Owen*. She gave a faltering note and wiped her daughter's face again. "Is that close?"

Angharad frowned, concentrating, thinking, her mind on the note now, to Della's relief. "No. This." She gave a note, the right one, just as her father would have.

"Very good," Della said, impressed. "I'll sing if I can. Might just have to say the words." She closed her eyes. "'Lead kindly light, amid the encircling gloom; lead thou me on,'" she sang.

"'The night is dark, and I am far from home; lead thou me on,'" Angharad added, joining in.

"'Keep thou my feet; I do not ask to see,'" they sang together, "'the distant scene—one step enough for me.'"

Della glanced at Saul, hoping she hadn't embarrassed herself in front of this much more sophisticated man, even if he did live in a mining town. She saw his struggle and touched his hand.

"That's all the hymn we need," Angharad said. She pillowed her head on her hands and closed her eyes. "I think I want to pray in my heart now."

Della leaned against the cot and bowed her head. *No more. No more.*

The night wore on as men took turns going down the shaft, working, and then trading off with other miners. The squeak of the hoist made Della want to find an oil can and grease the darned thing, and so she told Saul, who chuckled.

She started talking to Saul, who had wrapped himself in another blanket and leaned against the cot too, where Angharad slept. She told him about the Molly Bee, and that her father had died there when she was twelve. "I've wanted to go back to Hastings and leave something on my father's grave," she said. "I have just the thing too." She hesitated, wondering if she could even say Owen's name out loud.

"Owen . . . Owen carved me a plaque with 'Anders' on it," she said, her eyes blurring with tears again. For the last two hours tears had slid down her face with no effort at all. Her eyes were beginning to burn. "I would like to leave it on Papa's grave. His birthday is March 10. That would be a good time to go to Hastings."

"I think you should," Saul said.

She rested her face in her hands, weary beyond belief. In another moment, she was asleep.

It was poor sleep, or maybe it wasn't sleep at all. She was sitting in a classroom, her braids too loose because Papa wasn't any great shakes with hair. She knew she was supposed to be paying attention because they were parsing sentences, something she liked to do, except all she wanted now was to see Papa. But why?

She opened her eyes, puzzled, vexed, irritated with herself, wondering why she couldn't remember. Half awake, half asleep, she sat up with a gasp, wondering at a woman who would worry about something years ago when her husband was fighting for his life right now, or maybe dead like her father. What was the matter with her?

Silent, she looked around. Saul had wrapped himself into a tight ball and slept beside the cot. Angharad was insulated well against the cold. Her even breathing was peaceful.

One step enough. Della stood up quietly, unwilling to disturb anyone. She stared up the slope toward the headframe. Someone had rigged a row of battery-powered lights now. Men came and went, and the hoist squealed.

She wrapped the blanket around her like a shawl, wondering for the first time that evening why the sound of this steam whistle had not set her screaming. She wondered if she was getting good at pushing away thoughts that frightened her, and shook her head over what Saul's friend Sigi would think of her. Maybe Sigi could explain why she was dreaming of that classroom. To her surprise, she suddenly remembered the sentence they were parsing when the Molly Bee whistle blew.

"'The angry man whistled to his dog, who came to his side obediently,'" she whispered and started walking toward the headframe. *The night is dark, and I am far from home*, reverberated inside her skull as if it wanted out. To her fright, it wasn't music this time but an insistent voice getting louder and louder as she walked steadily toward the lights, one step at a time.

The miners had gathered around the hoist, looking down. Mindful of nothing except the urge to stand with them, she came closer, not even slowing down when a rescuer yelled at her to stop.

Della ignored him. As she shouldered her way through the crowd, the hand in her mind opened up finally, and released a tangle of thoughts and images.

She was twelve again.

Chapter 33

School had just started in Hastings. There hadn't been enough money for new shoes, so Della wore her old ones, and her feet hurt. Papa had promised shoes from the next pay envelope and she believed him, although not as quickly as usual. She wanted to tell him she was tired of everlasting flour and tinned milk pudding twice a day, and the embarrassment of crackers and one carrot in her lunch tin. She had taken to adding a few pebbles wrapped in cloth to the tin, so Miss March would think there was something more in the pail, if she happened to lift it or look inside.

It hadn't been a good morning. She had stormed up the slope and away from Papa after angry words about her shoes hurting and the fact that one of the girls in her class had a pendant locket and she wanted one. Papa had smiled, ducked his head, and said maybe they could manage something as extravagant as a locket closer to Christmas.

But this was September, and she wanted one now. Her feet hurt and she was hungry. She shouldn't have said what she did, but it came out anyway.

"Papa, I never want to see you again," she had shouted as they came to the path, school one way and Molly Bee the other.

"Oly, you'll change your mind by noon," he had called back. "I know you pretty well." He blew her a kiss and continued up the slope to the mine, where he was going to die in a few hours, even though neither of them knew it at the time.

"I'll never change my mind, Papa," she had shouted back. Head high, she continued to school, and sentences to diagram, and hunger until lunch.

But he was right. By noon, she could hardly wait until school was out to apologize to her father, a hard rock miner who in recent years had turned into more of a hard luck miner, as the Molly Bee began to play out. She knew he did his best, and she wanted to say she was sorry for angry words.

At 1:15 p.m., according to the Regulator on the schoolroom wall, the steam whistle at the Molly Bee began to shriek across the narrow valley. Everyone knew what it meant. Della screamed, leaped up from a spelling test, and ran out the door, calling for her father.

Halfway up the punishing slope to the Molly Bee, she tossed away her too-tight shoes and ran faster, stopping once for deep, heaving breaths.

She arrived at the Molly Bee headframe before some of the rescuers who were summoned from nearby mines. She backed away when any of the miners, and later the wives, tried to pull her away from the hoist. All afternoon, standing there in silence, with no one to comfort her, Della Olympia Anders kept her agonizing vigil by the hoist, waiting for Papa to reappear so she could throw herself into his arms and apologize for hot words spoken in anger that morning.

Her stomach was growling in earnest as the sky darkened and the high plateau air turned cool. Drooping but no less determined, her mind went into high alert when she heard murmured voices and then saw glances in her direction. As the hoist started to creak its way to the surface, she moved forward, hopeful.

She was thrust back and then led away screaming, but not before she caught a glimpse of blood-covered canvas spread over a body. She screamed all the way down the mountain, slung over a rescuer's back. She mercifully fainted, and then she woke up in her teacher's house, where she was told that Papa wasn't coming home any more. A week later, after the funeral, she was on her way to unknown relatives in Salt Lake City, her name and the Salt Lake address pinned to her coat, wearing another child's shoes.

That was it, but it was enough. The images went away and she was again standing at the Banner Mine. *I didn't need that*, Della thought. *Please God, no more. Not tonight.*

Doing her best to stay out of the way and quiet, Della remained by the silent hoist. *I will never do this again*, spooled in and out of her brain as the hours passed. She had brief moments of hope when the hoist moved down the shaft carrying new miners to shovel out the rock fall, and resurfaced with tired men who shook their heads and walked away for water first of all, then bread and jam.

Hope died away as the stars wheeled about in the sky and planets, those solitary travelers of Greek mythology, bowed out. Dawn was making a tentative effort when Della heard a shout from down in the shaft and the hoist creaked into life. She moved closer to the shaft.

"You shouldn't be here, Mrs. Davis," sounded surprisingly like, "Go away little girl." She shook her head, determined that no one would throw her over his shoulder this time and drag her away, no matter how frightful the sight. She grabbed onto one of the metal bars when one of the men attempted to move her.

"Don't touch me," she hissed. "My father will be here soon." Her words startled her.

Who am I? she asked herself. "I'm sorry. Please, what do you know?"

No one answered her, and it felt like the Molly Bee all over again. Her tired mind finally rebelled. She edged closer, desperate to see what was coming up in the hoist.

"Move that woman!"

"Don't you touch me!" she yelled back.

She knelt as the hoist rose until she could look inside the cage. How could she be twelve and twenty-five at the same time? She was anxious for her husband. She was also filled with guilt over angry words hurled at her father that she could not take back now.

"Steady," she heard as the hoist slowed. She held her breath; the voice sounded familiar.

She leaned closer to look inside and recoiled in horror at the sight of another bloody canvas. She pressed her hands to her face and screamed, moved forward on her knees, and was only stopped from falling into the shaft by a firm hand on her waistband that jerked her back and away. She lay there on the dusty ground, sobbing.

"*M cara?* My God, Della."

Devastated, she looked up as the bloody man climbed out of the hoist and two other men went in to crouch beside the figure under the canvas and then pick him up carefully.

Through tears and a glaze of weird memory, she now saw her father in the man who knelt beside her and took her so carefully in his arms. "Papa? I didn't mean what I said. Please believe me." She grabbed the front of his shirt and shook him. "Forgive me."

"Nothing to forgive, *m cara*," Owen said to her, "but Della, it's me."

She frowned, well aware of the enormity of her guilt. At least this time she wasn't alone on the slope, even if she knew she had earned a great scold from her father. But who was this man holding her close? He didn't seem like Frederick Anders, risen from the grave, when she knew he was truly dead and buried in Colorado.

Slowly, that hand in her mind, the one that had unloosed so many unwanted images, disappeared like smoke. The air was bitter cold, dawn was coming, and she was lying by the hoist at the Banner Mine, cradled in her husband's arms, the little girl gone.

Owen spoke over his shoulder to a man carrying a black bag. "It's not my blood," she heard. "I'm fine, Doctor. A bruise here and there. Take care of Aaron. His leg is badly broken. Send the hoist down again for the others. We cleared a passage through to Level Two."

She breathed deep into his shirt and realized finally that no matter how many times she had washed that particular old shirt, it was always going to smell a little like coal.

She looked into her husband's eyes, saw all the exhaustion, smelled the sweat and man odor, and felt the rock dust and grit against her skin. Without a murmur, she let him fold her into his arms. "Owen, I wanted to apologize to you this morning," she whispered. "I said hard things."

"So did I. Let's forget them."

With new strength, she clutched his bloody shirt, which she knew was going in the burn barrel at first opportunity. "You need to know the awful thing I did."

"Tell me. Tell me right now."

Too many people crowded around them. Della felt her breath coming in gasps as men blocked the breathable air. In misery, she listened as her husband quietly told everyone to back away and leave them alone. She heard what sounded like an argument, which he won handily. After the hoist came up the second time, she heard him speaking to the rest of his crew, telling them to go home and get some sleep.

"I'll see you three after Thanksgiving," he said. "You tell Aaron that I expect him there too, or we'll meet at his house. We have some planning to do."

She touched his cheek to get his attention. "Angharad and Mr. Weisman are sleeping by the bonfire."

"When you see the assayer on the way down, tell him all is well, and we will join him later. I'm busy now."

The last man left the slope, and the hoist was silent. Della started to shiver. Someone had kindly left several blankets. In a moment, Owen had cocooned them in the blankets.

She couldn't let her courage desert her, not now. "Owen, please listen to me. I did a terrible thing."

"How bad could it be?"

She put her hand on his chest, curling her fingers around the fabric of his shirt, hoping to keep him there, even though she knew he would be disgusted with her.

"I know what happened now. On the last day of his life, I quarreled with my father over a locket," she whispered, still too horrified to speak loud. "He said we couldn't afford it. I told him I never wanted to see him again."

When she started to weep, he said something low in his throat that maybe wasn't even words. He pulled her closer. Maybe he wasn't going to be upset with her beyond redemption. It gave her the courage to finish.

She didn't flinch when he wiped her eyes with his dirty hands, then pinched the mucus from her nose. "I felt wretched. I was going to be at the mine to apologize when he came off his shift."

She wailed out loud then. Owen rested his hand against her head and pulled her even closer to his heart. "I couldn't apologize! Will you forgive me?"

She didn't know who she was asking to forgive her. The chance with Papa was gone. She felt a burning need to make sure her husband knew how spiteful she had been. Maybe he would forgive her. Maybe he would not. She had kept this awful thing bottled up inside her for years and it had to come out, whether he liked it or not.

"Have you ever told anyone else this?" he asked quietly.

"No. I was so ashamed."

"Ashamed of what, my love?"

Why was this smart man so dense? Didn't he grasp what a fearful thing it was to wish her father dead and never be able to take it back?

"My cruelty, my hard words that I could not take back. Owen, you need to know what I did! It was shameful and spiteful."

She sat up quickly and felt immediately lightheaded when she tried to stand. She staggered and Owen pulled her down, his expression showing no disgust, only deep concern. How could he be so kind in the face of her petty spite aimed at someone who didn't deserve it?

"I *wanted* to tell someone," she said, knowing she might as well finish this mess.

"Why didn't you? I think I know. Think carefully. Breathe along with me."

She did as he said, until the ground she lay on quit spinning. She summoned back that mental hand and forced it open, remembering the sad-beyond-words child who arrived in Salt Lake City, thrown to the mercy of merciless people.

"Aunt Caroline wouldn't let me cry about my father," Della said at last, regretting the hardness of her tone but knowing that her husband deserved the truth. "She said he was a wicked man and good riddance. He wasn't wicked, Owen!"

"Certainly he wasn't. He was just trying to navigate life like all of us. She wouldn't let you cry?"

"No. I never could confess what I had said to him, that morning before he . . . Owen, please forgive me."

"There's nothing to forgive, Della Davis. Della Davis. I do like the sound of that," he said. "There's nothing to forgive. There never was."

She sat up, wondering how a man could be so dense. "Owen, I did a terrible thing! You're not taking this seriously."

"You did a *childish* thing. You were ready to apologize, weren't you?"

"So ready."

He kissed her cheek, must have liked it, and kissed it again. "Della, let me share something that every parent knows. I am confident you will know it someday too, with our own little ones. Shh, shh, we'll have them.

Right now, I have seven years of prior experience, so pay attention."

Owen sat up then. He straddled her, put his hands on her shoulders as she lay on the ground and put his forehead against hers. She couldn't have moved if she wanted to. "Della Davis, you were twelve years old and you were upset with your father."

"I was wicked and mean!"

"You were twelve," he repeated firmly. "There have been times when Angharad would have happily roasted me over an open flame for some infraction or another." He gave her head a gentle shake. "It passed." He repeated it more softly. "It passed. End of story. Done. Forgiven. Not remembered by either of us."

"Yes, but . . ."

"The only problem with your story was timing. I am certain your father had forgotten the whole matter hours before the rock fall. I am certain because I have been there with my daughter. Ask any parent."

She lay there in silence, absorbing his words. She wanted to believe him. She looked into his face, looked deep into the man she loved. She nodded.

"I don't really like myself right now," she admitted.

"I like you. I like you a lot. You'll like yourself again." He sat back on her. "I have my own challenges right now, and they put us at cross purposes. I'll admit it."

He turned toward the hoist. "I know precisely how to fix the Banner Mine. Level Three held quite well when that blast went off. We'll see how much timber Uncle Jesse will let me use on the *other* levels before he squawks."

"Owen, I can't stay here."

"No, you can't. You and Angharad are going to Provo."

She struggled to sit up, but he held her there. "You don't want me anymore?" she asked, her heart breaking again. Was it possible for a heart to break so much in one night?

"Nothing could be further from the truth."

"You're sending me away. You just said so."

"For your own good. For Angharad's good. I want you to return to Provo, get a job, enroll Angharad in the Maeser School, and do some calm thinking."

"But . . ."

He put his fingers to her lips. "Having trouble breathing?" he teased and got off her.

She sat up and he held her close. "There's one thing you need to do. No, two things. One at a time. You need to grieve for your father."

Della nodded. He was right. "The other?"

"You need to talk to your Uncle Karl and . . ."

"Never."

"Think about that one."

"Don't leave me."

"Never. Angharad is going with you. Would I send my precious child with you if I planned to abandon you? You know I would not."

She couldn't deny that. "And you'll be here in this mining camp, a place I hate like no other?" There, she admitted it. "No more mines for me."

"I have a job to finish right here. When it's done, we'll have to talk."

She saw the tears on his face. It was her turn to kiss his cheek, like it, and kiss him again.

She felt a welcome flash of understanding. Maybe she finally understood what he had been saying, almost ever since the disaster at Winter Quarters. "You're grieving for your friends by making the Banner Mine safe. And I am grieving too, but differently. Neither way is wrong, is it?"

"No, miss," he said. She heard all the sorrow. "We both need a little time and space. We're going to Provo tomorrow."

Chapter 34

To Owen's great relief, it was surprisingly easy to leave Knightville for a few days. They were on the afternoon train to Spanish Fork and then Provo with time to spare.

After he and Della walked from the Banner Mine's headframe, arms around each other's waists—not sure who was holding up whom—they made it off the mountain by moving slowly enough for Angharad and Mr. Weisman.

After bidding Mr. Weisman goodnight (or good morning because the sun was up), they took the train to Knightville. They stumbled into bed, clothes and dirt in all.

Della needed no encouragement to pack. After a short visit to the hospital in Eureka, where Aaron, his injured crewmember, was dopey but doing well, Owen gathered the rest of his men in the carpenter's building, shut down the equipment, and said he would be back on Monday to begin again.

Comrades now, where they had been boss and crew before, they sat together, comparing notes on what they had seen. Even the Lithuanian, silent mostly because of language challenges, drew a diagram of possibilities, giving Owen more ideas of how to make a successful timbering even better.

Mr. Weisman's sorrowful expression as he lamented the loss of his secretary meant more diplomacy in the assayer's office. Once Owen told him all that Della had been harboring up in her mind for years, Saul give him his blessing and a mild threat.

"She needs this time, no doubt," he said, and then he shook his finger at Owen. "You had better do some thinking of your own, or someone else will take your place."

"She already has her champions," Owen said, thinking of Dr. Isgreen. "I'm a tenacious man and she chose me, remember." He patted Saladin and put Della's pay envelope in his pocket. It felt suspiciously heavy, but he knew better than to object and trade on Mr. Weisman's dignity and kind heart.

He did borrow a few dollars from the envelope in Silver City's Western Union office to send a lengthy telegram to the Knights and hope for the best from that quarter. When he arrived in Knightville, his women were packed and ready to go. He overpaid the Tates' two boys to carry their luggage to the tracks. Owen carried Angharad's dollhouse, with its small door locked and board slid in place in the back to keep the little inhabitants and their furniture inside.

When Della and Angharad waited on the platform, Owen went back to snatch up some clothing for himself. He looked around. Except for Angharad's absent dollhouse, everything was still in place. He walked to the bedroom he shared with his wife and sighed to think how much he was going to miss the simple warmth of her in bed. One more look confirmed his worst fear—when a woman leaves a home, it might as well be a castle sacked by Norsemen and abandoned.

Owen held Angharad all the way to Provo, Della tucked close to his side. He wanted to hold her too, but this was a train with other passengers, and they might think he was taking liberties. Each turn of the wheels made him second-guess the wisdom of letting Della and Angharad out of his sight.

He had no doubt now that a mining camp, any mining camp, was no place for either of his girls. How could he convince Della that he would never leave her? He knew she wanted to believe him, but seriously, when had people who should have cared for her *not* let her down?

He had let her down too, let her down hard, dragging her right back to a mining camp when he said he was done with them. He wasn't proud of that, but to his way of thinking, he owed safer mines to the memory of his friends. His late mother would have rolled her eyes and made a stringent comment about *that* being the question for the ages. He didn't let himself think what Richard Evans would say.

He let his ladies sleep against him, not proud of the tracks of tears on both faces, and truth to tell, his own. From the wary glances that came his way, other travelers must have wondered why this little trio was so tightly bound together and sorrowful. Let them wonder.

When Della woke up, she started and gasped, as if wondering for a second where she was. "You're fine, I'm here," he whispered. He felt his insides curl as he watched the relief on her face turn wary and sad. Maybe this was how she looked on that trip from Colorado to Salt Lake twelve years ago.

After the train pulled into Spanish Fork and they changed trains for Provo, he won a small victory, mainly because he had no intention of losing this round.

"I am giving you forty dollars for the rest of November," he whispered. "I'll send more in December. You needn't find a job."

"Oh, but I want to work," she countered.

Aha. He had her. "Very well, if you must, but I'm still giving you forty dollars." That was the bigger issue in his mind, anyway. "No argument on that, Della Anders Davis," he said.

"Oh, the dreaded three names," she teased, just a mild tease, but the only one in days. "Very well. I accept."

He had kept the extra key to their house in Provo. He opened the door, remembering how he had carried her across the threshold in May.

He carried Angharad's dollhouse into her old room, pulled out the hooked board, and left her there to rearrange her family and furniture. By then Della had wandered into their bedroom. She took her hat off with a sigh, unbuttoned her traveling suit, took off her shoes, and lay down. He covered her with a blanket, told Angharad he was walking over to the Knights, and left his ladies.

Their faces serious, Uncle Jesse and Amanda sat him down in the parlor and heard the whole story. When he finished, he regarded Amanda's tears, followed by remorse.

"I can't help my regret that I did not do more. After all, Caroline is my cousin."

"Della hid it well because she was told to. She was only twelve and did not understand how to manage her feelings," he said. Frustrated, he smacked his fist into his other hand. "The Anders could have helped her though this so easily!" He shook his head. "I'm sorry."

"And we are too," Jesse said. "Heartily so." He rested his hand on Owen's shoulder. "We can take it from here."

He nodded, grateful for the Knights. "Sir, I'm heading back Sunday afternoon. I need your permission to order more lumber. That second drift needs the work."

"You have it," Jesse said promptly.

"I might be working myself out of a job."

"Not for long. I have other mines." Uncle Jesse peered closer. "There's more involved here than a mine, isn't there?"

"Considerably, sir, and now I'll visit my sister-in-law. Over the carriage house?"

He found Mabli Reese in a wonderfully cozy apartment. With no preamble, he told her everything. She took it all in, sighed when he sighed, and reminded him he was still her brother-in-law. "Bring Angharad over here Friday night and Saturday night. You and Della need the house to yourselves."

He could have blushed, but why? The smart money in dealing with Welsh women was not to appear gormless and without a functioning brain. "Aye, we do need that time, Della and I. I'll see you tomorrow."

She took his arm before he could leave and held tight to him. "And while you are alone there in Tintic, you need to ask yourself just how much you owe your departed friends," she said, as serious as he had ever seen her.

He had to admit it was a good question. He also understood the other side of the coin, the side Mabli didn't mention. "And which is more important: those friends or my wife, eh?"

"I believe that to be true," she said. "Be wise, little Owen."

What could he say to that?

"Dinner is at two o'clock," she told him, her expression more kindly now. "If Angharad would like to help me, send her over by half nine, young Owen."

Thoughtful, he walked home, pleased to see his house well lit now, and smoke coming from the chimney. Never mind that supper was crackers and geriatric jam found in the back of the pantry, plus some apples and cheese that the neighbors had brought over, seeing the house lit again and wondering why, since Mabli was gone.

This modest meal was followed an hour later by Mabli herself, bearing a loaf of oat bread that made Della cry. Owen walked Mabli back to the Knights' while Della heated water in the tin tub, brought in from the back porch and readied for Angharad. His daughter was clean and in her nightgown when he returned, ready for a kiss and bed.

"Mam's washing," his daughter said. "She told me she needed her back scrubbed. I told her I could, but she wanted you."

He kissed her, heard her prayers, and tucked her in, listening as she sang "Ar Hyd y Nos," then took himself into the kitchen in time to scrub his wife's back.

With wisdom he didn't know he possessed, Owen did nothing more than hold Della that night, and the night after, content to talk about Wales and his mother and father, and the brothers who died in Abercarn, and his baptism when he was eight. He talked and Della listened, chuckling a little at the funny stories, but more often sleeping a deep and solid sleep, which gave him unfathomable peace.

When he headed for the depot after Sacrament Meeting on Sunday, he left Angharad smiling and ready to start school Monday morning. Della was on the verge of tears, so he took her hand and led her into the kitchen. He flipped the calendar to December and tapped it.

"I don't know when I'll be back, but I will be back. Never doubt me, Della."

She nodded, unable to speak. She held out her hands to him in a pleading gesture that went right to his heart, then lowered them to her sides, her dark eyes deep pools of worry. He took her by the shoulders, running his hands down them, committing to memory the feel of her, as if he could ever forget.

"Go to Winter Quarters and talk to Dr. Isgreen. Tell him everything that happened to you."

"I won't. You can't make me."

"Then I'll write him a letter and tell him to come here," he said, knowing he was riding roughshod over the woman he adored. "Let me give you another unwelcome task. Talk to Uncle Karl. Make him tell you everything about your father. Learn all you can."

"I will not talk to Uncle Karl," she said, and her chin went up. The look she gave him told Owen that a few thousand years ago, the Greeks must truly have struck terror in the Medes and Persians.

"Think about it, *m cara*. Above all, it's time for you to grieve a good man. And write to me. I'm going to miss you and your lovely bones."

She laughed at that, which suggested all was not lost, not if he did what he said he would and did not add to his felonies by continuing to like mining.

He kissed her hard on the mouth, and she threw her arms around him and kissed him back. "I still won't visit my uncle," she said, but she softened her words with another kiss, and one more for good luck.

She took his hand and pressed it to her heart. "Be careful, and for heaven's sake, my love, start singing."

"Only if you do what I ask." He could bargain with the best of them. He wasn't Welsh for nothing.

"*Ask?*" She gave him that flinty glare again. "You are making demands on me. I will remind you that women have the vote in Utah, and I am not entirely powerless."

Hardly. What she lacked in logic, she made up for with another kiss.

"I will visit Dr. Isgreen, and you will return here singing," she said.

"And your uncle?" He was enjoying this Della.

"I have my limits. You're at the outer edge right now, my man."

He smiled at that. He picked up his valise, put on his hat, doffed it in a grand gesture, and left without a backward glance. He was on his outer edge too, and it would never do to look back.

He did look back at the corner. She still stood on the porch, even though the wind had picked up and blew cold. She raised her hand in farewell. He waved to her. He stood there until she went inside and closed the door.

Chapter 35

Take that, Owen Davis, you bully, Della thought as she walked Angharad to Maeser School on Monday morning and enrolled her, to Principal Holyoke's delight.

After escorting them to the door of Miss Wilkins's classroom, where Angharad's teacher greeted her with a beaming smile, Mr. Holyoke walked Della to the main door and promised to see what he might find in the way of school district employment for her.

She started for her house, then let the realization wash over her that there was no need to hurry anywhere. Owen was back in Knightville and probably eating crackers and old cheese. He was a terrible cook. Unwilling to deprive Mrs. Tate of the weekly two dollars, she had ordered Owen to continue the arrangement, except that this time Mrs. Tate would provide him with supper and a lunch for his tin pail.

She knew he would follow through, because he was Owen, well aware how much the Tates needed the extra money, and he did like to eat. And because he was Owen, she knew he would find a way to increase his weekly tab to three dollars.

Della switched from a walk to an amble. She allowed herself a flash of anger at Owen Davis. Too bad *she* couldn't give Mrs. Tate a few dollars more to rail at him regularly for thinking he could bring back dead friends by making a mine safer somewhere far distant from Winter Quarters.

She wanted to stay angry with him, but she couldn't. She loved the rascal to distraction, and she honestly admitted that he had every right to grieve for his friends in his own way, as she now had the right and duty to grieve for her father, even after all these years.

Her amble took her to the park. The leaves were gone now and the creek dried up, but she sat there anyway, bowed her head, and cried for Frederick Anders.

She began with a silent plea for his forgiveness, something she had done countless times. To her surprise, this time her mind didn't turn her into a child again and force her to relive the quarrel, flouncing away from her father and shouting angry, unforgettable words, a sorry spectacle never repeated out loud until she shared them with her husband at the Banner Mine. She acknowledged she felt sad and wounded, and perhaps that was all right too.

Hands to her face, she allowed herself the privilege of mourning a good man. She thought of her years in an even harder apprenticeship in Salt Lake City, sad beyond belief and then filled with anger that Papa would dare die and leave her at the mercy of his relatives. Fearsome remorse for even thinking she could feel such anger against the man she loved always followed. Who understood that? She didn't then, but she began to understand a little now because she was almost twenty-five and thoughtful, and not twelve and ruled by younger emotions.

All these conflicting feelings bombarded her and left her shaken. Maybe she did need to visit Dr. Isgreen in Winter Quarters. Maybe she needed a medical opinion on her brain, if he could offer one.

Back home, she wrote a letter to Dr. Isgreen, asking when she and Angharad could come to Winter Quarters, because she needed to talk. She found a stamp and walked to the post office, breathing deep of the winter air. She sent the letter on its way and discovered there was mail for her.

"Been saving it, Mrs. Davis," the man behind the counter said. "I didn't have a forwarding address."

She arranged for delivery again and took the mail. One letter for Owen was from Gomer Thomas in Salt Lake City that she forwarded to Knightville. She wanted to toss it because she remembered Mr. Thomas was Utah's chief mine inspector. What business could he have with her rascal husband?

The other letter was addressed to her, a thick envelope on fine paper, from Mrs. Kristina Aho. She gave a gasp of delight—she knew Auerbach's sold wonderful stationery for all occasions, including weddings—and opened it on the spot.

"Kristina, you did it," Della said out loud. She found a bench by a wall of mailboxes and opened the inside envelope, an invitation to a wedding at the First Presbyterian Church in Salt Lake.

She glanced at the date, afraid she had missed it, but no, Kristina Aho, widowed too young by coal, wished the pleasure of Mr. and Mrs. Owen Davis and Angharad Davis's company at a wedding this coming Saturday. Still in the post office, Della bought a penny card and accepted with equal pleasure for her and Angharad. She sent the postcard on its way, pleased that Kristina's life would be easier and that Pekka and Reet would have a father.

A wedding coming right up meant a trip to Provo Cooperative Mercantile Institution, where her practical nature reigned triumphant with bath towels and wash-cloths. Gift wrapping only cost a dime, so she indulged.

Her indulgence continued with a stop at the Palace Drug Store, where she indulged again with a cherry phosphate, enjoyed it, and drank another one. *See here, Della, you are frittering,* she told herself, and felt not even slightly repentant, although she did burp a lot on the walk home.

Sitting at the kitchen table that night while Angharad finished a page of addition, Della wrote her first letter to her husband, describing how she had frittered. She hesitated only a moment before telling him she had written to Dr. Isgreen, requesting an appointment. She hesitated a little longer and then decided not to mention that she also wrote to ask the doctor about fertility. It was easier to include a paragraph on Kristina Aho's upcoming wedding to Mr. Whalley and describe the gift of towels.

She had no hesitation in telling him that, all in all, it was a good day, even if she had cried for her father and wallowed in some misery. She set down her fountain pen, wondering if it really was misery. There was no one she had to hide her tears from, no Aunt Caroline to shake her and remind her that tears were a waste of time for a scoundrel. All she had to do was feel sad for a good man gone, and not worry about the Aunt Carolines of the world.

She continued the bedtime ritual she and Owen had established for Angharad, with the usual prayer and then singing "Ar Hyd y Nos."

She did something different then and lay down with her stepdaughter, asking her if there was anything she wished to talk about. "It is like this, Angharad," she said. "I always wanted someone to ask me about my day, and if I had any problems. No one ever did, but you may tell me about your day, if you'd like. Any subject."

Angharad considered the matter. "One of the boys teased me because I don't talk like everyone else," she said finally. "He said I have an accent."

"What did you say to that?"

"I gave him my best smile and told him that it is a privilege to be Welsh," Angharad said. "I told him I can speak two languages." She laughed. "I asked him how many languages *he* could speak. He didn't bother me after that."

"Bravo, Angharad," Della said, impressed. She had enough room on the bottom of her letter to Owen to include that and compliment him on raising a forthright child.

She could have died with the loveliness of the next moment, when Angharad patted her cheek and asked, "How was your day, Mam?"

"I thought about my father and cried a little," Della told her, touched to her heart. "I've already told you about the wedding we are going to on Saturday."

"Will Mrs. Aho wear a beautiful white dress with a train?" Angharad asked.

"Probably not, because she has been married before and white is for first-time brides," Della replied. "I know it will be lovely because Mrs. Aho has impeccable taste and an artist's eye."

Angharad nodded. "Did you miss Da today?"

"With all my heart."

"Why does he want us here and not in Knightville?"

"Because it is too hard for me and you," Della said, after gathering up her diminished stock of courage, weighing it and finding it not so wanting that she could not provide an honest answer. "We worry too much when he is in the mine."

"What will he do?"

"I don't know," Della said frankly. No sense in lying to a child. "I hope when this project is done he will join us."

"Doesn't he know that we need him here with us?"

"He's remembering his friends who are gone now and wants to make mines safer for others too," Della said.

Angharad sighed. She raised her arms, spread her fingers and looked through them. "*We* need him."

"We do. Angharad, would you like me to tell you about my father, at least, when I learn more about when he was a boy?"

"Aye, Mam."

Angharad closed her eyes and settled herself for sleep. Della lay beside her until she slept, then went to the kitchen. She sat a long moment with paper and fountain pen in front of her, then wrote to Karl Anders, the man she was never going to see or write or think of again.

Maybe she had been hasty about that.

Chapter 36

With a tip of his hat, the postman delivered three letters to Della on Friday afternoon: one from Knightville, one from Scofield, and the other from Salt Lake City. She opened the one from Knightville first.

As onerous it was to have a perfectly serviceable husband living at some distance, she felt a layer of callous around her heart drop away at his salutation: My Darling. He wrote in Welsh next, then added in English that he wouldn't translate it until they were together again.

My word, Owen, she thought, as she read another paragraph of love, in English. Food followed love, as he went into a paragraph rhapsodizing Sister Tate's cooking. Business was next, with a cut-and-dried sentence or two about measurements on Level Two, which had been cleared of rock and rubble now and was the focus of the carpenter work. She couldn't help that her heart raced a little faster.

Compassion followed, with a report on Aaron's broken leg, and how Mr. Weisman had put Owen's youngest crew member to work learning to type. *Aaron is already whining about Saul's handwriting*, she read.

He asked if she had found a job yet and then asked about Angharad's first week of school, said he hoped they would have a pleasant time in Salt Lake at Mrs.

Aho's wedding, and concluded with a paragraph that made her frown. *The letter you forwarded from Gomer Thomas fair amazed* me, he wrote. *He has invited me to be his assistant mine inspector for the state of Utah, with a salary of one hundred dollars a month. I told him I would think about it, but I shouldn't, should I?*

"No, you shouldn't, you duplicitous man," Della said out loud, and not softly either, because the boy playing pick up sticks on his porch next door looked up, startled.

He had enclosed a letter for Angharad, so she set it by Angharad's place at the table, after a peek inside to see what he had drawn for his daughter. She smiled to see a perfectly dejected-looking Saladin—snout on paws, eyes mournful—with a thought bubble reading, "I want to hoooowl without my girls."

What now? The letter from Dr. Isgreen, or the one in the envelope from Anders, Court and Landry? That was no contest. She opened Emil's letter, pleased to read that he would be at the wedding tomorrow and they could talk then. *What you're telling me is intriguing, indeed. I believe I can enlighten you about Sigi*, she read. *See you at the First Presbyterian Church.*

Stop by my office, Uncle Karl's letter began, with no preamble. *You know I work on Saturdays. I want to see you.* That was all. Owen's letter went under her pillow, Emil Isgreen's on her bureau, and Uncle Karl's in the trash.

Considering that the Interurban was leaving at six the next morning, Della stayed up too late answering Owen's letter. The letter wasn't long, because she knew she would write more after the wedding. She finally closed her eyes and dreamed of nothing more frightening than catching the train.

Angharad was so excited about the double delight of riding the train to Salt Lake and going to a wedding that she had trouble sitting still as the Interurban chugged its way through the small towns between Provo and the capitol.

"We're going to a wedding," Della confided to the lady across the aisle, who, from the expression on her face, seemed to think children should neither be seen nor heard.

Della knew Angharad liked a good story and could probably sit still with the proper encouragement. "My darling, you will agree that I am an amateur at raising a daughter."

"I believe you're doing fine, Mam," Angharad said generously.

"You'll think I'm a complete idiot, but let me tell you something I did once to my poor father."

There was no need to drag out the entire story, not with her stepdaughter's father possibly even underground as they sat there on the Interurban, but she held Angharad close and told her about an angry twelve-year-old who scolded her father for not buying her a locket on a chain.

"I was furious at him, and I said some things I shouldn't have," she concluded. "I worried about it for years, until your father told me that he made mistakes too, in raising a daughter. Maybe I shouldn't have worried so much. What do you think?"

"Da is right," Angharad said with no hesitation. She sighed. "I shouted at him a few times, but that was a long time ago. I think I was four. Maybe five." Her brow puckered as she seemed to consider the matter. "He has learned a lot in the last two years. I haven't needed to yell much."

Della smiled inside at that, knowing Angharad's artless reasoning would go into a letter headed to Knightville soon. "What does he do to make you smile?"

In answer, Angharad took out the little notebook and pencil she always carried in her handbag, the bag Owen had told Della belonged to Gwyna. Bracing her arm against the rhythmic swaying of the railcar, she drew a circle and quick lines and dots and then held the notebook out to Della.

"This is me sometimes." She turned the circle upside down, and Della saw the frown. "Da turns it over, and look." The smiling face grinned at them both. "We both do this. If I am angry about something, he waits a while, and then I find a smiling face somewhere. He says I can do it too, whenever I want."

What a lovely man I have married, Della thought, charmed by the drawing. "I haven't seen one of these around the house. This is new to me."

"We've been happy," Angharad said simply, which filled Della's cup to overflowing. "Now tell me about the locket. Did you ever get one?"

"Alas, no."

"Do you still want one?"

Did she? "I'm not certain," Della replied.

A glance at Angharad's face told her that was an insufficient answer, so Della did better. "What I wanted was a heart-shaped locket. All the girls in my classroom had them—well, if I am honest, it was one girl, and her father was the mine foreman. She opened the locket and showed us a lock of her hair. Angharad, I envied her because she had long blonde hair, and it was straight. Imagine that!"

Her stepdaughter laughed out loud. "Sometimes this summer when I should have been asleep, I heard you and Da laughing in your room. I asked him what was so funny, and he said he laughed because you made faces when you tried to comb your hair."

"My hair is no laughing matter," she said, feigning irritation, which made Angharad laugh louder and earn a glare from that censorious woman across the aisle who probably never knew what it was like to have fun with a child.

Trust Angharad to focus on the matter. "Was it the locket or the straight hair you wanted?"

"Probably both." Della couldn't help a laugh of her own. "As it was, I got neither, and somehow I survived."

They looked at each other with real charity. *Gwyna, I will do my best to help raise your lovely child*, she thought as she put her arm around Angharad. *She is my treasure too.*

When they reached Salt Lake City, a glance at her timepiece told Della that not even a brisk walk would get them to the church on time. Not entirely sure what to do, she took Angharad by the hand and walked quickly to the curb. She was familiar with trolleys from her days of teaching at the Westside School, but they had just missed the one headed north on State Street. She had enough money, but how did one hail a cab?

"It appears you could use some help."

She turned around, surprised, then smiled. "Oh my goodness, are you here to rescue us, Dr. Isgreen?"

"Nothing simpler. Just arrived myself, ready for a wedding."

Angharad clapped her hands. "Dr. Isgreen, I still have that menu you gave me from Scofield!"

"I hoped you would keep that," he said, and he tipped his hat to her and Della. "I enjoyed squiring two of my favorite ladies to dinner." He glanced at Della with a rueful smile. "Seems so long ago."

It was years and years, Della thought, struck by how long ago mere months seemed, when so much had happened between that pleasant evening and this moment. "Emil, it's so good to see you."

He winked at her and stepped into the street, holding up his hand. An automobile with the sign "Taxi" fixed prominently to the roof pulled up and stopped. Angharad stared, her mouth open. She grabbed Della's hand.

"Mam, I have never been in one of these. Is it *safe*?"

Dr. Isgreen leaned down. "We'll tell the cabby to drive carefully." He opened the rear door. "Better climb in. We have a wedding to go to, and brides don't like to wait, or so I have been told."

They crowded into the taxi and Emil gave directions. He leaned back and clapped his arm around Angharad. "Are you ready for an adventure?"

"My stars," was all the child could say.

As the taxi pulled into traffic and darted ahead, Emil turned his attention to Della. She saw all the kindness on his open face, and also that probing doctor look, the one she needed to see.

"What about you, Mrs. Davis? Ready for an adventure?"

Chapter 37

Dressed in a pale-gray gown with lace on the bodice, and with a smile on her face, Kristina Aho became Mrs. James Whalley. Their faces serious, Pekka and his little sister Reet stood beside their mother as she quietly made her vows in front of the altar with the tall man whose heart was so generous that Della had to reach for her handkerchief and then share it with Angharad.

She sniffed and thought about how the practically magisterial Mr. Whalley had overlooked her own clumsiness in Auerbach's Menswear until she got the hang of selling stockings, collars, shirts, and braces to gentlemen, a perfectly wonderful summer job. She had heard the whispers in the break room of the dignified man's own heartbreak of a wife dead in childbirth years earlier, and furthered her own education about sorrow that the eye can't see.

And here he was, smiling as she had never seen Mr. Whalley smile, and gazing down at all the loveliness beside him that came with an instant family. Della wanted for Owen to be seated beside her so she could hold his hand and lean against him. She watched as the four of them walked down the aisle to a triumphal march, and she silently begged her husband to give up mines. She remembered the tears on Kristina's face as she buried her Matti in Scofield's now-overcrowded cemetery. She saw no tears now, only love for the new husband beside her.

"Time has a way of moving us on, hasn't it?" Dr. Isgreen said on her other side.

She nodded, too full of all kinds of emotion to speak. She wanted to be here; she wanted to be in Knightville with Owen. She remembered Matti's funeral a little over a year ago in the fall of 1899, her first brush with death in the mines. She wanted to soak in all the love and beauty right here and right now and forget the sight of Matti's body under a bloody piece of canvas.

Her mind seemed to race back and forth, tugging at her sleeve, as she thought of all the miners who died in May. She repeated her own agony of placing paper flowers her students had made on the bodies as they lay in the makeshift morgue that her classroom had become. Later in the church's reception room, she watched Kristina throw her bouquet of real flowers toward an eager handful of ladies. All the images jumbled in her mind until she had to sit down and try not to shake, try not to appear anything but joyous, in this room of happy people.

She wanted to be alone, but Emil Isgreen sat beside her. "It's not easy," was all he said, which gave her permission to turn her face into his sleeve and cry.

"Why am I remembering the hardest things right now?" she managed to say finally. Thank the Almighty that everyone's attention, even Angharad's, was focused on a new bride cutting a cake. She took Emil's handkerchief gratefully.

"Because you're human," he said. "Because you care deeply. Don't be afraid of it, Della."

In a quiet corner of the reception hall, after Pekka and Reet had taken Angharad to their table for cake and ice cream, Della quickly told Emil Isgreen everything that had happened in Knightville. She glossed over nothing and he listened.

By the time she finished, she felt her heart resume its normal speed. She wiped her eyes, wished they weren't so red, but knew she could manage.

"I know I told you some of this in my letter. Should I be embarrassed for telling you all of this?" she asked.

"Not at all. Allow me a liberty."

She nodded and he put his arm around her shoulder. "I say this as your physician, Della. You may not agree with me, but what you're doing is normal and natural, and by golly, so painful."

She nodded again.

"Let me tell you something else, dear friend. I made my own vow that awful week in Winter Quarters Canyon. With Bishop Parmley's approval, I sent a letter to all the widows, telling that I would provide them and their children a lifetime of free medical care."

Della chuckled at that, a watery sound, but a welcome one to her own ears. "Emil, you're never going to make your fortune treating diseases of the rich, are you?"

He laughed out loud at that, throwing back his head and letting loose with a real guffaw, loud enough for heads to turn in their direction, which appeared to bother him not a bit. If he was anything, the Pleasant Valley Coal Company's doctor was a confident man.

"Guilty as charged, Della," he said. "And you're one of my patients too."

"Thank you," she said simply. "I needed that."

"This is no time for lengthy mental therapy, but I have to share something with you."

"Share away. I think Angharad is on her second or third piece of cake. I'll have to pry her off the ceiling, but that'll keep."

"You're a good mother," he teased. "In your letter, you mentioned Saul Weisman and his Viennese friend Sigi's theories about dreams." He reached in his suit pocket and pulled out two sheets of closely typed paper. "It hasn't been translated entirely into English yet, but there is a Viennese doctor named Sigmund Freud who is making quite a splash in the world of . . . I hardly know what to call it . . . well, I don't know what to call it except mind studies. I have a few excerpts in English, and I look forward to reading the whole work someday. That's your Sigi."

"Sigi," Della repeated, enchanted. "Saul told me that when we sleep, our dreams have a way of expressing events we wouldn't want to talk about."

"He's right. Sitting around in a Viennese coffeehouse, Sigi taught him well. Keep doing what you're doing, Della. You're on the right track. You are healing from a tragic personal loss, and you're talking about it."

She said a silent prayer of thanksgiving for Dr. Isgreen. "And the other matter I wrote you about?" She couldn't help that her face went hot and red. Was there a time when a lady wouldn't blush?

"You're so impatient," Emil said. "Your mind is busy healing now. You have plenty to do." He leaned closer. "Never doubt that, Della. You're on a good path." He laughed again, but softly this time. "In a few years when you're wiping snotty noses and trying to manage a brood of little ones, you'll wonder what you worried about. Feel free to write and tell me about it. I mean, you'll probably want to give some of them away to gypsies."

It was her turn to laugh. "All right! I should quit worrying?"

"Absolutely." He took his arm out from around her shoulder. "I still wish *I* were the lucky man, but I'll find someone as charming as you."

"I have no doubt about that," she told him, and held out her hand.

He shook her hand and stood up with her. "I had better go say something to the pretty bride and give her a kiss, if I dare. Then I'm off to Tooele to visit my mother. On the way back, I'm stopping in Knightville to visit another person who is my patient. He just doesn't know it yet."

She kissed his cheek, grateful beyond measure for the Emil Isgreens of the world. "Emil, is it permissible for me to love you a little bit?"

"You'd better. I'd hate to think I wasted all those years in medical school if there wasn't some adulation involved."

"Oh, you! Do be serious."

"I *am* serious. More than you know. Let me know how things go with you. Write to me if I can help you in any way."

She watched him walk away and quietly closed a chapter in her book of life. She might have closed it sooner, but watching him cross the reception hall, Della knew she had needed Emil Isgreen precisely now.

The next chapter promised to be harder, so she softened it with a pleasant stop first. After her own hug, tears, quick words with Mrs. Whalley, and the promise to visit in a few weeks, she took Angharad to Auerbach's, first for cream cheese and date nut bread and then to the floor with offices.

They walked slowly past the row of pictures her lovely Winter Quarters students had drawn for the good man who was her supreme boss a summer ago. Her stepdaughter paused the longest time in front of her own picture, the one Da had helped her with, showing the two of them drawing a Welsh dragon.

"Da needs a dragon," Angharad said and put her hand in Della's. "He needs a singing dragon."

"Then you'd better draw him one for Christmas," Della said, managing to speak around the lump in her throat.

"I'm all out of Magic Paper," Angharad reminded her.

"I think a dragon for Da deserves something better than the inside paper lining in a man's shirt," she said. "I know just the place."

And I had better find myself a job next week to finance my impulsive whims, Della thought as she led Angharad to Stationery and turned her over to Mr. Hovey, who presided over paper and pens and envelopes and all things artistic.

"Mr. Hovey, we need an artist's sketchbook and colored pencils," she said.

They left Auerbach's two dollars lighter, buoyed up by Mr. Hovey's assurance that nowhere, not even in ZCMI, could they have found better art supplies. Mr. Hovey took the liberty of whispering that he had applied her Auerbach's employee discount, which told her he was going to supply the ten percent difference when she and Angharad left his department. Did a lowly, former Menswear clerk deserve such friends? She decided she did. Dr. Isgreen would have approved.

Anders, Court and Landry, Attorneys at Law. She read the discreet and utterly elegant wrought iron title, collected herself, and opened the door.

Chapter 38

The lobby was empty. Her heart thumping against her corset, Della sat Angharad down and pulled up a wooden chair. "You can use this as your drawing table," she instructed.

She handed the child the copy of Dickens's *The Posthumous Papers of the Pickwick Club* that she had bought from Mr. Hovey for Owen's Christmas present. Owen had told her once how much he loved the book, but he didn't have a copy. "Look through these pages and copy some of the illustrations. We can use that as wrapping paper for Da's gift. I won't be long."

"Where are you going?" Angharad made herself comfortable and took the sketchbook from the bag.

"I need to see my Uncle Karl for a few minutes. It might be longer." She took her cream cheese date bread sandwich from the bag and pointed to the drinking fountain nearby with its column of pointed paper cups. "Keep yourself busy, my love. I'll be back."

The steps to the second floor seemed extra steep, but not steep enough to prevent her from ultimately standing in front of her uncle's office door with the frosted window. She knocked, wincing at how loud it sounded in the silent building.

"Come in."

She opened the door and peered through the area where his secretary ordinarily sat and into the office of

Karl Anders, well-known railroad lawyer, who never lost a case and never cared one iota what happened to the only child of his black-sheep brother.

Perhaps she was too harsh. He greeted her with a pleasant smile and gestured toward his office. He went to close the door, but she stopped him, wondering where her courage came from, she who usually turned so quiet and biddable around her Anders relatives.

In fact, she walked back through the secretary's office and opened the outside door, leaving herself a clean path if she felt like leaping up and running. To his quizzical expression, she merely stated, "Angharad needs to know where I am. I set her to drawing downstairs, but she's just a child. You understand." *Or do you?* she asked herself as he indicated that she sit. *You were never around your own daughters too much. A pity. They turned out much like their mother.*

"I won't monopolize your time, Uncle Karl," she said. "I'm only here because I've been thinking a lot about my father lately. Do you ever think about him?"

She hadn't meant to ask that. At least she said it politely. "I know he was the family ne'er-do-well, but he took good care of me, and I loved him."

Still nothing. She found the gumption to look him full in the face and saw all the uncertainty there and something else. She doubted it was remorse—maybe a second cousin to remorse. Better just forge ahead. "I never thanked you for sending me that letter you probably should have given me years earlier. It made a difference in my life. Imagine what it might have done if I had been able to look for and find my mother."

She had memorized the letter. Even now, it lay in the top drawer of the bureau in her Provo home, nestled among her underthings. "All those years I thought, or was taught to think, that my mother had abandoned me and your brother. Imagine my surprise to learn that she had been dragged away from us by her father, who, I can only assume, had a smaller heart than even you and Aunt Caroline."

He made a sound in his throat that sounded so jarring that it startled her. If she didn't know him better, she might have thought it *was* remorse.

There. She had wanted to say that for years. Through lonely nights that turned into years in the Anders mansion, she had wanted to sob out her sorrow over her father's death, her guilt at their final exchange of words, the shock of thinking her mother had abandoned her. No one in the Anders household had ever wanted to listen. After Aunt Caroline commanded her to be silent, Della had no choice but to bury all the hurt in her mind.

Until now. Until she stood over another hoist in another state, staring down at her own husband helping a wounded man to the surface. As she calmly talked to her uncle, she felt sudden liberation. It was nearly euphoric.

"Anyway, I want to ask you a few things about my father. Can you tell me something about his childhood? I'd like to know a little more, if you please. I'll leave you alone then. I know your time is valuable. If you can just send me a little note now and then, when you remember some childhood incident, I'd like that."

She gave him her brightest smile, because he suddenly looked so sad, so old, so beaten down. She hadn't planned to do this, but she quickly came around his desk and kissed his cheek, amazed at how good that made her feel.

She was almost out the last door when he called to her. She turned around, already thinking ahead to getting a trolley for the ride back to the Interurban depot, her mind on a long, long letter to Owen tonight. "Yes?"

"Sit down for a few minutes. I have something to tell you."

Probably only days ago, a sentence like that from her uncle would have churned her insides into jelly. As it was, she sat, interested but not involved.

"Before he went to the Colorado Plateau, your father did a singular thing for me." He sat down, or rather seemed to fall into his chair, as though his legs were suddenly strangers.

"Uncle?" she asked, worried.

He waved a hand at her. "I'm fine. No, no, I'm not. I should have told you this years ago, and what's more, I should have done something about it."

How bad could it be? Della knew she could handle whatever venom or vitriol he had stockpiled somewhere. She gave him her interested face.

"I always wanted to go to law school," he began, and glanced at the elaborate diploma from the University of Pennsylvania, with its fancy calligraphy, elaborate scrollwork, and Latin phrases. He managed a smile. "Your father thought that was vaguely unmanly. He was a freight hauler then, from Salt Lake to where Fort Duchesne is now. He worked hard and I know he played hard, to your grandfather's distress."

"Aunt Caroline told me years ago he was the black sheep," Della said, remembering all the venom.

"That's not strictly true, Della. Let me tell you what he did." He leaned forward, folded his hands in front of him on the desk, tried to make eye contact, and failed.

As she watched him struggle, she slowly began to realize that of the two brothers, Frederick was not the weak one.

"Father and Fred had a flaming quarrel one night. Fred ran upstairs to pack." Karl managed a self-deprecating laugh with no humor in it. "I was cowering in my room, the good son. Before he left, never to return, he pushed an envelope full of greenbacks under my door. He wrote on it, 'For Law School. I'll send it every year.' There was one hundred dollars in that envelope, Della. He sent it every year until I passed the bar and returned to Utah Territory."

Della stared at him, unable to speak. Her heart breaking, she thought of her own experience with Aunt Caroline, who informed her over breakfast one morning that there was no money for her to go to the University of Utah, and she would have to do it by herself, if at all. Reared in the hard curriculum of Aunt Caroline University, Della hadn't expected any help, but her porridge went down hard, because she was sitting with her cousins, who had elevated the smirk to a fine art. *That* did hurt.

She had only been able to afford a one-year teaching course, and she earned her way through by working summers and after class and on weekends at her old library job. Sitting there in Uncle Karl's office, she realized, to her surprise, that she had managed quite well.

Uncle Karl had to have known what she was thinking. His face had gone pale and he looked away from her.

"I owed Fred four hundred dollars. When I could afford to pay it, I told Caroline I was sending it to him. She said your father would only spend it on liquor and bad women." He bowed his face to his desk. "I listened to her and kept it. I promised myself that you would have it for college someday, if you wanted to go. You were probably about eight then."

There was nothing to say to that, and no force compelling her to sit there and hear more. She got up quietly and left the office. She was halfway down the stairs when she heard Uncle Karl call her name. She looked up at the landing to see him silhouetted there, not quite a man, not quite a shadow.

"Della, come to my house. You and . . . I can't pronounce her name . . . can spend the night. Maybe even visit with Caroline, if she feels up to it."

Quite possibly when Hades freezes over, Della thought. *Why yes, that's when I'll visit.*

"I think not, Uncle Karl," she heard herself say, sounding so kind. "I would only upset her. You two have a Merry Christmas, though."

Angharad had saved Della half of the date bread sandwich, which Della ate as they strolled along toward the depot. The afternoon shadows announced the end of another December day, but there wasn't any breeze and the brisk air felt good after Uncle Karl's office.

On the train, she admired Angharad's *Pickwick* drawings. "We can glue them together and have more than enough to cover the box for Da's book," she said.

"I'll draw him a dragon after I practice a bit more. I want to get it right."

"You will. I think we should roll it up and mail it to him," Della said and found herself unprepared for the worried look Angharad gave her. "Dearest, what's the matter?"

Oh goodness, what to do now? She felt suddenly helpless and stupid when Angharad started to cry. Was this how Frederick Anders and Owen Davis felt, when left to manage a little girl's tears? Being a parent was not for the faint of heart, evidently. She gave her own father a silent round of applause as she worried about this child.

"He's not coming home for Christmas?" Angharad managed to say.

Della pulled her close on her lap as the train swayed on through the darkness. "I know he is coming, my love. I want you to send him that dragon early, as a reminder. He must know how badly we need him." Was it true? Was it wishful thinking? How could she know? Still, there was a child needing comfort, and Della Davis was the duly appointed adult.

She felt Angharad nod against her breast, grateful from her hat to her shoe tops that they could cry and worry and hold each other and never, never be left alone to cry in the darkness.

At that precise moment, she realized she would never think of Angharad as her stepdaughter ever again. They were bound together in this life, and together they would manage whatever came. "Stepdaughter" was for sissies. She closed her eyes against the sight of Uncle Karl sitting in his expensive office with the fancy diploma, paid for by her father, one freight load at a time, and later, one ton of ore at a time.

Papa, you were the best, she thought. *I couldn't be more proud of you if I tried, from now until I die.*

Chapter 39

Her letter to Owen that weekend felt heavy enough to require block and tackle to get to the post office on Monday morning. She drew a Christmas wreath at the bottom of her letter, not to call undue attention to the holiday rapidly approaching but more of a gentle reminder from a wife.

Angharad had covered the kitchen table with dragons: big ones, little ones, dragons with music bubbles and notes coming from fiery maws, the kind of dragons that had probably kept the weaker English away from Wales for centuries, or so Angharad reckoned as she picked one for her teacher and set off to school.

Della reminded her daughter not to be alarmed if she came home and the house was empty. "Uncle Jesse has some scheme he wants to tell me about, and I do not know what to expect."

In Sunday school yesterday, Uncle Jesse had whispered for her to visit him in his new digs in the Knight Building. It had snowed the night before, so she picked her way carefully down Center Street to the red brick building on the corner and inquired within at Knight Investment Company.

No question about it: Uncle Jesse knew how to design an office for maximum effect. He had the corner tower with a view, plus a comfortable sofa—probably to lull would-be investors into somnolence—and a fireplace giving off welcome warmth. He smiled and gave an abracadabra wave of his hand, which made her laugh and put her entirely at ease. She knew this man.

He didn't waste a minute. "Della, I need a typist. You are elected at thirty dollars a month. There is no answer but yes, or *aye*, as your husband would say."

"Aye then," she said promptly. "When do I start?"

"I could use you right now. I visited with Owen last week in Silver City, and he assured me you can read any handwriting on the planet, as long as it is not composed by orangutans."

That sounded just like her man. "I can try. How is he doing? I get two letters a week, sometimes three, but I haven't laid eyes on him and I miss him."

That was blunt enough, but she knew this marvelous man well.

"He's determined to finish shoring up Level Two—what a mess *that* was—and completing Level Three before Christmas. He has hired four more carpenters, and he is training them for world domination, or so he tells me. Do all Welshmen have the gift of tongues?"

"I believe they do. And then?"

Uncle Jesse's eyes were full of sympathy as he shook his head. "I don't know. He's playing his cards close to his vest." He set his hands down on his desk and gave her a level appraisal. "And we will let him, eh, Mrs. Davis? Give me a smile, if you have one, and I'll show you where you'll be working."

She spent the afternoon practicing on the brand new Underwood Number Five typewriter on the second floor where the company lawyers and Jesse's son William presided. She went to work happily, wishing only that Saladin lay at her feet, his long nose resting on her shoe as often as not. She never minded a little slobber.

The end of the day came almost too soon because the work was interesting, with correspondence going to Canada mainly. Will Knight had come out of his office at the end of the day to chat and hand her another letter for tomorrow. She looked at the mailing address. "My goodness, the prime minister of Canada?" she asked and squinted at the paper. "Sir Wilfrid Laurier?"

"Yes, indeed. Pa's involved in a major land deal in the Alberta District of the Northwest Territories." Will rubbed his hand together. "Sir Wilfrid is interested in expansion, and what do you know, so are we."

He must have recognized the wonder in her eyes. "As well as you think you know my father, that's a different man upstairs, the single-minded businessman."

He took his coat from the rack by the door and shrugged into it. "Care for a ride home? I'm going past your house."

He let her off with a smile and a tip of his hat, as charming a gentleman as his father. She went inside to a warm house with the light on in the kitchen and Angharad putting the final touches on her Christmas dragon for Da.

Della kissed her cheek. "I have a job typing for Uncle Jesse. He's already told me that means a Christmas ham, even if I am a new employee. Thirty dollars a month, Angharad. No oatcakes this winter."

It was a family joke and Angharad beamed at her. "We will become as rich as coal mine owners, Mam. Aunt Mabli asked if I could help her in the kitchen on Fridays and the two weekends before Christmas at fifty cents a night. The Knights have a lot of dinner parties, she says."

"Will that be enough for your Christmas plans?" Della asked, remembering her own days in Colorado when she and Papa cut out pictures from the Sears Roebuck Catalog and gave them to each other during lean months in the mine.

"Aye. Aunt Mabli said she will help me shop, because she knows the best places in Provo. We will be provident. That is one of my new spelling words."

They spent a pleasant evening in the kitchen, Della reading aloud from *Pickwick Papers*, careful not to break the spine of the new book, since it was Owen's Christmas present, and Angharad coloring in the last of the red on the dragon.

"Uncle Jesse is going to the Tintic District tomorrow, and he said he could give your dragon to Da," Della told her. She looked at the notes, sharps and flats coming out of the dragon's thought bubble, and had an idea.

"My dear, let us write the words to 'Lead, Kindly Light' on the back. You know, just to remind Da."

"He's not going to forget us, is he?" Angharad asked, all the anxiety there, as if it were lodged barely under her skin and ready to pop out at the first opportunity.

"No, he is not," Della said firmly. Whatever doubts she felt, she could save them for later, when the lights were out, Angharad slept, and she was free to stare at the empty space beside her in the bed and wonder when, or if, her man was coming home.

"You write the words, Mam. You still have teacher handwriting."

Della smiled at that and wrote the words, finding herself humming along to the old hymn by Cardinal

Newman. She took special care with, 'The night is dark, and I am far from home; Lead thou me on!' remembering times Owen had sung to her. She panicked for a moment, searching her heart for the sound of his voice, wondering how long she would remember it if he never returned.

She walked into the parlor and looked out on the falling snow, which hid the mountains to the east and Winter Quarters Canyon, where widows and fatherless children were carrying on with their lives, much as she and Angharad were doing here, some sixty-five miles to the west and four thousand feet closer to sea level. Silent, she walked through to the kitchen where Angharad worked and out to the back porch, facing west and south toward the Tintic Mining District. "'Keep thou my feet; I do not ask to see the distant scene—one step enough for me,'" she whispered.

The rolled-up tube with its singing dragon and words to the miners' hymn went on its way to Tintic with Jesse Knight the next morning. Della typed letters for Canada and listened when Will's brother Raymond came into his office and shared stories about the ranch Father had bought in Alberta District and more land he wanted to buy.

"What is your father planning?" she asked, feeling it was all right for her to interrupt them, since both men were lounging in her office and eating Christmas shortbread that someone from the mailroom had brought that morning. Besides, she knew the brothers from many a Sunday dinner at the Knights' house.

"Sugar made from beets," Ray said. "He is inviting farmers to settle on the prairie and raise sugar beets.

He'll build houses for farmers and workers and a factory to turn beets into sugar."

"My goodness, the expense!" Della said.

Raymond shrugged. "Father operates on the principle that money serves no purpose lying around in a bank vault. How can he help people that way?" He smiled at her expression. "I know! He takes some getting used to, doesn't he, Will?"

The brothers laughed, went into Will's office, and shut the door, leaving her to type another letter to the prime minister of Canada and wonder how it was some people had more vision than others. She couldn't even imagine borrowing more than an egg from her neighbor, let alone thousands of dollars from a bank.

She thought about that on her walk home, shaking her head over the offer of a ride from Will because she wanted to stretch her legs after a day confined to an office. She peered in windows on the way home, past the wreaths on the doors and into parlors, some with Christmas trees, some without, but everyone with a father and a mother, as far as she could tell.

Uncle Karl had sent her a letter yesterday, and she needed to thank him for the memory of her own father that he had included, just a simple story about picking up dried buffalo dung to make campfires on the long walk to Utah Territory. She would read it to Angharad tonight and then tuck it in her top drawer along with the letters from Owen and an earlier letter from Uncle Karl with another story about Indians, one in particular who had followed their wagon train for two days and offered three horses for a pretty Swedish woman with blond hair.

That one had led to questions from Angharad that shifted into a modest discussion about why the Indian wanted the Swedish girl, and where babies came from. This parenting business was onerous, indeed.

But she was content, knowing Angharad would have brought the mail in tonight and there would be a letter from Owen, because he was a man of regular habits.

To her surprise, there was no letter that night, or the day after, or the day after that. She had inquired at the post office to see if snow or road agents or some national calamity she was unaware of had stopped the mail between Provo and Silver City. All she got was a shrug and the suggestion that maybe she could be more patient. After all, it was nearly Christmas, and the post office was swamped with maybe a thousand letters going here and there.

Nothing. She wrote every other night anyway, and so did Owen's daughter. It was time to put on a brave face.

Chapter 40

"Mam, why isn't Da writing to us?"

"I am certain he is busy, dearest."

The week before Christmas could not possibly have been longer. Thank goodness for Mr. Auerbach, who insisted Della and Angharad come to Salt Lake for the annual employees' holiday party, which meant spending the night with Mr. and Mrs. Whalley, Pekka, and Reet at her former manager's house.

Who wouldn't enjoy a party at the department store? Angharad had sat on Santa's lap and whispered in his ear. Della felt her face go numb when she saw Santa look away, gather himself together, then turn back with a hearty "Ho ho!" and a candy cane.

Della wanted to sit on Santa's lap, give the big man a shake, and demand that he produce one Welshman who loved mines more than his family. A fervent letter to Dr. Isgreen had produced a prompt reply, urging her to hold on a little longer, even though it was difficult. She had to smile at his last few sentences. "'This may sound less than professional, but only a moron would stay away from a charming wife and daughter. You have my complete permission to smack him when he shows up. It might even be good, therapeutically, at least for you. Yours sincerely.'"

Long after Mr. Whalley and the children had gone to bed, Della sat up with Kristina in tears, wondering what to do. Kristina had hugged her, held her off, and looked at her with serious eyes full of hard-earned and unwanted experience. "Dearest Della, this is where women have to dig in and just keep breathing." She sighed and looked out a window that wasn't there in Mr. Whalley's parlor. "There were days, even here in Salt Lake when I started work, that the most ambitious task I set for myself was just to breathe. That always led to working and then to the children and fixing meals. I breathed."

Kristina couldn't help her laughter then. "If we were in the canyon, Eeva Koski would drag you into the sauna!"

"I would go gladly," Della said.

Kristina's eyes misted over. "There are times when I think of Matti." Her face went solemn. "Jim tells me to think all I want. Sometimes he likes to sit in the quiet and remember his Augusta. We keep breathing. You too."

It was good advice. She kept breathing when Kristina shyly announced before they returned to Provo that she was already in the family way. She kept breathing when Angharad sat so close to her on the train and in church, as if hanging on to the only permanent person in her life. Or maybe Della sat close to Angharad; it was hard to tell. She kept breathing at the school party, when Angharad and three friends sang "Adeste Fideles," and Della wished with all her heart that Owen sat beside her. She breathed and sent Uncle Karl one of Angharad's Christmas cards, with its small dragon beside a tree.

The Knights' office party was held in the boardroom at the Knight Investment Company. Uncle Jesse circulated with eggnog in one hand and Christmas bonuses in the other for everyone, even new employees. The promised ham was delivered, along with an already-decorated tree from the Payson ranch by Raymond's family.

There was always something in the air on Christmas Eve, no matter whether it was snowing or raining, or whether someone was there or not: a special feeling of peace and goodwill that came, free of charge, to anyone who needed it. Della needed it.

She sent Angharad ahead to the Knights' house, where everyone was gathering for the big night of hors' d'oeuvres and laughter and maybe a discreet rattling of packages. She promised to show up in an hour with her offering of Welsh cakes, the special kind made with sultanas and a dusting of sugar.

She never minded standing at the range and flipping the *cage bach* until they were nicely browned on both sides. The house was still. She breathed in the solitude and found it to her liking, in that way of Christmas that was going to come, no matter what. Granted, matters could have been better, but the ham would go in the oven to slow cook all night, and there was a respectable pile of presents under the tree, including Owen's copy of *Pickwick Papers* that she could always mail to him in a day or two if he decided not to come.

After Angharad went to bed, there would be an orange and handful of nuts for her stocking, plus a small package that Della intended to place on top, a gift from one grateful heart to another.

Hungry, she searched the neat pile of *cage bach* for one a little crooked, halt, or lame. She found it and popped it in her mouth, relishing the goodness.

Della looked at the clock and changed into her green wool dress with the lace collar that Owen had given to her from Gwyna's modest stash. A critical look at her hair reminded her that it wasn't going to change, and she could live with that, particularly since she had no choice.

She turned down the lamp in her bedroom, struck by the fact that she wasn't thinking of it as their bedroom. It was her bedroom. Maybe in the spring she would get a yellow bedspread.

Breathe, breathe, she told herself. She was reaching for her coat when she heard carolers in front of her house. She smiled, happy she had made extra cakes, and went into the kitchen for them.

She walked onto the porch, pleased to see such an assembly. She stood there, aware she was happy because they were singing and it was Christmas Eve and she was headed to a party with dear friends. Kristina and Dr. Isgreen were both right about taking each day one at a time. It would be a good New Year's resolution.

"Silent Night" blended into "Joy to the World" and her personal favorite, "O Little Town of Bethlehem." She listened in appreciation and watched the plumes of used-up air coming in puffs from each caroler. She rubbed her shoulders, wishing she had actually put on that coat she had taken from the closet.

The last song faded into the frigid air, and Della handed around the Welsh cakes. She stepped back, expecting them to hurry on, but they stood where they were. A caroler stepped forward and cleared her throat.

"We've been asked to hum a hymn just for you," she said, and then she glanced at the porch next door, where Della saw her neighbors listening too. "A note, please?"

Della's heart nearly stopped when she recognized the note. She reminded herself to breathe; then she closed her eyes as the carolers hummed and Owen Davis sang the miners' hymn to her.

She heard his voice coming closer and realized he had been standing on the porch with her neighbors, the duplicitous, conniving, clever, irritating man, the man she couldn't fathom living without. She opened her eyes.

Now he stood in the center of the carolers. He set down his valise and held out his arms. With a cry, she threw herself into his arms, trying to hug him everywhere.

"'The distant scene—one step enough for me,'" he sang right in her ear in his beautiful second tenor voice. "Della, Della, give me your answer true." He segued into "Daisy Bell," which made the carolers laugh, wish them a merry Christmas, and move away, leaving them alone in a snowy yard on a quiet street. "'I'm half crazy all for the love of you. It won't be a stylish marriage; I can't afford a carriage.'"

He stopped singing, held her off for a long look, and pulled her close and kissed her. He must have noticed that she was starting to wobble on uncertain legs because he picked her up and carried her up the steps and into their house, as he had done last May.

"Let's begin again, shall we?" he asked as he set her down. He took her by the shoulders, his dark eyes full of concern now. "Della, can you forgive me for being an idiot? I mean no ordinary idiot, but a certified, bona fide idiot."

She nodded, unable to say anything. She touched his face, outlining his profile almost as if she expected him to disappear, and she needed a reminder that would last awhile. The gesture brought tears to his eyes, which she flicked away, and then she kissed him.

"I'm to take hors' d'oeuvres to the Knights," she said, finding her voice.

"They won't miss them," he told her. "We're not going anywhere. I stopped there first and gave Angharad a great kiss. She scolded me and I deserved it. She also agreed to spend the night with Mabli and show up here tomorrow morning on the dot of eight o'clock to open presents. You're stuck with me."

"I have so many questions," she began but then realized not one of them mattered. Owen was here and he was singing again.

They stood in the front room, close but not touching. Words were needed now, and she waited for him to speak.

"One thing you need to know, Della, and not an hour from now, or tomorrow. I really stopped at the Knights' house first to hand Uncle Jesse my resignation. I am no longer connected to the Banner Mine, or any Knight mines."

She breathed deeply and filled her nostrils with the fragrance from his overcoat that would always smell of coal. Which reminded her . . .

It must have reminded her husband too. He tossed the coat he had been holding onto the sofa, his eyes lively. "I also sent a letter to Gomer Thomas, thanking him for the offer to work with him but telling him no.

I'm through with coal, *m cara*. Done with it. Come a little closer, if you wish."

"If I wish," she repeated. "I do wish. They won't miss us at the party?"

"Not even a little bit."

Chapter 41

"I hate to admit this, *m cara*, but I'm getting too old for an entire night of wild Welsh abandon with Greek women."

"Oh, and how many Greek women might there have been before me?" she teased back.

"I lost count after one."

"That's pretty much my score with Welshmen."

He turned onto his back, perplexed with himself. How can you tease a woman when all you want to do is apologize? "Della, I believe I could ask for your forgiveness every day for the rest of our lives, and it wouldn't be enough."

God bless the lady. She rested her head on his chest. "Once was enough." She poked him in the chest, but it turned into a caress and then a shy look when she rose up on her elbow. "I've finished apologizing to my father for being a demanding twelve-year-old." She smiled and he saw the wonder in her face. "My uncle has been sending me stories about his brother's life. Let me tell you the most amazing one."

He listened with astonishment as she told him how her father, the blackest of black sheep, if Aunt Caroline was to be believed, had financed the major portion of Uncle Karl's law school expenses.

Upset with Uncle Karl on a nearly visceral level, he couldn't speak for a moment when she finished. It was more pleasant to run his hand down her arm from shoulder to wrist and feel her softness. Maybe that was what real strength felt like. He had underestimated this wife of his, this kindest of gifts to a widower and his daughter.

"Della, you're not angry that he could easily have financed your own college education to pay his brother back? I am, and I don't mind admitting it to you."

She laughed. "And *that*, my love, is the reason the country is called England and not Wales! Why fret and stew and talk about it? I would never have met you if my way had been smooth, and that would be the greater loss."

She was right. He thought about that while he shaved and heard the homely sound of someone making breakfast in the kitchen. When he finished, he made their ruin of a bed and wondered if she would mind if he brought his carving tools in from the shed in the backyard and worked in the kitchen. He had some free time on his hands, now that he was out of work.

He leaned against the door in the kitchen and watched her efficiently moving from range to table. She had tugged her wild mop of hair back with a piece of heavy-duty string, from the looks of it. He admired her small waist and considered himself amply repaid for having the good sense to persist until he wore her down and she decided to give a Welshman a chance.

"Stare all you want," she said, and he realized she stood there with two plates in her hand and watched him. "It's nearly eight o'clock, and we have other things to do besides, you know . . ."

"You caught me," he told her with a laugh, taking the plates to the table. He looked at the clock. "Where is my child?"

"If I know Mabli, she's giving us another moment or two. Sit down. French toast waits for no man."

He blessed the food and they ate in companionable silence, Della going to the range to turn the sausages and then skewer one and drop it on his plate. He thought of mounds of oatcakes in lean times and realized there hadn't been any lean times since he married this treasure.

When she finished, she pushed back her plate. "I do need to know why you didn't write us."

Elbows on the table, he told her how he had moved Angharad's smaller bed into the carpenter's shop and slept there, working himself to the limit, measuring and sawing and hinging. "I suppose I was trying to punish myself for being a fool. I wanted to work myself to death, as if that would have brought one single friend back to life." Might as well admit the rest. "Dr. Isgreen told me you were making great progress, and I was not."

"He said he was going to visit you," she said, after a long pause in which he saw her gather herself together. "I'm glad he did."

"After Emil left, we fitted our first timbered unit on Level Two. It held tight, but we waited out a rock fall as everything settled. I was on one side of the rocks and my crew on the other. Between you and me, the Banner is the devil's mine. I have so informed Uncle Jesse in my letter of resignation. We'll see what he does with that information."

She reached for his hand, her dark eyes boring into his. He saw all the fear, all twelve years of it. For a small moment, she was a child again. He held his breath, relieved when the glimpse passed. He would have to ask Dr. Isgreen if that little girl from the Colorado Plateau might reappear now and then.

"I sat there in the dark and thought about my friends, from the Farishes to the Hunters to the Evans, of course."

"Did you pray?"

Did he pray? "Not at first. I knew the Lord was unhappy with me. Why bother an angry man?"

She shook her head slightly, but her eyes were kind. "I figured you would ask the Lord again for his will in the matter. You listened on May 1 and lived."

This wife of his was going to make him tell her the whole uncomfortable truth. He could see it on her face. He glanced at the clock. He was only going to say this once. Angharad didn't need to know how stupid her father was. Sufficient unto the day was the knowledge that his wife already had a sneaking suspicion.

"I did, finally."

"And?"

"I heard absolutely nothing this time, no eternal wisdom. Nothing." He saw the surprise on her face and took her hand again. "Della, it finally occurred to this genius you married that the Lord Almighty had already given me the tools I needed to make a smart decision. I made myself comfortable against the smoothest boulder and realized I didn't need another mine in my life. Not one more."

"Is that when you started to sing?"

God bless the ladies. "You know me pretty well, don't you?" he asked his particular lady. "I thought about the miners' song and realized I had it wrong all these years. I was still trying to see the distant scene, when all I needed was the 'one step enough' part. Who wouldn't sing after that?"

His cup of life filled to the brim when he heard Angharad's footsteps on the porch. He took Della by the hand and they opened the door together. His other treasure stood there, covered in snow.

"Heavens, Angharad, was there a blizzard between our house and Center Street that no one told us about?" Della asked as she stepped outside to unbutton Owen's daughter's coat, help her out of it, and then shake it off.

Owen prudently decided not to point out the obvious. The next Ice Age could have happened overnight and a husband and wife who hadn't seen each other in too long wouldn't have heard a thing.

"Mam, I made a snow angel on the lawn." She pointed to it.

Could his cup get any fuller? "Daughter, after breakfast I will put on my coat and make another one with you," Della said. "Come inside!"

She did, and he held out his hands to her. This lovely child who looked so much like her mother rested her hands in his. "*Nadolig Llawen*, Da."

He gave her fingers a squeeze. "*Ac i chithau, Angharad m cara*. And a happy new year," he added in English for Della's benefit.

He picked up Angharad and hugged her until she protested and he set her down. She went to the tree and frowned.

"Da, you already have my present, the singing dragon. I wish I had another gift for you."

"Why would I need anything else?" He glanced at Della. "If your mam won't cut up stiff, I plan to bring in some wood from my workshop and carve a suitable frame for it on the kitchen table. It's warmer in here."

"May I help?" Angharad asked after a glance at Mam, who nodded.

"I thought you would never ask."

He sat his ladies down on the sofa. "I have some presents too. Angharad, you won't mind if I give Mam's to her first?"

"Only if I am next to give her one."

"Very well."

Owen picked up a little box he had left under the tree before time and tide swept him into the bedroom last night. He handed it to Della with a flourish. "It's long overdue."

Her eyes full of questions, she opened the little thing. He held his breath, hoping it was right. He saw her eyes widen. She nodded and then held up a heart-shaped gold locket.

Could a man's heart melt? She put her two hands in his in the Welsh way, this gift of his, better than a present, from the Aegean. "*Rwy'n dy garu di*," then, "Did I say that right, daughter? Angharad taught me."

"You said it right." He could teach her *Ti Yw fy ngahriad* later, because the Welsh knew the difference between formal love and the more abandoned kind that he preferred. Poor Englishmen—one phrase for everything. Hard to believe they had conquered his country.

Angharad laughed. "My turn. Mam, you won't believe this!"

She went to the tree and held out her present to Della. It was another small box. Owen felt a great laugh of massive proportion growing inside him.

Della opened the box, took out another heart-shaped locket, and pulled Angharad down onto her lap. "You rascal!"

"You needed one, Mam. I could tell you did, almost as much as Da needed a dragon."

He watched in delight as Della and Angharad clung to each other. Della pointed to his daughter's Christmas stocking and a by-now-familiar small box sticking out of the top.

"What could that possibly be for you, dearest?" she asked as she pointed Angharad to the mantelpiece.

"Mam, you shouldn't have," Angharad teased after she opened the box and took out yet another locket.

Goodness, what a strange gift-giving this had become. Might as well continue it. "There is my present to you, Angharad," Owen said. "Better open it and look surprised."

His daughter picked up another small box and started laughing even before she removed the ribbon. Della leaned against him and laughed.

"Let me guess," Angharad joked, which set them off in another wave of merriment. When they had subsided into weak giggles, she tore off the ribbon and paper and held up a fourth, and hopefully final, heart-shaped locket.

"Heavens, what a bunch of sillies," Della said. "I love you both."

He was about to kiss her when someone knocked on the door. "Do you think we made so much noise that the next door neighbors called the constable?" he asked. "I'll go peacefully, but I expect bail as soon as the bank opens tomorrow."

Sure enough, a man in uniform stood at the door, but it was a delivery uniform of some sort. "Merry Christmas, sir. Does Mrs. Della Davis live here?"

Thank God she does, Owen thought. He looked down at the handsome cream-colored envelope the man held out to him. "Aye, you've come to the right home."

"Here you are then, and a Happy New Year too." He took a nickel tip from Owen and hurried back to his automobile, ready for other last-minute deliveries.

The package read "Della Davis," the address, and nothing more. He took it inside and plopped it in Della's lap. "At least we know it isn't a heart-shaped locket, *m cara*."

"Oh, please, my stomach hurts and I can't laugh anymore," she told him as she opened the envelope and peered inside.

He looked at her in alarm when her olive skin paled to a sickly white. She stared, covered her eyes, and wept. He picked up the envelope, ready to order Angharad to hunt for smelling salts, if they even had any.

He opened the envelope wider and knew why his wife sat there so stunned. He pulled out four one-hundred-dollar bills and a note. "'Long overdue, niece,'" he read out loud. "'I can never make it up, but this is a start. Forgive me, Uncle Karl.'"

Chapter 42

The cash went into their bank account two days later during Della's lunch break at Knight Investment Company. She also sent a letter on its way to Uncle Karl's law office, thanking him and assuring him she was paid in full and, more to the point, so was Frederick Anders.

She had kissed her husband goodbye, hair still uncombed, sitting at the kitchen table and already at work on a frame for Angharad's singing dragon. He hummed as he worked, which made her smile all the way down Center Street to her desk in the Knight Building, where more letters to Canada waited.

Her hand went to her neck, where she felt the one chain that bore two lockets now, one with a bit of hair from Owen's head on one side and hers on the other. They were the same color, but her curl had been subdued practically with a whip and chair into the tiny frame. The other locket carried Angharad's lighter hair and another curly offering of her own, mother and daughter.

Angharad's locket—the child vowed never to remove it—held Owen and Della's hair. By unanimous consent, the one remaining locket went on its way to Knightville with Uncle Jesse to the Tates' eldest daughter.

That night they discussed the unexpected windfall from her uncle. Owen assured Della the money was hers, along with all decisions relating to it. He had accumulated enough money working for Uncle Jesse to weather out unemployment, as long as it didn't last too long, and after all, she was employed.

Owen knew her too well. He looked at her reflection in the mirror as he brushed her hair. "You have something in mind, don't you?"

"It's perfectly selfish."

"I doubt that. Tell me or I'll tickle it out of you."

"You know precisely where that will lead," she said, and she laughed when he shrugged. "It's this, my man: My father's birthday was March 10. I want to take that Anders plaque you carved for me . . ."

"Back when you were still Anders."

". . . and somehow leave it on Papa's grave in Hastings," she concluded. "I've never been back. We can afford that, can't we?"

"That and more," he said. "If there is no headstone, we can make arrangements while we are there. March 10 it is."

She didn't expect either Will or Ray to come into the office, not during that week between Christmas and New Year's Day, but there they were one afternoon, the bearers of doughnuts and eggnog, which they insisted on sharing with her.

Before Ray left, he stopped at Della's desk. "Can you get Owen to drop by tomorrow morning?" he asked. "Dad has an idea, and we like it too."

"Certainly. Do you need some cabinets or flooring?"

"Something a little larger," Ray said. He took the last doughnut. "So glad neither of you like the black-and-white sprinkles. Have him drop by around eleven. He can take you to lunch when we're done."

"Whatever can the Knights be planning?" Owen asked over supper when Della announced the request from the Knight brothers. "No one mentioned mines, I am confident in assuming."

"Not one word."

"*M cara*, your face will freeze that way if you frown too often," he teased.

After he came out of Will's office the next day, he invited her to lunch with a handsome man, only she was not to tell her husband. Della put on her hat and coat and gave him her arm.

Without any consultation required, they walked to the Palace and sat at the counter, ordering grilled cheese sandwiches and cherry phosphates.

"If you don't tell me really soon what is going on, I can guarantee I will have a splitting headache tonight," Della threatened.

"Goodness. For a fairly new bride, you have a vast awareness of marriage politics," he teased.

"I mean it, Owen Rhys Davis."

"Horrors! Three names! They want me to spend the next two weeks in an architect's office in Salt Lake, first to learn more about blueprints, then next to visit a construction site. I'll be getting the same wages I earned in Tintic for those two weeks, and they'll put me up in a hotel."

"That won't be necessary," Della said. "I'll send a letter to Kristina and Mr. Whalley, and they'll be pleased to have you. What are the Knights planning?"

"Neither would say. They wanted me to assure you it did not involve mines and that I might be useful to them as a citizen of the Commonwealth."

"Canada," she said, interested. "Beet sugar."

"Is that a secret code?" he asked, amused. "I couldn't identify a beet if someone lobbed a handful at me. I didn't even know you could concoct sugar from beets." He made a face. "I never cared for beets. If you ever decide to serve them, *I'll* get a headache."

"Owen, I can't take you anywhere."

"Why would you want to, *m cara*? I'm so loveable at home."

A week later she kissed him goodbye at the Interurban depot and reminded him that he had extra collars and stockings in his valise. She hurried back to work, because most of those letters written before Christmas had turned into contracts to be typed. The Knights' lawyer on her second floor had left her a barely legible note, throwing himself on her mercy because his secretary had a toothache and he needed her.

She happily kept herself too busy, because neither Will nor Ray was especially communicative about their reasons for Owen's trip to Salt Lake. Better to tackle contracts than try to second-guess bosses who were being remarkably mum.

Owen came home from Salt Lake on Friday night and laughed out loud when Della served him beets. When Angharad asked why beets were so funny, he only smiled and changed the subject.

"It's a long week without you," he told her later, much later, when the house was dark. "The Whalleys don't help much. Della, if someone had told you that the ever-so-proper manager in Menswear would make a cake of himself over a pretty blond, would you have believed it?"

"No, but that's what love does to people apparently. I noticed you ate the beets, oh loving husband."

"No hardship." He pulled her closer. "That's better. I must tell you I spent two evenings at your favorite house in the avenues visiting your uncle. By the way, I am supposed to call him Karl and not Mr. Anders now."

"It's not a warm place, is it?" she asked and rubbed her arms, feeling a chill that had nothing to do with the temperature.

"It is not," he agreed, and then he took over the arm-rubbing duty.

"Were my cousins there?"

"Karl mentioned they were both back east, one of them in Vassar and the other at Boston College. I wonder what *that* tuition costs."

She had to know. "Did you see my aunt?"

"I did not," he said with a shake of his head. "Karl is worried about her. A nurse lives there now."

He kissed her cheek. "He wants you to visit."

"No."

"I told him it would be your decision. I think he wanted to argue the matter, but I had to leave." He gave her a pat. "Do you know those architects have been giving me homework? How fortunate that I like blueprints."

"As much as you like me?"

Della thought he would laugh, but he didn't. "Some things I don't joke about," he said, and he kissed her.

He returned to Salt Lake for the final week, this time to visit the construction site of a brewery. Halfway through the morning on Wednesday, Uncle Jesse's private secretary hurried into the office.

"Della, you have a long-distance telephone connection waiting upstairs. Please hurry."

Every dark moment of her life seemed to flash through her brain like a burst of lightning, and then she calmed herself. Long distance meant it wasn't Angharad. Owen wasn't in a mine. Who else did she know?

"I've never received a telephone call," she said, "never mind a long distance one."

The secretary touched her arm. "No fears, Della. I can ask who it is. Come on."

She hurried upstairs, too distracted to think of a prayer fit for a modern device.

The secretary sat down and indicated a chair by her desk. She spoke to the operator, waited a moment, and then asked, "Who is this, please? Owen Davis? I'll put your wife on."

Della sighed with relief and took the receiver from the secretary. "Owen? Owen?"

"The very man of your dreams," came a tinny voice. "Should I sing one verse of 'Men of Harlech' to prove it?"

She swallowed. If he could joke, nothing was seriously wrong. "What's the matter?" Maybe she could tease too. "Did you forget your train fare?"

"I wish it were that simple, *m cara*. I shouldn't be joking, but I knew you would be frightened to hear from me this way. It's your Aunt Caroline. There's no easy way to say this: she's dying, and she wants you here."

Chapter 43

Owen knew dubious when he heard it, even through a telephone receiver fifty miles away. He also knew reluctance when he heard it, but had enough confidence to stand on the Interurban platform four hours later, waiting for his wife.

How to cajole or console the woman he adored? He understood her supreme reluctance. He had tried one more tack. Time was running out on this call, and so was Aunt Caroline.

"*M cara*, you're looking at the distant scene. Try the one step enough. It worked for me in the mine. I'll stay right beside you the whole time."

"I'm to do this for you?"

He could hear her heart breaking, and he knew he had broken her heart enough. "No. You're to do this for you. I'll see you in four hours."

And so he stood on the platform in the rain that turned to sleet that turned to snow. Four and a half hours later, the train pulled in, delayed either by weather or by one frightened woman dragging her feet. When he saw the lights of the Interurban, he stepped from the depot and opened his umbrella.

There she hesitated, looking for him through the late afternoon gloom. When she saw him, she started to run, picking up her skirts and flashing a bit of ankle to other commuters, some of whom appeared appreciative. He knew *he* was.

He dropped the umbrella, grabbed her shoulders, and held her close. "I don't want to be here," she sobbed.

"I'll be with you every step of the way."

She gave him that intense gaze of hers, the one that excited him, energized him, chastened him, and humbled him, depending on the place and the occasion. This time it was a train platform, and he felt her terror.

She broke the gaze first. "You're standing here getting cold. If you catch a bilious fever and die, I will be forced to earn my living forever at a typewriter."

She looked too serious, so he knew better than to laugh. "We're both tougher than that," he assured her as he led her through the depot to the taxi stand, where he hailed a cab and gave the avenue address.

She was silent until they turned onto the street where the Anderses lived, and where he knew she had been force-fed spite and contempt for years, all because she was poor and defenseless, the daughter of the family black sheep, illegitimate, and she didn't look like the tall, blond Anders clan.

"I never wanted to see her again," she murmured into his overcoat.

What could he say to that? He held her close.

She started to shake as he rang the doorbell. "With you every step," he reminded her as the door opened.

In shirtsleeves but somehow managing to look like a guest in his own home, Karl ushered them inside. Owen heard Della's quiet intake of breath as she took in the gray and drawn man before her, and he knew her heart opened, because she was kind.

She touched her uncle's cheek and said nothing. Karl sobbed and put his hand over hers. They stood in silence, not close together but not far apart either, until Karl pulled away.

"She told me to get you here," he said, tucking Della's hand in his and leading her toward the stairs. "She's waiting."

Alarmed, she looked back at Owen and pulled her hand free. He was by her side in two strides, his arm around her waist as she clutched his belt.

Karl watched them. Owen saw a handful of emotions cross his face, paramount among them shame, and then the baldest kind of remorse that made him look away and collect himself.

Her face so serious, Della glued herself to Owen's side. Maybe some day if he ever got the nerve, he would ask her how she managed to live in that house without a champion beside her. He didn't need to ask. He already knew her deep well of courage that he had dipped from himself not so long ago.

Uncle Karl went into the room first, closing the door behind him. Owen heard the murmur of low voices. In a moment, a woman in a cap and apron came out, her face troubled. "She has been talking and talking to me," she said, and Owen heard all the weariness. "I'll be downstairs."

Karl ushered them inside. Owen had to give Della a gentle tug to set her in motion again.

The room smelled of sickness and decay, no matter how tidy it appeared. If death had an odor, Owen breathed it now. Della looked at him, fear in her eyes. He took her hand to his lips, happy to breathe in her own fragrance for a fleeting moment.

Karl indicated a chair for Della beside the bed and a distant one for Owen. She shook her head at that, and Owen pulled his chair close to hers.

Aunt Caroline's eyes fluttered open. She seemed not to know where she was for a moment, and then she locked onto Della's face, her gaze unwavering. With a jolt, Owen felt himself yanked back a few years to a day in Number Four when a snake crawled out from the seam of coal where he was shoveling, stared at him with that same hypnotic gaze, hissed, and slid away to terrify three or four Farishes mining beside him.

The Farishes had laughed about it later, but they hadn't seen what Owen saw. He never forgot that tightening of his gut. He felt it now. Slowly he put his hand into Della's waistband this time, ready to jerk her back if the woman in the bed made a move of any kind.

This is no repentant soul, he thought. He whispered, "We can leave right now."

Della shook her head, not taking her gaze from the dying woman. She swallowed a few times. "I'm here, Aunt Caroline," she said clearly. "What is it you want from me?"

"I can't stay here!"

Owen turned around in surprise as Karl backed away from the bed, seeing his own demons, or maybe a reflection of his own cowardice for his years of neglecting his niece when she needed an advocate, any advocate, and no one had taken her side.

"I can't." His voice sounded weak; he *was* weak.

"Then don't, uncle," Della said calmly, her eyes never leaving her aunt's face. They appeared to be locked in a battle of wills. Owen saw Aunt Caroline's expression quite clearly. He couldn't see Della's, but he could imagine it.

"I'll . . . I'll be right outside the door," Karl said. "Call me if you need me."

Della laughed softly, but Owen heard no mirth. "You always said that. You'll be more comfortable downstairs in your office."

"I would, Della, thank you," Karl said, sounding relieved, as if she had given him permission to be a coward and he was happy with it.

What kind of a household is this? Owen asked himself in disgust. Karl nearly ran for the door.

Della turned her attention back to Aunt Caroline. "There, now. Do you have something to say to me? I don't want to wear you out."

Owen stared in dumbfounded fascination as the stick-thin woman in the bed opened and closed her mouth several times. No sound passed her dry and cracking lips. She seemed to be forming words, and oddly enough, her face appeared as animated as if she spoke. Nothing.

He watched the weirdest sort of dumb show, with Caroline Anders forming words with nothing behind them. Her eyes were stormy and placating by degrees. He didn't understand any of this. The nurse had said she could speak. Why didn't she?

"Della, what do you make of this?" he asked softly.

She turned her gaze on him now, the same look she must have been giving to Aunt Caroline. If he lived to be a hundred, he knew he would never see such tenderness in anyone's eyes. Della had looked at him like this before, as she held him up as he stood beside the grave of his best friend Richard Evans and sobbed, again across the altar in Manti, and more recently as he stood in the snow with the carolers and prayed that she wouldn't leave him there to pick up his valise and walk away.

"I think Aunt Caroline can't bring herself to apologize," she whispered back. "Poor soul. The words won't come out. If we leave right now, she will die alone, and I won't have that on my conscience. Sit across from her and take her other hand."

He did as she directed, picking up the paper-thin hand that seemed composed of hummingbird bones. She was cold to the touch, and he thought of that reptile in the mine again. If Welshmen had a fault, it was a superstitious nature.

"Let's sing to her," Della said, her voice normal now. "I like 'Nearer, My God, to Thee.' Pitch it."

He did, and they sang. Because of the season, the hymns turned into carols. He found himself relaxing, soothed because singing always made him complete. He had been a fool to stop singing. Della frowned but followed him when he sang, "Let Us Oft Speak Kind Words to Each Other," which he noticed made Aunt Caroline flinch and look away, her jaw working again. *So there, you old trot*, he said to himself, and he didn't feel much remorse. *Would it have killed you to show kindness to Della Anders?*

Heavenly Father must have given him a cosmic smack on the head. Oh no, it was Della leveling one of her patented appraisals in his direction, looking remarkably like Saladin. He quickly sang "Sweet Is the Work," which got him out of the theological doghouse.

Then it was over. Della leaned closer with a warm cloth, wiping around her aunt's eyes, closed now. She stopped when Caroline opened her eyes and slowly raised her hand to Della's cheek. Owen watched, alert for trouble, but he needn't have worried. One gentle pat, another one, and she died.

The hand he held relaxed, and he set it carefully on the sheet. He leaned back as Della gently closed her aunt's eyes and folded her hands neatly together.

"We can leave now," she said.

He helped her from the room and closed the door on death and malice and perhaps, just perhaps, grace, because that deathbed needed grace. Della had been full of it. Maybe if he stayed around his woman long enough, he would become a better man. He resolved to find out.

At the foot of the stairs, he helped her into her coat and opened the door. She breathed deep of the bracing air, midnight air.

They walked down the front steps, and she turned around at the bottom to look up at the elegant house. "I never have to go back there, do I?"

"You do not."

"I'm tired," she said simply, and she sank down to the sidewalk almost before he could catch her.

Owen picked her up, unsure of what to do because he had no intention of returning to the Anderses' mansion for assistance. Through some manifestation of divine providence, a taxi came by and stopped.

"Need some help there, sir?"

"I do." He gave the cabbie the Whalleys' address. Within the half hour, Della was tucked in bed and sound asleep, while he explained to his kind hosts with the worried eyes what had happened that evening.

An hour later, he unwound enough to lie down next to the darling of his heart. She woke up enough to give him her extra-tender look, so he had to ask her. "Was I wrong in insisting you go there?"

"Not at all," came her drowsy answer. "I learned something tonight."

"More like yesterday now," he teased gently. "What did you learn?"

"That I was always the strongest person in that house. Who would have thought it?"

Chapter 44

Thoughtful, Della returned to Provo in the morning after a lingering kiss on the Interurban platform that should have embarrassed her, but didn't. She gave her husband an equally tender kiss at the end of the week when he returned to Provo, valise in hand.

The following week, Owen finished the frame for his dragon and secured a piece of beveled glass to it. He debated with Della whether to glue "Lead, Kindly Light" to the back, but asked her to print it smaller, so he could put it in the front. "In case I need to remind myself," he told her. She obliged, and he was satisfied.

He borrowed a tea towel and arranged an elaborate unveiling ceremony when Angharad returned from school one afternoon. "Oh Da," turned into a hug, an ample reward.

"This is going to hang in every house we live in," he announced to them over cake, because Della knew what an artist's unveiling required. "In the front room."

In the end of January, her man answered a summons to the Knight Building for a conference with the Knight brothers. Uncle Jesse was still traveling, seeking investors for that project to the north involving major construction.

Owen left the house wearing his suit and Angharad's favorite dark green cravat, going to the Knight Building for a Saturday meeting, auspicious enough in itself. After watching his rollicking walk toward Center Street, Della went to her knees to pray.

One hour. Two hours. She baked a mound of Welsh cakes, unable to stop herself. She put them to good use, because three little girls had joined her daughter down the hall and were rearranging the furniture in the dollhouse already legendary in the neighborhood.

When everyone was fed, she went back to her bedroom and prayed again. If she thought she was well acquainted with deity before Aunt Caroline's death, she had learned something more, something she wished Caroline Anders had known. "His grace is sufficient," she told Owen one night after family prayer. He understood.

She felt it now, but that didn't prevent her from standing by the front room window, equal parts anxious and aggravated with herself. She reminded herself that she had a job and their nest egg was cooling its heels in the bank. How long she would keep her job was an unknown, but she knew her man would never fail her, not now.

And there he was. The door was closed against the cold, but he was singing, never a bad sign. She opened the door and he struck a pose.

What are you up to? she thought, enchanted.

"'The Maple Leaf, our emblem dear; The Maple Leaf forever,'" he sang to her. "'God save our King and Heaven bless The Maple Leaf forever!' That's just the chorus, *m cara*, and yes, it's King Edward now. I'm going to Canada with Raymond. I'll learn the other verses."

She whooped and ran down the steps, her arms out. He grabbed her and swung her around. "Uncle

Jesse is in Canada right now, making a deal with someone named McGrath. No guarantee for me yet, but things are leaning in my favor. The architect gave me a favorable report, so we shall see. You're cold! Doesn't your husband take good care of you, little lady? Is he around?"

"You are very nearly certifiable," she scolded, her hands on her hips.

"Not around?" He winked at her. "Better and better for me."

Arm in arm, they walked inside. "What *is* the job?" she asked.

"Building a sugar beet factory." He sank down on the sofa and pulled her with him. "My goodness, I can't believe I just said that. Me, a coal miner."

"Tell me what happened in the meeting."

"Not until you snuggle up. Ah, better. Uncle Jesse is negotiating with said Mr. McGrath right now. He's a former member of Canadian parliament and now an official with the Northwest Irrigation Company. Jesse just bought a thirty-thousand-acre ranch."

Owen grabbed her apron and fanned himself with it, which made her giggle, since she was still attached to the apron. "*M cara*, Ray said the transaction took a half hour. There's already a township on the land and some houses."

"I spend a half hour just mulling over the purchase of two yards of cloth," Della said, "and he buys how much land?"

He laughed and squeezed her shoulder. She leaned back and watched his enthusiasm, a far remove from the blank-faced man with red eyes who buried his best friends last May.

He was watching her face now. "So much has happened," she said simply. "I have changed. You have changed."

"For the better, or the better or worse?"

She considered what he was asking. "Maybe both. Marriage might be bliss, but it comes in little doses." She sat up. "You said you're going to Canada *when*?"

"By Friday at the latest. Jesse wants us to meet with Mr. McGrath in Lethbridge, where the depot is. For some reason, they think a man with an accent like mine might reassure the good chap that the Yankees come in peace, with lots of greenbacks."

"You will never cease to amaze me," she teased. "And to think you are mine for a *really* long time."

"Better or worse, *m cara*. I wonder . . . Do you think Mr. Holyoke would mind if I walked Angharad to school tomorrow and asked to look at a map of Canada?"

Since the Knight brothers and Owen were going to spend a day in Salt Lake City consulting with another lawyer before taking the night train toward Canada, Della took Owen's measurements one night and telephoned Mr. Whalley in Menswear. Informed that her man was a pretty standard size, she put Owen under orders to stop there first thing for a fitting and alteration if needed. Mr. Whalley had just the suit, a black worsted wool, for five dollars and fifty cents.

"If you're going to be talking to Mr. McGrath, and heaven knows who else, you need to look your best." She kissed his cheek. "The green cravat is entirely for luck, my darling."

She and Angharad saw the men off for Salt Lake and points north before school on Thursday. On Saturday she received a telegram at the office from Ray

Knight, who assured her all was well and they were in Lethbridge with his father for talks.

And then they waited, which was less onerous than usual. Amanda Knight invited them over one evening to pull taffy, talk about books, and worry a little, at least on Della's part.

"I don't know how you take all this in stride," Della asked. "I mean, these huge amounts of money!"

"I used to worry. What woman wouldn't?" Amanda replied. She took Angharad's stretched-out taffy and began to cut it into bite-sized pieces on her marble slab. "Did my husband ever tell you about his vision?"

Della shook her head. Chin in her hands, she listened as Amanda told her of the time Jesse and Will were climbing up the side of Godiva Mountain, ready to work the Humbug claim, a bold venture for a man in modest circumstances, and one scoffed at by others.

"We had the Payson Ranch," Amanda said. She arranged the taffy on little plates, a faraway look in her eyes. "My goodness, we were in debt, and here was this mine that a prospective investor had called a humbug." She shook her head, almost as if she still didn't believe what happened.

"Call it what you will—an epiphany, a vision, inspiration—Jesse told our son that pretty soon we were going to have all the money we wanted, if we would see it as a stewardship to help others." She rested her hands in her lap. "Sure enough, they struck a rich vein in the Humbug, and that started the company."

Della took over from her hostess and continued cutting the taffy. "I have to tell you that Owen and I have joked about Uncle Jesse, wondering if he starts each day deciding who to help."

They laughed together. "I think he does," Amanda said. She turned kind eyes on Della. "He's been watching over the Davises."

"We thought so," Della said. She swallowed down her tears, wondering why she was so emotional lately. "He's moving mountains for us, and we know it."

She thought about Amanda's words with every letter Owen sent, describing the land of the Alberta District, the soil perfect for wheat certainly, but also for sugar beets, according to experts. *Mind you, I know nothing about agriculture*, he wrote, *but I'm starting to believe in this land. Home soon, I hope.*

She hoped the same, watching the calendar slide toward the end of a short month anyway, wondering if she should remind him of his promise to take her to Hastings for her father's birthday anniversary on March 10.

She had a bigger interest, something on her mind since early January, something she tried not to think about, until it was all she thought about. A few shy words to Amanda had directed her to David Smoot, M.D., whose office was a block north of the Knight Investment Company. Lying on his examination table in a too short cotton gown, she answered his questions, asked a few of her own, and let him prod a bit, somewhat south of her belly button.

When he measured her hips and smiled at the caliper reading, Dr. Smoot gave her a hand up into a sitting position and nodded to his nurse.

"Mrs. Davis, I predict you'll be washing diapers in about the middle of September," he said. "Congratulations."

She burst into tears, babbling about waiting and waiting for just such news until her husband had told her to stop marking *X*s on the calendar.

"My dear, you look so young. How long have you been married? Has it been years?"

"Since last May!" she wailed.

He laughed. "Then you are an impatient soul, indeed." He shook his finger at her. "You have about seven more months to grow this little one, and nothing needs to rush that. Make an appointment to see me once a month." He shook her hand and left the room, still laughing.

Della wondered whether to write such news in a letter. She stewed over the matter and then realized late that night as she tossed in bed that she was terrible at keeping secrets. She got up, dragged herself into the kitchen, and wrote a letter to her man, to the father of this tiny being inside her. She wrote of her love, reminded him of his Colorado promise, and asked him what he thought about having a little Canadian in the family this coming September, if the Knights decided he was the man for the job.

On her walk to work—Dr. Smoot had assured her that walking was excellent exercise for a lady-in-waiting—she debated long and hard over mailing the letter. She held the letter suspended over the postbox until a woman waiting behind her cleared her throat loud enough to remind her that other people lived in the universe and mailed letters. In it went.

On the first of March, Della was ready to strangle the father of her child. "You promised to take me to Hastings," she told his miner's round lunch bucket, the one with the two compartments, one for a meal and the larger one for water, that she had started using earlier in the week when the queasy feeling in her stomach revolted and attacked. It had a useful handle and lid, which meant she could carry it to the toilet for disposal.

Angharad had caught her early that morning, heaving up everything except the birthmark on her ankle. "Mam! Are you ill?"

Once Della had eaten a few saltines and the kitchen quit spinning, she sat her daughter down and told her what was going on. She watched the shy look Angharad gave her and held out her two hands in the Welsh way. With a delighted smile, Angharad placed her hands in Della's, never taking her eyes from Della.

"Does Da know?"

"I sent him a letter. I want him home soon."

That morning, Uncle Jesse's secretary showed her a telegram from her boss. *Tonight at six*, it read. "Why use ten words when three will do?" the woman said. "Is that how the rich stay rich?"

Della remembered what Amanda had told her about Uncle Jesse's mandate from heaven. He stayed rich by helping others. The secretary was new; maybe she hadn't heard it yet.

They were waiting at six when the Union Pacific railroad steamed its way toward the Provo station and hissed to a stop. She waved to Uncle Jesse and Ray and then stood still, too shy to wave at Owen Davis, the man who knew her better than anyone on earth—the father of their baby, the singer, the coal miner, and maybe now a builder on Canada's vast prairie.

Angharad hurried to him and he hugged her. He took her hand, bent down and sent her ahead to walk with Uncle Jesse. Her heart thumping loud, Della walked toward Owen. He came faster, and then he stopped directly in front of her.

"I was going to grab you and swing you around, but maybe I shouldn't, *m cara*," he told her.

He set down his valise and gently folded her in his arms.

"I'm not made of porcelain. Baby's tucked in there pretty safely," she whispered in his ear. "I think maybe since Christmas. Maybe that night you came home. The night you sang to me. Well?"

Della's reminder of her durability notwithstanding, he held her off from him just as carefully. "Baby Davis will be a Canadian. Della, I'm to facilitate building a town and a sugar factory. My stars, but life is strange, is it not?"

Chapter 45

Owen had purchased tickets on the D&RGW for Colorado when they stopped in Salt Lake on the way home. After Della's letter that he read over and over in his hotel room in Lethbridge, he made sure they were Pullman tickets. No pregnant wife of his needed the discomfort of sitting in a parlor car for such a distance. He remembered how tired Gwyna had been in those first few months. Better to let Della stretch out, for all that she protested how good she felt, barring an early-morning heave.

When she heard the news about the baby, the job, and the trip, Mabli had clapped her hands, hugged them, and said she would be happy to let Angharad stay with her while they traipsed off to Colorado. She packed a prodigious box lunch and handed it over when they dropped off Angharad the next evening and caught the night train to Grand Junction and points east.

A man of obvious efficiency, the porter had already made up the bed in the sleeping car. "My goodness, we have our own compartment," Della said after he left. "I was just hoping for partitioned curtains."

"You're worth a compartment," he said.

"And you're an overly protective man I adore," she said. "I am quite fine."

She could protest all she wanted. By the time he had helped her into her nightgown, bracing her against the motion of the moving car, she was drooping noticeably and yawning. "I'll just rest my eyes," she told him as she lay down close to the window and patted the space beside her. Before he could unbutton his shirt, she was asleep.

Della barely made a sound when they pulled into Grand Junction, patting Owen's shoulder before she returned to sleep. In the light from the depot, he watched her, touched by how her hands already cupped her belly even though she wasn't showing yet. Gwyna had done the same thing. How kind of the Lord Almighty to bless him with two wives who loved their little ones, no matter how small. Maybe all mothers did that. How would he know?

By the time they changed trains and headed south on a track reminiscent of Utah's winding canyon routes, she was wide awake and nervous. To distract her from the great drop-off to the river far below, he told her all over again about his new job, and the wide-open prairie that was the District of Alberta.

"There are mountains in the distance, and at this moment, that's probably close enough for you, eh? I've never seen anything quite like the Alberta District," he said. "One of the local leaders told us that a dog could run away in Alberta, and you'd be able to see him for three days."

She laughed. "Owen, with no mountains close, are there any mines?"

"Cross my heart I didn't ask," he said. She could find out for herself later that there was a town by Lethbridge called Coaldale.

"Fences, more ditches, and houses come first. Then comes the sugar factory, which is already contracted for its first load of beets in 1903," he said. He tucked her close, because he knew from experience in Scofield how trains in canyons terrified her. "If you came right now or even in May when school is out, you'd be living in a tent, and I won't have it."

Tears welled in her eyes, which made him doubt his own resolve. The last thing he wanted was to leave her in Provo while he worked in Canada, but a coming baby had changed things. "I'll build you the first house," he promised. "Uncle Jesse and Ray will be advertising across Canada's southern district and Utah for settlers. There's space and room to grow." He peered closer. "Are you unhappy with me?"

"Not precisely," she said, which made him smile.

"Do you at least like me?" They had traveled this road before.

"Quite a lot. Could we perhaps consider a tent for the summer? I'm healthy and I'm strong, and Angharad is already such a help." Her words came out in a rush then. "My heart will break if I am not with you."

He sighed and kissed her hair. "We'll think about it."

"That's all I ask," she told him quietly before she drifted to sleep. He could tell her later that she was probably going to win this argument. His lonely time in Knightville was not something he wanted to repeat, not ever.

By mid-morning they reached La Perla, where the next step was to find a way to Hastings, which proved to be simple enough. Someone was always going to Hastings, only ten miles away. It was a simple matter of finding the freight yard and asking around.

"Does any of this look familiar to you yet?" he asked her.

Della nodded, her face solemn.

The freighter providing the ride looked at her with interest. "You lived here, Mrs. Davis?"

"My father mined in the Molly Bee."

"It's been closed for years," he told her, and then he looked over his shoulder to Owen. "Give your lady a hand up and we'll be going."

"What do people do around here now?" she asked after the driver clucked to his team and they started up the graded incline.

"Ranching, mostly." He pointed to the southeast with his whip. "The Wilson ranch that way. Bob Wilson's been here the longest and he has quite a spread. I think he runs three thousand cattle."

Hastings was much what he expected: a modest town with some abandoned buildings, two churches, more saloons than churches, and a schoolhouse smaller than the one where Della taught in Winter Quarters Canyon.

She pointed due south toward a steeper road looking overgrown and neglected now. "That's the way to the Molly Bee." Della shivered, but Owen didn't think she was cold, since the sun shone.

"May I ask—my wife tells me I'm nosy—what are you folks planning to do here?"

"My father died in a rock fall when I was a child. I haven't been back since, and I wanted to visit his grave before we move to Canada," Della said, adding, ". . . this summer," with a pointed look at Owen. "Is there still only the one burying ground between the two churches?"

"The very same," he said. "I can take you there now, or maybe you might want to have some lunch."

"Lunch," Owen said at the same time Della said, "Burying ground."

They laughed. "I suppose we should eat," Della conceded.

The teamster laughed at them. "No harm meant, Mrs. Davis, but your father will keep." He pointed with his whip toward a two-story building needing paint like all the others. "How about I drop you there with your luggage? It's not much, but I hear the sheets are clean with no bedbugs, and there's a nice café."

Owen doubted they would remain in Hastings much beyond a visit to Frederick Anders's grave, but he agreed. Wife and luggage on the boarded walk now, he waved to the teamster who left them there. The man promised someone was always leaving Hastings in the morning and they would have no difficulty leaving too.

The hotel was much as described. Della looked around the room he rented and nodded her guarded approval. With a pang, Owen realized that even this shabby room looked far more promising than a tent in Raymond.

Della opened her suitcase and retrieved the Anders name he had carved for her last year. She held it up for a good look and then cradled it in her arms. Her eyes were bright when she smiled at him. "Let's go. My father has waited years for this."

No, you have, he thought.

"I have to tell you, Owen: the first time I saw the Scofield cemetery, it gave me quite a jolt," she said as she led him toward the open ground between the churches. "Papa has a wooden marker just like those. Can we think about a regular headstone?"

"Your wish is my command, fair lady. Let's make arrangements on the way back to the train. I can carry that for you."

"I know you can," she said, hugging the Anders carving closer. "It's my job, though."

There weren't many graves in the Hastings Cemetery. Della scanned the burying ground and pointed toward the row of wooden markers. "Over there." Her voice seemed to shrink. He waited, hoping she wouldn't begin to use that eerie child's voice, and she didn't. A full-grown, confident woman walked beside him. He couldn't have been more grateful. He would have to write to Saul Weisman and tell him Sigi was right.

She was in no hurry, stopping every few feet and looking around. She must have thought her slow pace deserved an explanation. "I doubt I will ever be here again. I want to remember this moment."

He nodded, thinking that in a few days on their return trip he would probably do the same thing when they stopped in Scofield. Through the years, he had managed to save enough for a granite memorial for Gwyna. He planned to spend more than a moment by her again, explaining why he was moving so far away to the plains of Alberta District. He knew Gwyna would understand, but he needed to tell her.

They reached the row at the back with ten wooden markers and one granite headstone with flowers in front of it.

"That's odd," Della said. "I thought Papa's was the one on the end, but I suppose there were more miners' deaths." She leaned against him. "Clumsy of me to say that, especially when I think of May 1. Certainly there were more deaths."

"There will always be miners' deaths," he said, and he braced himself against the wave after wave of agony that broke over him that awful day when the Number Four blew, and which had troubled him for months. He waited; it didn't happen.

Instead, he felt an odd sort of peace settle on him, followed by a shower of wonderful memories of friends gone, but friends still. He had come full circle in his own personal grief. This thing in May that was far bigger than he was had become at least an ally, if not a friend. He could live with that.

"Owen. *Owen.*"

He must have closed his eyes for his tender epiphany. When he opened them, Della stood before a granite marker, staring down. To his astonishment, she dropped the carving she carried and fell to her knees.

He was at her side in moment, looking where she pointed.

"Frederick Soiseth Anders," he said out loud. "Eighteen Fifty-one to Eighteen Eighty-six. Della, who did this?"

She shook her head and held out her arm so he could help her stand. She leaned closer to touch the flowers, then pulled back her hand as though it burned.

"They're fresh! Someone must have left these today, on his birthday. Who would do this?"

As surprised as she was, Owen shook his head. "Do you have any relatives here?"

"Not one."

He saw the bewilderment on her face. She picked up his carving and leaned it against the headstone, staring down.

"You don't . . . you don't think your uncle did this, do you?" he asked her. "Surely he would have said something."

"Aunt Caroline would never have allowed such a kindness. These are fresh flowers. We must have just missed whoever it was that left them."

They stared at each other, and he held out his hand. "Do you know *anyone* in town?"

"Not a soul." She took his hand and they started by silent agreement for the front of the cemetery, walking fast.

Chapter 46

A bell tinkled when Owen opened the door to Hastings Dry Goods and ushered her inside. The sharp tang of dried herring made Della's stomach lurch. *Not now, Baby Davis,* she thought, half amused, half exasperated. *I don't have time to puke.*

"Is anyone here?" Owen asked. "Please?"

"Over here."

They turned together and saw who they guessed must be the owner, sitting in a rocking chair by a pot-bellied stove and, of all things, knitting. He noticed their surprise and held up the ball of yarn.

"The wife calls this a winter project," he said. "I knit socks. That's all. Learn one thing and do it well is what I say. Can I help you folks?"

Owen looked at Della and gave her a little push forward. "I don't even know what to ask," she whispered to her ever-helpful man.

"Let's try this," that ever-helpful man whispered back. "Sir, we were noticing the flowers on that grave in the back row of the cemetery."

"Nice, aren't they?" The proprietor put down the latest sock and came closer. "She does it every year on his birthday."

"*Who* does?" Della and Owen asked at the same time.

It was the owner's turn to raise both hands against their sudden intensity. "Hey, hey, slow down! Tig Wilson."

Della's heart plummeted. She couldn't put a finger on what she had suddenly been hoping, but someone named Tig Wilson wasn't it. "Owen, I don't know anyone named Tig Wilson."

"She's the wife of Bob Wilson, the biggest rancher in these parts," the man in the shadows said. "I'm Ed Sanford and I own this place." He chuckled. "Business is always slow, but we like Hastings. Been here for years."

Sanford came closer and it was his turn to stare, wide-eyed, at Della. He looked her up and down so thoroughly that Della wondered if she had a leaf plastered to her face, or maybe her shirtwaist was unbuttoned.

Apparently too thoroughly for Owen's taste. "Um, Mr. Sanford, this is *my* wife," he said firmly, emphasizing the word. "We're the Davises. We stopped here today to leave something . . ."

Della clapped her hand on Owen's arm. "Do you think you know me?" she asked, hardly breathing.

The proprietor was obviously a man not prone a rude stare. He nodded to Owen. "Beg pardon, sir, but your wife bears a remarkable resemblance to Mrs. Wilson. That's all. Could happen to anyone. All the same . . ."

"Tig? That's her name?" Della asked.

"No. Only part of it. I can't remember the rest." With a glance of apology, Sanford peered more closely at Della. "Ma'am, you look pale. Want to sit down? Maybe unbutton your coat? I'd hate to have you keel over into the tobacco twists."

She made no objection when both men took her by the arm and led her to a bench by the entrance, where the sun shone in and warmed the room a little. Della did as he said, unbuttoning her coat then untying the strings to her winter hat and removing it because everything felt too tight, too *everything.*

Sanford gasped, swore, and immediately apologized. "Jeez, ma'am, I'm not one to pop off like that, but your hair!"

"I. Like. It," Owen said, equally firm again.

Sanford threw up his hands. "I'm making an idiot of myself, but ma'am, Tig Wilson has a head of hair just like yours. Gray, of course, but . . ."

"Please, please, what is her real name?" Della asked. This was no time to cry, not now. The doctor had told her she might be more skittish, but this was no time for Baby Davis to complicate matters.

The pressure of Owen's hand on her shoulder calmed her. "Can you recall her real name?" he said.

"No, no. As I remember, Mrs. Wilson came to town about seven or eight years ago, after the Molly Bee closed. The town was bigger then, but I'd never seen anyone like her before. What a beauty," he told them, "and what a resemblance."

"Her whole name?" Della prompted, but kindly.

Sanford tipped his head back, maybe hoping for an answer to appear in the rafters. "Something Greek. That's all I know."

"Tig. Tig. I don't know," Della said, hopeful and not hopeful at the same time. She had looked at pictures of Greek statues and knew something about relative resemblance. Welsh were short and dark-eyed. Greeks were olive with curly hair.

Mr. Sanford snapped his fingers. "Antigone! That was it. Antigone. Anyway, she got a job cooking at the Wilson Ranch. I think she took care of Mrs. Wilson, who died a year or two later." He shook his head. "The first Mrs. Wilson was quite a lady, I assure you, and the whole town mourned. I guess Bob didn't want to lose a good cook, and truth to tell, there are lots of men who wouldn't have minded someone as pretty as Tig in their house. She wasn't young, but she was charming. We all like her."

"She lives here?" Owen asked.

"Out at the ranch. She comes in now and then, but she never misses March 10, when she leaves flowers on some miner's grave."

Della put her hands to her face and sobbed out loud. With a creak to the bench, Owen sat next to her, wrapped her arms around her and held her tight.

"It might not be her, *m cara*. I mean, you said your mother's name was Olympia."

Blindly she took the handkerchief Owen held out to her and blew her nose.

"It is. But Owen, what else don't I know?"

"Your mother? Seriously?" Sanford asked.

Alert, Della watched him as he looked up, brightened visibly and pointed through the open door. "We can solve this in a minute. I see Mrs. Wilson right now, coming out of the milliner's. It's usually her last stop before she leaves town. How about I go get her?"

He didn't wait for an answer. "Breathe, Della," Owen said. "Just breathe. Close your eyes."

What could she say to that? Della breathed in and out slowly. The dried herring still bothered her, but her mind was miles away, remembering another child.

As she watched in her brain, the little girl smiled and waved at her, blew a kiss, and then faded.

The door opened. She heard Owen's sudden intake of breath. Della opened her eyes, and her mother stood before her.

Della sat still, unable to move and breathe at the same time. The woman with her face gazed with Della's eyes into Della's face. The woman closed those same deep-set eyes and bowed her head.

"Della Olympia Anders," she said finally. "You've come home to me."

Della leaped to her feet and they were in each other's arms, her mother patting her back and caressing her as if she wanted to make up all at once for so many long years without her baby.

"Well I'll be," Sanford said. "No one's going to believe this."

"Mama," Della managed to gasp out. "Mama. But your name . . ."

"Olympia Antigone Stavrakis, now Wilson." She smiled at her daughter. "Bob—Mr. Wilson—calls me Tig." She held her off to see Della better. "I know you have a birthmark on your ankle."

Della started to laugh. They hugged each other.

"And my hair is the great trial of my life," Della said, which must have sounded like the funniest thing ever because Mrs. Wilson nodded and laughed too.

"I told Frederick, your father—blessed be his memory—I told him I would put a little olive oil on a comb because that would help." Her face clouded over. "Did he, after I left? Tell me he did!"

"He did," Della said softly. Because of the long-overdue letter that her Uncle Karl gave her last year in Winter Quarters, she knew this woman standing so close to her had an additional layer of anguish. Mrs. Wilson needed to know every tiny detail of her child's life that she had missed, when her father dragged her away from her baby. Della had so much to tell her, so she started with the simplest thing. "He always used a little olive oil."

"Della still does." Owen held out his hand to Mrs. Wilson. "I'm Owen Davis, and I believe you are my mother-in-law."

"What is this shake?" Mrs. Wilson asked. "That's not the Greek way."

Della watched in delight as her mother grabbed Owen, kissed one cheek and the other, and then threw her arms around him. She glanced at Mr. Sanford, who, from the gleam in his eyes, enjoyed every second of the drama playing out in front of him. She had no doubt that word would spread within minutes, giving the citizens of Hastings something to talk about for years.

"I didn't know your middle name was Antigone," Della said. "There is so much I don't know about you, and I want to know everything."

"And what happened to you in the past years? I hope you have had a lovely life."

What to tell her mother about life with the Anderses, her hard work scratching for an education, and her impulsive "escape" to Winter Quarters, where everything changed? She held out her hand to her husband, who was having his own struggle with her mother's question.

She watched her mother, her beautiful face wreathed in worry, likely concerned that maybe Della hadn't had a good life because she wasn't answering right away. Looking from husband to mother, found at last, Della thought of all the awful times, the times when she thought she could not live another minute. She weighed them against the depth of her love for Owen Davis and Angharad, and friends who never wished her anything but well, and she dismissed the hard times forever.

In the deepest part of her soul, she knew beyond all logic and reason that every good moment and every bad moment had conspired to bring her right here to Hastings, Colorado, at the perfect time. Bishop Parmley had told her once that the Lord was mindful of her; he was right.

"I have been greatly blessed, Mama," she said quietly.

Chapter 47

Owen knew Tig Wilson wouldn't even consider that her dear child spend a night in the Hastings Hotel. He wasn't surprised in the least when she insisted they come home with her for a few days. He had no plans to argue the decision apparently made without words between mother and daughter. He knew he was going to relish every moment of this reunion.

Still, Uncle Jesse needed a telegram explaining why they would be a little late, considering that Owen and Ray were due to head north again almost immediately to negotiate the purchase of lumber for the new town of Raymond.

In the telegram, he asked Uncle Jesse to inform Mabli that Angharad was going to be her guest for a little longer. Telegram sent, he squared with the hotel, retrieved their luggage, and climbed in the back of Mrs. Wilson's buckboard, ready to enjoy the next few days of being the onlooker, watching a mother and daughter find themselves in each other.

He was aided and abetted by Bob Wilson, a powerful rancher, from the look of his land and holdings, but a man little more than putty in the capable hands of Antigone. Owen couldn't help but wonder if such would be his fate under Della's management. He sincerely hoped it was.

Once he recovered from the amazement and shock of seeing his wife's veritable twin, Bob Wilson took the whole thing in stride. "Sometimes things get a little slow this far from town. We'll have plenty to talk about, from here on out to the finish line."

"You're calmer than I was when they met," Owen said. "I may never recover."

Mr. Wilson was obviously made of sterner stuff. "Just when you think you've seen it all, you realize, well, no, you haven't." Or possibly not so stoic. Owen watched the old rancher dab at his eyes then look away for a long moment. Or maybe not too serious either. When he turned back to Owen, he motioned to the ladies. "Pretty wife you've got there, son. One of a kind." They laughed together.

After giving her husband a smile unparalleled in its brilliance, Tig sat Della down by the fireplace. No words spoken, the mother and daughter simply held hands and looked at each other.

"Owen, let me tell you a few things about Tig. I know she'll tell Della, but it's a hard story."

Owen nodded. No need to inform this genial rancher that he had hard stories of his own.

"Tig's father took her away to Trinidad and another mine."

"That's not so far from here," Owen said, and let out his breath in a whoosh. "That's where she was all these years?"

"It might as well have been the moon. He forced her to marry an older Greek. He didn't live too long, but when her father died, she was gone the next day. Frederick Anders meant everything to her."

What could he say to that?

As time ticked away, Mr. Wilson gently reminded his wife that night was coming and asked about supper.

"I can cook. What about you, Bob?" Owen said, which brought both women to their feet immediately.

"Oh, no," the women said together, and then they looked at each other and said in unison, "Yours too?"

Fixing the meal took longer than usual, with the ladies talking nonstop and then lapsing into silence as they stared at each other and fell into each other's arms.

Owen found himself grinning like a fool one moment and then deadly serious the next, trying to imagine what would have happened if they had arrived in Hastings five minutes later. The merchant had said Mrs. Wilson stopped at the milliner's on the way out of town. Owen had noticed the hatbox on her arm when Mr. Sanford stopped her. In a bare minute or two, she would have left Hastings, none the wiser. Better not think about it.

While the women did the dishes, Bob Wilson took Owen with him to make sure the hired man had finished his chores. Owen admired the neatness and order he saw everywhere. "You've been here a while, haven't you?"

Wilson nodded. He rested his arms on the corral fence. "Maudie and I came here pretty early in the game. Raised two sons. Buried two others." He nodded toward another ranch house on the other side of the field. "Our eldest lives there with his family. I'll take you to meet them tomorrow. Our younger is enrolled in the animal husbandry program at Colorado Agricultural College."

"And Antigone?"

"She's been a blessing. It was tough when Maudie died," he said simply.

"I have to know, unless this is not my business. Did *you* put up the stone marker for Della's father?"

"Sure did. When I hired Tig to begin with, she told me straight up what had happened to her. When I married her, that marker seemed like a good idea. She visits Fred's grave and I visit Maudie's." He glanced at Owen. "Surprised?"

"I am not. My first wife died in childbirth when our daughter was born. I visit Gwyna's grave. Della tells me I'd better keep doing that, or it's curtains for me."

"Then we're both lucky men."

Mother and daughter talked long into the evening. When the grandfather clock struck ten, Bob got to his feet and stretched.

"Let's you and I each get a hot water bottle," he said. "It gets chilly here at night, and I'm no fan of cold feet."

Owen looked at Della, her head on her mother's shoulder. "You're suggesting we might not have anyone to put our feet on tonight?"

"Sure am. Do they look like they're going anywhere?"

When Owen came downstairs in the morning, mother and daughter were curled up together on the sofa, Antigone's hand protectively draped over Della, and Della's hand gentle on her belly, mothers and children—three generations.

"I'm an ogre, but I have to be in Provo by the end of the week," Owen told Della two mornings later when they packed to leave. The Wilsons were driving them to Hastings for a last visit to Fred's grave and then down to the railroad in La Perla.

"No need to feel that way, my love," Della said. "They've promised to visit me at least once in Provo after you leave for Canada again." She put her hands on his chest. "And Angharad and I are coming north when school is out in May."

"You are. I won't argue," he said, and he kissed her right before he put his dirty socks on her head, which made her laugh and swat at him. "Mr. Wilson told me that sometimes the path of least resistance is the way to deal with Greeks. I'll bow to his superior knowledge."

In Hastings, Della and her mother stood for a long moment looking down at Frederick Anders's grave. Arm in arm, they returned to the buckboard for a quiet ride to La Perla.

They stood close together as the train approached, and then they wiped each other's tears. Antigone kept looking back as they left the Davises at the depot. Owen's hands gentle on her shoulders, Della waved until her mother was out of sight.

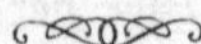

A day later, they left the D&RGW and rode the short line from Colton to Scofield. "I told Uncle Jesse we'd be back in Provo tomorrow. We have some friends to visit, *m cara*."

The first friends lay in the cemetery, their wooden headstones already showing wear from the scouring wind. Some of the bereft had already exchanged wood for stone markers. The bare patches in the ground signaled gophers hard at work as usual, but some early spring grass poked up here and there.

"Time works on it, but I doubt this will ever be a beautiful cemetery," Owen said later, looking down at Gwyna's grave and talking to her in Welsh. He glanced over the rows to see Della still standing by Richard's plot. She touched the wooden marker and moved toward David Evans's little allotment of American real estate in this place so far from the green hills of Wales.

"Going to Canada, Gwyna," he said. "I'll come back and tell you about it someday."

Would he? He smiled inside, knowing in his heart that the other woman lodged there would insist upon it. He would be back to visit. He patted Gwyna's headstone and walked toward Della. Those gopher holes were hard to spot, and he didn't want her to trip.

They spent the afternoon in Clear Creek with Martha Evans and her three little ones, directed there by Rees Phillips, a miner Owen already knew: a good and patient Welshman from Monmouthshire. After Phillips left for his own place, Martha told them they were making plans for June.

"I hope you don't think it's too early," she told Owen, while Della read to the children. "My little ones need a father, and he's a good man."

"He is," Owen agreed, understanding more than he thought he ever would about moving on, whether with coal or mines or matters of the heart—maybe all three.

Visiting the Koskis meant hugs for Della and threats for Owen if he didn't treat Della right. Owen thought it prudent not to mention a tent in the summer. Eeva bubbled over with news from Montana about Mari Luoma and her baby, ten months old now and already pulling himself up to furniture.

"She named him Vihtori Heikki, and he is thriving," Eeva said. "There's a man name of Adolph Hill too, who is keeping her company." She gave a sigh of exasperation. "The clerk at Ellis Island couldn't pronounce his Finnish name, much less spell it, so he became Hill."

Moving on. They spent the night back in Winter Quarters with the Parmleys, who had invited Emil Isgreen for dinner too. A few months ago, it might have bothered him when the doctor took Della aside for a few words. It didn't bother him now; he knew his wife's heart. Besides that, the good doctor shook his hand and patted his back. "I knew you had it in you, Owen," he said cheerfully and blew a kiss to Della as he left.

"He's a rascal, to be sure, but he ordered me to let you do any heavy lifting and to walk for exercise," Della said. She leaned against him and whispered, "I didn't tell him about the tent."

Owen got up before Della in the morning. With a sigh of pleasure, she moved into his warm spot. He joined Bishop Parmley on the porch as Winter Quarters came alive for another shift in the mines.

"In case you didn't know, there was a strike here in January."

"There was a small article in the *Herald* about it. A wildcat strike, wasn't it?"

"Aye. Not much planning. All the same, change is coming to the coalfields. You think you'll miss mining?"

"Now and then, if I'm honest. I have a lot to do in Canada, though."

"From what you said last night, it's sound ambitious enough for a Welshman."

"Aye, sir. Life takes us down strange paths."

Bishop Parmley nodded. "One step at a time makes the journey." He clapped a hand on Owen's shoulder. "But you know that."

He did.

Chapter 48

"Insist all you wish, dearest, but this little one might be a boy. Perhaps you should entertain the possibility, however remote, so you are not gravely disappointed in September."

"I want a sister, Mam," Anghard said. "Besides, Da *knows* girls."

"He knows boys too. He *is* one," Della reminded her. "Angharad, you should be a lawyer when you grow up, for you can certainly argue a case. Oh, I think the word I mean in Canada is barrister. Or is it solicitor?"

"A girl," Angharad said firmly. She sighed. "I am a terrible traveler."

Della laughed inside, unwilling to trample on her daughter's innate dignity. "Lean close to me and you might feel a little tap from your brother or sister."

"Sister. But are we almost there?"

"You are exasperating."

"I want to see Da in just about the worst way. I *need* him."

You and me, Della thought. Owen's visit in April had been too short. He had breezed in like a breath of spring, ruffled Angharad's hair, and then lay with his head in Della's shrinking lap, the better to feel the activity within. His eyes had filled with tears and she called him an old softy.

When they were comfortable in bed later, he told her about the brand new and raw little town of Raymond, which was already attracting settlers, many from Utah looking for land and a better life.

"That is all Uncle Jesse ever wants," Owen said, the wonder still in his voice, even though he knew the man better than most. "A better life for us too."

"And now you've hired Saul Weisman?" she asked, drowsy but unwilling to go to sleep and waste a single sweet moment with her absentee husband.

"He should be in Raymond soon, along with Saladin. Sugar beets need analysis too, for content and moisture. He said he was glad to leave Silver City." He kissed her throat. "Told me he's going to make certain I treat you right and stay out of mines." He kissed her shoulder. "Between Saul and Saladin, Eeva Koski, my newly found mother-in-law, and the ever-watchful Dr. Isgreen, I am doomed forever to toe the mark."

"Welsh drama. Kiss me again and go to sleep."

"Aye, miss. Still awake?"

"Barely."

"I've put the men to work digging foundations and wells for the houses to come. With any luck, I'll start on our house next month."

Two letters later he was already apologizing for the tent it would have to be until at least August. "But there will be a wooden floor," he added in a postscript. "Do you still like me?"

Don't be silly; certainly I do, she remembered saying to the letter. She patted her belly and looked out the window at the District of Alberta. They had transferred to the Canadian Pacific a few hours ago at the Montana border. Angharad had stared out the window. "Are we really in Canada? It looks just like Montana," had been her only comment before she returned to her book. No, Angharad was not a traveler.

Della absorbed the view and found herself relishing the miles of empty rolling prairie with the Canadian Rockies in a haze to the west. *The distant scene*, she thought. *All I want is a home—canvas or otherwise—with my husband. No distant scene, thank you.*

Her only regret on this journey north was that she could not have spent more time in Salt Lake between trains. As it was, she had to hurry to Auerbach's to tell Mr. A. goodbye and try not to cry. He had sent Angharad with his secretary to the mezzanine snack bar, which gave him time to stroll with Della past his gallery of Winter Quarters art done with Franklin Rainbow Colors drawn on Magic Paper.

"It seems so long ago," she said, remembering brave children, some scattered across the West to new mines with living fathers, or to relatives with only memories to comfort them. "So much has happened."

He led her to the newest drawing, still on Magic Paper so it matched the others, of a tall man dressed formally in tails, with a pretty blond lady by his side, and two children standing next to her at an altar.

"My goodness, Pekka drew the wedding," she said. "We're all moving on, I suppose."

"As you should." He kissed her cheek. "*Shalom*, Della. Visit us when you can."

She hurried downstairs to Menswear, with only enough time for a breathless hello and goodbye to Mr. Whalley. "Give all my love to Kristina," she said, her eyes tearing up because the manager looking back at her had changed too. "Let us know when your baby comes."

"And you do the same for us, Della," he said. He leaned toward her. "You know, I wondered if I could love another man's children. Silly me, I do."

What could she say to that? She knew what he meant because she couldn't imagine life without Owen's daughter, even if the child wasn't much of a traveler and liked to discuss things at length. Della blew a kiss to Mr. Whalley and hurried from the store.

Angharad in tow, she nearly didn't stop at Anders, Court and Landry, half hoping Uncle Karl would be out. "I won't be long," she told Angharad in the lobby. "There's a train to catch but I should do my duty."

The secretary directed her to the boardroom, where she found her uncle surrounded by papers and from the look of concentration on his face, trying to make sense of it all. There he was, one of Salt Lake's most successful attorneys, given a chance by his older brother's toil of freighting and mining ore.

He raised bleak eyes to her face. He had lost weight, and looked almost frail. "I could have done so much for you," was his greeting.

He didn't invite her to sit down. She sat anyway, telling him of finding Antigone Wilson in Hastings, Colorado, whether he wanted to know or not.

"Owen is working in Canada, and we are on our way to join him." She held out her hand. "I wish you well, Uncle Karl," she said quietly.

"I don't know why you should," he replied, his voice barely audible.

"I'm your niece, and that's enough reason. Goodbye and God keep you."

Keep you far from me, she thought on the way downstairs, then felt ashamed of herself. Maybe she would write to him from the distance of Alberta District. She knew Owen would encourage her to write, but never force her.

"I am a terrible traveler too," she told Angharad when the child woke up, glanced at more of the same prairie, and sighed. "All I want is to see Da, same as you."

Weary of travel, Della looked out the window. Suddenly, it wasn't the same prairie where the buffalo grass was still new after winter.

Instead, she saw fields of grain the dull gold color of late summer, when the harvest neared. The grain waved in ripples—fickle Alberta wind—and turned into an ocean of wheat that stretched for miles, at least where it wasn't intersected with the deep green of sugar beets. As she watched in fascination, the green leaves of the sugar beet tops spread throughout the prairie and then turned back into golden grain.

Startled, she sat back, unsure of what it meant, but delighted with the view in her mind's eye. It was most assuredly a distant scene, maybe sort of vision or epiphany that Uncle Jesse had experienced as he climbed the side of Godiva Mountain and knew that if he used the wealth coming his way for helping others, he would never fail. In that moment, she knew, as surely as Uncle Jesse had known, that *her* wealth would be children and friends and a man with songs in his heart.

She thought of all the steps that had brought her to this precise moment in her life, a future she had never considered when she took the train to Winter Quarters almost two years ago and everything changed, most things for the better, some for the worse, but all part of the tapestry that was a life, *her* life. Her gratitude knew no bounds.

Buoyed up by her glimpse of the future, she looked out the window and saw the prairie of May again and the promise before her now. It was enough, and she was content.

Grumpy, hopeful, irritable, joyful, and anxious, Della held Angharad's hand as the train entered Lethbridge and started to slow down. Della rolled her eyes when she saw a long line of coal cars on a parallel track—so much for no coal mining nearby. Was there truly an honest Welshman?

She saw the depot, but no husband. Della looked up at the flag, standing out stiff, but Owen had already warned her about the wind. Some of her exhaustion left her as she admired the brilliant red with the Union Jack in the left corner. She squinted, trying to make out the block of color toward the center. Never mind. Owen could probably tell her what it represented.

With a lump of boulder proportion in her throat, she shifted herself in the railcar and looked south, trying to glimpse one last time the land of the red, white, and blue and the Fourth of July and the Declaration of Independence. She patted the Canadian in her belly. One step enough. Her epiphany had told her she would come to love this land.

When she turned back to look out, Owen stood on the platform, Saladin leaning against his leg, both of them seeming to search the windows for their people. Owen stepped back in mock surprise when Angharad began to wave wildly. Della wondered if an expectant lady was too old to wave with an eight-year-old's abandon. She decided to be prudent.

There's going to be a tent with a wooden floor, Della thought as she and Angharad stood up to be the first passengers off the train. *Maybe a well. The wind is going to blow forever, and I am already wondering about the winter.*

Did it matter? Suddenly shy, she watched from the top step as Angharad launched herself into Owen's arms and he hugged her. They stood close together, father and daughter who had been through rough times together, always together, but happy to share their lives with her.

Angharad knelt to pet Saladin, who waved his feathery tail in polite greeting. Owen came toward Della and held out his hands. This had become a year to remember, or maybe forget, or at least remember selectively. *Sometimes all's well that ends*, she thought with a smile. *Or begins.*

"You're home now, Della Davis," her husband said as he took her hands and helped her down so carefully.

"So are you, Owen Davis. I'm here."

Epilogue

September 12, 1901

Dearest Mama and Bob,

My goodness, such a time we had last week. We have a son now, and we named him Frederick Jesse Davis. Angharad is reconciling herself to a brother. She told me only this morning that he will do, since there is nothing better right now.

Fred came early, so we were still in the tent. His arrival coincided with a blizzard on September 4, which meant no doctor from Lethbridge. My husband has proved himself to be the master of many trades, apparently. He told me to breathe steadily and evenly, and he walked Angharad to Saul Weisman's tent for something called a "frameygram." He told her not to return without it. Saul took it from there and they searched for the frameygram until Fred squalled his way into life an hour later, delivered by his father and a neighbor lady. They never did find the frameygram. No need for Angharad to have more education at her tender years than she needs.

Poor Owen. After he cleaned up Fred and put him in my arms, he cried. When he could speak, he told me what a difference this was from Angharad's birth, when everything went wrong. I've assured him several times that I feel fine, if a little sore, and happy to be up and about.

Mr. Weisman and Angharad lugged over a beet scale. Fred weighs seven pounds and ten ounces. He's twenty inches long and has curly black hair, which pleased Owen. Fred enjoys his meals. There's plenty to suck, so we are all content.

Owen can't get enough of something as simple as watching Fred nurse. He is finally starting to relax and realize that he is married to a healthy woman who had a baby: no more, no less. As I watch him watching us, I begin to understand the emotions that charged Gwyna's death and Angharad's birth immediately after.

We're in our house. Even two rooms (for now) and a lean-to kitchen are an improvement on the tent. More houses are going up, and soon Ray and Owen will put out a bid for contractors to begin construction of the sugar factory. There is no school yet, but after life settles down with Fred, I'll teach Angharad and anyone else who wishes to join us.

Come soon for a visit, Mama, if you can. I think you'll be pleased with what you see here in Raymond, our home on the prairie. I can't imagine being anywhere else now. Owen taught us to sing "The Maple Leaf Forever" and "God Save the King." He sings all the time. He is happy, and so am I.

Fred is tuning up, so it's time for another grab at Mam, who feels like a Jersey cow these days. Owen often lies down with us and reads aloud from *Pickwick*. Saladin divides his time between Saul's tent and our front step, where he guards us from all intruders. Angharad and the other little girls play with her dollhouse.

Mama, this is my life now. I want no other.

Your daughter,
Della Olympia

Afterword

As a writer of historical fiction, I enjoy rubbing shoulders with history's intriguing characters, some well-known, some not.

I'm often asked which people in *My Loving Vigil Keeping*, and now *One Step Enough*, actually lived. The answer is many. In fact, I've never used so many real people in works of fiction as in these two books.

One way to make historical fiction come to life is to write the real people alongside fictional ones. Richard Woodman, author of the Napoleonic Era nautical series featuring Nathaniel Drinkwater, wrote:

"This [series] sprang from my desire to truly reflect the reality of the sea-life of the period and not some romanticized version of it, but also from a strong urge to insert my imaginary naval protagonist into the very fabric of recorded history. That is what I believe an historical novel should attempt."

I agree. When I place my fictional characters (Della and Owen) next to actual people (Thomas Parmley, Jesse Knight, and Richard Evans) the reader more easily makes the leap to considering the fictional characters real.

The real people mean as much to me as my fictional creations, if not more. I have tried mightily to "use" them appropriately and accurately. I made some errors, and these errors are mine. Sometimes I have left out details from their actual lives, simply because the details couldn't further the story. The writer of historical fiction must be ever-mindful that as fascinating as history is, the story comes first. It must.

Not surprisingly, it was after the publication of *My Loving Vigil Keeping* that I began to hear from descendants of some of these real people. To a person, they have been both appreciative and supportive of my efforts to "borrow" their relatives. They also politely set me straight when I went far afield.

The difficulty in finding out more at the time of writing *Vigil* lay in the reality that most of the wives who became widows remarried and took other last names. Since they were mainly peripheral characters, I couldn't spend hours of research time finding them. For the most part, I was accurate, but not always.

In this vein, let me share a little with you about the real people in this book I came to appreciate and—I don't mind admitting it—to love. Novelists roll that way.

Thomas Jennison Parmley (1855–1947)

Affectionately known as Uncle TJ among his descendants, Thomas Parmley was the son of a coal miner. Born in Durham, England, in 1855, he went into the mines at the age of ten. His father had died when TJ was six, and his mother remarried George Watson.

At some point, the family listened to missionaries from The Church of Jesus Christ of Latter-day Saints and joined the Church. TJ remained in Durham until the age of twenty-six, when he came to the United States, going first to coal mines in Iowa and eventually to Utah. In 1882, he became mine superintendent in Winter Quarters Canyon, located quite close to Scofield, Utah, in Carbon County.

Following his 1885 marriage to Mary Ann Carrick, an English convert like him, TJ also became the bishop of the Pleasant Valley Ward, located in Winter Quarters Canyon. He remained both bishop and superintendent until Mary Ann's death in 1919. The Parmleys were the parents of seven children, three of whom died young and were buried in the family plot in Scofield Cemetery with Mary Ann. You can find them there as I did.

Well-known in mining circles, TJ Parmley remained an influence in Utah coal mines all his life. In 1922, he married Mary Margaret Whiting. He died in Provo, Utah, in 1947 at the age of ninety-one, and is buried in Salt Lake City.

Jesse Knight (1845–1921)

Jesse Knight was born September 6, 1845, in Nauvoo, Illinois, the sixth child of Newel K. Knight and Lydia Goldthwaite Knight, two of the LDS Church's early stalwarts.

His first memories centered around hardship and persecution of the Saints, who were forced from New York, to Missouri, to Illinois and assembled in Winter Quarters, Nebraska, preparatory to moving west. Sadly, Newel Knight died there before he could make the journey. Lydia and her children eventually arrived in Utah Territory in 1850.

Jesse's was a childhood of poverty. He made the trek west as a six-year-old, walking mainly and gathering dried buffalo chips for firewood. In Utah, he recalled digging pigweed and sego lily roots to help feed the family. By the age of eleven, he hauled firewood with a team of oxen.

Marrying Amanda McEwan in 1869, Jesse did a little bit of everything to support his own family. His faith waned for a time, but a series of health crises among his children reminded Jesse of earlier promises he had made to the Lord. Jesse's life changed forever after that, as he accepted what he called his "stewardship to the Lord."

A rancher in Payson, Utah, Jesse took an interest in the land, in particular the limestone in which valuable ore often formed. He found a promising outcrop of limestone on the eastern slope of mountains forming the Tintic Mining District, and convinced investors to join him.

Tintic wasn't new. In 1869, George Rust, cattle rancher from nearby Tooele County, founded it, and fortunes were already being made on that western side, which some claimed held all the wealth. Jesse wasn't convinced, because he had seen limestone outcroppings on the eastern side that suggested otherwise.

This wasn't Jesse's first venture in Tintic. He had found ore in his June Bug Mine and sold it for $14,000, which had the purchasing power of $388,967.03 in 2018 dollars. Jesse proceeded to give all of it away to others in need. He was a soft touch, and he knew it. He learned the hard way the necessity of combining wisdom with generosity

Here was his chance to try again on that eastern slope. One possible investor said no, calling the whole thing a humbug and declaring Jesse would never strike it rich. But Jesse possessed a dogged faith that gave him the courage to move forward, plus real skill in locating potential ore deposits. While walking on Godiva

Mountain with his son William, he had a vision that if he used wealth to do good for others, he would never lack for his family.

Sure enough, the jokingly named Humbug Mine proved out successfully in 1896 as one of the richest lead deposits in the West. After the mine's success, Jesse told his family that from now on, he would work with his brains instead of his hands to provide others with honest livings for their families. He had also learned a valuable lesson about how to help people by creating jobs, and not just handing out the wealth, as he had done with the proceeds of the June Bug sale.

As the Knight Corporation, Jesse and his sons eventually formed sixty-five companies, many of them mines delivering lead, copper, iron, coal, gold, and silver. He established canning and woolen mills, more ranches, and a sugar beet factory in Raymond, Alberta, which figures prominently in this story.

In addition to employing many, Jesse's philanthropy extended to Brigham Young Academy (later Brigham Young University). Timely gifts at opportune moments kept the school afloat and helped it become the magnificent school it is today. I'm a BYU graduate, and I recall a class or two in the Jesse Knight Building.

In the early days of the twentieth century, Jesse furnished equally timely loans to the LDS Church as it struggled to recover from years of persecution at the hand of the federal government. Jesse's loans were paid in full, as the Church moved forward in coming years.

Through it all, Jesse Knight became known as "Uncle Jesse" because of his many unsung kindnesses to people who struggled and needed a little help to succeed. There is hardly anyone in Utah's history more deserving of acclaim than the modest man who took his stewardship from the Lord seriously. As his son William wrote in the memoir, *The Jesse Knight Family: Jesse Knight, His Forebears and Family*: "[Jesse] believed that the surest way to express love for God was by doing good to God's children."

Martha Evans Evans Phillips (1872–1923)

No people in both *My Loving Vigil Keeping* and *One Step Enough* meant more to me than Richard Thomas and Martha Evans. I felt a certain kinship to Richard Evans because he was the choirmaster of the Pleasant Valley Ward Choir in Winter Quarters Canyon. At the time I wrote *Vigil*, I was choir director in our congregation in Wellington, Utah. I occasionally wondered what Richard would think of my little choir. Richard had a lovely high tenor voice, documented by many, and was the best friend of my fictional Owen Rhys Davis.

I told Richard's story in *Vigil*. Let me add here that nothing I have ever written was harder than writing of his death in the Number Four mine. I probably would have written the sequel to *Vigil* sooner had I not felt so keenly the loss of Richard. Because I felt it, so did Owen. That's how novelists work.

I have visited Richard's grave many times. I left him a Welsh dragon medallion once. I hope it is still there.

But what of Martha? Her story after her husband's death is the story of many women who became widows on May 1, 1900. She was born in 1872 in Spanish Fork, Utah, to Welsh parents named Evans. At the age of seventeen, she married Welshman Richard Thomas Evans in the Manti Utah Temple. The Evanses were the parents of five children, three of whom were living at the time of Richard's death. Martha was twenty-seven.

Superintendent/Bishop Thomas Parmley hired Martha to run a miners' boardinghouse in Clear Creek, located about eight miles south of Winter Quarters Canyon. She moved there with her three children.

On June 20, 1901, Martha Evans married Rees Phillips, a Welsh coal miner from Monmouthshire, located on the English/Welsh border. Also a convert to the LDS Church, Rees proved to be an excellent second husband. Martha's daughter Catherine said he was a wonderful stepfather. Martha and Rees became the parents of six children. Of the eleven children born to Martha, seven were alive at the time of her death in 1923.

In November 1922, Martha was stricken with what was diagnosed as stomach cancer. She suffered greatly but never alone. Always with her were her children, her friends, and her husband Rees. She died on March 4, 1923, at the age of fifty.

Like her first husband, Richard, Martha was known for her lovely voice, singing at many church and town gatherings. She could be counted on to tend the sick and needy and help wherever she could.

After her death, Rees carried on, eventually moving his little family to Castle Gate, Utah, not far from Helper, Utah. One of their children wrote, "We were always one big, fun family that looked out for each other."

Maria Elvina Luoma (1869–1941)

I called her Mari in both books. I knew little to nothing about Maria, except that she was the wife of Heikki

Vihtori Luoma (1871–1900), one of numerous sons, brothers, nephews, and cousins—eight Luomas in all—who died in the mine disaster.

This loss of life among so many family members is one of the striking aspects of the Scofield [Winter Quarters] Mine Disaster. The Number One and Number Four mines, among the oldest coal mines in Utah, were considered the safest, to the extent that they were known as "married men's mines."

The Luoma story is particularly poignant. The Luomas were mining successfully in the canyon and decided to send for their parents to join them in America. Aaprami and Kaissa Luoma arrived in January 1900, only to see so many of their descendants die May 1, 1900, in the mine disaster. They returned to Finland with a widowed daughter.

The Luomas were among many whose whole families were affected by the disaster. Gatherums, Hunters, Padfields, Davises, Farishes, Evanses, Strangs, and others felt similar loss of life among relatives on a wide scale.

But what of Mari and Heikki? I didn't really know anything about them, but in *My Loving Vigil Keeping*, they became the newly married couple who come to Della Anders and ask if Mari can sit in class and learn a little English that way. I also assigned Mari the dubious job of being the new widow who tries to commit suicide by walking in front of a coal train and is saved by Dr. Isgreen and Della. (Incidentally, Emil Isgreen's descendants think they know who that really was.)

As it turned out, about a year after *Vigil*'s publication, I heard from Doug Kero, who lives in Oregon and is a descendant of Heikki and Mari Luoma.

Doug was kind. Seldom have I got a story more wrong. According to Doug, when Heikki and Maria arrived in the United States, they already had two children: Rauha, age four, and Juho, age two. Doug is descended from Rauha, also called Ellen. Maria and Heikki are his great-grandparents.

After Heikki's death, Maria had a posthumous child and named him Vihtori Heikki, after her late husband. She soon moved to Belt, Montana, and lived with relatives. While in Belt, she met Adolph Hill, another Finn, and married him. In 1911, the Hills bought a dairy farm in Menlo, Washington, and moved there. Maria Luoma Hill died in 1941. The land is still in the family. Doug owns five acres of it and has a cabin there.

Emil Isgreen, MD (1865–1945)

One day when I was volunteering at the Western Mining and Railroad Museum in Helper, Utah, I was contacted by Robert Johnson, who identified himself as the son-in-law of Emil Isgreen, MD, who plays a strong role in both *My Loving Vigil Keeping* and now *One Step Enough*.

Bob had heard about the novel and wanted to meet me on his next trip up from Silver City, New Mexico. Later, I had breakfast with Bob and his son Tom, and daughter Kristina Moody, and learned more about the charming doctor and his life before and after Winter Quarters.

Bob was married to Emil and Minnie Isgreen's youngest child, Patricia Jane (1922–2012). He knew Dr. Isgreen well and commented that he was a serious man who lived by this precept: "There is always satisfaction in a duty performed and a noble deed done."

Emil Isgreen was born in Tooele, Utah, the son of Swedish parents who came to Utah after joining the LDS Church. He graduated from Brigham Young Academy in 1887. He taught in the department of natural and physical sciences from 1887 to 1892, when he became president of Weber Stake Academy (now Weber State University) in Ogden, Utah.

After a year, he resigned and went to the University of Michigan, followed by Chicago's Rush Medical College, where he received his medical degree in 1897. Returning to Utah, Emil was first hired by the Union Pacific Railroad as a resident physician in Helper, Utah.

A year later, he became resident physician for the Pleasant Valley Coal Company, located in Winter Quarters Canyon. It is here that Emil Isgreen became part of my first novel, *My Loving Vigil Keeping*, as a suitor to the fictional Della Anders. As mentioned in that novel, Emil served on the board of directors for the Winter Quarters School, where Della taught the lower grades. In actual fact, one improvement he initiated was to replace the log schoolhouse with a frame one. At the time of the mine disaster, the Winter Quarters School was one story high. A few years later, a second story was added. By the time the mines closed in 1928, there was a two-story brick building. Emil Isgreen cared deeply about education.

Following the mine disaster, Dr. Isgreen continued as resident physician. By 1907, Dr. Isgreen left the employ of the Pleasant Valley Coal Company/Utah Fuel and practiced medicine in Salt Lake City and also part-time in Tooele. At the age of forty-three, he married Minnie Peterson of Logan, Utah. The Isgreens had five children, two of the sons becoming physicians, as well.

Bob Johnson gave ample testimony to the upright character and innate goodness of his father-in-law. What touched me the most was the pledge of lifetime free medical care Dr. Isgreen made to the many widows and fatherless children of the Number Four and Number One disasters. That Emil Isgreen honored this pledge I have no doubt.

Acknowledgments

I owe a massive debt of gratitude to R. Craig Johnson, Salt Lake City attorney with his own interest in mining and mining disasters, about which he has written too. Craig kindly arranged for us to visit the Tintic Mining District, long-fabled in Utah mining lore, and located in and near Eureka, Utah. The Johnsons were the perfect hosts.

On a brisk spring day in 2017, Craig, his wife Nancy and son Robert met me and my friend Kemari Rawlings for an ATV tour of the area, guided by Nick Castleton, mayor of Eureka. We all learned a lot during those two days.

Mayor Castleton has a vast knowledge of mining lore and is an unabashed booster of his little town. He took us all around the Tintic Mining District, entertaining and educating us with wonderful stories about the mines that employed many hard rock miners and made the owners wealthy. Nick's grandparents came to Eureka/Silver City in the early 1900s, and he has spent years in this interesting historic area.

Roaring around on ATVs, we saw a number of boarded up mines and the foundations of Knightville, Jesse Knight's community built for his Mormon miners and their families. As far as anyone knows, it was the only mining town in Utah with no saloons. Uncle Jesse understood what his co-religionists wanted. He also knew how to treat his miners, working them six days a week and paying them for seven.

Nick took us to one of the headframes near Eureka, several of which dot the area. And yes, they do look like gallows. The headframes, the hoists, and the various mining buildings still in place outside of Eureka stand as mute testimony to the vigor of Utah's early nineteenth-century mining community and the great wealth found there. Eureka's museum and other historic buildings told their own stories of life both above and under the ground. Nick was a most helpful guide, and I'm pleased to count him and the Johnsons as friends.

Nick also read this novel in manuscript form. His comments on the Tintic Mining District strengthened the narrative. I know a fair bit about historic coal mining, but hard rock mining is not within my comfort zone. Thanks, Nick. I owe you dinner. Ditto to you too, Doug Kero and Craig and Nancy Johnson.

About the dedication: Elam Jones, son of Derk and Julie Jones, died in Rhino Mine in Emery County, Utah, in 2013. He left behind his parents, a wife, Jaqlynn, and two sons. Elam has been on my mind for years, partly because I was allowed inside Rhino when I was researching *My Loving Vigil Keeping*. I knew if I ever wrote a sequel to *Vigil*, I would dedicate it to him.

And Darren and Verena Beazer of Cardston, Alberta? There is good-natured joking between Cardston and nearby Raymond that Cardston grooms find their brides in Raymond. Well, it happened with Darren and Verena. Justin, Ryan, Cameron, Michael and Madison Beazer are pleased, I am certain! Thanks, guys, for being good friends to the Kellys.

Carla Kelly, 2018

About the Author

Photo by Marie Bryner-Bowles,
Bryner Photography

Carla Kelly is a veteran of the New York and international publishing world. The author of more than forty novels and uncounted novellas for Donald I. Fine Co., Signet, and Harlequin, Carla is the recipient of two Rita Awards (think Oscars for romance writing) from Romance Writers of America and two Spur Awards (think Oscars for western fiction) from Western Writers of America. She is also a recipient of Whitney Awards for *Borrowed Light*, *My Loving Vigil Keeping*, and *Softly Falling*.

Recently, she's been writing Regency romances (think *Pride and Prejudice*) set in the Royal Navy's Channel Fleet during the Napoleonic Wars between England and France. She comes by her love of the ocean from her childhood as a Navy brat.

Carla's history background makes her no stranger to footnote work, either. During her National Park Service days at the Fort Union Trading Post National Historic Site, Carla edited Friedrich Kurz's fur trade journal. She also wrote a short history of Fort Buford, where Sitting Bull surrendered in 1881.

The Kellys have lived in Idaho Falls, Idaho, since 2014 and have no particular plans to move again. On a clear day, they can see the Tetons from their neighborhood and enjoy proximity to Yellowstone National Park. Carla enjoys speaking at book clubs, visiting friends and family, and writing, always writing.

She owes a tremendous debt to Miss Jean Dugat, her English and journalism teacher at A.C. Jones High School in Beeville, Texas. "She was a dragon," Carla remembers. "She made us work hard to find the right phrase, the correct sentence, the accurate footnote." Carla also remembers her epiphany at the end of her sophomore year. "I decided that if I worked hard and listened to Miss D, I might be a writer some day. What a teacher."

Scan to visit

carlakellyauthor.com